The
Seven Sisters

Maia's Story

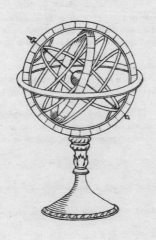

LUCINDA RILEY

PAN BOOKS

First published 2014 by Macmillan

First published in paperback 2015 by Pan Books

This edition first published 2018 by Pan Books
an imprint of Pan Macmillan
20 New Wharf Road, London N1 9RR
Associated companies throughout the world
www.panmacmillan.com

ISBN 978-1-5290-0345-1

3 5 7 9 8 6 4

A CIP catalogue record for this book is available from the British Library.

Printed and bound by CPI Group (UK) Ltd, Croydon, CRO 4YY

Visit **www.panmacmillan.com** to read more about all our books
and to buy them. You will also find features, author interviews and
news of any author events, and you can sign up for e-newsletters
so that you're always first to hear about our new releases.

For my daughter, Isabella Rose

*'We are all in the gutter, but some of us
are looking at the stars.'*

Oscar Wilde

Cast of characters

ATLANTIS

Pa Salt – *the sisters' adoptive father (deceased)*
Marina (Ma) – *the sisters' guardian*
Claudia – *housekeeper at Atlantis*
Georg Hoffman – *Pa Salt's lawyer*
Christian – *the skipper*

THE D'APLIÈSE SISTERS

Maia
Ally (Alcyone)
Star (Asterope)
CeCe (Celaeno)
Tiggy (Taygete)
Electra
Merope (missing)

Dear Reader,

Welcome to the Seven Sisters – and Maia's story!

When I first had the idea of writing a series of books based on the Seven Sisters of the Pleiades, I had no idea where it would lead me. I was very attracted to the fact that each one of the mythological sisters was a unique and strong female. Some say they were the Seven Mothers who seeded our earth – there is no doubt that, in their stories, they were all highly fertile! And I wanted to celebrate the achievements of women, especially in the past, where so often their contribution to making our world the place it is today has been overshadowed by the more frequently documented achievements of men.

However, the definition of 'feminism' is equality, not domination, and the women I write about, both in the past and present, accept that they want and need love in their lives. Not necessarily in the traditional form of marriage and children, but the Seven Sisters series unashamedly celebrates the endless search for love and explores the devastating consequences when it is lost to us.

As I travel round the world, following in the footsteps of my factual and fictional female characters to research their stories, I am constantly humbled and awed by the tenacity and courage of the generations of women who came before me. Whether fighting the sexual and racial prejudices of times gone by, losing their loved ones to the devastation of war or disease, or making a new life on the other side of the world, these women paved the way for us to have the freedom of thought and deed that we enjoy today. And so often take for granted. I never forget that this freedom was won by thousands of generations of remarkable women, perhaps leading right back to the Seven Sisters themselves . . .

I hope you enjoy Maia's journey – according to legend, she was the most beautiful of all the sisters, but also the most solitary. Somehow, she must find the inner strength to no longer hide away from the world, but trust in it – and love – in order to live again.

The Seven Sisters

Maia's Story

Maia

June 2007

First Quarter

13; 16; 21

1

I will always remember exactly where I was and what I was doing when I heard that my father had died.

I was sitting in the pretty garden of my old schoolfriend's townhouse in London, a copy of *The Penelopiad* open but unread in my lap, enjoying the June sun while Jenny collected her little boy from nursery.

I felt calm and appreciated what a good idea it had been to get away. I was studying the burgeoning clematis, encouraged by its sunny midwife to give birth to a riot of colour, when my mobile phone rang. I glanced at the screen and saw it was Marina.

'Hello, Ma, how are you?' I said, hoping she could hear the warmth in my voice too.

'Maia, I . . .'

Marina paused, and in that instant I knew something was dreadfully wrong. 'What is it?'

'Maia, there's no easy way to tell you this, but your father had a heart attack here at home yesterday afternoon, and in the early hours of this morning, he . . . passed away.'

I remained silent, as a million different and ridiculous thoughts raced through my mind. The first one being that

Marina, for some unknown reason, had decided to play some form of tasteless joke on me.

'You're the first of the sisters I've told, Maia, as you're the eldest. And I wanted to ask you whether you would prefer to tell the rest of your sisters yourself, or leave it to me.'

'I . . .'

Still no words would form coherently on my lips, as I began to realise that Marina, dear, beloved Marina, the woman who had been the closest thing to a mother I'd ever known, would never tell me this if it *wasn't* true. So it had to be. And at that moment, my entire world shifted on its axis.

'Maia, please, tell me you're all right. This really is the most dreadful call I've ever had to make, but what else could I do? God only knows how the other girls are going to take it.'

It was then that I heard the suffering in *her* voice and understood she'd needed to tell me as much for her own sake as mine. So I switched into my normal comfort zone, which was to comfort others.

'Of course I'll tell my sisters if you'd prefer, Ma, although I'm not positive where they all are. Isn't Ally away training for a regatta?'

And as we continued to discuss where each of my younger sisters was, as though we needed to get them together for a birthday party rather than to mourn the death of our father, the entire conversation took on a sense of the surreal.

'When should we plan on having the funeral, do you think? What with Electra being in Los Angeles and Ally somewhere on the high seas, surely we can't think about it until next week at the earliest?' I said.

'Well . . .' I heard the hesitation in Marina's voice. 'Perhaps

4

the best thing is for you and I to discuss it when you arrive back home. There really is no rush now, Maia, so if you'd prefer to continue the last couple of days of your holiday in London, that would be fine. There's nothing more to be done for him here . . .' Her voice trailed off miserably.

'Ma, of *course* I'll be on the next flight to Geneva I can get! I'll call the airline immediately, and then I'll do my best to get in touch with everyone.'

'I'm so terribly sorry, *chérie*,' Marina said sadly. 'I know how you adored him.'

'Yes,' I said, the strange calm that I had felt while we discussed arrangements suddenly deserting me like the stillness before a violent thunderstorm. 'I'll call you later, when I know what time I'll be arriving.'

'Please take care of yourself, Maia. You've had a terrible shock.'

I pressed the button to end the call, and before the storm clouds in my heart opened up and drowned me, I went upstairs to my bedroom to retrieve my flight documents and contact the airline. As I waited in the calling queue, I glanced at the bed where I'd woken up this morning to Simply Another Day. And I thanked God that human beings don't have the power to see into the future.

The officious woman who eventually answered wasn't helpful and I knew, as she spoke of full flights, financial penalties and credit card details, that my emotional dam was ready to burst. Finally, once I'd grudgingly been granted a seat on the four o'clock flight to Geneva, which would mean throwing everything into my holdall immediately and taking a taxi to Heathrow, I sat down on the bed and stared for so long at the sprigged wallpaper that the pattern began to dance in front of my eyes.

'He's gone,' I whispered, 'gone forever. I'll never see him again.'

Expecting the spoken words to provoke a raging torrent of tears, I was surprised that nothing actually happened. Instead, I sat there numbly, my head still full of practicalities. The thought of telling my sisters – all five of them – was horrendous, and I searched through my emotional filing system for the one I would call first. Inevitably, it was Tiggy, the second youngest of the six of us girls and the sibling to whom I'd always felt closest.

With trembling fingers, I scrolled down to find her number and dialled it. When her voicemail answered, I didn't know what to say, other than a few garbled words asking her to call me back urgently. She was currently somewhere in the Scottish Highlands working at a centre for orphaned and sick wild deer.

As for the other sisters . . . I knew their reactions would vary, outwardly at least, from indifference to a dramatic out-pouring of emotion.

Given that I wasn't currently sure quite which way *I* would go on the scale of grief when I did speak to any of them, I decided to take the coward's way out and texted them all, asking them to call me as soon as they could. Then I hurriedly packed my holdall and walked down the narrow stairs to the kitchen to write a note for Jenny explaining why I'd had to leave in such a hurry.

Deciding to take my chances hailing a black cab on the London streets, I left the house, walking briskly around the leafy Chelsea crescent just as any normal person would do on any normal day. I believe I actually said hello to someone walking a dog when I passed him in the street and managed a smile.

No one would know what had just happened to me, I thought, as I managed to find a taxi on the busy King's Road and climbed inside, directing the driver to Heathrow.

No one would know.

Five hours later, just as the sun was making its leisurely descent over Lake Geneva, I arrived at our private pontoon on the shore, from where I would make the last leg of my journey home.

Christian was already waiting for me in our sleek Riva motor launch. And from the look on his face, I could see he'd heard the news.

'How are you, Mademoiselle Maia?' he asked, sympathy in his blue eyes as he helped me aboard.

'I'm . . . glad I'm here,' I answered neutrally as I walked to the back of the boat and sat down on the cushioned cream leather bench that curved around the stern. Usually, I would sit with Christian in the passenger seat at the front as we sped across the calm waters on the twenty-minute journey home. But today, I felt a need for privacy. As Christian started the powerful engine, the sun glinted off the windows of the fabulous houses that lined Lake Geneva's shores. I'd often felt when I made this journey that it was the entrance to an ethereal world disconnected from reality.

The world of Pa Salt.

I noticed the first vague evidence of tears pricking at my

eyes as I thought of my father's pet name, which I'd coined when I was young. He'd always loved sailing and often when he returned to me at our lakeside home, he had smelt of fresh air and of the sea. Somehow, the name had stuck, and as my younger siblings had joined me, they'd called him that too.

As the launch picked up speed, the warm wind streaming through my hair, I thought of the hundreds of previous journeys I'd made to Atlantis, Pa Salt's fairy-tale castle. Inaccessible by land, due to its position on a private promontory with a crescent of mountainous terrain rising up steeply behind it, the only method of reaching it was by boat. The nearest neighbours were miles away along the lake, so Atlantis was our own private kingdom, set apart from the rest of the world. Everything it contained was magical . . . as if Pa Salt and we – his daughters – had lived there under an enchantment.

Each one of us had been chosen by Pa Salt as a baby, adopted from the four corners of the globe and brought home to live under his protection. And each one of us, as Pa always liked to say, was special, different . . . we were *his* girls. He'd named us all after The Seven Sisters, his favourite star cluster. Maia being the first and eldest.

When I was young, he'd take me up to his glass-domed observatory perched on top of the house, lift me up with his big, strong hands and have me look through his telescope at the night sky.

'There it is,' he'd say as he aligned the lens. 'Look, Maia, that's the beautiful shining star you're named after.'

And I *would* see. As he explained the legends that were the source of my own and my sisters' names, I'd hardly listen, but simply enjoy his arms tight around me, fully aware of this rare, special moment when I had him all to myself.

I'd realised eventually that Marina, who I'd presumed as I grew up was my mother – I'd even shortened her name to 'Ma' – was a glorified nursemaid, employed by Pa to take care of me because he was away such a lot. But of course, Marina was so much more than that to all of us girls. She was the one who had wiped our tears, berated us for sloppy table manners and steered us calmly through the difficult transition from childhood to womanhood.

She had always been there, and I could not have loved Ma any more if she had given birth to me.

During the first three years of my childhood, Marina and I had lived alone together in our magical castle on the shores of Lake Geneva as Pa Salt travelled the seven seas to conduct his business. And then, one by one, my sisters began to arrive.

Usually, Pa would bring me a present when he returned home. I'd hear the motor launch arriving, run across the sweeping lawns and through the trees to the jetty to greet him. Like any child, I'd want to see what he had hidden inside his magical pockets to delight me. On one particular occasion, however, after he'd presented me with an exquisitely carved wooden reindeer, which he assured me came from St Nicholas's workshop at the North Pole itself, a uniformed woman had stepped out from behind him, and in her arms was a bundle wrapped in a shawl. And the bundle was moving.

'This time, Maia, I've brought you back the most special gift. You have a new sister.' He'd smiled at me as he lifted me into his arms. 'Now you'll no longer be lonely when I have to go away.'

After that, life had changed. The maternity nurse that Pa had brought with him disappeared after a few weeks and Marina took over the care of my baby sister. I couldn't understand how the red, squalling thing which often smelt and diverted attention from me could possibly be a gift. Until one morning, when Alcyone – named after the second star of The Seven Sisters – smiled at me from her high chair over breakfast.

'She knows who I am,' I said in wonder to Marina, who was feeding her.

'Of course she does, Maia, dear. You're her big sister, the one she'll look up to. It'll be up to you to teach her lots of things that you know and she doesn't.'

And as she grew, she became my shadow, following me everywhere, which pleased and irritated me in equal measure.

'Maia, wait me!' she'd demand loudly as she tottered along behind me.

Even though Ally – as I'd nicknamed her – had originally been an unwanted addition to my dreamlike existence at Atlantis, I could not have asked for a sweeter, more loveable companion. She rarely, if ever, cried and there were none of the temper-tantrums associated with toddlers of her age. With her tumbling red-gold curls and her big blue eyes, Ally had a natural charm that drew people to her, including our father. On the occasions Pa Salt was home from one of his long trips abroad, I'd watch how his eyes lit up when he saw her, in a way I was sure they didn't for me. And whereas I was shy and reticent with strangers, Ally had an openness and a readiness to trust that endeared her to everyone.

She was also one of those children who seemed to excel at everything – particularly music, and any sport to do with water. I remember Pa teaching her to swim in our vast pool and, whereas I had struggled to stay afloat and hated being underwater, my little sister took to it like a mermaid. And while I couldn't find my sea legs even on the *Titan*, Pa's huge and beautiful ocean-going yacht, when we were at home Ally would beg him to take her out in the small Laser he kept moored on our private lakeside jetty. I'd crouch in the cramped stern of the boat while Pa and Ally took control as we sped across the glassy waters. Their joint passion for sailing bonded them in a way I felt I could never replicate.

Although Ally had studied music at the Conservatoire de Musique de Genève and was a highly talented flautist who could have pursued a career with a professional orchestra, since leaving music school she had chosen the life of a full-time sailor. She now competed regularly in regattas, and had represented Switzerland on a number of occasions.

When Ally was almost three, Pa arrived home with our next sibling, whom he named Asterope, after the third of The Seven Sisters.

'But we will call her Star,' Pa had said, smiling at Marina, Ally and me as we studied the newest addition to the family lying in the bassinet.

By now I was attending lessons every morning with a private tutor, so my newest sister's arrival affected me less than Ally's had. Then, only six months later, another baby joined us, a twelve-week-old girl named Celaeno, whose name Ally immediately shortened to CeCe.

There was only three months' age difference between Star and CeCe, and from as far back as I can remember, the two of them forged a close bond. They were akin to twins, talking in their own private baby language, some of which the two of them still used to communicate to this day. They inhabited their own private world, to the exclusion of us other sisters. And even now in their twenties, nothing had changed. CeCe, the younger of the two, was always the boss, her stocky body and nut-brown skin in direct contrast to the pale, whippet-thin Star.

The following year, another baby arrived – Taygete, whom I nicknamed 'Tiggy' because her short dark hair sprouted out at strange angles on her tiny head and reminded me of the hedgehog in Beatrix Potter's famous story.

I was by now seven years old, and I'd bonded with Tiggy from the first moment I set eyes on her. She was the most delicate of us all, suffering one childhood illness after another, but even as an infant, she was stoic and undemanding. When yet another baby girl, named Electra, was brought home by Pa a few months later, an exhausted Marina would often ask me if I would mind sitting with Tiggy, who continually had a fever or croup. Eventually diagnosed as asthmatic, she rarely left the nursery to be wheeled outside in the pram, in case the cold air and heavy fog of a Geneva winter affected her chest.

Electra was the youngest of my siblings and her name suited her perfectly. By now, I was used to little babies and their demands, but my youngest sister was without doubt the most challenging of them all. Everything about her *was* electric; her innate ability to switch in an instant from dark to light and vice versa meant that our previously calm home rang daily with high-pitched screams. Her temper-tantrums resonated through my childhood consciousness and as she grew older, her fiery personality did not mellow.

Privately, Ally, Tiggy and I had our own nickname for her; she was known among the three of us as 'Tricky'. We all walked on eggshells around her, wishing to do nothing to set off a lightning change of mood. I can honestly say there were moments when I loathed her for the disruption she brought to Atlantis.

And yet, when Electra knew one of us was in trouble, she was the first to offer help and support. Just as she was capable of huge selfishness, her generosity on other occasions was equally pronounced.

After Electra, the entire household was expecting the arrival of the Seventh Sister. After all, we'd been named after Pa Salt's favourite star cluster and we wouldn't be complete without her. We even knew her name – Merope – and wondered who she would be. But a year went past, and then another, and another, and no more babies arrived home with our father.

I remember vividly standing with him once in his observatory. I was fourteen years old and just on the brink of womanhood. We were waiting for an eclipse, which he'd told me was a seminal moment for humankind and usually brought change with it.

'Pa,' I said, 'will you ever bring home our seventh sister?'

At this, his strong, protective bulk had seemed to freeze for a few seconds. He'd looked suddenly as though he carried the weight of the world on his shoulders. Although he didn't turn around, for he was still concentrating on training the telescope on the coming eclipse, I knew instinctively that what I'd said had distressed him.

'No, Maia, I won't. Because I have never found her.'

As the familiar thick hedge of spruce trees, which shielded our waterside home from prying eyes, came into view, I saw Marina standing on the jetty and the dreadful truth of losing Pa finally began to sink in.

And I realised that the man who had created the kingdom in which we had all been his princesses was no longer present to hold the enchantment in place.

2

Marina put her comforting arms gently around my shoulders as I stepped up onto the jetty from the launch. Wordlessly, we turned to walk together through the trees and across the wide, sloping lawns that led up to the house. In June, our home was at the height of its beauty. The ornate gardens were bursting into bloom, enticing their occupants to explore the hidden pathways and secret grottos.

The house itself, built in the late eighteenth century in the Louis XV style, was a vision of elegant grandeur. Four storeys high, its sturdy pale pink walls were punctuated by tall multipaned windows, and topped by a steeply sloping red roof with turrets at each corner. Exquisitely furnished inside with every modern luxury, its thick carpets and plump sofas cocooned and comforted all who lived there. We girls had slept up on the top floor, which had superb, uninterrupted views of the lake over the treetops. Marina also occupied a suite of rooms upstairs with us.

I glanced at her now and thought how exhausted she looked. Her kind brown eyes were smudged with shadows of fatigue, and her normally smiling mouth looked pinched and tense. I supposed she must be in her mid-sixties, but she didn't seem it. Tall, with strong aquiline features, she was an elegant, handsome woman, always immaculately attired, her effortless chic reflecting her French ancestry. When I was young, she used to wear her silky dark hair loose, but now she coiled it into a chignon at the nape of her neck.

A thousand questions were pushing for precedence in my mind, but only one demanded to be asked immediately.

'Why didn't you let me know as soon as Pa had the heart attack?' I asked as we entered the house and walked into the high-ceilinged drawing room that overlooked a sweeping stone terrace, lined with urns full of vivid red and gold nasturtiums.

'Maia, believe me, I begged him to let me tell you, to tell all you girls, but he became so distressed when I mentioned it that I had to do as he wished.'

And I understood that if Pa had told her not to contact us, she could have done little else. He was the king and Marina was at best his most trusted courtier, at worst his servant who must do exactly as he bade her.

'Where is he now?' I asked her. 'Still upstairs in his bedroom? Should I go and see him?'

'No, *chérie*, he isn't upstairs. Would you like some tea before I tell you more?' she asked.

'To be quite honest, I think I could do with a strong gin and tonic,' I admitted as I sat down heavily on one of the huge sofas.

'I'll ask Claudia to make it. And I think that, on this occasion, I may join you myself.'

I watched as Marina left the room to find Claudia, our housekeeper, who had been at Atlantis as long as Marina. She was German, her outward dourness hiding a heart of gold. Like all of us, she'd adored her master. I wondered suddenly what would become of her and Marina. And, in fact, what would happen to Atlantis itself now that Pa had gone.

The words still seemed incongruous in this context. Pa was always 'gone' – off somewhere, doing something, although none of his staff or family had any specific idea of what he actually did to make his living. I'd asked him once, when my friend Jenny had come to stay with us during the school holidays and been noticeably awed by the opulence of the way we lived.

'Your father must be fabulously wealthy,' she'd whispered as we stepped off Pa's private jet which had just landed at La Môle airport near St Tropez. The chauffeur was waiting on the tarmac to take us down to the harbour, where we'd board our magnificent ten-berth yacht, the *Titan*, and sail off for our annual Mediterranean cruise to whichever destination Pa Salt fancied taking us.

Like any child, rich or poor, given that I had grown up knowing no different, the way we lived had never really struck me as unusual. All of us girls had taken lessons with tutors at home when we were younger, and it was only when I went to boarding school at the age of thirteen that I began to realise how removed our life was from most other people's.

When I asked Pa once what exactly it was he did to provide our family with every luxury imaginable, he looked at me in that secretive way he had and smiled. 'I am a magician of sorts.'

Which, as he'd intended, told me nothing.

As I grew older, I began to realise that Pa Salt was the master illusionist and nothing was as it first seemed.

When Marina came back into the drawing room carrying

two gin and tonics on a tray, it occurred to me that, after thirty-three years, I had no real idea who my father had been in the world outside Atlantis. And I wondered whether I would finally begin to find out now.

'There we go,' Marina said, setting the glass in front of me. 'Here's to your father,' she said as she raised hers. 'May God rest his soul.'

'Yes, here's to Pa Salt. May he rest in peace.'

Marina took a hefty gulp before replacing the glass on the table and taking my hands in hers. 'Maia, before we discuss anything else, I feel I must tell you one thing.'

'What?' I asked, looking at her weary brow, furrowed with anxiety.

'You asked me earlier if your father was still here in the house. The answer is that he has already been laid to rest. It was his wish that the burial happen immediately and that none of you girls be present.'

I stared at her as if she'd taken leave of her senses. 'But Ma, you told me only a few hours ago that he died in the early hours of this morning! How is it possible that a burial could have been arranged so soon? And *why*?'

'Maia, your father was adamant that as soon as he passed away, his body was to be flown on his jet to his yacht. Once on board, he was to be placed in a lead coffin, which had apparently sat in the hold of the *Titan* for many years in preparation for such an event. From there he was to be sailed out to sea. Naturally, given his love for the water, he wanted to be laid to rest in the ocean. And he did not wish to cause his daughters the distress of . . . watching the event.'

'Oh God,' I said, Marina's words sending shudders of horror through me. 'But surely he knew that we'd all want to say goodbye properly? How could he do this? What will I tell the others? I . . .'

'*Chérie*, you and I have lived in this house the longest and we both know that where your father was concerned, ours was never to question why. I can only believe,' she said quietly, 'that he wished to be laid to rest as he lived: privately.'

'And in control,' I added, anger flaring suddenly inside me. 'It's almost as though he couldn't even trust the people who loved him to do the right thing for him.'

'Whatever his reasoning,' said Marina, 'I only hope that in time you can all remember him as the loving father he was. The one thing I do know is that you girls were his world.'

'But which of us knew him?' I asked, frustration bringing tears to my eyes. 'Did a doctor come to confirm his death? You must have a death certificate? Can I see it?'

'The doctor asked me for his personal details, such as his place and year of birth. I said I was only an employee and I wasn't sure of those kinds of things. I put him in touch with Georg Hoffman, the lawyer who handles all your father's affairs.'

'But *why* was he so private, Ma? I was thinking today on the plane that I don't ever remember him bringing friends here to Atlantis. Occasionally, when we were on the yacht, a business associate would come aboard for a meeting and they'd disappear downstairs into his study, but he never actually socialised.'

'He wanted to keep his family life separate from business, so that when he was at home his full attention could be on his daughters.'

'The daughters he adopted and brought here from all over the world. Why, Ma, why?'

Marina looked back at me silently, her wise, calm eyes giving me no clues as to whether or not she knew the answer.

'I mean, when you're a child,' I continued, 'you grow up accepting your life. But we both know it's terribly unusual – if not downright strange – for a single, middle-aged man to adopt six baby girls and bring them here to Switzerland to grow up under the same roof.'

'Your father *was* an unusual man,' Marina agreed. 'But surely, giving needy orphans the chance of a better life under his protection couldn't be seen as a bad thing?' she equivocated. 'Many wealthy people adopt children if they have none of their own.'

'But usually, they're married,' I said bluntly. 'Ma, do you know if Pa ever had a girlfriend? Someone he loved? I knew him for thirty-three years and never once did I see him with a woman.'

'*Chérie*, I understand that your father has gone, and suddenly you realise that many questions you've wanted to ask him can now never be answered, but I really can't help you. And besides, this isn't the moment,' Marina added gently. 'For now, we must celebrate what he was to each and every one of us and remember him as the kind and loving human being we all knew within the walls of Atlantis. Try to remember that your father was well over eighty. He'd lived a long and fulfilling life.'

'But he was out sailing the Laser on the lake only three weeks ago, scrambling around the boat like a man half his age,' I said, remembering. 'It's hard to reconcile that image with someone who was dying.'

'Yes, and thank God he didn't follow many others of his age and suffer a slow and lingering death. It's wonderful that you and the other girls will remember him as fit, happy and healthy,' Marina encouraged. 'It was certainly what he would have wanted.'

'He didn't suffer at the end, did he?' I asked her tentatively, knowing in my heart that even if he had, Marina would never tell me.

'No. He knew what was coming, Maia, and I believe that he'd made his peace with God. Really, I think he was happy to pass on.'

'How on earth do I tell the others that their father has gone?' I entreated her. 'And that they don't even have a body to bury? They'll feel like I do, that he's simply disappeared into thin air.'

'Your father thought of that before he died, and Georg Hoffman, his lawyer, contacted me earlier today. I promise you that each and every one of you will get a chance to say goodbye to him.'

'Even in death, Pa has everything under control,' I said with a despairing sigh. 'I've left messages for all my sisters, by the way, but as yet, no one has called me back.'

'Well, Georg Hoffman is on standby to come here as soon as you've all arrived. And please, Maia, don't ask me what he'll have to say, for I haven't a clue. Now, I had Claudia prepare some soup for you. I doubt you've eaten anything since this morning. Would you prefer to take it to the Pavilion, or do you want to stay here in the house tonight?'

'I'll have some soup here, and then I'll go home if you don't mind. I think I need to be alone.'

'Of course.' Marina reached towards me and gave me a hug. 'I understand what a terrible shock this is for you. And I'm sorry that yet again you're bearing the burden of responsibility for the rest of the girls, but it was you he asked me to tell first. I don't know whether you find any comfort in that. Now, shall I go and ask Claudia to warm the soup? I think we could both do with a little comfort food.'

After we'd eaten, I told Marina to go to bed and kissed her goodnight, for I could see that she too was exhausted. Before I left the house, I climbed the many stairs to the top floor and peered into each of my sisters' rooms. All remained as they had been when their occupants left home to take flight on their chosen paths, and each room still displayed their very different personalities. Whenever they returned, like doves to their waterside nest, none of them seemed to have the vaguest interest in changing them. Including me.

Opening the door to my old room, I went to the shelf where I still kept my most treasured childhood possessions. I took down an old china doll which Pa had given to me when I was very young. As always, he'd woven a magical story of how the doll had once belonged to a young Russian countess, but she had been lonely in her snowy palace in Moscow when her mistress had grown up and forgotten her. He told me her name was Leonora and that she needed a new pair of arms to love her.

Putting the doll back on the shelf, I reached for the box that contained a gift Pa had given me on my sixteenth birthday; I opened it and drew out the necklace inside.

'It's a moonstone, Maia,' he'd told me as I'd stared at the unusual opalescent stone, which shone with a blueish hue and was encircled with tiny diamonds. 'It's older than I am, and comes with a very interesting story.' I remembered he'd hesitated then, as if he was weighing something up in his mind. 'Maybe one day I'll tell you what it is,' he'd continued. 'The necklace is probably a little grown up for you now. But one day, I think it will suit you very well.'

Pa had been right in his assessment. At the time, my body was festooned – like all my schoolfriends' – with cheap silver bangles and large crosses hanging from leather strings around my neck. I'd never worn the moonstone and it had sat here, forgotten on the shelf, ever since.

But I would wear it now.

Going to the mirror, I fastened the tiny clasp of the delicate gold chain around my neck and studied it. Perhaps it was my imagination, but the stone seemed to glow luminously against my skin. My fingers went instinctively to touch it as I walked to the window and looked out over the twinkling lights of Lake Geneva.

'Rest in peace, darling Pa Salt,' I whispered.

And before further memories began to engulf me, I walked swiftly away from my childhood room, out of the house and along the narrow path that took me to my current adult home, some two hundred metres away.

The front door to the Pavilion was left permanently unlocked; given the high-tech security which operated on the perimeter of our land, there was little chance of someone stealing away with my few possessions.

Walking inside, I saw that Claudia had already been in to switch on the lamps in my sitting room. I sat down heavily on the sofa, despair engulfing me.

I was the sister who had never left.

3

When my mobile rang at two in the morning, I was lying sleepless on my bed, pondering why I seemed unable to let go and cry over Pa's death. My stomach performed an abrupt one hundred and eighty degree turn as I saw on the screen it was Tiggy.

'Hello?'

'Maia, I'm sorry to call so late, but I only just picked up your message. We have a very patchy signal up here. I could tell from your voice something was wrong. Are you okay?'

The sound of Tiggy's sweet, light voice thawed the edges of the frozen rock that currently seemed to have taken the place of my heart.

'Yes, I'm okay, but . . .'

'Is it Pa Salt?'

'Yes,' I gulped, breathless from tension. 'How did you know?'

'I didn't . . . I mean I don't . . . but I had the strangest feeling this morning when I was out on the moors searching for one of the young does we'd tagged a few weeks back. I found her dead, and then for some reason, I thought of Pa. I brushed the feeling off, thinking that I was just upset over the doe. Is he . . . ?'

'Tiggy, I'm so, so sorry, but . . . I have to tell you that he died earlier today. Or should I say, yesterday now,' I corrected myself.

'Oh Maia, no! I can't believe it. What happened? Was it a sailing accident? I told him only last time I saw him that he shouldn't be skippering the Laser alone any longer.'

'No, he died here at the house. It was a heart attack.'

'Were you with him? Did he suffer? I . . .' There was a catch in Tiggy's voice. 'I couldn't bear to think of him suffering.'

'No, Tiggy, I wasn't here. I'd gone to visit my friend Jenny in London for a few days. In fact' – I drew in my breath as I remembered – 'it was Pa who persuaded me to go. He said it would do me good to get away from Atlantis and have a break.'

'Oh Maia, how awful for you. I mean, you leave so rarely, and the one time you do . . .'

'I know.'

'You don't think he knew, do you? And wanted to spare you?'

Tiggy voiced the same thought that had flitted across my mind in the past few hours.

'No, I don't. I think it's called Sod's Law. Anyway, don't worry about me. I'm far more concerned about you and the dreadful news I've just had to tell you. Are you okay? I wish I was there with you to give you a hug.'

'To be honest, I can't tell you how I feel just now, because it's simply not real. And perhaps it won't be until I'm home.

I'll try to get on a flight tomorrow. Have you told the others yet?'

'I've left them endless messages asking them to call me urgently.'

'I'll be back as soon as I can to help you, darling Maia. I'm sure there'll be a lot to do with a funeral to arrange.'

I couldn't bring myself to share the news that our father was already buried. 'It'll be good to have you here. Now try to sleep, Tiggy, if you possibly can, and if you need to talk at any time, I'm here.'

'Thank you.' The wobble in Tiggy's voice told me she was on the verge of tears as the news began to sink in. 'Maia, you know he hasn't gone. No spirit dies, they just move on to another plane.'

'I hope that's true. Goodnight, darling Tiggy.'

'Keep strong, Maia, and I'll see you tomorrow.'

As I pressed the button to end the call, I lay back exhausted on the bed, wishing that I shared Tiggy's fervent spiritual beliefs about the afterlife. But just now, I could not think of a single karmic reason why Pa Salt had left the earth.

Perhaps once upon a time, I *had* believed that there was a God, or at least some power beyond human understanding. But somewhere along the line, that comfort had been wiped away.

And if I was honest with myself, I knew exactly when that had happened.

If only I could learn to *feel* again, rather than simply being an automaton who was outwardly a calm, functioning human being. The fact that I didn't seem to be able to react to Pa's death with the kind of emotion it deserved told me more than anything about how deep my problem went.

And yet, I mused, I had no problem comforting others. I knew all my sisters saw me as the family touchstone, the one who would be there for them if there were a problem. Maia; always practical, sensible, and, as Marina had said, supposedly the 'strong' one.

The real truth was that I was filled with more fear than any of them. Whereas all my sisters had taken wing and flown the nest, I had remained, hiding behind the need for my presence here now that Pa was getting older. And using the added excuse that it suited perfectly the career I had chosen, which was a solitary one.

Ironically, given the emptiness of my own personal life, I spent my days in a fictional and often romantic world, translating novels from Russian and Portuguese into French, my first language.

It had been Pa who had first noticed my gift, how I could imitate parrot-fashion any language that he cared to speak to me in. As an expert linguist himself, he enjoyed switching from one to the other and seeing if I could do the same in reply. By the time I was twelve, I was tri-lingual in French, German and English – all languages spoken in Switzerland – and was already proficient in Italian, Latin, Greek, Russian and Portuguese.

Languages were a real passion for me, a challenge that was endless, because however good I became, I could always be better. Words and the correct use of them absorbed me, so when it came to thinking about what I might study at university, the choice was an obvious one.

I turned to Pa for advice on which languages I should focus on.

He'd looked at me thoughtfully. 'Well, Maia, it's for you

to choose, but perhaps it shouldn't be the one you're currently most in command of at present, as you'll have three or four years at university to learn and perfect it.'

'I really don't know, Pa,' I'd sighed. 'I love them all. That's why I'm asking you.'

'Well then, I'll give you a logical view, and tell you that in the next thirty years, the world's economic power is going to radically shift. So if I were you, seeing how you're already fluent in three major western languages, I'd look further afield.'

'You mean countries like China and Russia?' I'd queried.

'Yes, and India and Brazil, of course. All countries that have vast untapped resources, and fascinating cultures too.'

'I've certainly enjoyed Russian, and, in fact, Portuguese. It's a very' – I remember searching for the words – 'expressive language.'

'Well then, there you are.' Pa smiled and I could see he was pleased with my answer. 'Why don't you study both languages? With your natural gift as a linguist, you could easily cope. And I promise you, Maia, that with either or both of those under your belt, the world will be your oyster. There are few people presently who have the vision to see what's coming. The world is changing, and you'll be at the vanguard of it.'

My throat felt parched and dry, and I rolled off the bed and padded into the kitchen to pour myself a glass of water. I thought about how Pa had hoped that I, armed with my unique skills, would step out confidently into the new dawn he was sure was coming. And back then, I'd thought that was almost certainly what I would do too. Apart from anything else, I'd been desperate to make him proud of me.

But as with so many people, life had happened to me and sent me spinning off my planned trajectory. And instead of providing a launch pad into the wider world, my skill-set had enabled me to hide away in my childhood home.

Whenever my sisters fluttered in from their varying existences across the world, they would tease me about my reclusive life. They told me I was in danger of ending up an old maid, for how was I ever to meet someone if I refused to set foot outside Atlantis?

'You're so beautiful, Maia. Everyone who meets you says the same, and yet you sit here alone and waste it,' Ally had chided me the last time I'd seen her.

And it was probably true that it was my outer packaging that made me stand out in a crowd. Coming from a family of six sisters, we'd all been given our labels when we were younger, the key features that made us special:

Maia, the beauty; Ally, the leader; Star, the peacemaker; CeCe, the pragmatist; Tiggy, the nurturer; and Electra, the fireball.

The question was this: had the gifts we'd each been given brought us success and happiness?

Some of my sisters were still very young and hadn't lived enough of their lives for them to know, or for me to judge. But for myself, I knew that my 'gift' of beauty had helped to bring about the most painful moment of my life, simply because I was too naive at the time to understand the power it wielded. So now, I hid it away, which meant hiding myself.

When Pa had been to visit me in the Pavilion lately, he'd often asked me if I was happy.

'Of course, Pa.' I'd always answered in the affirmative. After all, outwardly I had little reason *not* to be. I lived in total comfort, with two pairs of loving arms only a stone's throw away. And the world, technically, *was* my oyster. I had no ties, no responsibilities . . . yet how I longed for them.

I smiled as I thought of Pa, only a couple of weeks ago, encouraging me to visit my old schoolfriend in London. And because it was Pa who suggested it, and I'd spent my adult life feeling that I'd disappointed him, I agreed. Even if I couldn't be 'normal', I hoped he'd think I was if I went.

And so I'd gone to London . . . and returned to find that he had gone too. Forever.

By now it was four in the morning. I returned to my bedroom and lay down, desperate to drift into sleep. But it wouldn't come. My heart began to beat against my chest as I realised that with Pa's passing, I could no longer use him as an excuse to hide here. It might even be that Atlantis would be sold. Pa had certainly never mentioned anything to me about what would happen after his death. And as far as I knew, he'd said nothing to any of my sisters either.

Until a few hours ago, Pa Salt had been omnipotent, omnipresent. A force of nature that had held us all securely aloft.

Pa used to call us his golden apples. Ripe and perfectly rounded, just waiting to be plucked. And now the bough had been shaken, and all of us had been sent tumbling to the ground, with no steady hand to catch us as we fell.

I heard someone knocking at my front door and stumbled groggily from the bed to answer it. In desperation a few hours earlier, as dawn was breaking, I'd searched for the sleeping pills I'd been prescribed years ago and taken one. As I glanced at the clock in the hall and saw it was past eleven, I wished that I hadn't succumbed.

As I opened the door, Marina's concerned face appeared from behind it. 'Good morning, Maia. I tried your landline and mobile and there was no answer, so I came to check that you're all right.'

'Sorry, I took a pill and it knocked me out. Come in,' I said, embarrassed.

'No, I'll let you wake up properly, then perhaps when you've taken a shower and got dressed, you could come over to the house? Tiggy called to let me know she's arriving at around five tonight. She managed to get in touch with Star, CeCe and Electra, so they're on their way home too. Any news from Ally?'

'I'll check my mobile and if not, I'll call her again.'

'Are you all right? You don't look well at all, Maia.'

'I'll be fine, Ma, really. I'll be over later.'

I closed the front door, and scuttled into the bathroom to throw some cold water on my face to jog me awake. As I looked in the mirror, I could see why Marina had asked if I was all right. Lines had appeared overnight around my eyes and there were huge blueish marks underneath them. My normally shiny, dark brown hair hung lank and greasy around my face. And my skin, usually an unblemished honey-brown that needed little make-up, looked puffy and pale.

'Hardly the beauty of the family this morning,' I muttered to my reflection, before searching in the tangled bedclothes for my mobile. Eventually finding it under the duvet, I saw there had been eight missed calls. I listened to my sisters' voices, with their varying messages of disbelief and shock. The only sister who had still not responded to my SOS was Ally. Yet again I spoke to her voicemail and asked her to call me urgently.

Up at the house, I found both Marina and Claudia changing sheets and airing my sisters' rooms on the top floor. I could see that Marina, despite her grief, was happy about her flock of girls returning to the roost. It was a rare occurrence these days for us all to be together under one roof. The last time had been in July, eleven months earlier, on Pa's yacht, cruising round the Greek islands. At Christmas, only four of us were here at home, as Star and CeCe had been travelling in the Far East.

'I've sent Christian off on the boat to collect the food and supplies I've ordered,' said Marina as I followed her downstairs. 'Your sisters are all so fussy these days, what with Tiggy being a vegan, and goodness knows which faddy diet Electra is on,' she grumbled, part of her enjoying every second of the sudden chaos, which reminded her, I knew, of the days when we'd all been in her care. 'Claudia's been up since dawn in the kitchen but I thought we'd keep it simple tonight and have pasta and salad.'

'Do you know what time Electra's arriving?' I asked her as we reached the kitchen where the mouth-watering smell of Claudia's baking brought back a wave of childhood memories.

'Probably not until the early hours. She's managed to get on a flight from LA which takes her to Paris, and she'll fly to Geneva from there.'

'How did she sound?'

'She was crying,' Marina said. 'Hysterically.'

'And Star and CeCe?'

'As usual, CeCe was in charge of their joint arrangements. I didn't speak to Star. CeCe sounded utterly shocked, poor thing, like the wind had been taken out of her sails. They only arrived home from Vietnam ten days ago. Have some fresh bread, Maia. I'm sure you haven't eaten anything yet this morning.'

Marina put a slice slathered with butter and jam in front of me. 'I dread to think how they're all going to be,' I murmured as I took a bite.

'They will all be as they always are, and react in their own, different ways,' replied Marina sagely.

'And of course, they all think they're coming home for Pa's funeral,' I said with a sigh. 'Even though it would have been a hugely upsetting event, at least it would also have been a rite of passage, a chance for us all to celebrate his life, put him to rest and then hopefully begin to move on. Now, they'll arrive home simply to find their father gone.'

'I know, Maia. But what's done is done,' said Marina sadly.

'Surely, at the very least, there are friends or business associates that we should tell?'

'Georg Hoffman said he would be doing all that. He called me again this morning to find out when you'd all be here, so he can arrange to come and see you. I told him I'd let him know as soon as we'd been in touch with Ally. Perhaps he can shed some light on the mysterious workings of your father's mind.'

'Well, I hope someone can,' I muttered grimly.

'Now, do you mind if I leave you to eat alone? I have a thousand things to do before your sisters arrive.'

'Of course. Thank you, Ma,' I said. 'I don't know what we'd all do without you.'

'Or I without you.' She patted me on the shoulder and left the kitchen.

4

Just after five that evening, after an afternoon of wandering aimlessly about the gardens, then trying to settle down to some translation work in an attempt to take my mind off Pa, I heard the motor launch pulling in at the jetty. Relieved that Tiggy had finally arrived and that at least I'd no longer be alone with my thoughts, I flung open the front door and ran across the lawns to greet her.

I watched her as she emerged gracefully from the boat. Pa had often suggested that she take ballet lessons when she was younger; for Tiggy didn't walk, she floated, carrying her lithe, slim body so lightly, it was as if her feet didn't touch the ground. She had an almost other-worldly presence, with her huge liquid eyes, framed by thick eyelashes, dominating her heart-shaped face. As I watched her, I was suddenly struck by her resemblance to the fragile young deer she so ardently took care of.

'Darling Maia,' she said, stretching out her arms towards me.

We stood for a moment in a silent embrace. When she pulled back from me, I saw her eyes were brimming with tears.

'How are you?' she asked.

'Shell-shocked, numb . . . You?'

'The same. Still unable to take it in,' she replied as we began to walk towards the house, our arms clasped tightly around each other's shoulders.

Tiggy stopped abruptly on the terrace and turned to me.

'Is Pa . . . ?' She glanced at the house. 'If he is, I just need to prepare myself for a moment.'

'No, Tiggy, he's not in the house any longer.'

'Oh, I suppose they've taken him to a . . .' Her voice tailed off miserably at the thought.

'Let's go inside, have a cup of tea and I'll explain everything.'

'You know, I tried to feel him . . . I mean, his spirit,' Tiggy said with a sigh. 'But there's simply a void; nothing there.'

'Maybe it's too soon to feel anything,' I comforted, used to Tiggy's strange ideas and not wishing to crush them with harsh pragmatism. 'I certainly can't,' I added as we walked into the kitchen.

Claudia was at the sink and as she turned to see Tiggy – who I'd always suspected was her favourite – I saw the sympathy in her eyes.

'Isn't it just terrible?' Tiggy said, giving her a hug. She was the only one of us who felt comfortable enough to physically embrace Claudia.

'Yes, terrible indeed,' agreed Claudia. 'You and Maia go to the drawing room. I will bring tea to you in there.'

'Where's Ma?' asked Tiggy as we made our way through the house.

'Upstairs, putting the finishing touches to all your bedrooms. And she probably wanted us to have some time together first,' I said as we sat down.

'She was here? I mean, she was with Pa at the end?'

'Yes.'

'But why didn't she contact us all sooner?' Tiggy asked, just as I had.

For the next half an hour, I went through the answers to all the same questions I had bombarded Marina with yesterday. I also told her that Pa's body had already been laid to rest in a lead box in the ocean, expecting her to be as outraged as I'd been. Tiggy simply gave a small shrug of understanding.

'He wanted to return to the place he loved and have his body rest there forever. And in some ways, Maia, I'm glad I didn't see him . . . *lifeless*, because now I can always remember him as he was.'

I studied my sister in surprise. Given she was the most sensitive of us all, the news of Pa's death had evidently not affected her – outwardly at least – as much as I'd envisaged. Her thick chestnut hair shone round her face in a glossy mane, and her enormous brown eyes with their habitually innocent, almost startled, expression were positively sparkling. Tiggy's calm perspective gave me hope that my other sisters might be as outwardly sanguine as she seemed, even if I wasn't.

'Ironically, you look wonderful, Tiggy,' I complimented her, voicing my thoughts. 'It seems all that fresh Scottish air must suit you.'

'Oh, it does, definitely,' she agreed. 'After all those years as a child when I had to stay indoors, I feel I've been released into the wild too. I absolutely love my job, even though it's hard work, and the cottage I'm staying in is incredibly basic. There's not even an indoor loo.'

'Wow,' I said, admiring her ability to eschew all creature comforts in order to follow her passion. 'So it's more fulfilling than working in the laboratory at Servion Zoo?'

'Oh God, completely.' Tiggy raised an eyebrow. 'To be honest, even though it was a great job, I hated it there, because I wasn't working with the animals themselves, just analysing their genetic make-up. You probably think I'm mad to give up a great career to tramp across the Highlands day and night for almost zero pay, but I find it so much more rewarding.'

She looked up and smiled at Claudia as she entered the drawing room carrying a tray, which she set down on the low table before retreating.

'I don't think you're mad, Tiggy. Really, I completely understand.'

'In fact, up until our phone call last night, I was feeling happier than I ever have.'

'It's because you've found your calling, I'm sure,' I smiled.

'Yes, that and . . . other things,' she admitted as I noticed a faint blush appear on her delicate cheekbones. 'But that's for another time. When are the others home?'

'CeCe and Star should be here by seven this evening, and Electra is arriving sometime in the small hours of the morning,' I said, pouring some tea into two cups.

'How was Electra when you told her?' Tiggy asked me. 'Actually, you don't need to answer that, I can imagine.'

'Well, it was Ma who spoke to her. I gather she was bawling her eyes out.'

'True to form, then,' said Tiggy, taking a sip of her tea.

Then she sighed suddenly, the light disappearing from her eyes. 'It feels so odd. I keep expecting Pa to walk in at any second. And of course, he never will again.'

'No, he won't,' I agreed sadly.

'Is there anything we should do?' Tiggy asked, rising suddenly from the sofa and walking to the window to stare out. 'I feel we should be doing . . . *something*.'

'Apparently, Pa's lawyer will come and see us when we've all arrived and explain things, but for now' – I shrugged despairingly – 'all we can do is wait for the others.'

'I suppose you're right.'

I watched as Tiggy pressed her forehead against the windowpane.

'None of us really knew him, did we?' she said quietly.

'No, we didn't,' I conceded.

'Maia, can I ask you another question?'

'Of course.'

'Do you ever wonder where you came from? I mean, who your real mother and father were?'

'Of course it's crossed my mind, Tiggy, but Pa's been everything to me. He *has* been my father. So I suppose I've never needed – or wanted – to think beyond that.'

'Do you think you'd feel guilty if you did try to find out?'

'Maybe,' I replied. 'But Pa has always been enough, and I couldn't imagine a more loving or caring parent.'

'I can understand that. You two always did have a special bond. Perhaps the first child always does.'

'But each one of us had a special relationship with him. He loved us all.'

'Yes, I know he loved me,' said Tiggy calmly. 'But that hasn't stopped me from wondering where I originally came from. I thought of asking him, but I didn't want to upset him. So I never did. Anyway, it's too late now.' She stifled a yawn and said, 'Would you mind if I went up to my room and had a rest? Perhaps it's delayed shock or the fact I haven't had a day off for weeks, but I feel totally exhausted.'

'Of course not. You go and lie down, Tiggy.'

I watched as she floated across the room to the door. 'I'll see you later.'

'Sleep well,' I called as I found myself alone once again. *And* oddly irritated. Maybe it was me, but Tiggy's other-worldliness, her air of being slightly removed from all that went on around her, seemed suddenly more pronounced. I wasn't quite sure what I wanted from her; after all, I'd been dreading my sisters' reactions to the news. I should be glad that Tiggy looked to be handling it so well.

Or was the real reason I felt unsettled the fact that each of my sisters had lives that went on above and beyond Pa Salt and their childhood home, whereas both he and Atlantis had comprised my entire world?

Star and CeCe stepped off the launch just after seven and I was there to greet them both. Never one to volunteer physical affection, CeCe allowed me to clasp her briefly in my arms before pulling away.

'Shocking news, Maia,' she commented. 'Star's very shaken up.'

'I'm sure,' I replied, watching Star as she stood behind her sister, looking even paler than usual.

'How are you, darling?' I asked, reaching my arms towards her.

'Devastated,' Star whispered, resting her head, with its glorious hair the colour of moonlight, on my shoulder for a few seconds.

'At least we're all together now,' I said, as Star moved away from me and towards CeCe, who immediately wrapped her own strong, protective arm once more around her.

'What needs to be done?' CeCe asked as the three of us walked up towards the house.

Again, I took both of them into the drawing room and sat them down. And once more, I repeated the circumstances of Pa's death and his wish to have a private burial with none of us in attendance.

'So who was it that actually put Pa over the side of the boat?' CeCe enquired, as clinically logical as only my fourth sister could be. I understood she didn't mean to be insensitive. CeCe just wanted the facts.

'It's not a question I've asked, to be honest, but I'm sure we can find out. It was probably a member of his crew on the *Titan*.'

'And where did it happen? I mean, near St Tropez where the yacht was moored, or did they sail out to sea? I'm sure they must have done,' added CeCe.

Both Star and I shuddered at her need for detail. 'Ma says he was buried in a lead casket which was already on board the *Titan*. But as to where, I really don't know,' I said, hoping that would be the end of CeCe's probing.

'Presumably, this lawyer will be telling us exactly what's in his will?' she persisted.

'Yes, I should think so.'

'For all we know, we're now destitute,' she said with a shrug. 'You remember how obsessed he was about us all earning our own living? I wouldn't put it past him to have left the lot to charity,' she added.

Even though I understood that CeCe's natural tactlessness was almost certainly more pronounced at this moment to help her cope with her current inner pain, I'd reached my limit. I didn't respond to her comment but instead turned to Star, sitting silently on the sofa next to her sister.

'How are you feeling?' I asked her gently.

'I—'

'She's in shock, like we all are,' cut in CeCe before Star could speak. 'But we'll get through this together, won't we?' she said as she reached a strong brown hand towards her sister and clasped Star's slender, pale fingers within it. 'It's such a shame, because I was about to tell Pa some good news.'

'And what is that?' I enquired.

'I've been offered a place in September on a year's foundation course at The Royal College of Art in London.'

'That's wonderful news, CeCe,' I said. Even though I'd never really understood her strange 'installations', as she called them, preferring a more traditional style to modern art, I knew it was her passion and I was pleased for her.

'Yes, we're thrilled, aren't we?'

'Yes,' Star agreed obediently, although she didn't look it. I could see her bottom lip was trembling.

'We'll base ourselves in London. That's if there are still funds available after we've met with this lawyer of Pa's.'

'Honestly, CeCe,' I said, my stretched patience finally

snapping. 'This is hardly the moment to be thinking of such things.'

'Sorry, Maia, you know it's just my way. I loved Pa very much. He was such a brilliant man and he always encouraged me in my work.'

Just for a few seconds, I saw vulnerability and perhaps a little fear appear in CeCe's hazel-flecked eyes.

'Yes, he was one of a kind,' I affirmed.

'Right, Star, why don't you and I go upstairs and get unpacked?' CeCe suggested. 'What time's supper, Maia? We could both do with something to eat soon.'

'I'll tell Claudia to have it ready as soon as possible. Electra isn't arriving for hours and I still haven't heard from Ally.'

'We'll see you in a while then,' said CeCe, standing up, with Star following suit. 'And anything I can do, you know you simply have to ask.' CeCe smiled at me sadly as she said this. For all her insensitivity, I knew she meant it.

After they left, I pondered the enigma that was the relationship between my third and fourth sisters. Marina and I had discussed it often, both of us concerned as they grew up that Star simply hid behind the strong personality that was CeCe.

'Star seems to have no mind of her own,' I'd said time and time again. 'I haven't a clue what she really thinks about anything. Surely it can't be healthy?'

Marina had agreed wholeheartedly with me, but when I'd mentioned it to Pa Salt, he'd smiled his enigmatic smile and told me not to worry.

'One day, Star will spread her wings and fly, like the glorious angel she is. You wait and see.'

This hadn't comforted me, for just as Star was reliant on CeCe, it was obvious that, for all CeCe's outward self-possession, the dependence was mutual. And if Star *did* one day do as Pa Salt had predicted, I knew CeCe would be completely lost.

Dinner that evening was a sombre affair as my three sisters began to adjust to being home, where everything around us served as a reminder of the enormity of what had been lost to us. Marina did her utmost to keep everyone's spirits up, but seemed uncertain how best to do so. She asked questions about what each of her precious girls were currently doing in their lives, but unspoken memories of Pa Salt brought sporadic tears to all our eyes. Eventually, the attempts at conversation gave way to silence.

'I'll just be glad when Ally's been located and we can move on with hearing whatever it is Pa Salt wanted to tell us,' Tiggy said with a long sigh. 'Excuse me, but I'm going up to bed.'

Kissing all of us, she left the room, followed by CeCe and Star a few minutes later.

'Oh dear,' sighed Marina, when it was just the two of us left alone at the table, 'they're all completely devastated. And I agree with Tiggy: the sooner we've located Ally and she's back, the faster we can all move on.'

'She's obviously out of mobile phone range,' I said. 'You must be completely exhausted, Ma. Go to bed and I'll stay up and wait for Electra to arrive.'

'Are you sure, *chérie?*'

'Yes, positive,' I confirmed, knowing how difficult Marina had always found dealing with my youngest sister.

'Thank you, Maia,' she said, acquiescing without further protest. She rose from the table, kissed me gently on the top of my head and left the kitchen.

For the next half an hour, I insisted on helping Claudia clear up from the evening meal, simply grateful for something to do while I waited for Electra. Used to Claudia's lack of small talk, tonight I found her steady and silent presence particularly comforting.

'Shall I lock up, Miss Maia?' she asked me.

'No, you've had a long day too. Go to bed and I'll see to it.'

'As you wish. *Gute Nacht*,' she said as she left the kitchen.

Wandering through the house, knowing it would be at least a couple of hours before Electra arrived and feeling wide awake due to my unusually long lie-in that morning, I arrived at the door to Pa Salt's study. I had an urge to feel him around me, so I turned the door handle, only to find that it was locked.

This surprised and disturbed me; during the many hours he'd spent in the room working from home, the door had always been freely open to us girls. He'd never been too busy to offer a welcoming smile at my timid knock, and I'd always enjoyed sitting in his study, which contained the physical and material essence of him. Even though banks of computers sat on his desk and a large video screen hung on the wall in readiness for satellite conference calls, my eyes always strayed to the personal treasures placed randomly on the shelves behind the desk.

These were simple objects that he'd told me he'd collected

during his constant travels around the world – amongst other things, a delicate gilt-framed miniature of the Madonna, which could fit in the palm of my hand, an old fiddle, a battered leather pouch and a tattered book by an English poet I'd never heard of.

Nothing rare, nothing particularly valuable that I knew of, just objects that all meant something to him.

Even though I was certain that a man such as Pa could have filled our home with priceless works of art and exquisite antiques if he'd so desired, in reality it did not contain many hugely costly artefacts. If anything, I'd always felt he'd had an aversion to inanimate material possessions of any great worth. He'd derided his wealthy contemporaries vociferously when they'd paid exorbitant sums for famous works of art, telling me that most of them ended up locked away in their strong rooms for fear of their being stolen.

'Art should be on display to all,' he'd said to me. 'It is a gift to the soul from the painter. A painting that has to be hidden from sight is worthless.'

When I'd dared to mention the fact that he himself owned a private jet and a large luxury yacht, he'd raised an eyebrow at me.

'But Maia, can't you see that both those things are simply a mode of transportation? They provide a practical service, a means to an end. And if they went up in flames tomorrow, I could easily replace them. It's enough for me to have my six human works of art: my daughters. The only things on earth worth treasuring, because you are all irreplaceable. People who you love *are* irreplaceable, Maia. Remember that, won't you?'

These were words he'd spoken to me many years before

and that had never left me. I only wished with every fibre in my body that I'd remembered them when I should have done.

I walked away emotionally empty-handed from the door of Pa Salt's study, and went into the drawing room, still wondering why on earth the room had been locked. I'd ask Marina tomorrow, I thought, as I walked across to an occasional table and picked up a photograph. It had been taken aboard the *Titan* a few years ago, and showed Pa, surrounded by all of us sisters, leaning against the railing on the deck of the yacht. He was smiling broadly, his handsome features relaxed, his full head of greying hair swept back by the sea wind, and his still toned and muscular body bronzed by the sun.

'Who *were* you?' I asked the photograph with a frown.

For want of anything better to do, I switched on the television and flicked through the channels until I found the news. As usual, the bulletin was full of war, pain and destruction and I was just about to switch channels when the newsreader announced that the body of Kreeg Eszu, a famous captain of industry who ran a vast international communications company, had been found washed up in a cove on a Greek island.

I listened intently, the remote control frozen in my hand, as the newsreader explained how his family had announced that Kreeg had recently been diagnosed with terminal cancer. The inference was that, given the diagnosis, he had decided to take his own life.

My heart began to beat faster. Not only because my father, too, had recently chosen to spend eternity at the bottom of the ocean, but because this story had a direct connection to *me* . . .

The newsreader stated that his son, Zed, who'd been working alongside his father for a number of years, would be taking over with immediate effect as Chief Executive of Athenian Holdings. An image of Zed flashed up on the screen and I instinctively closed my eyes.

'Oh God,' I groaned, wondering why fate had decided to choose this moment to remind me of a man I'd spent the past fourteen years desperately trying to forget.

So it seemed that, ironically, within the space of a few hours, both of us had lost our fathers to a watery grave.

I stood up, pacing the room, trying to remove the image of his face – which seemed if anything even more handsome than I'd remembered it – from my mind.

Think about the pain he caused you, Maia, I told myself. It's over, it was over years ago. Don't go back there, whatever you do.

But of course, as I sighed and sank down onto the sofa, drained of energy, I knew it could never truly be over.

5

A couple of hours later, I heard the soft humming of the motor launch heralding the arrival of Electra. I took a deep breath and tried to pull myself together. Walking out of the house and into the moonlit gardens, the dew warm under my bare feet, I saw Electra was already crossing the lawns towards me. Her beautiful ebony skin seemed to glow with a lustre in the moonlight as her endless legs made short work of the distance between us.

At over six feet tall, Electra always made me feel insignificant next to her statuesque, effortless elegance. As she reached me, it was she who clasped me tightly to her, my head fitting snugly into her chest.

'Oh Maia!' she moaned. 'Please tell me it isn't true? He can't have gone, he simply can't have. I . . .'

Electra began to sob loudly and I decided that, rather than disturb the other sisters currently sleeping in the house, I'd take her into the Pavilion. I steered her gently in its direction, and she continued to cry pitifully as I closed the door behind us, led her into the sitting room and sat her down on the sofa.

'Maia, what will we all do without him?' she asked me, her glowing amber eyes entreating me to give her the answer.

'There's nothing we can do to take away the pain of his loss, but I hope at least that with all of us being here together, we can comfort each other,' I said, hurriedly taking a box of tissues from the shelf and putting them next to her on the sofa. She took one and wiped her eyes. 'I haven't stopped crying since Ma told me. I just can't bear it, Maia, I simply can't.'

'No, none of us can,' I agreed. And as I watched and listened to her outpouring of grief, I thought how her arresting, sensuous physical presence was so at odds with the vulnerable little girl who inhabited her soul. Often I'd see photos of her in magazines on the arm of a film star or a rich playboy, looking fabulous and totally in control, and I'd wonder if it could really be the same woman as the emotionally volatile sister I knew. I'd come to believe that Electra craved constant displays of love and attention to satisfy some inherent deep-seated insecurity.

'Can I get you something to drink?' I asked, during a hiatus from her sobbing. 'A brandy perhaps? It might help calm you down.'

'No, I haven't had a drink for months now. Mitch is on the wagon too.'

Mitch was Electra's current boyfriend, known to the rest of the universe as Michael Duggan, a world-famous American singer who was currently on a sold-out international tour, playing huge arenas packed to the rafters with screaming fans.

'Where is he at the moment?' I asked, wondering if talk of him would divert Electra from another teary outburst.

'Chicago, and then next week he plays Madison Square

Garden. Maia, can you tell me how Pa Salt died? I really need to know.'

'Are you sure, Electra? You're obviously very upset and you've had such a long flight. Perhaps after a good night's sleep you might feel calmer.'

'No, Maia.' Electra shook her head and made a visible effort to pull herself together. 'Please tell me now.'

So, for the third time, I repeated what Marina had told me, swiftly covering as much ground as I could. Electra sat quietly and listened intently to every word I said.

'So, have you thought about arrangements for the funeral? Mitch did say that if it was next week, he might be able to fly over and help me get through it.'

For the first time, I was actually relieved that Pa had chosen to be laid to rest privately. The thought of the media circus that would have ensued had Electra's megastar boy-friend made an appearance at Pa's funeral sent shudders through me.

'Electra,' I began, 'we're both tired now and—'

'What is it, Maia?' said Electra, immediately picking up on my hesitation. 'Tell me, please.'

'Okay, I will, but please try not to upset yourself again.'

'I'll do my best, I promise.'

So I told her that the funeral of sorts had already taken place. And, to her credit, even though I saw her knuckles were white as she balled her fists in tension, she did not cry again.

'But why would he have done that?' she asked me. 'Surely it's cruel to deny us all a chance to say goodbye to him properly? You know' – Electra's yellow-gold eyes flashed angrily – 'it's so typical of him. I think it's a really selfish thing to have done.'

'Well, we have to believe that he felt the opposite and wanted to spare all of us the pain of saying goodbye to him.'

'But how can I ever feel he's gone? How can any of us? In LA, they talk about "closure" all the time and how important it is. How can that ever happen for us now?'

'To be honest, Electra, I don't think you ever achieve closure after losing someone you've loved.'

'Maybe not, but this doesn't help.' Electra glared at me. 'Well, Pa Salt and I never did see eye to eye on most things. I mean, it was obvious he disapproved of how I earn my living. I think he's the only person who ever thought I had a brain. You remember how furious he was with me when I flunked all my school exams.'

I *did* remember vividly the stand-up arguments that would reverberate from his study over Electra's appalling school reports and other elements of her life as she grew up. Electra only ever saw rules as things to be broken and she was the only one of us who'd stand toe to toe with Pa and fight it out. Yet at the same time, I'd seen the glint of admiration in Pa's eyes when he talked of his fiery youngest daughter.

'She's certainly spirited,' he'd said to me on more than one occasion, 'and that will always mark her out from the crowd.'

'Electra, he adored you,' I comforted her. 'And yes, perhaps he did want you to use your brain, but then, what father doesn't? And let's face it, you've become more successful and famous than any of us. Look at your life compared to mine. You have everything.'

'No I don't,' she sighed suddenly. 'It's all smoke and mirrors, no substance to it really, but there we are. I'm tired, Maia; would you mind if I slept here in the Pavilion with you tonight?'

52

'Of course not. The spare bed is made up. Sleep as late as you want tomorrow, because until we've got hold of Ally, there's nothing any of us can do except wait.'

'Thank you. And I'm sorry I got so emotional. Mitch has put me in touch with a therapist who's trying to help me with my mood swings,' she confessed. 'Can I have a hug?' she asked as she stood up.

'Of course you can.'

I took her into my arms and held her to me. Then she picked up her overnight case and walked towards the sitting room door, halting in front of it. 'I have a terrible headache,' she said. 'Do you have some codeine by any chance?'

'No, sorry, but I think I've got a couple of paracetamol.'

'Don't worry.' Electra gave me a weary smile. 'See you tomorrow.'

As I switched off the lights in the Pavilion and walked towards my bedroom, I reflected that, just as I'd been surprised by Tiggy's muted reaction, so Electra had given me food for thought. There seemed to be an underlying air of desperation about her tonight that concerned me.

As I settled under the bedclothes – perfectly restructured by Claudia after my restless night – I thought how Pa Salt's death might well prove a seminal moment for us all.

None of my sisters were up the following morning when I went to see Marina to enquire if she'd heard anything from Ally.

'No,' she said helplessly.

'Pa would have known what to do. He always did.'

'Yes,' Marina agreed. 'How was Electra?'

'Shocked, devastated and very angry about not being able to say goodbye to Pa properly, but she managed to keep her emotions under control. Just.'

'Good. Georg Hoffman called me again to see if we'd found Ally yet and I had to say no. What can we do?'

'Nothing, except try to be patient. By the way, Ma,' I said as I made myself some tea, 'when I tried to get into Pa's study last night, I found the door was locked. Do you know why?'

'Because your father asked me to lock it for him just before he died. And then insisted I give him the key straight afterwards. I've no idea where he put it and, to be honest, with everything being so . . . difficult, it slipped my mind.'

'Well, we'll obviously have to find it. I'm sure that Georg will need to get in there. It's almost certainly where Pa kept all his papers.'

'Of course. Now, seeing that none of your sisters have managed to appear yet and it's nearly noon, I thought that Claudia should cook a brunch,' said Marina.

'Good idea,' I agreed. 'I'll go back to the Pavilion and see if Electra's awake.'

'All right, *chérie*.' Marina threw me a sympathetic smile. 'The waiting will be over soon.'

'I know.'

I walked out of the house and was heading towards the Pavilion when, through the trees, I glimpsed a lone figure sitting on the jetty staring out across the lake. I walked towards her and tapped her gently on the shoulder, trying not to startle her.

'Star, are you okay?'

'Yes, I suppose so,' she said, shrugging.

'Can I join you?'

She gave an almost imperceptible nod in response, and as I sat down and swung my legs over the edge of the jetty, I glanced at her and saw her face was streaked with tears.

'Where's CeCe?' I asked.

'Still sleeping. She likes to sleep when she's upset. Last night I couldn't sleep at all.'

'No, I'm struggling to as well,' I admitted.

'I simply can't believe he's gone, Maia.'

I sat next to her silently, knowing how rare it was for her to talk openly about her feelings to anyone other than CeCe. And I wanted to say nothing that might cause her to clam up.

'I feel . . .' she said eventually '. . . lost. I always knew somehow that Pa was the only person who really understood me. I mean *really* understood.'

She turned to me then, her striking, almost ghostly features distorted into a mask of despair. 'Do you know what I mean, Maia?'

'Yes,' I said slowly. 'I think I do. And please, Star, if you ever need someone else to talk to, I'm always here. Remember that, won't you?'

'I will.'

'There you are!'

Both of us jumped instinctively and turned round to see CeCe striding along the jetty towards us. Perhaps I imagined it, but I'm sure that I saw the tiniest hint of irritation pass fleetingly across Star's opalescent blue eyes.

'I came to get some fresh air because you were asleep,' Star said as she stood up.

'Well, I'm awake now. And so is Tiggy. Did Electra arrive

last night? I just looked into her bedroom and there were no signs of anyone having slept in there.'

'Yes, she stayed at the Pavilion with me. I'll go see if she's woken up,' I said, standing up and following my two sisters back across the lawns.

'Presumably, you had a tough night last night, Maia, dealing with Electra's usual histrionics?' said CeCe.

'As a matter of fact, for Electra, she was relatively calm,' I answered, knowing there was little love lost between my fourth and sixth sisters. Each was the antithesis of the other: CeCe so practical and loath to show any emotion, and Electra so volatile.

'Well, I'm sure it won't be for long,' CeCe sniffed. 'See you later.'

I headed back to the Pavilion, pondering Star's distress. Although she hadn't actually voiced it, it was the first time I'd ever had an inkling that CeCe's domination of her was a problem. Entering the Pavilion, I heard sounds of movement from the kitchen.

Electra, looking astonishing in an emerald silk robe, was filling the kettle.

'How did you sleep?' I asked her.

'Like a baby. You know me, I always do. Would you like some tea?'

I eyed the teabag warily. 'What is it?'

'Virgin green. Everyone's drinking it in California. Mitch says it's meant to be very good for you.'

'Well, you know me, I'm addicted to good old caffeine-fuelled English Breakfast tea,' I smiled as I sat down, 'so I think I'll pass.'

'We're all addicted to something, Maia. I wouldn't worry too much about tea. So, any news of Ally?'

I related to her exactly what Marina had told me up at the house.

'I know patience isn't one of the virtues that I possess, as my therapist never ceases to remind me, but are we all simply meant to hang around here until Ally turns up? If she's out at sea, it could be weeks.'

'I really hope not,' I said as I watched her sashaying gracefully around the kitchen. Even though I was considered the beauty of the family, I'd always thought that the title should have gone to Electra. Just out of bed, her hair hanging loose around her shoulders in a tangled, tightly curled mane, her face needed not a hint of make-up to highlight her incredible cheekbones and full lips. Coupled with her athletic yet feminine body, she reminded me of an Amazonian queen.

'Have you anything in here that isn't full of additives?' she queried, pulling open the fridge and studying its contents.

'Sorry. Ordinary mortals like me don't scrutinize the fine print on labels,' I retorted, hoping she'd take the joke.

'Well, let's face it, Maia, it hardly matters what you look like, when you barely see another human from one day to the next, does it?'

'No, you're right, it doesn't,' I replied equably. After all, it was quite true.

Electra finally decided on a banana for her breakfast, opened it and bit into it disconsolately. 'I have a big shoot for *Vogue* in three days' time, which I hope I don't have to cancel.'

'I hope not either, but who knows when Ally will appear? Last night, I googled sailing regattas taking place at the moment, but I couldn't find any. So we can't even send out a message to the maritime authorities to contact her. Anyway,' I suggested, 'the others are awake up at the house so, when you're dressed, why don't we go across and see them?'

'If we must,' said Electra nonchalantly.

'Listen, I'll see you in a bit,' I said, rising from the table, knowing that in a mood like this, Electra was best left alone. I went into the room I used as my study, sat down behind the desk and turned my computer on. I saw I had a sweet email from a Brazilian author, Floriano Quintelas, whose beautiful novel, *The Silent Waterfall*, I'd translated from Portuguese a few months ago. I'd corresponded with him during the translation process when I'd been struggling over a particular phrase – I had wanted to convey as authentically as I could the poetic, ethereal quality of his writing – and we'd periodically exchanged emails ever since.

He was emailing to tell me that he'd be flying over for publication of his book in Paris in July and he'd love me to attend the launch party. He'd also attached the first chapters of his new book, asking me to read them if I had time.

His email warmed my heart, for sometimes translation could be an anonymous and correspondingly thankless task. So I treasured the rare occasions when an author contacted me directly and I felt a connection with them.

My attention was diverted from my computer by the sight of a familiar figure running up the lawns from the jetty.

'Ally,' I breathed in surprise, as I sprang up from my desk. 'Electra, Ally's arrived!' I called as I hurried out of the Pavilion to greet her.

My other sisters had obviously seen her arrive too, and by the time I reached the terrace of the main house, CeCe, Star and Tiggy were already clustered around her.

'Maia,' Ally said as she saw me, 'isn't it absolutely awful?'

'Yes, just ghastly. But how did you hear? We've been trying to contact you for the last two days.'

'Shall we go inside?' she asked us all. 'And then I'll explain.'

I lagged behind slightly while my other sisters crowded around Ally as they walked into the house. Even though I was the eldest and the one they looked to individually if they had a problem, as a group, it was Ally who always took command. As I let her do now.

Marina was already at the bottom of the stairs, ready and waiting with open arms. Once Ally had embraced her too, she suggested we all head into the kitchen.

'Good idea. I really am desperate for some coffee,' Ally said. 'It's been a long journey home.'

As Claudia prepared a large pot of coffee, Electra sidled in and was warmly welcomed by everyone apart from CeCe, who made a point of merely nodding in her direction.

'Right, I'm going to tell you what happened, because to be honest, I'm still confused about it,' said Ally as we all sat down around the table. 'Ma,' she said to Marina, who was hovering, 'you should hear this too. Maybe you can help explain.'

Marina sat down at the table with us.

'So, there I was, down in the Aegean Sea, training for the Cyclades Regatta next week, when a sailing friend of mine asked me if I wanted to join him on his motor yacht for a few days. The weather was fantastic and it was great to actually relax on the water for a change,' Ally acknowledged with a rueful smile.

'Whose boat was it?' asked Electra.

'I told you, just a friend,' Ally responded abruptly, and each one of us raised our eyebrows in disbelief.

'Anyway,' she continued, 'there we were a couple of afternoons ago, when my friend told me that another sailing mate of his had radioed him to say he'd spotted the *Titan* anchored off the coast of Delos. My friend obviously knew the boat belonged to Pa, and we both decided it would be fun to surprise him and rendezvous with him. We were only an hour or so away if we stepped on it, so we raised anchor and set off.'

Ally took a sip of her coffee before continuing.

'I saw the *Titan* through the binoculars as we neared it and radioed Hans, Pa's skipper, to tell him we were close by. But' – Ally sighed – 'for reasons that I didn't understand at the time, no message came back. And in fact, we could see that the boat was already moving away from us. We did what we could to catch it, but as you all know, Pa's boat can shift when it wants to.'

I watched my sisters' rapt faces around the table, all clearly intrigued by Ally's story.

'The signal on my mobile was dreadful and it was only yesterday when I was able to pick up all your messages asking me to call you urgently. And one from you, CeCe, telling me exactly what had happened.'

'Sorry, Ally.' CeCe lowered her eyes in embarrassment. 'I didn't think there was any point beating about the bush. We needed to get you home as fast as possible.'

'And I came. So please,' Ally entreated us, 'can somebody tell me what on earth was going on? And why Pa Salt's boat was down in Greece when he was already . . . dead?'

All eyes at the table turned to me, including Ally's. So, as concisely as I could, I told her what had happened, referring occasionally to Marina for confirmation. Ally's face drained of colour when I explained where and how our father had wanted to be laid to rest.

'Oh my God,' she whispered. 'So the chances are that I happened upon his private funeral. No wonder the boat sped off as fast as it could away from me. I . . .'

Ally put her head in her hands and the other girls stood up and gathered around her. Marina and I shot each other painful glances from opposite ends of the table. Finally, Ally recovered her composure and apologised for her instinctive display of emotion.

'It must be an awful shock for you to realise what was actually happening,' said Tiggy. 'We're all so sorry for you, Ally.'

'Thank you,' she said, nodding. 'But now I think about it, Pa did tell me once when we were out sailing together that his wish was to be buried at sea. So I suppose it all makes sense.'

'Apart from the fact that none of us were invited to be in attendance when it happened,' commented Electra mutinously.

'No. We weren't,' Ally sighed. 'And yet, totally by coincidence, there I was. Listen, would you all mind terribly if I had a little time alone?'

My sisters and I all agreed she should, and with messages of support called after her, Ally left the kitchen.

'How dreadful for her,' said Marina.

'Well, at least we all know approximately where Pa Salt decided to be buried,' said CeCe.

'Jesus, CeCe, is that really all you can think of?' shot Electra.

'Sorry, ever practical, that's me,' CeCe replied, unperturbed.

'Yes, I'm rather glad we *do* know his whereabouts,' countered Tiggy. 'We all know he had a huge soft spot for the Greek Islands, the Cyclades in particular. Perhaps this summer we should take his yacht out and drop a wreath at sea, wherever it was that Ally spotted the boat on the radar.'

'Yes,' Star ventured. 'That's a beautiful idea, Tiggy.'

'Now, girls, can anyone manage some brunch?' asked Marina.

'Not for me,' said Electra. 'I'll have some salad, if there's any green stuff going in this house.'

'I'm sure we can find something to suit you,' said Marina patiently, signalling to Claudia that she should begin preparing the food. 'Now that Ally's home, should I call Georg Hoffman, and ask him to come here as soon as he can?'

'Absolutely,' said CeCe, before I could answer. 'Whatever Pa Salt wanted us to know, let's hear it as soon as soon as possible.'

'Do you think Ally will be up to it?' said Marina. 'She's had a horrible shock today.'

'To be honest, I think, like all of us, she'd prefer to get it over with,' I said. 'So yes, Ma, call Georg.'

6

Ally didn't appear for lunch and we all left her alone, knowing she'd need some time to comprehend what had happened.

Marina arrived in the kitchen as Claudia was clearing the plates from the table. 'I've spoken to Georg, and he's arriving just before sunset tonight. Apparently, your father was specific in his requests, time-wise.'

'Right. Well, I could do with a breath of fresh air after that huge lunch,' said CeCe. 'Anyone up for a quick trip out on the lake?'

The rest of the sisters, perhaps eager to escape the growing tension, agreed.

'I won't join you, if you don't mind,' I said. 'One of us should be here for Ally.'

When the four of them had departed on the launch with Christian, I told Marina I was going back to the Pavilion, and that if Ally needed me, that was where I'd be. I curled up on the sofa with my laptop and began to read the opening chapters of Floriano Quintelas's new book. Like his first one, the prose was exquisitely crafted and exactly the kind of narrative that I loved. It was set a hundred years ago, near the Iguazu Falls, and told the story of a young African boy released from the tyranny of slavery. Engrossed, I must have relaxed so much that I actually dozed off, as the next thing I knew, my laptop had slipped to the floor and someone was calling my name.

Waking with a start, I saw it was Ally.

'I'm sorry, Maia. You were asleep, weren't you?'

'I guess I was,' I agreed, for some reason feeling guilty.

'Ma says that the other girls have gone out on the lake, so I thought I'd come and speak to you. Do you mind?'

'Not at all,' I said, trying to shake off the torpor of my impromptu afternoon nap.

'Shall I make us both a cup of tea?' Ally asked me.

'Yes, thank you. The usual English Breakfast for me.'

'I know,' she smiled, raising her eyebrows slightly as she left the room. When she returned with two steaming cups and sat down, I saw that, as she lifted hers to her mouth, her hands were shaking.

'Maia, I need to tell you something.'

'What is it?'

Ally put her cup down abruptly in its saucer. 'Forget the tea. Have you got anything stronger?'

'There's some white wine in the fridge,' I said and went into the kitchen to retrieve the bottle and a glass. Given that Ally rarely drank, I knew that whatever it was she wanted to share with me must be serious.

'Thank you,' she said as I handed the glass to her. 'It's probably nothing,' she said as she took a sip. 'But when we arrived at the spot near where Pa's boat had been and saw it speeding off into the distance, there was another large boat still moored there.'

'Well, surely that's not unusual, is it?' I queried. 'It's late

June, and the waters in the Mediterranean are bound to be crowded with holidaymakers.'

'Yes, but . . . this was a boat that both I and my friend recognised. It was the *Olympus*.'

My teacup was halfway up to my mouth as Ally said this. I clattered it back into its saucer.

'And of course, you've almost certainly heard what happened on the *Olympus*. I read about it in the newspaper on the plane.' Ally bit her lip.

'Yes, I saw it on the news.'

'Don't you think it's strange that Pa had obviously picked this particular place in which to be laid to rest? And that probably, at about the same time, Kreeg Eszu was choosing to take his own life close by?'

Of course I thought – for more reasons than I could ever tell Ally – that it was a ridiculous, almost obscene coincidence. But anything more than that? It couldn't be.

'Yes,' I said, doing my best to hide my distress. 'It is. But I'm sure there's no link. They didn't even know each other, did they?'

'Not as far as I'm aware,' said Ally. 'But what *did* we know about Pa's life beyond this house and his yacht? We met so few of his friends, or his business associates. And it stands to reason that they may well have come across each other in the past. After all, they were both hugely rich and successful men.'

'Yes, Ally, but I'm sure that this was simply a coincidence. After all, you were in the vicinity too on your boat. Delos is simply a very beautiful island that many boats head for.'

'Yes, I know that. But I can't get the thought out of my mind that Pa is lying alone on the seabed there. And of course, at the time I didn't even realise he was dead. Let alone that he was somewhere beneath that incredible blue sea. I . . .'

I stood up and went to put an arm around my sister. 'Ally, please, forget about the other boat being there – it's irrelevant. But the fact you were there to see the area where Pa chose to be buried is actually comforting. Perhaps, as Tiggy suggested, in the summer we can all take a cruise together and lay a wreath on the water.'

'The worst thing is' – Ally was sobbing now – 'I feel so guilty!'

'Why?'

'Because . . . those few days on the boat were so beautiful! I was so happy, happier than I've ever felt in my life. And the truth is, I didn't want anyone to contact me, so I turned off my mobile. And while it was off, Pa was dying! Just when he needed me, I wasn't there!'

'Ally, Ally . . .' I stroked her hair back from her face as I rocked her gently. 'None of us were there. And I honestly believe it's the way Pa wanted it to be. Please remember I live here, and even I had flown the nest when it happened. From what Ma has said, there really was nothing that could have been done. And we must all believe that.'

'Yes, I know. But it feels as though there are so many things I wanted to ask him, to tell him, and now he's gone.'

'I think we all feel that way,' I said ruefully. 'But at least we have each other.'

'Yes, we do. Thank you, Maia,' Ally said gratefully. 'Isn't it amazing,' she sighed, 'how our lives can turn on their heads in a matter of hours?'

'Yes, it is,' I agreed fervently. 'Anyway, at some point, I'd like to know the reason for your happiness.'

'And at some point, I'll tell you, I promise. But not just yet. How are you, Maia?' she asked me suddenly, changing the subject.

'I'm okay,' I shrugged. 'Still in shock like everyone.'

'Yes, of course you are, and telling our sisters can't have been easy. I'm sorry that I wasn't here to help you.'

'Well, at least the fact that you're here now means we can meet with Georg Hoffman and begin to move on.'

'Oh yes, I forgot to say that Ma has asked us to be up at the house in an hour. He's due here any minute, but wants to have a chat with her first, apparently. So,' Ally said, 'can I please have another glass of wine while we wait?'

At seven o'clock, Ally and I walked back to the house and found our sisters sitting in the late evening sun on the terrace.

'Has Georg Hoffman arrived?' I asked them as we both sat down.

'Yes, but we've been told to wait here. He and Ma have disappeared off somewhere. Typical Pa Salt, mysterious to the last,' Electra commented acerbically.

The six of us sat waiting tensely until Georg eventually appeared on the terrace with Marina.

'Sorry to keep you so long, girls; there was something I had to organise. My condolences to you all,' he said stiffly, reaching out his hand around the table and shaking each of ours in the usual formal Swiss manner. 'May I sit down?'

'Of course,' I said, indicating the chair next to me. I studied him, dressed immaculately in a dark suit, the creases on his tanned face and his receding silver-grey hair telling me he was probably in his early sixties.

'I'll be inside if anyone needs me,' said Marina with a nod, before walking off in the direction of the house.

'Well, girls,' Georg said. 'I am so very sorry that the first time I meet you in person is under such tragic circumstances. But of course, I feel as though I know each of you very well through your father. The first thing I must tell you is that he loved you all very much. Not only that, but he was passionately proud of who you have all become. I spoke to him just before he . . . left us, and he wanted me to tell all of you this.'

I was surprised to see a glint of tears in Georg's eyes – I knew how unusual it was for a man such as he to show any emotion, and I warmed to him somewhat.

'The first thing to do is to get the finances out of the way and reassure all of you that you will be provided for, at some level, for the rest of your lives. However, your father was adamant that you should not live like lazy princesses, so you will all receive an income which will be enough to keep the wolf from the door, but never allow you to live your lives in luxury. That part, as he stressed to me, is what you must all earn yourselves, just as he did. However, your father's estate is held in trust for all of you and he has given me the honour of managing it for him. It will be down to my discretion to give you further financial help if you come to me with a proposition or a problem.'

All of us remained silent, listening intently to what Georg was telling us.

'This house is also part of the trust, and Claudia and Marina have both agreed that they are happy to stay on and take care of it. On the day of the last sister's death, the trust will be dissolved and Atlantis can be sold and the proceeds divided between any children you may have among you. If there are none, then the money will go to a charity of your father's choice. Personally,' Georg commented, 'I think what your father has done is most clever: making sure the house is here for the rest of your lives, so you know you have a safe place to return to. But of course, your father's ultimate wish is for all of you to fly away and forge your own destinies.'

I watched the other sisters exchanging glances, unsure whether they were pleased with Pa's decision or not. For myself, I realised that practically and financially, little had changed. I still had the Pavilion, for which I paid a nominal rent to Pa, and my career would provide comfortably for any other immediate needs.

'Now, there is one further thing that your father has left you, and I must ask you all to come with me. Please, this way.'

Georg stood up and, instead of walking towards the front door of the house, he traversed the side of it and we followed him, like lambs after a shepherd, through the gardens. Eventually, we arrived in a hidden garden that sat behind a wall of immaculately clipped yews. It looked directly onto the lake, with a spectacular uninterrupted view of the sunset and the mountains on the other side.

From the terrace that sat in the centre of it, there were steps leading down to a small, pebbled cove where we sisters had swum often in the summer in the clear, cool waters. I also knew that it was Pa's favourite spot in the gardens. If I couldn't find him in the house, I'd usually find him sitting here, with the sweet smell of lavender and the scent of roses emanating from the well-tended flower beds.

'So,' said Georg, 'here we are. And this is what I wish to show you.'

He pointed to the terrace and we all stared at the strange but beautiful sculpture that had appeared in the centre of it.

Gathering round, we studied the object in fascination. It consisted of a stone plinth rising to just below hip height, with an unusual circular structure set on top of it. As I peered at it, I saw that the shape was made up of an intricate series of slender, overlapping bands, enclosing a small golden ball at their centre. On closer inspection, I realised that the ball was in fact a globe, with the outline of the continents engraved upon it, and that it was skewered by a slim metal rod with an arrow at one end of it. Around the circumference was a further band, depicting the twelve astrological signs of the zodiac.

'What is it?' asked CeCe, speaking for all of us.

'It is an armillary sphere,' said Georg.

Seeing that we looked none the wiser, Georg continued. 'The armillary sphere has existed for thousands of years. The ancient Greeks originally used them to determine the positions of the stars, as well as the time of day. These,' he said, indicating the golden bands encircling the globe, 'all depict the equatorial, latitudinal and longitudinal lines of the earth. And the meridian line, which encircles all of them, and has the twelve signs of the zodiac inscribed on it, runs from north to south. The central rod points directly to Polaris, the North Star.'

'It's beautiful,' breathed Star, bending over to take a closer look.

'Yes, but what does it have to do with us?' asked Electra.

'It isn't part of my remit to explain that,' said Georg.

'Although, if you look closely, you'll see that all of your names appear on the bands I pointed out just now.'

We all bent in closer, and saw that Georg was right.

'Here's yours, Maia,' said Ally, pointing to it. 'It has numbers after it, which look to me like a set of coordinates,' she said, turning to her own and studying them. 'Yes, I'm sure that's what they are. It's what we use to navigate on the sea all the time.'

'And there are inscriptions too, but they seem to be engraved in a different language,' commented Electra.

'They're in Greek,' I said, immediately recognising the lettering.

'What do they say?' asked Tiggy.

'I'd have to get some paper and a pen and write them down to work them out,' I said, looking closely at my own inscription.

'Okay, so this is a very nice sculpture and it's sitting on the terrace. But what does it actually mean?' asked CeCe impatiently.

'Once again, that is not for me to say,' said Georg. 'Now, Marina is pouring some champagne on the main terrace, as per your father's instructions. He wanted all of you to toast his passing. And then after that, I will give you each an envelope from him, which I hope will explain far more than I am able to tell you.'

Once again, we followed him back through the gardens, all of us stunned into silence. Arriving on the terrace, we did indeed find two chilled bottles of Armand de Brignac champagne and a tray of crystal flutes. As we settled ourselves, Marina clucked around us and poured some for each of us.

Georg raised his glass.

'Please join me in celebrating your father's remarkable life. I can only tell you that this was the funeral he wished for: all his girls gathered together at Atlantis, the home he was honoured to share with you for all these years.'

Like robots, we all lifted our glasses. 'To Pa Salt,' I said.

'To Pa Salt,' the rest of my sisters chorused.

We all took an uncomfortable sip, and I looked up to the heavens and then out to the lake and mountains beyond and told him I loved him.

'So, when do we get these letters?' asked Ally eventually.

'I'll go and get them now.' Georg stood up and left the table.

'Well, this has to be the most bizarre wake I've ever attended,' said CeCe.

'Trust Pa Salt,' Electra said with a wan smile.

'Can I have some more champagne?' asked Ally.

And Marina, noticing we'd all drained our glasses, topped us up.

'Do you understand it, Ma?' asked Star nervously.

'I know nothing more than you do, *chérie*,' she replied, her usual enigmatic self.

'Well, I just wish he was here,' said Tiggy, her eyes suddenly filling with tears, 'to explain in person.'

'But he isn't,' Ally reminded her quietly, 'and somehow I feel this is fitting. For something so awful, he made it as easy as possible. And now we must take strength from each other.'

'You're right,' agreed Electra.

I looked at Ally and wished that I could find the right words – as she always seemed able to do – to rally our sisters.

By the time Georg returned, the champagne had relaxed us all a little. He sat back down and placed six thick cream-coloured vellum envelopes on the table. 'These letters were lodged with me approximately six weeks ago. And in the event of your father's death, I was instructed to hand one to each of you.'

We all eyed them with equal amounts of interest and suspicion. 'May I have a refill of champagne, as well?' asked Georg in a voice that sounded strained.

I realised then how difficult all this had to be for him too. Telling six grieving daughters of their father's unusual legacy would have taxed even the most pragmatic individual.

'Of course, Georg,' Marina said, as she poured a glass for him.

'So,' said Ally, 'are we meant to open them now, or later, when we're alone?'

'Your father made no stipulation on this point,' Georg replied. 'All he said was that you should open them whenever each of you is ready and feels comfortable to do so.'

I studied my letter. My name was written in the beautiful script I knew intimately as my father's writing. Just the sight of it made me want to weep.

We all looked at each other, trying to work out how everyone else felt.

'I think I'd prefer to read mine privately,' said Ally.

There was a general murmur of agreement. I knew that, as usual, Ally had instinctively read our collective feelings correctly.

'So, my job is now done.' Georg drained his glass, then reached into his jacket pocket and pulled out six cards, which he distributed around the table. 'Please don't hesitate to contact me, any of you, if you need my help. And rest assured I'll be available to you day and night. But I'm sure that, knowing your father, he will have anticipated already what it is that you might all need. So, now it is time for me to leave you. Once again, girls, my condolences to you.'

'Thank you, Georg,' I said. 'We all appreciate your help.'

'Goodbye.' He stood and nodded to us all. 'You know where I am if you need me. There's no need to see me out.'

We watched him leave in silence, then I saw Marina rise from the table too.

'I think we could all do with something to eat. I'll tell Claudia to bring supper out here,' she said and disappeared inside the house.

'I'm almost frightened to open this,' said Tiggy, fingering her envelope. 'I have absolutely no idea what it contains.'

'Maia, do you think you could go back to the armillary sphere and translate the quotations on it?' asked Ally.

'Of course,' I said, seeing Marina and Claudia walking towards us with plates of food. 'After supper, I will.'

'I hope you guys don't mind, but I'm not hungry,' said Electra, standing up. 'I'll see you later.'

As she left, I knew that every one of us wished we had the courage to do the same. We all wanted time alone.

'Are you hungry, Star?' asked CeCe.

'I think we should eat something,' Star answered quietly, her hands clasped tightly around her envelope.

'Okay,' said CeCe.

All of us valiantly forced down our food, lovingly prepared by Claudia. And then, one by one, my sisters began to stand up and walk silently from the table, until only Ally and I were left.

'Do you mind, Maia, if I go to bed too? I feel completely exhausted.'

'Of course not,' I answered, 'You were the last one to hear and you're still getting over the shock.'

'Yes, I think I am,' she agreed, standing up. 'Goodnight, darling Maia.'

'Goodnight.'

As I watched her leave the terrace, my fingers closed around the envelope that had been sitting by my plate for the past hour. Finally I stood up and walked towards the Pavilion. In my bedroom I put the envelope under my pillow, then went into my study to gather some paper and a pen.

Armed with a torch, I walked back across the gardens to study the armillary sphere. Night was truly descending, and the first stars were emerging. Pa Salt had shown me The Seven Sisters many times from his observatory, when they hung directly over the lake between November and April.

'I miss you,' I whispered to the heavens, 'and I hope that one day I understand.'

Then I turned my attention to the golden bands circumnavigating the globe. Copying down the Greek words as best I could with the torch held in my left hand, and thinking that I must return tomorrow to make sure that I had them all exactly right, I counted the inscriptions I had.

There were six.

But there was still one band I had not yet looked at. As I shone the torch onto the seventh, searching for the inscription, I saw that it was blank apart from a name: 'Merope'.

7

I spent the small hours translating the quotes on the armillary sphere. Whether each one was relevant to the other girls, I didn't feel it was my place to investigate. I left mine until last, almost too frightened to know what it said. When I'd finished translating it, I took a deep breath and read it.

Never let your fear decide your destiny

I knew that the seven words Pa Salt had left me could not have described me and who I was any more accurately.

The next morning, after making my requisite cup of tea, I returned to the bedroom, tentatively pulled the envelope from under my pillow, and carried it into the sitting room. I studied it for a while as I sipped my tea.

Then, taking a few deep breaths, I picked it up and tore it open. Inside was a letter, but also something else; as I reached inside to grasp it, it felt solid, yet somehow also soft beneath my fingers. As I drew it out, I saw it was a triangular-shaped stone tile, creamy in colour but with a green hue to it. I turned it over and saw there was an illegible faded inscription on the back of it.

Unable to decipher it, I set it down, and, with trembling hands, I unfolded Pa's letter and began to read.

Atlantis
Lake Geneva
Switzerland

My dearest Maia,

I'm sure as you sit and read this that you'll be feeling confused and sad. My beloved first-born girl, I can only tell you what a joy you have been to me. Even though I can't claim to be your natural father, I beg you to believe that I have loved you as though I was. And I must tell you that it was you who inspired me to continue to adopt your beautiful younger sisters, and that all of you have given me more pleasure than anything else in my life.

You have never asked me to tell you about your true heritage, the story of where I found you and the circumstances that led up to your adoption. Rest assured, I would have told you if you had, as one of your sisters did a few years ago. But as I leave this earth, I feel it is only right to allow you the freedom to discover it in the future if you wish.

None of you came to me with a birth certificate, and as you know, all of you are officially registered as my daughters. No one can take that away from you.

However, at the very least, I can point you in the right direction. After that, only you can choose to take the journey back into your past if you so wish.

On the armillary sphere, which you have now seen, are a set of coordinates indicating exactly where on this planet your story began. And there is also a small clue inside the envelope to help you further.

Maia, I can't tell you what you'll find if you do decide to return to the country of your birth. But what I can tell you is that your true family and their story touched my life.

I'm sad that there is no time left for me to relate my own story to you, and that perhaps you sometimes felt that I kept many things to myself. What I did, I did to protect you all. But of course, no man, or woman, is an island. And as you grew up, I had to set you free to fly.

We all hold secrets inside us, but please believe me when I say that family is everything. And that the love of a parent for a child is the most powerful force on earth.

Maia, it's understandable that I look back on my life and regret many of the decisions that I've made during it. Of course, it is the human condition to make mistakes, as that is how we learn and grow. But my dearest wish is to at least pass on any wisdom that I've gathered to my precious daughters.

I think there is a part of you that, because of your life experience so far, has led you to lose your faith in human nature. My dearest Maia, please know that I too have suffered from the same affliction and it

78

blighted my life at times. However, I have learnt over the many years I've spent on this earth that for every one bad apple, there are thousands more whose hearts are full of kindness. And you must trust to the intrinsic goodness inside each of us. Only then will you be able to live and love fully.

I will leave you now, my dearest Maia; I'm sure I have given you and your sisters much to think about.

I am watching over you always from the heavens.

Your loving father,

Pa Salt x

I sat holding the letter, and saw that my hands were shaking. I knew I needed to read it again, and probably a third or a fourth time, but one phrase stuck in my mind.

Had he known?

I called Marina on her mobile and asked her if she could come and see me at the Pavilion. She arrived five minutes later, and saw the distress on my face.

Following me into the sitting room, she glanced at the letter lying open on the coffee table.

'Oh Maia,' she said, holding out her arms to me. 'I'm sure you must be very distressed, having heard your father's voice speaking to you from the grave.'

I didn't move to accept her embrace. 'Ma, please, you must tell me if you ever told Pa Salt about our . . . secret?'

'Of course not! Please believe me, I would never betray you!'

I could see the hurt in Marina's kind eyes.

'So he never knew?'

'No. How could he have done?'

'In the letter, he says something that made me think he *must* have known . . .'

'May I take a look at it?'

'Of course. Here.' I picked up the letter and handed it to her, watching intently as she read it.

Eventually, she looked up at me, her expression calmer now. She nodded in understanding.

'I can see why you've reacted as you have, but I honestly think that your father was simply sharing with you his *own* truth.'

I sat down abruptly on the sofa and put my head in my hands.

'Maia.' Marina shook her head and sighed. 'As the letter from your father says, we all make mistakes. We simply do what we think is right at the time. And you, out of all the girls, have spent your life putting the feelings of others first. Especially your father's.'

'I just never wanted to let him down.'

'I know, *chérie*, but all your father wished for each one of you was that you were happy and felt secure and loved. Please, today of all days, don't forget that. But perhaps it's time, now that he's gone, for you to think about yourself and what *you* want.' Marina shook herself briskly and rose. 'Now, Electra has announced she's leaving, as has Tiggy. CeCe called Georg Hoffman first thing this morning and has gone off with Star to visit him at his office in Geneva. And Ally is busy on her laptop in the kitchen.'

'Do you know if any of them have read their letters yet?' I asked, trying to pull myself together.

'If they have, they haven't shared the information with

me,' Marina confirmed. 'Perhaps you'd like to join us up at
the house for lunch, before Electra and Tiggy leave?'

'Of course. And I'm sorry, Ma, for ever doubting you.'

'It's completely understandable, given the letter. Now, you
take some time alone to calm down, and I'll see you up at the
house at one o'clock.'

'Thank you,' I whispered as Marina headed out of the
room. Before she reached the front door, she paused and
turned back to face me.

'Maia, really, you are the daughter I wish I'd had. And just
like your father did, I love you as such.'

After she left, I sat on the sofa and sobbed my heart out. It
was as if a torrent of long-buried emotions were begging to
be released and, to my shame, I lost control of myself in a
tidal wave of self-pity.

I knew I was crying for *me*. Not for Pa and his unexpected
death and the pain he must have suffered during it, but for
my own pain at his loss and the awful realisation that I had
proven myself unworthy by not trusting him enough to tell
him the truth.

What kind of a person was I? What had I done?

And why was I feeling all these things now, things that in
so many ways were not connected with Pa's death?

I'm behaving like Electra, I told myself, hoping that would
bring me up short. But it didn't. And the tears just wouldn't
stop. I lost track of time, and when I finally looked up, I saw
Tiggy standing in front of me, her face a picture of concern.

'Oh Maia, I just came here to say that Electra and I are

leaving shortly and we wanted to say goodbye. But I can't leave you like this . . .'

'No,' I snuffled. 'Sorry, I . . .'

'What do you have to apologise for?' she said as she came to sit next to me and took my hands in hers. 'You're a human being too. I think you sometimes forget that.'

I saw her glancing at the letter from Pa still sitting on the coffee table and I grabbed it protectively.

'Was it very upsetting?' she asked.

'Yes . . . and no . . .'

I knew I couldn't explain myself to her. And of all the sisters who could have been here at this moment, Tiggy was the one I'd mothered most, who had relied on me and for whom I had always been there. The role reversal was not lost on me.

'You missed lunch, by the way,' she said.

'I'm sorry.'

'Please, can you stop apologising? We all understand, we all love you. And we know what Pa's death means to you.'

'But look at me! I'm the "coper", the person who sorts everyone else out! And it's me who's falling apart. Have you opened your letter?' I asked her.

'No, not yet. I think – or at least I *feel* – that I want to take it back with me to Scotland. And stand on the moors in my special, private place and read it there.'

'Well, this is my home, where I belong, so I opened mine here. But I feel so guilty, Tiggy,' I confessed.

'Why?'

'Because . . . I've been crying for myself. Not for Pa, but for *me*.'

'Maia,' she sighed, 'do you really think there's any other reason why people cry over the death of a loved one?'

'Yes, of course. They cry for a life cut short, for the pain the person suffered, surely?'

'Well . . .' Tiggy gave a small smile. 'I know that you find it difficult to believe what I believe, that there *is* life after death and that our souls live on. But I can imagine Pa is now in the universe somewhere, released from his inadequate human body – free for the first time. Because I could see so often in his eyes that he must have suffered a lot during his life. And all I can say is that when one of my deer dies and is released from the pain of living, I understand that I'm crying at my own loss, because I will miss the animal so badly. Maia, please, even if you can't believe in anything beyond this earth, try to understand that grief is all about the people left behind. About *us*. We're all grieving for ourselves and our loss. And you really mustn't feel any guilt about it.'

I looked at my sister, feeling her calm acceptance. And I silently acknowledged that the part of me she'd called a 'soul', I'd consciously buried for many years.

'Thank you, Tiggy, and I'm sorry I wasn't there for lunch.'

'You didn't miss much. In the end, it was only Ally and me. Electra was packing and said she'd eaten far too much junk anyway, and CeCe and Star are still in Geneva. They went to see Georg Hoffman this morning.'

'Ma told me. Presumably CeCe went about money?'

'I'd assume so. I'm sure you know she has a place on an art course in London she wants to take. They'll need somewhere to live and that will cost money.'

'Yes.'

'Obviously Pa's death affects your circumstances far more

than any of us. I mean, we all know you stayed here to keep him company and watch over him.'

'Tiggy, that's not really the truth. It's because I had nowhere else to go,' I admitted bluntly.

'As usual, I think you're being incredibly hard on yourself. Pa *was* part of the reason you were here. Now he's gone, surely the world is your oyster? You have a job you can do anywhere, you could go wherever you wanted.' Tiggy looked at her watch. 'I really must go and pack. Goodbye, darling Maia,' she said as she threw her arms round my shoulders. 'Please take care of yourself. You know I'm always at the end of the phone if you need me. Why don't you think about coming to visit me up in the Highlands at some point? The landscape is so beautiful and the atmosphere unbelievably tranquil.'

'Maybe, Tiggy. Thank you.'

Soon after she left, I roused myself to go and say goodbye to Electra. But as I was walking across the gardens to the jetty, Electra herself appeared right in front of me.

'I'm off,' she said. 'My agency said they'll sue me if I'm not there at the shoot tomorrow morning.'

'Of course.'

'Hey.' Electra cocked her head to one side. 'Are you okay?'

'Yes, I'm fine.'

'Listen, now you have no Pa to mind here, why don't you pop over to La-La Land and come and stay with me and Mitch for a while? There's a great little guest house in the garden, and really, you're welcome to it anytime.'

'Thanks, Electra. Keep in touch, won't you?'

''Course I will. So, see you soon,' she said as we reached the jetty and saw that CeCe and Star were just getting off the boat.

'Hi guys,' said CeCe, and her smile told me that her mission in Geneva had obviously been successful.

'Are you leaving, Electra?' Star asked.

'I have to get back to LA. Some of us have to work for a living, you know,' she said pointedly and I knew the comment was meant for CeCe.

'Well, at least some of us are using our brains, not our bodies to earn it,' CeCe retorted, as Ally arrived on the jetty with Tiggy.

'Now, now, girls, surely this is the moment to be there for each other? Bye, Electra.' Ally walked to her sister and kissed her on both cheeks. 'Let's try to arrange to see each other soon.'

'Sure,' Electra agreed as she kissed Star, but ignored CeCe. 'Are you ready, Tiggy?'

'Yes,' Tiggy said, having embraced the rest of her sisters and made her way over to Star. As she hugged her, I saw Tiggy whisper in Star's ear and Star whisper back.

'Right, let's get going,' ordered Electra. 'I can't afford to miss my flight.'

I watched as Tiggy and Electra stepped onto the boat and, as the engine hummed, we four remaining sisters waved them off, then turned and walked back up to the house.

'I think Star and I might be on our way later too,' commented CeCe.

'Really? Couldn't we stay a little longer?' asked Star plaintively.

'What's the point? Pa's gone, we've seen the lawyer and we need to get to London as soon as possible to find somewhere to live.'

'You're right,' said Star.

'What will you do with yourself in London while CeCe's at art school?' asked Ally.

'I'm not quite sure yet,' replied Star.

'You're thinking of taking a cordon bleu course, aren't you, Star? She's an amazing cook, you know,' CeCe added to me. 'Right, I'm off to see about flights. I know there's an eight o'clock from Geneva to Heathrow, which would suit us perfectly. See you later.'

I stood with Ally as we watched both girls walk into the house.

'Don't say it,' I sighed, 'I know.'

'I always thought it was a positive thing that they were so close when we were all growing up,' said Ally. 'They're the middle girls and it was good they had each other.'

'I remember Pa suggesting they go to separate schools, and then Star sobbing hysterically and begging him to let her go with CeCe,' I mused.

'One of the problems is that no one ever gets a chance to talk to Star by herself. Is she okay? She's looked awful since she's been here.'

'Ally, I have absolutely no idea. In fact, sometimes I feel I hardly know her,' I admitted.

'Well, if CeCe is going to be busy with her art course, and if Star decides to do something separately too, perhaps that will give them both a chance to disentangle themselves a little. Now, how about you and I go and sit on the terrace and I'll ask Claudia to bring out some sandwiches for you? You look pale, Maia, and you missed lunch. And I have something I want to discuss with you.'

I acquiesced and sat down in the sun, its warmth caressing

my face and relaxing me. Ally reappeared and sat down next to me.

'Claudia's bringing you something to eat,' she said. 'Maia, I don't want to pry, but did you open your letter last night?'

'Yes, I did. Well, this morning actually,' I confessed.

'And it's obviously upset you.'

'Initially yes, but I'm okay now, Ally, really,' I replied, not prepared to discuss it any further. Tiggy's sweet concern had comforted me, but I knew Ally's attention might make me feel patronised. 'How about you?'

'Yes, I opened mine,' Ally said. 'And it was beautiful and it made me cry, but it also uplifted me. I've spent the morning looking the coordinates up on the internet. I now know exactly where all of us originally came from. And there are a few surprises in there, I can tell you,' she added as Claudia brought out a plate of sandwiches and placed them in front of me.

'You know exactly where we were born? Where *I* was born?' I clarified.

'Yes, or at least, a clue to where Pa found us. Do you want to know, Maia? I can tell you, or I can leave it to you to look up yourself.'

'I . . . I'm not sure,' I said, aware of a nervous fluttering in my stomach.

'All I can say is, Pa certainly got around.'

I looked at her and I only wished that I could be as calm as she seemed in this paradox of mysterious death and revelations of birth.

'So you know where you're from?' I asked her.

'Yes, though it doesn't make sense just yet.'

'What about the others? Did you tell them you know where they were born?'

'No, but I've explained to them how to look up the co-ordinates on Google Earth. Shall I explain to you too? Or just tell you?' Ally's beautiful blue eyes were fixed on me.

'At the moment, I'm simply not sure.'

'Well, as I said, it's very easy to look it up yourself.'

'Then I'll probably do that when I'm ready,' I said firmly, feeling yet again one step behind my sister.

'I'll write down the details of how you pinpoint the co-ordinates, in case you decide you want to know. Did you have a chance to translate any of the quotes that were engraved in Greek on the armillary sphere?'

'Yes, I have them all.'

'Well, I'd really like to know what Pa chose for me,' Ally said. 'So would you tell me, please?'

'I can't remember exactly, but I can go back to the Pavilion and write it down for you.'

'Thank you.'

I bit into one of the sandwiches Claudia had put in front of me, wishing for the thousandth time I could be more like Ally, who took everything in her stride, who was never afraid of anything life threw at her. The career she had chosen – full of danger and often solitary, facing waves that could knock over in an instant the fragile craft in which she sailed – was a perfect metaphor for who she was. Out of all of us, I thought she was the most comfortable in her own skin. Ally never succumbed to negative thinking; she saw any setbacks as positive life lessons, and then she moved on.

'So it seems that between us, you and I can provide the rest of the sisters with the information they need if they wish to explore their past,' Ally mused.

'We can, but perhaps it's too soon for any of us to think

whether we'll go back and follow the clues Pa has given us.'

'Maybe so,' Ally sighed. 'Besides, the Cyclades race is starting and I'm going to have to leave here as soon as possible to join the crew. To be honest, Maia, after what I saw a couple of days ago, getting back on the water is going to be hard.'

'I can imagine,' I said. After all I'd just been thinking about her, I was surprised to sense Ally's sudden vulnerability. 'But you'll be fine, I'm sure.'

'I hope so. It's honestly the first time I've had cold feet since I began racing competitively.'

'You've put everything into your sailing for years, Ally, so you mustn't let it faze you.'

'You're right. I'll do my best to help us win. For him. Thanks, Maia. You know, I was thinking earlier how I've allowed it to dominate my life. Remember how desperate I was to become a professional flautist when I was younger? But by the time I got to music school, the sailing bug had taken over.'

'Of course I remember,' I smiled. 'You're talented at so many things, Ally, but I must admit, I miss hearing you play the flute.'

'Funny, I'm actually beginning to realise that I miss it too. Anyway, will you be okay here by yourself?'

'Of course I will. Please don't worry about me. I have Ma, and my work. I'll be fine.'

'Well, perhaps later on in the summer, you'd like to come out on my boat for a few days? We can sail anywhere you fancy; perhaps down the Amalfi Coast. It's so beautiful there, one of my favourite places. And maybe I'll bring my flute on board with me,' she said with a faint smile.

'That's a lovely idea. But we'll have to see. I'm very busy with translation work at the moment.'

'We've managed to get two seats on a flight to Heathrow,' crowed CeCe, bursting onto the terrace behind us. 'Christian is taking us to the airport in an hour.'

'Then I might see if I can get a last-minute flight to Nice and come with you. Don't forget to write out the quotation for me, will you, Maia?' said Ally as she rose from the table and disappeared inside the house.

'Everything go all right at Georg's office?' I asked CeCe.

'Fine.' CeCe nodded. 'I take it you've translated the quotations?' she asked as she pulled out a chair and sat down.

'Yes.'

'Ally told me that she also had all our coordinates.'

'Have you opened your letter yet?' I asked.

'No. Star and I have agreed we'll pick a quiet moment together and open them then. But it would be very helpful if you could write down our quotations, put them in an envelope and give them to me before we leave. I've asked Ally to do the same with the coordinates.'

'I can certainly give you yours, yes, CeCe. But Pa said explicitly in his letter to me that I must only hand over the translated quotes to the sister in question. So I'll give Star's directly to her,' I said, surprising myself with the smoothness of the lie.

'Okay,' CeCe shrugged. 'But obviously we'll share.' She glanced at me suddenly. 'Are you going to be okay here by yourself, what with Pa gone? What will you do?'

'I do have my work to keep me busy,' I reiterated.

'Yes, but we all know you were living here because of him. Anyway, it would be great if you could come to London and visit us once we have our new apartment. I've already contacted some rental agencies. Both of us would love to have you.'

'That's very kind of you, CeCe. I'll let you know.'

'Good. Maia, can I ask you something?'

'Of course you can, CeCe.'

'Do you . . . do you think that Pa liked me?'

'What a strange question! Of course he did. He loved us all, equally.'

'It's just that . . .'

I saw CeCe's stubby fingernails moving like a pianist's on the tabletop.

'What is it?' I asked her.

'Well, to be honest, I'm scared to open the letter. I mean, as you know, I'm not the most emotional person and I never felt the relationship I had with Pa was very close. I'm not stupid, I know that people think I'm brusque and too practical – except Star, of course – but I *do* feel everything inside. Do you understand?'

CeCe's unexpected revelation made me instinctively reach out a hand to touch hers. 'I understand completely. But CeCe, I remember you coming home as a baby and Ma being shocked because your arrival here was so soon after Star's. When I asked Pa why we'd had another sister so quickly, he said that it was because you were so special, he simply had to bring you home with him. And that's the truth.'

'Really?'

'*Really.*'

For the first time since I'd known her, my fourth sister looked as though she was about to cry.

'Thank you, Maia,' she said gratefully. 'Now, I must go and find Star and tell her that we're leaving soon.'

As I watched her stand up and walk inside, I thought how Pa's death had changed all of us already.

An hour later, having handed each sister a copy of the inscription I'd translated for her, I was yet again on the jetty saying goodbye. I watched Ally, CeCe and Star skim across the water in the launch, on their way back to their own lives. In the Pavilion, I poured myself a glass of wine, thinking how each one of my sisters had offered me space in her life; if I chose, I could literally spend the next year traversing the globe and inhabiting their various worlds.

But here I was, still living in my childhood home. And yet, I thought, there had been somewhere before this place. A life I didn't remember and knew nothing about.

I walked determinedly to my office and switched on my laptop. Maybe now it was time to discover who *I* was. Where I came from. And where I belonged.

My hands trembled slightly as I accessed Google Earth. Carefully typing in the coordinates as Ally had instructed me, I held my breath, waiting for the laptop to tell me where to find my heritage. Finally, after the small circle on the screen had spun for an eternity – like a globe on its axis – the details appeared in front of me. And the place of my birth was revealed.

8

Surprisingly, that night I slept a deep, dreamless sleep, from which I awoke refreshed. I lay staring at the ceiling of my bedroom, processing what I'd learnt yesterday.

I felt the information I'd discovered had not been shocking – it was as if I'd always known it somewhere in my DNA. And in fact, purely coincidentally, my life had already encompassed a part of it. I could hardly believe that I had actually viewed the very house in which I might have been born. The aerial view on Google Earth made it seem enormous and very grand, and I wondered why, given its apparent splendour, I'd been removed from it by Pa Salt as a baby.

As I climbed out of bed, my mobile rang, and I grabbed it to try to answer before it rang off. I saw on the screen it was an unknown number and probably a cold call, so I left it and walked into the kitchen to revive myself with my usual morning mug of English Breakfast tea.

As I sipped it, I mused that it really was incredible to think that if I so wished, I could simply jump on a plane tomorrow and within twenty-four hours, I could be knocking on the door of my past.

A Casa das Orquídeas, Laranjeiras, Rio de Janeiro, Brazil.

I searched my mind for the exact details of the conversation I'd had with Pa before deciding on my university degree. There was no doubt he'd encouraged me to take up Portuguese as one of my languages, and I remembered how learning it had come as easily to me as my mother tongue, French. I wandered into the sitting room to find the small, triangular-shaped tile that had been in the envelope, pulled it out and studied the faded inscription on the back.

Looking at it now made far more sense, because I realised it was written in Portuguese. I could make out some of the letters, and a date – 1929 – but I couldn't decipher the rest of it.

A sudden shiver of excitement ran through me, but I stifled it immediately. Surely it would be ridiculous to simply up and go to Brazil?

And yet, would it?

I pondered the thought over a second cup of tea. Once I had calmed down I decided that yes, perhaps sometime in the future I would make the journey. After all, I had a valid reason to go there, given that I translated Brazilian authors into French. I could arrange to visit the Brazilian publishers of Floriano Quintelas – the author who'd contacted me only recently – to see if they would recommend me to work with other authors who needed my services.

My mobile rang again. I stood up and went to retrieve it from the bedside table, and heard the voice alerting me to a message from the earlier missed call. I put the handset to my ear as I walked back to the kitchen, as another, all too familiar voice spoke to me.

'Maia, hi, it's me, Zed. I hope you remember who I am,' he said with a casual chuckle. 'Listen, I don't know whether you've heard the dreadful news about my father; so terribly tragic. To be honest, we're all just getting over the shock. I wouldn't have called, but I heard about your father yesterday through a sailing friend of mine. Apparently, he just passed away too. Anyway, I have to come to Geneva in the next few days, and I just thought how good it would be to see you. Perhaps we can cry on each other's shoulders. Life is bizarre, isn't it? I've no idea if you're even still living in Geneva, but I've got your home number somewhere. So when I arrive, I'll give you a buzz, or even try my luck and call in at the famous Atlantis if I don't hear back from you after this message. I'm so sorry about your father. Take care.'

A beep alerted me to the end of the message as I stood, rooted to the spot, the shock of hearing his voice for the first time in fourteen years rendering me immobile.

'Oh my God,' I breathed, as I processed the thought of Zed turning up here on the doorstep in a couple of days. I felt like a rabbit caught in the headlights; part of me wanted to crawl under the bed and hide, just in case he was already in Geneva and would arrive here any second and find me.

I realised that Marina or Claudia might well pick up the telephone at the house and innocently tell him that I was indeed at home. The thought of this sent shock waves through me. I had to go up to the house immediately and warn them not to tell *anyone* who called that I was here.

But what if Zed simply appeared on the doorstep? He knew exactly where Atlantis was. I'd described its location in detail to him once.

'I'll have to go away,' I whispered to myself, my legs finally obeying my command to carry me into the sitting room, where I paced restlessly, thinking which of my sisters' offers I'd take up.

Not a single one appealed, so I wondered whether I should simply go back to London, and hole up with Jenny until it was safe to return.

But for how long? Zed might well be in Geneva for an extended period of time; I would have taken a bet that his father's vast wealth lay in the hands and the vaults of the Swiss banks.

'Why now?' I wailed to the heavens. Just as I needed some time to regroup, to calm down, I knew I had to leave. Seeing him again would break me completely, especially given my current fragile state of mind.

I looked down at the coffee table and my fingers reached out instinctively to touch the smooth surface of the triangular tile. I stared at it as my brain processed the thought that had just appeared in my mind.

If I wanted to put distance between myself and him, with no one knowing where I was, then Brazil certainly fitted the bill. I could take my laptop with me and work there on my current translation. Why not?

'Yes, Maia, why not?' I asked myself.

An hour later, I walked into the kitchen and asked Claudia where Marina was.

'She went into Geneva on some errands, Maia. Can I give her a message for you when I see her?'

'Yes,' I said, digging deep to find the courage to say the words. 'Tell her that I'm leaving tonight, for a couple of weeks at least. And, Claudia, if anyone calls for me, either on the landline or in person, you can tell them I'll be away for some time.'

Claudia's usually impassive face registered an expression of surprise.

'Where are you going, Maia?'

'Just away,' I said neutrally.

'Good,' she said.

I waited for her to continue, but she didn't.

'So, I'm going back to the Pavilion to pack,' I said. 'And perhaps you can let Christian know when he comes back that I need the launch to take me to Geneva at around three o'clock.'

'Shall I prepare some lunch for you?'

'No thanks,' I said, knowing my stomach was churning enough as it was. 'I'll pop in and say goodbye before I leave. And remember, Claudia, if anyone calls for me from now on, I'm not here.'

'I know, Maia, you've already said.'

Two hours later, having booked flights and a hotel and with a hurriedly packed suitcase in hand, I left Atlantis. As the launch carried me smoothly across the water to Geneva, it suddenly struck me that I had no idea whether I was running *away* from my past or towards it.

9

Due to the five hours' time difference, I found myself on Brazilian soil at six o'clock the following morning. Expecting to step out into the glaring South American sun, I was disappointed to arrive to a cloudy sky. Of course, I realised, I'd arrived in their winter, which – even though the temperature was still in the high seventies – meant the absence of the intense tropical heat I'd anticipated. As I emerged into the arrivals hall, I saw a man holding a board with my name upon it.

'*Olá, eu sou Senhorita D'Aplièse. Como você está?*' I asked in Portuguese as I approached the driver, and enjoyed the look of surprise on his face.

As he led me to the car and we drove out of the airport towards Rio, I gazed through the window with avid interest. This was the city – apparently – of my birth. Even though I'd travelled to Brazil during my second year at university, the exchange programme had been based at a university in São Paulo, and my travels had taken me up to the old capital of Salvador. Stories of Rio and its crime, poverty and wild nightlife had made me wary of visiting, especially as a single woman. But now, here I was, and if Pa Salt's information was correct, I was part of its DNA and it was part of mine.

The driver, happy to have a rare foreigner who spoke fluent Portuguese in his car, asked me where I was from.

'Here. I was born here,' I replied.

He surveyed me in the rear-view mirror.

'Why, of course! Now I can see you look Brazilian! But your surname is D'Aplièse, so I presumed you were French. You're here to visit relatives?'

'Yes, I suppose I am,' I replied, the truth of the words resonating in my brain.

'Look.' The driver pointed upwards to a high mountain on which a white statue stood, arms wide open, embracing the city. 'There is our *Cristo Redentor*. I always know I'm home when I see Him for the first time.'

I gazed up at the pale, elegantly sculpted figure, who seemed to be hovering amidst the clouds like an angelic apparition. Even though, just like the rest of the world, I'd seen the image countless times in the media, the reality was breathtaking and surprisingly moving.

'You have been up to visit Him?' my driver asked.

'No, I haven't.'

'Then you are a true native of Rio – a *carioca*!' he said with a grin. 'Even though he's one of the modern Seven Wonders of the World, we in Rio take the statue for granted. It's the tourists who flock to it.'

'I will definitely go,' I promised, as we disappeared into a tunnel and *Christ the Redeemer* vanished from view.

Forty minutes later, we pulled up at the Caesar Park Hotel. Across the wide road lay Ipanema Beach, deserted for the present due to the early hour but simply magnificent, stretching as far as the eye could see.

'Here is my card, Senhorita D'Aplièse. My name is Pietro

and I will be on call for you any time you wish to go out in the city.'

'*Obrigada*,' I said, thanking him, and I handed him some reais as a tip before following the porter into the lobby to check in.

A few minutes later, I was installed in a pleasantly spacious suite with a wonderful view of Ipanema Beach from the large front windows. The room was ridiculously expensive, but was all they'd had available at such short notice. And given that I rarely spent anything from my earnings, I didn't feel guilty. Depending on what happened in the next few days, if I decided to stay on for longer, I'd simply rent an apartment.

And what *would* happen in the next few days?

The past twenty-four hours had been such a whirlwind, propelled only by how panicked and desperate I'd felt to remove myself from Switzerland, I hadn't really thought through what I'd do when I actually arrived. But for now, having slept so badly on the plane, and feeling exhausted from the trauma of the past few days, I decided to hang the *do not disturb* sign on the door, then slipped between the fresh, sweet-smelling sheets and went to sleep.

Waking up a few hours later, and discovering that I was hungry but also eager to see the city, I took the lift up to the top-floor restaurant. Sitting on the small terrace that had a wonderful vista of both the sea and the mountains, I ordered a Caesar salad and a glass of white wine. The clouds had blown away like a memory, and below me the beach was now crowded with bronzed bodies sunning themselves.

Once I'd eaten, I felt my brain begin to clear enough to allow me to think about what was best to do. I studied the address pinpointed by the coordinates, which I'd copied into my mobile, and conceded there was no guarantee that my original family was still occupying the house. I didn't know their names, or anything about them. I couldn't help a nervous chuckle at the thought of turning up on the doorstep and announcing I was searching for my long-lost family.

But then, I mused, trying to honour Pa Salt's quote on the armillary sphere, the worst they could do was to slam the door in my face. Perhaps the glass of wine and the jet lag were providing me with an unusual feeling of courage. So I returned to my suite, and before I changed my mind, called downstairs to see if Pietro, the driver who had collected me from the airport, was available to take me to the address I wanted.

'No problem,' said the concierge. 'Do you wish for the car immediately?'

'Yes.'

And so it came to pass that ten minutes later, I was back in Pietro's car, heading slowly out of the centre of the city.

'This house, A Casa das Orquídeas, I think I know it,' he commented.

'I don't,' I confessed.

'Well, if it's the one I think it is, it is most interesting. It's very old and used to be inhabited by a rich Portuguese family,' he said as we came to yet another grinding halt in the traffic jams he'd told me never ceased.

'The house may have new owners,' I mused.

'This is true.' He eyed me in the mirror, and I knew he sensed my tension. 'Are you searching for a relative?'

'Yes,' I answered honestly, glancing up as we drove and immediately seeing *Christ the Redeemer* hovering above me. Never having been particularly religious, somehow at that moment I felt an extraordinary sense of comfort from His all-encompassing, outstretched arms.

'So, we will pass the address you want in a couple of minutes,' Pietro advised me fifteen minutes later. 'I doubt you can see much from the road, because it is surrounded by a high hedge to give it privacy. This used to be a very exclusive neighbourhood, but now, sadly, much development has taken place around it.'

I could see that the road was indeed lined with a mixture of industrial buildings and apartment blocks.

'The house is there, senhorita.'

I followed Pietro's pointed finger and saw a long stretch of overgrown hedge, wild flowers poking their pretty but destructive heads through the leaves. Compared to our immaculately maintained garden in Geneva, this one looked to me as if it had not seen a tender pair of hands caring for it in a very long time.

All I could see above the hedge was a set of old-fashioned chimneys; their original brick-red colour had been covered by years of soot and had faded to blackness.

'Maybe the house is unoccupied,' shrugged Pietro, immediately assessing, as I had, the unkempt look of the outside.

'Maybe,' I agreed.

'Shall I park here?' he asked me, slowing down and pulling over to the side of the road a few metres past the property.

'Yes please.'

Bringing the car to a halt, he switched off the engine and turned to face me. 'I shall be here waiting for you. Good luck, Senhorita D'Aplièse.'

'Thank you.'

I climbed out of the car and slammed the door with far more force than necessary, preparing myself for what might come. As I walked along the pavement, I told myself that, in fact, whatever occurred in the next few minutes of my life didn't matter. I'd always had a loving father and de facto mother, and I'd had my sisters. And if anything, the reason I was here was less to do with whatever I might find hidden behind these hedges, and far more to do with what I'd instinctively run away from.

With this thought giving me the confidence I needed, I turned through the large, open wrought-iron gates into the drive. And for the first time, I laid eyes on the house where the coordinates had told me my story had originally begun.

It was an elegant eighteenth-century mansion, its formal square shape and white stuccoed walls, with their intricate plaster corbels and mouldings, redolent of Brazil's colonial past. Yet as I drew nearer, I could see the stucco was shabby and cracked and the paintwork on the dozens of tall casement windows had peeled away in many places to reveal bare wood.

Garnering my courage, I walked towards it, passing around the base of a carved marble fountain, where rivulets of water must once have played. I saw that most of the shutters on the windows were tightly closed and began to wonder whether Pietro was right and that this house was no longer occupied.

Walking up the wide set of steps to the front door, I pressed the antiquated bell. But it elicited no sound from within. After trying it twice more, I knocked on the door as confidently as I dared. I waited for a response, but there was no sound of footsteps inside. I decided to knock again more loudly.

Having now stood on the doorstep for a good few minutes, I realised it was fruitless and that no one would be answering the door. Looking upwards, and again noting the closed shutters across the windows of the rooms above, I deduced the house was probably not lived in.

I descended the steps, deciding whether to walk straight back down the drive to Pietro and forget the whole idea, or whether to have a prowl around to see if I could at least see through a crack in one of the shutters. Deciding eventually on the latter, I crept around the side of the house.

I realised that it was far longer than it was wide, the side wall of the house stretching towards what I could see had once been a beautiful garden. I kept walking along its length, disappointed to find no visible peephole through which I could spy. As I reached the far end of the wall, it brought me on to a moss-covered terrace.

My eye was immediately caught by a stone sculpture of a young woman in the far corner of it, amidst some cracked terracotta plant pots. She was in a sitting position, staring straight ahead. And even though as I approached I saw the nose was chipped, the clean, simple lines of the woman were starkly beautiful.

I was about to turn to survey the back of the house when I noticed a figure sitting under a tree in the garden below the terrace.

My heart began to pound in my ears as I shrank back against the wall out of sight and peered round the corner to study the figure. From this distance, it was hard to form an exact physical description; all I could tell was that she was female and, from the way she sat in the chair, very elderly.

The sight of her sent a thousand thoughts shooting through my synapses. Never good at making immediate decisions, I stood there cowering, half an eye cocked towards the old woman who might or might not be related to me.

I looked up above me to the heavens and knew instinctively that Pa had never shrunk away from moments such as this. And for the first time in my adult life, neither would I.

I stepped out into full view of the woman and walked towards her. She didn't turn her head towards me as I drew nearer. And when I was finally close enough to see her properly, I saw her eyes were closed and that she appeared to be asleep.

This gave me the opportunity to look at her face in more detail. I wondered if I should recognise some features of my own, but I knew there was every chance she would be a total stranger – someone who had occupied the house for the thirty-three years I'd been away from it.

'*Desculpe?* Can I help you, senhorita?'

I almost jumped out of my skin as I heard a soft voice behind me and turned around. A stick-thin, elderly African woman with wiry greying hair and dressed in an old-fashioned maid's uniform was looking at me suspiciously.

'I'm sorry,' I said quickly. 'I couldn't get any answer at the front door . . .'

The woman put a finger to her lips. 'Hush, she is sleeping. Why are you here?'

'Because I . . .' How on earth did I encapsulate the truth to this woman in a few whispered words? 'I've been told I have a connection to this house and I'd like to speak to the owner.'

I felt her appraise me and there was a sudden flicker of her eyes as her gaze came to rest on my neck.

'Senhora Carvalho is seeing no one. She is very sick and in much pain.'

'Well, perhaps you can tell her I called.' I opened my bag and looked inside for one of my cards, which I handed to the maid. 'I'm staying at the Caesar Park Hotel. Can you say I very much want to talk to her?'

'I can, but it will make no difference,' the maid said abruptly.

'May I ask how long the lady in the chair has lived in this house?'

'For all of her life. Now, I will see you out.'

Her words sent shivers through me and I threw one last glance at the old woman in the chair. If Pa Salt and his co-ordinates were correct, it *must* mean that she was somehow related to me. I turned, and the maid began to escort me back across the terrace. We'd reached the corner of the house when a weak voice echoed towards us.

'Who is she?'

We both stopped and turned round, and I saw the glint of fear in the maid's eyes.

'Forgive me, Senhora Carvalho, I did not wish to disturb you,' she answered.

'You are not. I have been watching you for the last five minutes. Bring her over. We can't have a conversation one hundred metres apart.'

The maid did as her mistress asked and reluctantly walked me back across the terrace and down the steps into the garden. She ushered me in front of the old woman, and then read out the details of my card.

'She is Senhorita Maia D'Aplièse and she is a translator.'

Now face to face with the woman, I could see she was emaciated, her skin a deathly grey, as though her life force was slowly ebbing away. But as her gimlet eyes swept over me, and a fleeting look of recognition and shock passed across them, I knew she was mentally alert.

'Why are you here?' she asked.

'It's a long story.'

'What do you want?'

'Nothing, I . . .'

'Senhorita D'Aplièse told me that she had an association with this house,' said the maid, almost, I thought, encouragingly.

'Really? And what kind of association would that be?'

'I've been told that this was the house in which I was born,' I said.

'Well, I'm sorry to disappoint you, senhorita, but there have been no babies born under this roof since my own child, over fifty-five years ago. Isn't that so, Yara?' she said to her maid.

'*Sim*, senhora.'

'So, who gave you this information? Someone who wishes to form a relationship with me so that they can inherit this house when I am dead, no doubt?'

'No, senhora, I promise that this has nothing to do with money. That's not the reason I'm here,' I said firmly.

'Then please explain more clearly why you *are*.'

'Because . . . I was adopted as a baby. My adoptive father died last week, and wrote me a letter saying that this house was where my family once lived.' I stared at her, hoping the truth of what I'd said was visible in my eyes.

'I see.' Again she surveyed me carefully, seeming to hesitate before she replied. 'Then I must tell you that your father has made a terrible mistake and you have had a wasted journey. I am sorry to be of no further help. Goodbye.'

As I finally allowed the maid to lead me away, I knew with absolute certainty that the old woman was lying.

10

Even though it was only eight in the evening when I arrived back at the hotel, my body was telling me it was after midnight and I made the mistake of falling into a deep and dreamless sleep, waking up with the dawn at five the following morning.

I lay in bed contemplating what I had seen and learnt yesterday. Despite the old woman's vehement denials, every instinct I had was telling me that Pa Salt had not been wrong. However, I thought ruefully, I had no idea what I could do about it. Whatever both the woman and her maid knew, they'd made it obvious they weren't going to share it with me.

I pulled the tile out of my handbag, again trying to decipher the writing upon it, but I soon up gave up. What was the use? All I had was a few illegible faded words and a date. A moment in time sitting on the reverse of a piece of triangular stone.

Turning to my laptop to distract me, I looked at my emails and saw a message from the Brazilian publisher I had been working for, whom I'd contacted during the long three-and-a-half-hour wait in transit at Charles de Gaulle airport in Paris.

Dear Senhora D'Aplièse,

We are delighted you have decided to visit Brazil. Our offices are located in São Paulo, so it may not be convenient for you to travel here to see us, but we would be thrilled to make your personal acquaintance if you do. However, we have forwarded your email to Floriano Quintelas, the author himself, as he lives in Rio. I'm sure he would be happy to meet you and assist you during your time in our beautiful country. Please don't hesitate to ask if there is anything you need.

With best regards,
Luciano Baracchini

The friendliness and warmth of the email brought a smile to my lips. I remembered from my last visit how different the culture was from the far more formal Swiss style. I was in no doubt that if I had a problem of any kind, these people who didn't know me at all would welcome and assist me in any way possible.

I lay back on the bed, looking out of the window as the sun rose over the sea and the wide road beneath me began to thunder with early morning traffic. The city was waking up.

The question was, after yesterday, should I attempt to dig deeper to discover the secrets Rio was keeping from me?

Given the only alternative I had – returning to Geneva, which I knew was an impossibility for now – I decided to stay on for at least a few more days and play the tourist. Even if I'd already come to a dead end in finding my heritage, I could at least discover the city in which I might have been born.

I dressed, then took the lift downstairs and walked out of the hotel, crossed the road and found myself on Ipanema

Beach. It was deserted because of the early hour and as I walked towards the waves crashing against the soft sand beneath my feet, I turned back and looked at Rio from the sea's perspective.

A mass of buildings – all different heights and sizes – jostled for position along the seafront, with the tops of the hills behind just visible above the city skyline. To my right, the long sweep of the sandy bay ended in a rocky headland, while to the left, there was a stunning view of the twin peaks of Morro Dois Irmãos.

And there, standing completely alone, I felt an energy passing through my veins, and a sudden sense of lightness and release.

This is part of me, and I am part of it . . .

Instinctively, I began to run along the beach, my toes clenching to take hold of the slippery sand and support me as I threw my arms out to either side in a moment of sheer exhilaration. I came to a halt, panting and doubled over, laughing at my uncharacteristic behaviour.

I left the beach, crossed the road and began to walk deep into the city, noting the mixture of colonial and modern buildings forced to become stablemates along the streets due to changing architectural fashions.

I rounded a corner and found myself in a square where vendors were already setting up an early morning fruit and vegetable market. Stopping at a stall, I picked up a peach and the young man behind it smiled at me.

'Please, take it, senhorita.'

'*Obrigada*,' I said, and walked away, my teeth piercing the tender, succulent flesh of the fruit, my footsteps halting as I looked up suddenly and saw the white figure of the *Cristo* yet again hovering above me.

'That's what I'm going to do today,' I announced to myself.

Suddenly realising I had no idea where I was or how far I'd strayed from the hotel, I simply followed the sound of the waves, and, like a homing pigeon which already had a map of the area imprinted upon it, I eventually found my way back.

I ate breakfast upstairs on the terrace, and, for the first time since Pa had died, found myself with an appetite. Arriving back in my room, I saw there were a number of messages on my mobile. I took the decision to ignore them, not wanting any form of reality to spoil the exhilaration I'd felt so far this morning. However, I did see an email in my inbox, the sender of which attracted my attention. It was from Floriano Quintelas.

> My dear Senhorita D'Aplièse,
>
> My publisher has told me the surprise that you are here in Rio. It would be my pleasure to meet with you in person and perhaps to take you to dinner or lunch to say thank you for your translation work on my book. My French publishers have high hopes that it will sell very well. Or perhaps you simply wish to see my beautiful city through a true *carioca's* eyes. My mobile phone number is at the bottom of this email. And if I am honest, I would be most offended if you did not contact me during your stay.
>
> I am at your disposal.
> With kind regards,
> Floriano Quintelas

The email made me chuckle; due to our various communications over the past year about *The Silent Waterfall*, I had already gleaned he did not like to waste words unnecessarily.

So, I thought, *would he contact me if he was in Geneva, and I'd offered to show him the city?*

And would I be offended if he did not?

The answer to both questions was yes.

I decided the best and most passive way to contact him was by text. I'm not sure how many minutes I spent composing it, then editing and rewriting, but finally I was happy with it and pressed 'send'.

The moment it had gone, I of course reread it.

Dear Floriano, I am delighted to be here in Rio and it would be nice – *I'd deleted 'a pleasure'* **– to meet up at some point. I'm going up to Corcovado now to play the tourist, but you can contact me on this number. With best wishes, Maia D'Aplièse.**

Satisfied that I had managed to convey warmth and distance at the same time – I was a writer too, after all – I went to visit the concierge in the hotel lobby to discover how I could travel up to see *Christ the Redeemer*.

'Senhorita, we can offer you either the luxury or the real experience, the latter being the one I would personally advocate,' the concierge told me. 'Take a street taxi to Cosme Velho – tell them you're going to visit the *Cristo* – and then take the train up Corcovado Mountain.'

'Thank you.'

'My pleasure.'

Ten minutes later, I was in a taxi on my way to Cosme

Velho and the *Cristo*. My mobile rang in my bag and I answered, seeing it was Floriano Quintelas.

'Hello?'

'Senhorita D'Aplièse?'

'Yes.'

'It's Floriano here. Where are you?'

'In a taxi on my way to see the *Cristo*. I'm just near the train station now.'

'May I join you?'

I hesitated and he heard it.

'If you prefer to visit alone, I understand.'

'No, of course. I'd be glad of a local's guidance.'

'Well, why don't you take the train up the mountain and I'll meet you by the stairs at the top?'

'Okay,' I agreed. 'But how will you recognise me? There are bound to be many people there.'

'I'll recognise you, Senhorita D'Aplièse. I've seen your photograph on the internet. *Adeus.*'

I paid the driver and stepped out in front of the Estação do Corcovado, the tiny station at the foot of the mountain, wondering what Floriano Quintelas would be like in person. After all, I'd never met him, only fallen in love with the way he wrote.

After buying my ticket, I climbed aboard the two-carriaged train, which reminded me of the fragile Alpine railways that snaked up the mountains in Switzerland. I sat down and heard a cacophony of different languages – notably, none of them Portuguese. Eventually, the train began moving upwards and I looked out at the densely forested hillside, in awe that a jungle such as this could lie so close to a big city. It would never be allowed in Geneva.

I felt my head tilting backwards as we ascended, amazed at man's ability to create a vehicle that could take me and my fellow passengers up what seemed like a near-vertical mountainside. The views became more and more spectacular, until finally we came to a halt at a tiny station and everyone alighted from the train.

I looked up and saw the heels of *Christ the Redeemer*, mounted on a high plinth. The sculpture soared so far above me I could barely take in the rest of it. Watching my fellow passengers begin to mount the stairs, I wondered whether Floriano had meant that we should meet at the top or the bottom of them. But not wanting to waste any further time, I began to climb. And climb. Hundreds of steps later, I caught my breath, panting in the warmth of the day after my exertion.

'*Olá*, Senhorita D'Aplièse. It's a pleasure to finally make your acquaintance in the flesh.'

A pair of warm brown eyes smiled into mine, a hint of amusement in them at my obvious surprise.

'You're Floriano Quintelas?'

'Yes! Don't you recognise me from my author photograph?'

My gaze swept briefly over the handsome, tanned face, the full lips parted in a broad grin revealing very white, even teeth. 'I do, but . . .' – I gestured towards the steps beneath me – 'how on earth did you arrive faster than I did?'

'Because, senhorita, I was already up here.' Floriano grinned.

'How? Why?' I asked him, confused.

'Obviously, you have not read my author biography in

detail. If you had, you would know that I am an historian by profession. And that I can also be occasionally employed as a guide, by anyone of distinction who wishes to share my superior knowledge of Rio.'

'I see.'

'Actually, the truth is that my book is not yet earning me enough money to live on, so this is how I supplement my writing,' he admitted. 'But it isn't a hardship at all, showing and telling visitors about my wonderful city. This morning, I had a group of wealthy Americans who wanted to be up here before the crowds. You can see that now it is already very busy.'

'Yes.'

'So, Senhorita D'Aplièse, I'm at your disposal.' Floriano gave a mock bow.

'Thank you,' I said, still feeling flustered at his immediate and unexpected appearance.

'Are you ready for the history of Brazil's most iconic landmark? I promise you, you don't need to tip me at the end,' he quipped, as he led me through the crowds and we stood on the terrace, facing the statue. 'This is the best view of Him. Isn't He incredible?'

My eyes soared upwards to the *Cristo*'s gentle face, as Floriano talked to me of how the statue had been constructed. My brain was so full of the visual image, I hardly took in the spoken details he was relating.

'The miracle is that no one was killed during the construction . . . Another interesting fact is that the project manager began work on the *Cristo* as a Jew, but then converted to Christianity by the end of it. Senhor Levy wrote down all his family's names and secured them in the heart of the *Cristo* before it was sealed into the statue with concrete.'

'What a lovely story.'

'There are many moving stories such as that. For example' – he beckoned me forward and we walked right up to the statue – 'the whole of the outside of the *Cristo* is made up of a mosaic of triangular pieces of soapstone. Society women spent many months sticking them on to mesh netting to make large panels, which meant the outer coating was flexible and therefore the statue would not be prone to wholescale cracking. An old lady who was present during the process told me that many of the women used to write the names of their loved ones and a message or a prayer on the back of the tiles. And there they are, sealed forever onto the *Cristo*.'

My heart missed a beat, and I stared at him in amazement.

'Senhorita Maia, are you okay? Was it something I said?'

'It's a very long story,' I managed, eventually finding my voice.

'Well, you can imagine that those are my favourite type,' he said with a mischievous smile, before searching my face for one in return. On doing so, his expression changed to a look of concern. 'You are suddenly pale, senhorita. Perhaps it's too much sun. We will take a photograph – of course you must stand in front of the *Cristo* with your arms open wide in imitation – and then we will go downstairs to the café and get you some water.'

So, like many hundreds of thousands of tourists before me, I posed as Floriano requested, feeling very stupid standing there, arms spread and trying to force a smile onto my features.

That accomplished, he led me back down the steps and into a shady café, instructing me to take a seat at one of the tables. He returned shortly and sat down opposite me, placing a bottle of water in front of us then pouring some into two glasses. 'So, tell me . . . what is your story?'

'Floriano, it really is very complex,' I sighed, unable to say any more.

'And I am a stranger to you and you are uncomfortable sharing this with me. I understand,' he said, nodding phlegmatically. 'I would feel the same. So, may I ask you just two questions?'

'Of course.'

'Firstly, is your "very complex story" the reason you are here in Rio?'

'Yes.'

'And secondly, what was it I said that has shaken you?'

I pondered his question for a few seconds as I sipped my water. The problem was that if I told him, I'd end up having to explain everything. But as he was probably one of the few people who could tell me if the smooth, triangular tile with the faded writing on the back of it had once been destined for the *Cristo*, it seemed I didn't have much choice.

'I have something I'd like you to see,' I said eventually.

'Then show me,' he encouraged.

'Actually, it's back at the hotel in my safe.'

'It is valuable?' Floriano raised an eyebrow.

'No, not financially anyway. Just to me.'

'Well, given I have been at the *Cristo* for three long hours already, I suggest I drive you to your hotel and you collect whatever the object is and show it to me.'

'Really, Floriano, I don't want to put you to any trouble.'

'Senhorita Maia,' he said, rising from the table, 'I too have to get down the mountain, so you might as well accompany me. Come, we go.'

'Okay, thank you.'

Surprisingly, he didn't head for the train, but instead to a small minibus parked near the café. Climbing aboard, he greeted the driver and clapped him on the back. There were other passengers already aboard it and within minutes, we'd settled ourselves in our seats and the bus took off down a winding road, bordered by thick jungle. A few minutes later, we arrived in a car park and Floriano marched towards a little red Fiat and unlocked the door.

'Sometimes my clients don't wish to take the scenic route on the train, so I bring them directly to here,' he explained. 'So, Senhorita Maia, where are we headed?' he asked me.

'The Caesar Park Hotel in Ipanema.'

'Perfect, because my favourite restaurant is just around the corner and my stomach is telling me it's lunchtime. I like to eat,' he stated as we set off fast down the next section of the steeply curving jungle road. 'I must admit I'm fascinated to discover what it is you wish to show me,' he said as we emerged from Corcovado and joined the ceaseless flow of traffic heading through Cosme Velho into the centre of the city.

'It's probably nothing,' I said.

'Then you have lost nothing by showing me,' he answered equably.

As we drove, I glanced surreptitiously at my new friend. I always found it an odd moment when I met someone in the flesh, having only ever corresponded with them previously.

And, in fact, Floriano was almost exactly as I'd imagined him to be from his novels and emails.

He was extraordinarily good-looking – far more attractive in person than in his author photograph, because of his easy charm and energy. Everything about him – from his abundant black hair and sun-kissed skin, to a body that was muscular and strong – spoke to me of his South American heritage.

But ironically, he wasn't my type. I'd always found myself drawn to the polar opposite – Western males, with their fair colouring and pale skin. Perhaps, I thought, given my own dark looks, the polar opposite to *me* too.

'So,' he said as he pulled up on the forecourt of the hotel, 'you run upstairs and retrieve whatever it is, and I'll wait here for you.'

In my suite, I combed my hair and added a dab of lipstick, then took the triangular tile from my safe, stowing it in my handbag.

'Now we go for lunch,' announced Floriano as I climbed back into his car and we sped off. 'It's only round the block, but it could take me time to find somewhere to park.' A couple of minutes later, he pointed to a white, colonial-style house with tables laid out on its pretty terrace. 'That is where we are going. You get out and secure us a table. I will join you shortly.'

I did as he'd asked and was led by a waitress to a shady spot. I sat people-watching and taking a moment to retrieve my messages on my mobile. My heart pounded again as I heard the sound of Zed's voice, saying he'd called Atlantis and the housekeeper had said I was abroad. He was sorry to miss me, he said, as he was leaving for Zurich tomorrow.

Which meant it was now safe to return home . . .

'*Meu Deus!* I leave you alone for a few minutes and again you turn a strange colour,' exclaimed Floriano, appearing at the table and looking at me quizzically as he sat down opposite me. 'What is it now?'

I was amazed he'd noticed my tension for a second time. And I realised it would be difficult to hide anything from this man, who seemed to have a natural, laser-like intuition.

'Nothing, really,' I said, tucking my mobile into my handbag. 'In fact, I feel very relieved.'

'Good. Now I'm having a Bohemia beer. Will you join me?'

'I'm not really a fan of beer, to be honest.'

'But Maia, you're in Rio! You must drink a beer. It's that, or a *caipirinha* cocktail, which I can assure you is far stronger,' he added.

I agreed to the beer, and when the waitress came over, we both ordered the steak sandwich Floriano recommended.

'The beef is Argentinean, and although we hate them for beating us at football all too often, we love eating their cows,' he said with a grin. 'Now I don't think I'm able to wait any longer until you show me this precious object of yours.'

'Okay.' I brought the tile out of my bag and placed it carefully on the rough trestle table between us.

'May I?' he asked as his hands reached towards it.

'Of course.'

I watched him as he picked it up with care and studied it. He then turned it over and glanced at the faded words on the back.

'So,' he breathed, and I sensed his surprise. 'Only now can I understand what it was that shocked you. And yes, before you even ask, it looks to me as if this was once destined to adorn the body of the *Cristo*. Well, well,' he commented, the presence of the triangular tile cowing him into silence. Eventually he said, 'Can you tell me how you came by it?'

So, as our beers arrived and then our steak sandwiches, I told Floriano the whole story. He listened patiently, only interrupting occasionally if he needed a fact explained. By the time I'd finished talking, Floriano's plate was empty and mine was barely touched.

'So, now we swap. You will eat while I talk.' He indicated my plate and I did as I was bid. 'I can certainly help you on one point, and that is with the name of the family who live in A Casa das Orquídeas. The Aires Cabrals are a very well-known Rio family – aristocratic, in fact. Descended from the old and now redundant Portuguese royal family themselves. Various Aires Cabrals have featured throughout the past two hundred years of Rio's history.'

'But I have no proof to show the old woman that I'm anything to do with her family,' I reminded him.

'Well, we can't be sure of that yet. Or, in fact, of anything until we have completed a proper investigation,' said Floriano. 'Firstly, it's very easy for me to trace their history through birth, marriage and death records. With a Catholic family as prominent as theirs, I'm sure the records would have been kept meticulously. And then we need to try to decipher the names on the tile, and see if they match the names of any of the Aires Cabrals.'

I was feeling woozy and jet-lagged now after the beer and my early morning wake-up. 'Is it worth it?' I asked him. 'Even if the names did match, I doubt the old woman would admit to anything.'

'One step at a time, Maia. And please, try not to be so

defeatist. You have flown all the way to Rio to discover your history and you can't give up after a day. So, with your approval, while you go back to your hotel and take a nap, I will play detective. Yes?'

'Really, Floriano, I don't wish to put you to any trouble.'

'Trouble? To an historian like me, this is a gift! But I warn you, parts of it may end up in my next book,' he replied with a smile. 'Now, may I take this with me?' He indicated the tile. 'I might pop into the Museu da República to see if any of my friends are around in the lab with their magic UV imaging equipment. They can almost certainly help me decipher the inscription on the back of the tile.'

'Of course,' I agreed, feeling it would be churlish to refuse. I suddenly noticed two young women in their twenties hovering shyly behind Floriano.

'Excuse me, but are you Senhor Floriano Quintelas?' asked one of the girls, drawing closer to the table.

'Yes, I am.'

'We just wanted to say how much we loved your book. And can we please ask for your autograph?' The girl offered Floriano a small diary and a pen.

'Of course,' he smiled as he signed the diary, then chatted easily to the girls. They eventually walked away, blushing in pleasure.

'So, you're famous?' I teased him as we rose from the table.

'In Rio, yes,' he shrugged. 'My book was a bestseller here, but only because I paid people to read it,' he joked. 'Many other countries have bought it for translation and will publish it in the next year. So we will wait and see if I am able to give up my profession as a tour guide and write full-time.'

'Well, I thought it was a beautiful, moving book and I think it will do very well indeed.'

'Thank you, Maia,' he said. 'Now, your hotel is close by,' he added as he pointed out the direction. 'And I want to get going before the various departments I need at the Museu da República are closed for the day. Shall I meet you in your hotel lobby tonight at around seven o'clock? I might have some answers for you by then.'

'Yes, if you have the time.'

'I do. *Tchau.*'

He waved goodbye, and I watched him walk purposefully down the street. As I turned in the opposite direction, I realised this man – historian, writer, celebrity and occasional tour guide – was a human being who was full of surprises.

11

'So . . .'

I could see Floriano was brimming with excitement a few hours later as we took the lift to the terrace bar on the top floor of the hotel. 'I have news for you. And as it is good news, I believe this is the moment for you to indulge in your very first *caipirinha*.'

'Okay,' I said, as we took a table at the front of the terrace, and I watched the sun setting over the beach, gently lowering itself behind the Twin Brothers mountains as a balmy dusk began to fall.

'Here.' He handed me a sheet from a plastic wallet. 'Take a look at that. It is a list of every recorded birth, marriage and death in the Aires Cabral family since 1850.'

I glanced down at the list of names, still unable to believe they held any relevance to me.

'So, you will see there that Gustavo Aires Cabral married Izabela Bonifacio in January 1929. They then had a baby girl in April 1930 called Beatriz Luiza. There is no death certificate recorded for her, so we should presume for now that she is the old woman you met at the house yesterday.'

'And did she have any children?' I ventured.

'Yes, she did. She married Evandro Carvalho in 1951 and they too gave birth to a baby girl by the name of Cristina Izabela in 1956.'

'Carvalho was the old woman's surname! I heard her maid call her that. And Cristina? What happened to her?'

'That's where the line seems to end, as far as any recorded births or deaths in Rio are concerned,' Floriano continued. 'I can find no further records regarding any child that Cristina may have given birth to. But then we don't know the surname of the father, or indeed, whether she ever married. Sadly, the office was closing and I didn't have time to cross-check everything.'

'So . . . if I am related to this family, and it's a big "if", then Cristina is the obvious candidate to be my mother,' I said quietly as my drink arrived. '*Saúde*,' I said, toasting Floriano and taking a healthy slug of the cocktail, nearly choking as the potent, bitter liquid slid down my throat.

Floriano chuckled at my discomfort. 'Sorry, I should have warned you that it is strong,' he said, sipping his own *caipirinha* as if it was water. 'I also ran across to the Museu da República and asked my friend to take a quick look at the inscription on the back of the tile with his special UV machine. The only thing he could tell me for certain is that the first name on the tile is "Izabela". Who, from the records I found, would technically be your great-grandmother.'

'And the other name on the tile?'

'That's much more faded and my friend is running further tests. Although he has made out the first three letters.'

'And are they the first three letters of my possible great-grandfather, Gustavo Aires Cabral?' I queried.

'No, they aren't. Here, he's written down for you what

he's deciphered so far.' Floriano passed me another sheet of paper from the plastic wallet.

I studied them. '*L a u* . . . ?' I looked at him askance.

'Give Stephano another twenty-four hours and I'm sure he'll have deciphered the rest of the name. He's the best, I promise. Want another one?' he asked me, indicating my *caipirinha*.

'No thanks. I think I'll have a glass of white wine instead.'

After Floriano had ordered further drinks for both of us, he stared at me intently.

'What is it?' I asked him.

'I have something else to show you, Maia. And if it isn't ultimate proof that you are indeed related to the Aires Cabrals, I don't know what is. Are you ready for this?'

'It's nothing awful, is it?' I asked him apprehensively.

'No. I think it's something very beautiful. Here.' Another piece of paper was passed across to me. This time, the entirety of it taken up with a grainy photograph of a woman's face.

'Who is she?'

'Izabela Aires Cabral, whose first name is on the back of your tile, and who may well be your great-grandmother. Surely, Maia,' he encouraged, 'you must see the resemblance?'

I stared at the woman's features. And yes, even I could see my own face mirrored there. 'Perhaps,' I shrugged.

'Maia, it's uncanny,' Floriano stated categorically. 'And I can tell you that there's a lot more where that came from. There's an entire archive of Izabela's photographs from old newspapers, which I accessed on microfiche in the Biblioteca Nacional do Brasil. She was thought at the time to be one of the most beautiful women in Brazil. She married Gustavo

Aires Cabral at the cathedral here in Rio in January 1929. It was the society wedding of the year.'

'Of course, it could simply be coincidence,' I said, feeling uncomfortable at Floriano's implicit comparison between me and the society beauty of her day. 'But . . .'

'Yes?' he said, eager for me to continue.

'When I was at A Casa das Orquídeas, I noticed a sculpture sitting in the corner of the terrace. It stuck out because it was so unusual and not the kind of thing you'd normally expect to find in a garden. It was of a woman sitting on a chair. And looking at this photograph, I'm sure it was the same woman. And yes, at the time I remember thinking that she looked familiar.'

'Because she looks like you!' he said, as the waitress took the drinks from her tray and placed them on the table. 'Well, I feel that we've already made some progress.'

'And I'm very grateful, Floriano, but I still don't think the old woman I met yesterday wishes to tell me anything, or would ever acknowledge me. Why should she? Wouldn't you behave the same in the circumstances?' I challenged him.

'Admittedly, if a complete stranger walked into my garden, even if she *did* bear an uncanny resemblance to my mother, and then announced she'd been told she belonged to my family, I would indeed view her with suspicion,' Floriano agreed soberly.

'So, where do we go from here?' I asked him.

'Back to see her. I think I should accompany you. It will help give you some gravitas when she hears my name.'

I couldn't help a wry smile at Floriano's total conviction that the old woman would know who he was. South Americans, I'd noticed, seemed to have a refreshingly unabashed openness and honesty about their own gifts and achievements.

'I also want to see that sculpture you mentioned, Maia,' Floriano continued. 'Would you mind if I came with you?'

'Not at all. You've been so good helping me with all of this.'

'I can assure you, it's been a pleasure. After all, you are the spitting image of one of the most beautiful women Brazil ever produced.'

I blushed, feeling uncomfortable at the compliment. My cynical mind turned immediately to whether he'd expect favours in return for his help. Casual sex was the norm these days, I knew, but not something I could ever contemplate.

'Excuse me,' he said as his mobile rang and he spoke in fast Portuguese to someone he called '*querida*'. 'No problem,' he said. 'I'll be with you in fifteen minutes.' He looked at me and sighed. 'Sadly, I have to leave you,' he said, draining his *caipirinha*. 'Petra, the girl I live with, has managed yet again to lose her key.' He rolled his eyes and signalled for the bill.

'No,' I said firmly, 'this is on me, as a thank you for all your help.'

'Then I say thank you too.' He nodded graciously. 'What time should I collect you tomorrow?'

'Whenever suits you. I have no plans.'

'Then I suggest ten thirty, before Senhora Beatriz Carvalho has lunch and an afternoon nap. Don't get up,' he said as he rose from his chair. 'Stay here and finish your wine. Until tomorrow, Maia. *Tchau.*'

He walked away from me, nodding easily at the waitress who was staring at him with a look of appreciative recognition. I sipped my wine, feeling ridiculous that, just for a moment, I'd imagined he would want to sleep with me.

But, just like everybody else, he had his own life. Well, I thought as I lifted my wine glass to my lips, perhaps I was about to find mine.

12

Floriano arrived promptly in the lobby of the hotel the following morning and we took off in his red Fiat. He weaved through the incessant traffic confidently, as I caught my breath at the near misses.

'Where do you come from?' I asked him, to take my mind off his terrifying driving. 'Are you a true Brazilian?'

'And what do you think *is* a true Brazilian?' he asked me. 'There is no such thing. We are a race made up of half-breeds, different nationalities, creeds and colours. The only "real" Brazilians were the original *nativos* that the Portuguese began murdering after they arrived here five hundred years ago, claiming the riches of our country for themselves. And many more who didn't die a bloody death succumbed to the diseases the settlers brought with them. To cut a long family history short, my mother is descended from the Portuguese and my father is Italian. There's no such thing as a pure bloodline here in Brazil.'

I was learning fast about the country that might have produced me. 'So what about the Aires Cabrals?'

'Well, interestingly, they were pure Portuguese, until Izabela, your potential great-grandmother, arrived on the scene. Her father was a very rich man of Italian extraction, who, like many at the time, had made a fortune from coffee. And reading between the lines, I presume that the Aires Cabrals had fallen on hard times, like so many of the lazy, aristocratic families had. Izabela was very beautiful and from a wealthy family, and so one can only presume a deal was struck.'

'So it's fair to say your conclusions are supposition rather than fact at this point?' I asked him.

'One hundred per cent supposition. Which, apart from dates and the odd letter and diary, is always the case when one is first investigating an historical situation,' Floriano qualified. 'Nothing can ever be certain, because the voices one must hear from to confirm the story definitively are no longer with us. As an historian, you have to learn to put the pieces of a jigsaw puzzle together to create the whole picture.'

'Yes. I suppose you're right,' I mused, understanding what he meant.

'Of course, with the age of the internet and everything now recorded on it, history and the research of it will change. We are entering a new era where there will be fewer secrets, fewer mysteries that need to be uncovered. Thank God I'm also a novelist, because Mister Wikipedia and his friends have usurped my position as an historian. My memoirs when I'm old will be worthless; my story will be there for all to see on the web.'

I thought about this as Floriano – without even asking me to point him in the right direction – turned into the drive of A Casa das Orquídeas.

'How did you know exactly where it was?' I asked in amazement as he parked confidently in front of the house.

'My dear Maia, your potential long-lost family is famous in Rio. Every historian knows this house. It is one of the few remnants left of a lost era. So,' he said, switching off the engine and turning to me. 'Ready to go?'

'Yes.'

With Floriano leading the way, we approached the house and walked up the front steps.

'The bell doesn't work,' I told him.

'Then I will knock.'

And so he did. Loudly, as if to wake the dead. Receiving no response within thirty seconds, Floriano banged on the door again, even harder this time, which brought the sound of feet running on tiles towards it from the inside. I then heard bolts being drawn back and locks turned. Finally, the door was pulled open and I saw the grey-haired African maid whom I'd encountered on my last visit standing on the threshold of the house. As soon as she saw me, her features contracted in recognition and panic.

'Sorry for disturbing you, senhora, but my name is Floriano Quintelas. I am a friend of Senhorita D'Aplièse. I can assure you we do not wish to disturb or unsettle your mistress. However, we have some information that we think may well be interesting to her. I am a well-respected historian and also a novelist.'

'I know who you are, Senhor Quintelas,' the maid said, keeping her eyes on me. 'Senhora Carvalho is taking coffee in the morning room, but as I've already informed your friend, she is a very sick woman.'

As I listened to the formal way in which the maid spoke, I wanted to giggle. It was as if she was acting in a second-rate Victorian melodrama.

'Why don't we come in with you and explain to Senhora Carvalho who we are?' Floriano suggested. 'And then, if she feels she is not up to a conversation with us, I promise we'll go away.'

Floriano already had a foot over the threshold, which forced the flustered maid to back up and lead us both into a grand tiled entrance hall, with a sweeping curved staircase rising to the floors above. An elegant mahogany pedestal table sat in the centre of the floor and an imposing long-cased clock was positioned against one wall. Under the curve of the stairs, I could see a long narrow corridor running off the hall, which clearly led to the back of the house.

'Please be so kind as to lead the way,' Floriano invited the maid, adopting her formal tone.

She paused hesitantly, as though weighing something in her mind. Then she nodded to us and headed for the corridor, with the two of us following in her wake. However, as we all arrived outside a door towards the end of the dim passageway, the maid turned to us. And this time I could see she was adamant we would not gain entry until she had spoken to her mistress.

'Wait here,' she said firmly.

As the maid knocked and then entered the room, closing the door in our faces, I turned to Floriano.

'She's simply an old, sick lady. Is it right to upset her?'

'No, Maia, but equally, is it fair that she may be refusing to divulge the details of your true parentage? That woman behind the door may well be your grandmother. Her daughter, your mother. Do you really care if we are disturbing her morning routine for a few minutes?'

The maid emerged from the room. 'She will see you for

five minutes. No more.' Again I felt her glance at me closely as we walked into a dark room that smelt musty and damp. The decor clearly hadn't been altered for decades and, as my eyes became accustomed to the gloom, I noticed the thread-bare oriental rug beneath our feet and the limp, faded damask curtains that hung at the window. However, the general shab-biness was offset by the beautiful antique furniture of rose-wood and walnut, and the magnificent chandelier suspended overhead.

Senhora Carvalho was sitting in a high-backed velvet chair, a blanket across her knees. A jug of water and numer-ous pill bottles were sitting on the side table beside her.

'You're back,' she said.

'Please forgive Senhorita D'Aplièse for bothering you fur-ther,' began Floriano. 'But you can imagine that for her, finding her family is a serious business. And she will not be deflected.'

'Senhor Quintelas,' the old woman sighed, 'I told your friend yesterday that I cannot help her.'

'Are you sure, Senhora Carvalho? Surely you only have to look at that portrait that hangs on the wall above the fire-place to see that Senhorita Maia isn't here for some ulterior motive? She is not after money, but only wants to trace her family. Is that so wrong? Can you blame her for it?'

I glanced in the direction that Floriano had pointed and saw an oil painting of the woman I now knew to be Izabela Aires Cabral. This time there was no doubt in my mind. Even I could see I was the very image of her. 'Izabela Aires Cabral was your mother,' Floriano continued. 'And you also had a daughter, Cristina, in 1956.'

The old woman sat, her lips pursed together in silence.

'So you're not prepared to even consider the chance that you may, in fact, have a granddaughter? I have to tell you, senhora, that proof of Senhorita D'Aplièse's heritage is at this very moment being gathered by a friend of mine at the Museu da República. We'll be back,' Floriano promised.

The old woman continued to say nothing, not meeting Floriano's gaze. Suddenly she winced in pain. 'Please, leave me,' she said, and I saw the agony in her eyes.

'Enough,' I whispered to Floriano desperately. 'She's sick, it's not fair.'

Floriano acquiesced with a slight nod. '*Adeus*, Senhora Carvalho. I wish you a pleasant day.'

'I'm so sorry, Senhora Carvalho,' I said. 'We won't bother you again, I promise.'

Floriano turned tail and marched determinedly out of the room, with me following, embarrassed and near to tears, behind him.

We saw the maid was hovering in the hall and walked towards her.

'Thank you for letting us in, senhora,' said Floriano, as we followed her across the hall to the door.

'Keep her talking,' he whispered to me, 'there's something I want to see.'

As Floriano disappeared down the front steps, I turned to the maid, my face full of regret.

'I'm so very sorry to have upset Senhora Carvalho. I promise that I won't come back again without her permission.'

'Senhora Carvalho is very ill, senhorita. She's dying and has only a short time left, you see.'

As the maid hovered on the doorstep beside me, I sensed there was something else she wanted to say.

'I just wanted to ask,' I said as I pointed to the fountain that no longer played in the centre of the drive. 'Were you ever here to see this house in its full glory?'

'Yes, I was born here.'

I could see that she was reminiscing as she stared at the dilapidated structure with sadness in her eyes. Then she turned to me suddenly as, out of the corner of my eye, I saw Floriano disappear along the side of the house.

'Senhorita,' she whispered, 'I have something for you.'

'Excuse me?' My thoughts had been temporarily diverted by Floriano's disappearance, and I hadn't heard what the maid had said.

'I have something to give you. But please, if I entrust these to you, you must swear you will never tell Senhora Carvalho. She would never forgive me for my betrayal.'

'Of course,' I said. 'I understand completely.'

The maid drew a slim brown-paper package out of her white apron pocket and handed it to me.

'Please, I beg you, tell no one I've given you these,' she said, with a rasp in her voice. 'They were passed down to me from my mother. She said they were part of the history of the Aires Cabral family and gave them to me for safekeeping just before she died.'

I stared at her in wonder. 'Thank you,' I breathed, glad to note that Floriano had now reappeared and was standing by the car. 'But why?' I asked her.

With a long, bony finger, she indicated the moonstone hanging on its slim gold chain around my neck. 'I know who you are. *Adeus.*' She scurried back inside the house and closed the front door.

Dazed, I stuffed the package into my handbag and descended the steps towards the car.

Floriano was already inside it and had the engine running. I climbed in and we set off at his usual fast pace down the drive.

'Did you see the sculpture?' I asked him.

'Yes,' he said as we drove off down the road and away from the house. 'I'm sorry she refuses to acknowledge you, Maia, but my devious brain is now putting together the odd piece of the jigsaw puzzle. And I think I might understand her reticence. When we get back to the city, I'm going to drop you straight off at the hotel then go back to the Museu da República and the *biblioteca*. Shall I call you later with any news?' he asked as we arrived at the hotel.

'Yes please,' I said, as I climbed out of the car.

With a wave, he drove off along the street and I took the lift upstairs to my suite. Closing my door and hanging the *do not disturb* sign on it, I walked to the bed and took out the package. Inside was a bundle of letters held tightly together with string. I put it on the bed, untied the knot and picked up the first envelope, which I saw had been split open meticulously with a paper knife. Studying the writing on the front, I saw all the letters were addressed to a 'Senhorita Loen Fagundes'.

Painstakingly pulling out the letter inside, I felt the fragility of the tissue-thin paper beneath my fingers. I unfolded it and saw the address at the top was Paris and the date 30th March 1928. Checking through the next few letters I realised that the pile in front of me had not been put in any form of chronological order, as there were some letters sent in 1927 to Loen Fagundes at another address in Brazil. As I opened more of the envelopes, I saw the signature at the bottom of each of them was 'Izabela', the woman who may have been my great-grandmother . . . The maid's words came back to me.

I know who you are . . .

My fingers touched the moonstone necklace. All I could guess was that it had come with me as some kind of keepsake, perhaps from my mother, when Pa Salt had adopted me as a baby. He'd told me when he'd given it to me that there was an interesting story behind it. Perhaps he'd been subtly prompting me to ask him one day what it was; maybe at the time he hadn't wished to unsettle me by speaking of a direct connection to my past. He'd been waiting for me to ask. And I wished now with all my heart that I had.

For the next hour, I ploughed through the letters – of which there must have been over thirty – and set them in a pile in date order.

I was itching to begin reading the immaculate, beautifully scripted writing. My mobile rang, and I heard Floriano's voice on the other end of the line full of excitement.

'Maia, I have news. Can I come over and see you in an hour?'

'Would you mind if we met tomorrow morning? I think I may have picked up a stomach bug,' I lied guiltily, wanting the rest of the day to read the letters.

'Tomorrow at ten then?'

'Yes. I'm sure I'll be okay by then.'

'If there's anything you need, Maia, please call me.'

'I will, thank you.'

'No problem. Feel better,' he said.

Switching off my mobile, I called down to room service to

bring me two bottles of water and a club sandwich. Once they had arrived and I had distractedly wolfed down the contents, I picked up the first letter with trembling fingers and began to read . . .

Izabela

Rio de Janeiro

November 1927

13

Izabela Rosa Bonifacio was stirred from sleep by the scratchy pattering of tiny feet across the tiled floor. Sitting bolt upright, she looked down from her bed and saw the *sagui* staring up at her. In its hands – miniature, hairy facsimiles of her own – the monkey was holding her hairbrush. Bel couldn't help but let out a giggle as the *sagui* continued to stare at her, its liquid black eyes pleading with her to allow it to escape with its new plaything.

'So, you wish to brush your hair?' she asked it as she slithered forwards on her stomach to the bottom of the bed. 'Please' – she held out a hand towards the monkey – 'give it back to me. It's mine, and Mãe will be so cross if you steal it from me.'

The monkey inclined its head towards its escape route, and as Bel's long, slim fingers reached out to swipe the hairbrush back, the creature leapt daintily onto the windowsill and disappeared from view.

With a sigh, Bel fell back onto the bed, knowing she'd receive yet another lecture from her parents about keeping her shutters closed at night for this very reason. The hairbrush had been mother-of-pearl, a christening gift from her paternal grandmother, and as she'd told the monkey, her mother would not be amused. Bel wriggled back upwards and laid her head on the pillows, harbouring the vain hope that the *sagui* might drop the brush in the garden in its flight back to its jungle home on the mountainside behind the house.

A faint breeze blew a wisp of her thick, dark hair across her forehead, bringing with it the delicate scents of the guava and lemon trees that grew in the garden below her window. Even though the clock by her bedside told her it was only half past six in the morning, already she could feel the heat of the day to come. She looked up and saw there was not a single wisp of cloud marring the rapidly lightening sky.

Loen, her maid, wouldn't knock at her door for another hour to help her dress. Bel wondered whether she should finally pluck up the courage to creep out of the house while everyone slept and take a swim in the cool water of the magnificent blue-tiled swimming pool that Antonio, her father, had just had built in the garden.

The pool was Antonio's latest acquisition and he was very proud of it, as one of the first of its kind in a private house in Rio. A month ago he had invited all his important friends to see it, and everyone had stood dutifully on the surrounding terrace and admired it. The men were attired in expensively tailored suits, the women in copies of the latest Paris designs bought from the exclusive stores of the Avenida Rio Branco.

Bel had thought at the time how ironic it was that not one of them had brought their bathing suit, and she too had stood fully clothed in the burning heat, fervently wishing she could strip off her formal dress and dive into the cool, clear water. In fact, to this day, Bel had never seen anyone actually use the pool. When she had asked if she could take a swim in it herself, her father had shaken his head.

'No, *querida*, you cannot be seen in a bathing suit by all the servants. You must swim when they are not around.'

As the servants were *always* around, Bel had quickly realised that the pool was simply another ornament, a grand possession her father could show off to impress his friends. Another stop on his never-ending quest to achieve the social status he craved.

When she asked Mãe why Pai never seemed to be content with what he had when they lived in one of the most beautiful houses in Rio, dined often at the Copacabana Palace Hotel and even had a brand-new Ford motor car, her mother would shrug placidly.

'It is simply because, no matter how many cars or farms he owns, he can never change his surname.'

During Bel's seventeen years on earth, she had gleaned that Antonio was descended from Italian immigrants, who had arrived in Brazil to work on the many coffee farms on the verdant, fertile land surrounding the city of São Paulo. Antonio's own father had been not only hard-working but clever, and he had saved hard to buy his own parcel of land and begin his own business.

By the time Antonio was old enough to take over, the coffee farm was thriving and he was able to buy three more. The profits had made their family rich, and when Bel was eight years old, her father had bought a beautiful old *fazenda* five hours' drive outside Rio. It was the place she still thought of as her home. Tucked away high in the mountains, the large plantation house was tranquil and welcoming and contained Bel's most precious memories. Free in those days to roam and ride across the estate's two thousand hectares as she pleased, she had experienced an idyllic, carefree childhood.

However, although Antonio was now closer to Rio, this had still not been enough for him. She remembered having supper with her parents one night, and listening to her father explaining to her mother why they must one day move to the city itself.

'Rio is the capital, the seat of all power in Brazil. And we must be a part of it.'

As Antonio's business grew, so did his pot of gold. Three years ago, her father had arrived home and announced that he'd bought a house in Cosme Velho, one of the most exclusive districts in Rio.

'So now the Portuguese aristocrats will no longer be able to ignore me because they will be our neighbours!' Antonio had crowed as he'd thumped the table in triumph.

Bel and her mother had shared a horrified glance at the thought of leaving their mountain home and moving to the big city. However, her normally gentle mother was adamant that the Fazenda Santa Tereza must not be sold, so that at least there was sanctuary if they needed to escape the heat of a Rio summer.

'Why, Mãe, why?' Bel had wept later that evening as her mother had entered her room to kiss her goodnight. 'I love it here. I don't want to move to the city.'

'Because it is not enough for your father to be as rich as any of the Portuguese nobility in Rio. He wishes to be their equal in society. And to gain their respect.'

'But, Mãe, even I understand how the Portuguese in Rio look down on us Italian *paulistas*. Surely he will never achieve his aim?'

'Well,' her mother had said wearily, 'Antonio has achieved everything he has wished for so far.'

'But how will you and I know how to behave?' she'd asked. 'I have lived in the mountains for most of my life. We will never fit in as Pai wishes us to.'

'Your father is already talking about us meeting with Senhora Nathalia Santos, a woman from Portuguese aristocracy whose family has fallen on hard times. She earns a living by teaching families such as ours how to conduct themselves in Rio society. And she can make introductions for them too.'

'So we're to be turned into dolls, who wear the best clothes and say the right things and use the right cutlery? I think I would rather die.' Bel had made a choking noise to express her displeasure.

'That is about right, yes,' Carla had agreed, chuckling at her daughter's assessment, her warm brown eyes sparkling with amusement. 'And of course, Izabela, you, his beloved only daughter, are his goose who may lay the golden egg. You are already very beautiful, Bel, and your father thinks your looks will bring you a good marriage.'

Bel had looked up at her mother in horror. 'I am to be used as currency by Pai to gain social acceptance? Well, I won't do it!' She'd rolled over and thumped her pillows with her fists.

Carla walked towards the bed and settled her rotund figure on the edge of it, patting her daughter's rigid back with a plump hand. 'It's not as bad as it seems, *querida*,' she comforted.

'But I'm only fifteen! I want to marry for love, not for position. And besides, the Portuguese men are pale and scrawny and lazy. I prefer Italian men.'

'Come now, Bel, you cannot say that. Every race has its mixture of good and bad. I'm sure your father will find someone that you like. Rio is a big city.'

'I won't go!'

Carla bent forwards and kissed her daughter's shiny dark hair. 'Well, I'll say one thing for you, you have certainly inherited your father's spirit. Goodnight, *querida*.'

That had been three years ago and not a single thought that Bel had uttered to her mother then had changed since. Her father was still ambitious, her mother still gentle, Rio society as unbending in its traditions as it had been two hundred years ago, and the Portuguese men still deeply unattractive.

And yet, their current house in Cosme Velho was spectacular. Its smooth ochre-coloured walls and tall sash windows housed beautifully proportioned rooms that had been completely redecorated to her father's specifications. He had also insisted on installing every possible modern convenience, such as a telephone and upstairs bathrooms. Outside, the perfectly landscaped grounds could rival the splendour of Rio's magnificent Botanical Gardens.

The house was named Mansão da Princesa after Princess Isabel, who had once come to drink the waters of the Carioca River that ran through the grounds and were purported to have healing properties.

Yet despite the undeniable luxury of her surroundings, Bel found the brooding presence of Corcovado Mountain – which rose directly behind the house and towered over it

– oppressive. She often found herself longing for the wide open spaces and fresh clear air of the mountains.

Since arriving in the city, Senhora Santos, her etiquette tutor, had become part of Bel's daily life. She'd learned from her how to enter a room – shoulders back, head held high, *float* – and had the family trees of every important Portuguese family in Rio drummed into her head. And as she'd received instruction in French, piano, history of art, and European literature, Bel began to dream of travelling to the Old World herself.

The hardest part of her tutelage, however, was that Senhora Santos had insisted she forget the native language of her family which her mother had taught her from the crib. Bel still struggled to speak Portuguese without an Italian accent.

She often looked in the mirror and allowed herself a wry chuckle. For, whatever pains Nathalia Santos had taken to erase where she came from, her true heritage betrayed itself in her features. Her flawless skin, which up in the mountains had taken only a hint of sunshine to darken to a deep glowing bronze – Senhora Santos had warned her time and again to steer clear of the sun – was the perfect foil for the rich waves of dark hair and enormous brown eyes that spoke of passionate Tuscan nights in the hills of her true homeland.

Her full lips hinted at the sensuality of her nature, and her breasts protested daily when they were restrained inside a stiffly wired corset. As Loen tugged each morning at the back fastenings, endeavouring to tame the outward signs of femininity, Bel often felt that the constricting garment was the perfect metaphor for her own circumstances. She was like a wild animal, full of fire and passion, trapped in a cage.

She watched a tiny gecko run like a streak of lightning from one corner of the ceiling to the other and mused that, at any moment, it could make its getaway through the open window, just as the *sagui* had done. Whereas she would spend another day trussed up like a chicken ready to be placed in the burning heat of Rio's social oven, learning to ignore her God-given nature and instead become the society lady her father wished her to be.

And only next week, her father's plans for her future were to reach their crescendo. She would be eighteen, and launched into Rio society with a spectacular party at the beautiful Copacabana Palace Hotel.

After that, Bel knew that she'd be forced into the best marriage her father could find her. And the last vestiges of the freedom she had left would be gone forever.

An hour later, a familiar *tap-tapping* at the door alerted her to the presence of Loen.

'Good morning, Senhorita Bel. Is it not a beautiful one?' her maid asked as she entered the room.

'No,' Bel answered bad-temperedly.

'Come, you must get up and dress. You have a very busy day.'

'Do I?' Bel feigned ignorance, knowing full well what obligations her waking hours contained.

'Now, *minha pequena*, don't play games with me,' Loen warned, reverting as she often did in private to the pet name she'd given Bel as a child. 'You know as well as I do that you have your piano lesson at ten o'clock, then your French tutor arrives. And this afternoon, Madame Duchaine arrives for the last fitting of your ballgown.'

Bel closed her eyes and pretended not to hear.

Undeterred, Loen walked over to the bed and shook her shoulder gently. 'What is wrong with you? In only a week's time you will be eighteen and your father has organised you a wonderful party. Everyone in Rio will be there! Are you not excited?'

Bel did not respond.

'What do you wish to wear today? The cream or the blue?' persisted Loen.

'I don't care!'

Loen calmly went to the closet and drawers, then laid out her own choice of clothes on the end of Bel's bed.

Reluctantly, Bel roused herself and sat up. 'Forgive me, Loen. I'm sad because a *sagui* came in this morning and stole my hairbrush, a gift from my grandmother. I know Mãe will be angry with me for leaving my shutters open again.'

'No!' Loen was horrified. 'Your beautiful mother-of-pearl hairbrush gone to the monkeys in the jungle. How many times have you been told to keep the shutters closed at night?'

'Many,' agreed Bel companionably.

'I will tell the gardeners to search the grounds. They may find it yet.'

'Thank you,' Bel said as she lifted her arms to help Loen ease her nightgown from her body.

Over breakfast, Antonio Bonifacio was studying the invitation list to his daughter's party at the Copacabana Palace. 'Senhora Santos has indeed gathered the great and the good, and most of them have accepted,' Antonio commented with satisfaction. 'Although not the Carvalho Gomes family, nor the Ribeiros Barcellos. They are sad but they are busy elsewhere.' Antonio raised an eyebrow.

'Well, they do not know what they will miss.' Carla put a comforting hand on her husband's shoulder, knowing that these were two of the most important families in Rio. 'It will be talked of all over town, and they will hear of it, I'm sure.'

'I hope so,' Antonio grunted. 'It has cost enough. And you, my *princesa*, will be at the centre of it all.'

'Yes, Papa. I am very grateful.'

'Bel, you know you must not call me "Papa". I am "Pai",' Antonio chided her.

'Sorry, Pai, it's hard to change the habit of a lifetime.'

'So.' Antonio folded his newspaper neatly and stood up, nodding a goodbye to his wife and daughter. 'I'm off to the office to do the work that will pay for it all.'

Bel's eyes followed her father as he strode from the room and she thought how handsome he still was, with his tall, elegant physique and his full mane of dark hair, only slightly greying at the temples.

'Pai is so tense,' Bel sighed to her mother. 'Is he worried about the party, do you think?'

'Bel, your father is always tense. Whether it's over the yield of coffee beans on one of our farms or your party, he will always find something to worry about. It is just . . . who he is,' Carla shrugged. 'Now, I must go too. I'm meeting Senhora Santos here this morning to go through the final preparations for the reception at the Copacabana Palace. She will want you to join us after your piano and French lessons to go through the guest list.'

'But Mãe, I can already recite it front to back and upside down,' Bel groaned.

'I know, *querida*, but nothing must go wrong.'

Carla stood up to leave, then hesitated for a moment and turned back to Bel. 'There is one more thing I must tell you. My dear cousin Sofia is recovering from a very serious illness and I have invited her and her three children to stay at our *fazenda* while she recuperates. Since we only have Fabiana and her husband there, I must send Loen to attend to Sofia's children so she can rest. I'm afraid Loen will have to leave for the mountains by the end of the week.'

'But Mãe!' Bel gasped in dismay. 'My party is only a few days away. What will I do without her?'

'I'm sorry, Bel, but there is no choice. Gabriela will still be here and I'm sure she will give you all the help you need. Now, I must leave or I will be late.' Carla patted her daughter's shoulder comfortingly and left the room.

Bel slumped back in her chair and digested the unwelcome news. She was upset by the thought of being without her closest ally in the run-up to one of the most important events of her life.

Loen had been born at their *fazenda*, where her African forebears had worked as slaves on the coffee farm. When slavery had finally been abolished in Brazil in 1888, many freed slaves had downed tools that very day and left their former masters, but Loen's parents had chosen to stay. They had continued to work for the *fazenda*'s occupants at the time; a rich Portuguese family, until, like so many Rio aristocrats with no more slave labour to rely on to tend the coffee plants, they were forced to sell up. Loen's father had chosen that moment to promptly disappear into the night, leaving her mother, Gabriela, and nine-year-old Loen to fend for themselves.

When Antonio had bought the *fazenda* a few months later, Carla had taken pity on them and insisted they were kept on as maids. Three years ago, both mother and daughter had moved with the family to Rio.

While Loen was technically only a servant, she and Bel had grown up together on the isolated *fazenda*. With few other children of similar age to play with, the two of them had forged a special bond. Although barely older than Bel, Loen was wise beyond her years and an endless source of advice and comfort for her young mistress. Bel, in turn, had sought to repay Loen's kindness and loyalty by spending the long, languid evenings at the *fazenda* teaching her to read and write.

So at least, Bel reflected with a sigh as she sipped her coffee, they would be able to correspond while they were separated.

'Have you finished, senhorita?' asked Gabriela, interrupting her thoughts and giving Bel a sympathetic smile that indicated she had overheard Carla's announcement.

Bel glanced at the sideboard heaped with fresh mango, figs, almonds, and a basket of freshly baked bread. Enough to feed an entire street, she thought, let alone a family of three.

'Yes, you can clear the table. And I'm sorry for the extra work you will have while Loen is away,' she added.

Gabriela shrugged stoically. 'I know that my daughter too will be disappointed that she won't be here for your birthday preparations. But no matter, we will manage.'

After Gabriela had left, Bel reached for the *Jornal do Brasil* that was lying on the table and opened it. On the front page, there was a photograph of Bertha Lutz, the campaigner for women's rights, standing with her supporters outside City

Hall. Senhorita Lutz had started the Brazilian Federation for the Advancement of Women six years ago and was campaigning for all women in Brazil to have the vote. Bel followed her progress avidly. It seemed to her that times were changing for other women in Brazil, whereas here she was, with a father who was stuck in the past, still believing women should simply be married off to the highest bidder before producing a healthy brood of children.

Since their move to the city, Antonio had kept his precious daughter a virtual prisoner, never allowing her even to take a walk outside the house without an older female escort. He didn't seem to realise that the few girls of her own age she'd been introduced to at formal tea parties, and who had been deemed suitable as friends by Senhora Santos, were from families who were embracing the modern age, not fighting against it.

For example, her friend Maria Elisa da Silva Costa did indeed come from an aristocratic Portuguese heritage. But her family didn't, as Pai so misguidedly believed, just float from one social event to the next. The old Portuguese court Pai dreamed of his family being a part of had mostly faded into history, the last vestiges of it only championed by a few clinging on to a disappearing world.

Maria Elisa was one of the few young women Bel had met that she felt she had anything in common with. Her father, Heitor, worked for a living as a renowned architect and had recently won the honour of building the planned *Cristo Redentor* monument on top of Corcovado, the mountain that rose dramatically skywards behind their house. The da Silva Costas lived nearby in Botafogo and if her father was visiting the mountaintop to take measurements for his structure,

Maria Elisa would often accompany him as far as Cosme Velho and visit Bel while Heitor took the train up the mountain. Bel was expecting a visit from her later today.

'Senhorita, can I get you anything else?' Gabriela asked, hovering by the door with the heavy tray.

'No thank you, Gabriela, you may go.'

A few minutes later, Bel stood up and left the room after her.

'You must be so excited about your party,' said Maria Elisa as they sat in the shade of the dense, tropical forest that overhung the garden of the house. The foliage was kept in check by a small army of gardeners to prevent it invading the immaculate grounds, but beyond the perimeter, it surged untamed up the mountain.

'I think I'll be glad when it's over,' Bel replied honestly.

'Well, I'm looking forward to it, that's for sure,' Maria Elisa said, smiling. 'Alexandre Medeiros will be there and I have such a crush on him. I'll go to heaven if he asks me to dance,' she added as she sipped her freshly squeezed orange juice. 'Is there any young man who's caught your eye?' She looked at Bel expectantly.

'No, and besides, I know my father will want to choose a husband for me.'

'Oh, he's so old-fashioned! When I talk to you I feel lucky to have Pai, even though his head is in the clouds with his *Cristo* all the time. Do you know,' Maria Elisa said, lowering her voice to a whisper, 'my father is actually an atheist, and yet here he is, building the largest monument to Our Lord in the world!'

'Maybe this project will change his beliefs,' Bel suggested.

'Last night I heard him talking to Mãe about going to Europe to find a sculptor for the statue. As he'll be away for so long, he said we would all be travelling with him. Can you imagine, Bel? We will see the great sights of Florence, Rome and, of course, Paris.' Maria Elisa wrinkled her pretty freckled nose in pleasure at the thought of it.

'Europe?' exclaimed Bel as she turned to face her friend. 'Maria Elisa, at this moment, I can truly say that I hate you. It's been my dream forever to go to the Old World. Especially to Florence, where my family came from.'

'Well, perhaps, if it is confirmed, you could come with us, for some of the time at least? It would be better for me too, otherwise I'm stuck with only my two brothers for company. What do you think?' Maria Elisa's eyes were bright with excitement.

'I think it's a wonderful suggestion, but that my father would say no,' Bel stated flatly. 'If he doesn't even let me take a walk down the street here alone, I hardly think he would let me go across the sea to Europe. Besides, he wants me here in Rio, available to be married off as soon as possible.' Bel ground an ant beneath her shoe disconsolately.

The sound of a car pulling into the front drive alerted them to the fact that Maria Elisa's father had come to collect her.

'So,' she said, standing and giving Bel a warm hug, 'I shall see you next Thursday at your party?'

'Yes.'

'*Adeus*, Bel,' she said as she walked away across the garden. 'And don't worry, I promise we'll formulate a plan.'

Bel sat where she was, dreaming of seeing the Duomo and the Fountain of Neptune in Florence. Out of all the cultural lessons Senhora Santos had organised for her, history of art had been the one she'd most enjoyed. An artist had been employed to school her in the basics of line drawing and painting. Those afternoons when she'd sat in his airy studio in the Escola Nacional de Belas Artes had been some of the most pleasurable moments since she'd arrived in Rio.

The artist was also a sculptor, and had allowed her to try her hand with a lump of thick red clay. Bel still remembered the damp softness of it between her fingers, its malleability as she struggled to shape it into a figure.

'You have real talent,' the artist had nodded approvingly after she'd shown him what she considered a lamentably poor version of the *Venus de Milo*. But whether she had ability or not, Bel had loved the atmosphere of the studio, and when the lessons came to an end, she'd missed her weekly visits there.

She heard Loen's voice calling her in from the terrace, signalling that Madame Duchaine had arrived for the final fitting of the gown for her party.

Leaving thoughts of Europe and the glories it held in the jungle behind her, Bel stood up and made her way back through the garden and into the house.

14

On the morning of her eighteenth birthday, Bel woke to see heavy grey clouds scuttering across the horizon beyond her window and heard the sound of approaching thunder. This indicated a storm which would gather ominously in power as the sky was lit up with great bolts of lightning. Then suddenly, the heavens would open and unceremoniously drop their contents on Rio, drenching its unfortunate inhabitants.

As Gabriela bustled around the room, firing Bel's schedule for the day at her, she too turned to the window and studied the sky.

'We must only pray that the clouds decide to burst before your party and the rain is gone when your guests begin arriving. What a disaster it would be if your beautiful gown was mud-spattered as you stepped out of the car and into the hotel. I will go to the chapel and ask Our Lady to finish the rain before tonight, and for the sun to appear and dry up the puddles. Come now, Senhorita Izabela, your parents are waiting for you in the breakfast room. Your father wants to see you before he leaves for the office. It is a very special day for all of us.'

Much as she loved Gabriela, Bel wished for the hundredth

time that Loen was here to share this special day with her and to calm her nerves.

Ten minutes later, she walked into the breakfast room. Antonio rose from the table, his arms outstretched towards her.

'My precious daughter! Today you come of age, and I could not be prouder of you. Come, embrace your father.'

Bel walked into his strong, protective arms, smelling the comforting scents of the eau de cologne he always wore and the oil he used on his hair.

'Now, go and kiss your mother and we will show you the gift we have for you.'

'*Piccolina*,' said Carla, forgetting herself and using the old Italian endearment. She rose from the table and kissed her daughter warmly, then stood back and threw her arms wide open. 'Look at you! You are so very beautiful.'

'Inherited of course from your dear mother,' Antonio interjected, casting a fond glance at his wife.

Bel could see his eyes were filled with tears. It was rare to see her father display emotion these days and she was immediately transported back to when they were just a simple Italian family, before Pai had become very rich. The thought brought a lump to her throat.

'Come, see what we have bought for you.' Antonio reached down to the chair next to him and produced two velvet-covered cases. 'Look at this,' he said, reaching eagerly for the lid of the larger box to reveal what was inside. 'And these.' He opened the second, smaller box.

Bel gasped at the beauty of the emerald necklace and earrings in front of her. 'Pai! *Meu Deus!* They are exquisite.' Bel leant closer and with her father's nod of permission, lifted the necklace from its silk lining. It was formed of gold, with emeralds which graduated in size and culminated in a glorious, shining stone that would rest in the centre of her décolletage.

'Try it on,' her father urged her, motioning to his wife to fasten the necklace at the back.

When Carla had done so, Bel's fingers went to her throat and caressed the cool smoothness of the stones. 'Does it suit me?'

'Before you look, we must add the earrings,' said Antonio and Carla helped fasten the delicate teardrop-shaped gems to her ears.

'There!' Antonio steered Bel directly in front of the mirror which hung above the sideboard. 'They look wonderful!' he exclaimed as he surveyed his daughter's reflection, the jewels luminous against the creamy skin of her slender neck.

'Pai, they must have cost a king's ransom!'

'They are from the emerald mines of Minas Gerais and I myself inspected the uncut stones and chose the best.'

'And of course, *querida*, your gown of cream silk, embroidered with emerald thread, was planned especially to show off your birthday present,' Carla added.

'Tonight,' Antonio mused in satisfaction, 'there will be no woman in the room wearing adornments more beautiful or expensive. Even if they are wearing the crown jewels of Portugal themselves!'

Suddenly, all the girlish, natural joy at receiving such a magnificent present evaporated. As Bel stared in the mirror at her reflection, she realised that the jewellery had nothing to do with Antonio wishing to please his daughter on her birthday. It was just another way of impressing the many important people who would arrive tonight at her party.

Now, the gleaming green stones around her neck seemed vulgar, ostentatious . . . she was simply a canvas on which to exhibit the trappings of his wealth. And her eyes filled with tears.

'Ah, *querida*, don't cry.' Carla was immediately by her side. 'I understand you're overwhelmed, but you mustn't upset yourself on your special day.'

Bel reached instinctively for her mother and rested her head on her shoulder as fear for the future surged through her.

Bel looked back on her eighteenth birthday party at the Copacabana Palace – the night that she and, more importantly, her father were emphatically launched into Rio society – as a series of vivid, jumbled snapshots.

Gabriela had obviously made the right offering to Our Lady as, although the heavens had opened for the entire afternoon, at four o'clock, just as Bel had bathed and the hair stylist had arrived to pile her thick glossy mane on top of her head, the rain stopped. Strings of tiny emeralds – a further gift from her father – were woven through her chignon. And her gown, made of duchesse satin sent especially from Paris and expertly fitted by Madame Duchaine to accentuate her breasts, her slim hips and pan-flat stomach, clung to her like a second skin.

When she'd arrived at the hotel, a crowd of photographers, paid by her father to attend, had sprung into action as she'd emerged with Antonio from the car. A barrage of flashbulbs popped in her face as he led her inside.

The champagne fountain had flowed like water all evening, and rare beluga caviar, imported from Russia, had been handed round as freely as if it were cheap *salgadinhos* from a street vendor.

After an extravagant dinner of lobster thermidor accompanied by the best French wines, Rio's most fashionable dance band had performed on the terrace. The huge swimming pool had been covered over with boards so that the guests could dance under the starlight.

Antonio had refused point-blank to countenance any samba, which, although increasingly popular, was still considered the music of the poor in Rio. However, he had been persuaded by Senhora Santos to allow a couple of energetic maxixe numbers on the basis that the racy dance steps were these days considered the height of chic in the sophisticated clubs of Paris and New York.

Bel remembered being partnered on the dance floor by a series of men, their touch on her bare shoulder as insignificant as a mosquito she would immediately flick away.

Then Antonio himself had brought across a young man to meet her.

'Izabela,' he had said, 'may I introduce you to Gustavo Aires Cabral. He has been admiring you from afar and would like the pleasure of a dance.'

Bel knew immediately from his surname that this diminutive, whey-faced man represented one of the most aristocratic families in Brazil.

'Of course,' she had said, lowering her eyes deferentially. 'It would be my honour, senhor.'

She couldn't help noticing Gustavo was so short that his eyes were barely on a level with hers, and as he had bent to kiss her hand, she was afforded a view of the already thinning hair on top of his head.

'Senhorita, where have you been hiding yourself?' he'd murmured as he led her to the dance floor. 'You're surely the most beautiful woman in Rio.'

As they'd danced, Bel didn't need to look at her father to know that he was watching them with a self-satisfied smile on his lips.

Later, when her ten-tiered birthday cake had been cut, and everyone had been served a further glass of champagne from the fountain in order to toast her, a sudden blast of noise assailed Bel's ears. Like everyone else on the terrace, she had turned her head in the direction of it, to see a boat floating on the waves close to shore, firing off hundreds of catherine wheels, rockets and starbursts. The coloured fireworks lit up the night sky above Rio, and everyone had gasped at the spectacle. With Gustavo hovering at her shoulder, Bel could only muster a false smile of gratitude.

Bel woke at eleven the next day and, having written to Loen – whom she knew would be desperate to hear news of the party – at the *fazenda*, she emerged from her bedroom and made her way downstairs. The Bonifacio party had not arrived home until well after four in the morning, and she found her parents taking a late breakfast looking distinctly bleary-eyed.

'Look who it is,' Antonio crowed to his wife. 'The newly crowned *princesa* of Rio!'

'Good morning, Pai. Good morning, Mãe,' she said as she sat down and Gabriela moved to serve her. 'Just coffee, thank you,' she said, as she waved the offer of food away.

'How are you this morning, my dear?'

'A little weary,' she admitted.

'Perhaps you drank a little too much champagne last night?' said Antonio. 'I know I certainly did.'

'No, I only drank one glass all night. I'm simply tired, that's all. Are you not at the office today, Pai?'

'No. I thought that for once, I might just arrive late. And see here,' Antonio said, indicating a silver tray on the table, piled high with envelopes. 'Already a number of guests have sent their maids to deliver thank-you notes for last night and to invite you to lunch and supper. There's also a letter addressed to you personally. Of course, I haven't read its contents, but you can see who it's from by the seal on the back. Take it, Izabela, and tell your parents what it says.'

Antonio passed the envelope to her, and Bel saw the Aires Cabral insignia stamped in wax on the back of the envelope. She opened it and read the few lines on the thickly embossed notepaper.

'Well?' Antonio prompted.

'It's from Gustavo Aires Cabral, thanking me for last night and hoping he will meet me again soon.'

Antonio clapped his hands in glee. 'Izabela, what a clever girl you are! Gustavo is descended from the last emperor of Portugal himself and has one of the best pedigrees in Rio.'

'And to think, he has written to our daughter!' Carla clasped her hands to her bosom, she too carried away with the thought.

Bel surveyed her parents' animated faces and sighed. 'Pai,

Gustavo has simply sent me a thank-you card for the evening. This is not a proposal.'

'No, *querida*, but one day it might be.' Her father winked. 'I saw how taken he was with you. He told me as much himself. And why shouldn't he be?' Antonio held up the *Jornal do Brasil* with a photograph of a radiant Bel arriving at the party on the front of it. 'You are the talk of the town, my *princesa*. Your life and ours will be very different from now on.'

And indeed, in the next few weeks, as Christmas approached and the Rio social season got into full swing, Bel's feet hardly touched the ground. Madame Duchaine was called back to the house and instructed to make many further gowns for Bel to wear to dances, the opera and a number of dinners at private addresses. Perfectly trained by Senhora Santos, Bel acquitted herself on each occasion with aplomb.

Gustavo Aires Cabral, whom Maria Elisa and she had secretly nicknamed 'the ferret', because of his physical likeness to the animal and his habit of constantly nosing around Bel, was present at many of the events.

And on the opening night of *Don Giovanni* at the Theatro Municipal, he found her in the foyer and insisted she visit his parents' box at the interval so that he could formally introduce her to them.

'You should feel honoured.' Maria Elisa raised her eyebrows as Gustavo left Bel's side and walked through the crowd sipping champagne in the foyer before curtain up. 'His parents are the nearest thing to royalty we have left in Rio. Or at least,' she giggled, 'they behave as if they are.'

And indeed, when Bel was led into the box at the interval, she found herself making an impromptu curtsey, as if she'd been meeting the old Emperor himself. Gustavo's mother, Luiza Aires Cabral, haughty in demeanour and dripping with diamonds, surveyed her through cool, narrowed eyes.

'Senhorita Bonifacio, you are indeed as beautiful as everyone has remarked,' she said graciously.

'Thank you,' said Bel shyly.

'And your parents? Are they here? I don't think we have so far had the pleasure of making their acquaintance.'

'No, they are not attending tonight.'

'Your father has a number of coffee farms in the São Paulo region, I am told?' Gustavo's father, Maurício, an older replica of his son, asked her.

'Yes, senhor, he does.'

'And of course, he is becoming rich off the back of them. There is much new money to be made in the region,' said Luiza.

'Yes, senhora,' Bel agreed, understanding the implicit snub.

'Well,' said Maurício hurriedly, shooting his wife a warning glance, 'we must arrange for them to visit us for luncheon.'

'Of course.' Senhora Aires Cabral nodded at Bel, then turned her attention to her neighbour.

'I think they liked you,' said Gustavo as he led her back out of the box and escorted her to her own.

'Really?' Bel thought quite the opposite.

'Yes. They asked questions and were interested. That's always a good sign. I will remind them of their promise to entertain your parents.'

As Bel commented to Maria Elisa when she joined her afterwards, she fervently hoped Gustavo would forget.

The invitation, however, duly arrived for the three Bonifacios to attend a luncheon at the Aires Cabrals' home. Carla worried endlessly about what she should wear for such an occasion, trying on most of the dresses in her wardrobe.

'Mãe, please, it is only a lunch,' Bel pleaded with her. 'I'm sure the Aires Cabrals will not care what you wear.'

'Oh yes they will. Don't you see that we are there to be inspected? One negative word from Luiza Aires Cabral and the doors that have so far opened so easily for you in Rio will immediately be shut in our faces.'

Bel sighed and walked out of her mother's dressing room, wanting to scream that it didn't matter what the Aires Cabrals thought of her parents or her because she would not be sold like a parcel of flesh to *anyone*.

'Will you marry him if he asks you?' enquired Maria Elisa when she visited that afternoon and Bel told her of the invitation.

'Goodness! I hardly know him. And besides, I'm sure his parents want a Portuguese princess for their son's bride, rather than the daughter of Italian immigrants.'

'Perhaps they do, but my father says the Aires Cabrals have fallen on hard times. Like many of the old aristocratic families, they made their money from the gold mines of

Minas Gerais, but that was two hundred years ago. Then their coffee farms were bankrupted when slavery was abolished. My father says they have done little to remedy the situation since, and their fortunes have dwindled away.'

'How can the Aires Cabrals be poor when they live in one of the finest houses in Rio, and Gustavo's mother is laden with jewels?' asked Bel.

'The gems will be family heirlooms, and apparently the house hasn't had a lick of paint in fifty years. Pai went up there once to survey it because it was in such a bad state of repair. He said it is so damp, it has green mould growing up the bathroom walls. But when he presented Senhor Aires Cabral with a quotation, he gasped in horror and sent him packing.' Maria Elisa shrugged. 'I swear, they're only influential in name, not in wealth. Your father on the other hand is very rich.' She eyed Bel. 'However you try to deny it, you must see what's happening?'

'Even if he does ask, they can't make me marry him, Maria Elisa. Not if it makes me unhappy.'

'Well, I think your father would take a lot of persuading otherwise. Having a daughter with the Aires Cabral surname and his own grandchildren carrying on the line would be a dream come true for him. Anyone can see it's the perfect match: you provide the beauty and wealth, and Gustavo provides the noble lineage.'

Even though Bel had been assiduously avoiding thinking about the scenario, Maria Elisa's blunt words struck home. 'God help me,' she sighed. 'What can I do?'

'I don't know, Bel, I really don't.'

Bel changed the subject in an attempt to quell the desperation that threatened to overwhelm her, and voiced the thought

that had been in her mind since Maria Elisa had first mentioned it. 'When do you leave for Europe?'

'In six weeks' time. I'm so excited. Pai has already booked
our cabins on the steamer that will take us across the sea to
France.'

'Maria Elisa . . .' Bel reached out and grabbed her friend's
hand. 'I beg you to ask your father if he would be prepared to
speak to mine about me travelling to Paris with you? Convince him to persuade Pai that it will be beneficial for me to
finish my education with a tour of the Old World if I'm to
make a good marriage? Really, if I don't do something now,
you're right: my parents will have me married off to Gustavo
within the next few months. I have to escape, *please*.'

'All right.' Maria Elisa's steady brown eyes took in Bel's
distress. 'I will talk to Pai and see what he can do. But it may
already be too late. The fact the Aires Cabrals have now
invited you and your parents to their home tells me a proposal is imminent.'

'But I'm only just eighteen! Surely far too young to marry?
Bertha Lutz is telling us to fight for our independence, to
earn our own living, so that we don't need to sell ourselves to
the highest male bidder. And women are joining her in her
demands for equality!'

'Yes, Bel, they are, but those women aren't *you*. Now' –
Maria Elisa patted her friend's hand comfortingly – 'I promise
I will speak to Pai and we'll see if we can whisk you away
from Rio, at least for a few months.'

'And I might just never return,' Bel whispered to herself
under her breath.

The following day, Bel climbed into their car along with her parents and they were driven to A Casa das Orquídeas, the family home of the Aires Cabrals. Carla sat next to her, and Bel could sense her tension. 'Really, Mãe, it is only lunch.'

'I know, *querida*,' said Carla, staring straight ahead as the chauffeur drove through the tall wrought-iron gates and pulled into the drive of an imposing white mansion.

'It is indeed an impressive property,' remarked Antonio as he climbed out of the car and the three of them made their way to the porticoed front door.

Yet, despite the size of the house and its graceful classical architecture, Bel couldn't help remembering Maria Elisa's words as she noted the less than immaculate gardens and the weathered paintwork.

A maid greeted them and they were led through to an austere formal drawing room full of antique furniture. Bel sniffed the air. The room smelt of damp, and despite the heat of the day outside, she shivered.

'I will tell Senhora Aires Cabral you are here,' said the maid, indicating for them to sit down.

This they did, and after what seemed to be an inordinately long wait, during which the three of them sat in silence, Gustavo finally entered the room.

'Senhora and Senhor Bonifacio, and Senhorita Izabela, I'm so happy to have you here in our home. My parents are a little delayed, but will be joining us shortly.'

Gustavo shook Antonio's hand, and kissed Carla's, then took Bel's in his. 'And may I say how beautiful you're looking today, Izabela. Now, may I offer you some refreshment while we wait for my parents to join us?'

Finally, after ten minutes of stilted conversation, Senhora and Senhor Aires Cabral entered the room.

'My apologies, some family business held our attention, but we are here now,' said Senhor Aires Cabral. 'Shall we go through for luncheon?'

The dining room was impossibly grand, with a table that Bel thought could perhaps hold forty guests at its elegantly turned mahogany sides. But as she looked up above her to the ceiling, she saw large cracks in the once exquisite ornate cornicing.

'You find yourself well, Senhorita Izabela?' asked Gustavo, who was seated next to her.

'Yes, I am well.'

'Good, good.'

Bel racked her brain for a subject to discuss, having exhausted the obvious avenues of small talk with him on the previous occasions she had found herself next to him at dinner.

'How long has your family lived in this house?' she managed.

'For two hundred years,' Gustavo explained. 'And I think nothing much has changed in that time,' he noted with a smile. 'Sometimes, I feel it's like living in a museum, although a very beautiful one.'

'It is indeed beautiful,' Bel agreed.

'As you are,' Gustavo added graciously.

During the lunch, Bel caught Gustavo staring at her every time she turned her head towards him. His eyes were filled only with admiration, in contrast to his parents, who were not simply making polite conversation with the Bonifacios, but rather interviewing them. Bel saw her mother's face across the table, strained and pale, as Carla struggled to talk to Senhora Aires Cabral, and shot her a sympathetic glance.

However, as the wine eased the tension of the diners, Gustavo in particular began to talk more freely to her than he had previously. During that lunch, Bel learnt about his passion for literature, his love of classical music and his studies of Greek philosophy and Portuguese history. Having never worked a day in his life, Gustavo had filled his time with cultural learning and it was while discussing these subjects that he began to come alive. As he shared her own love of art, Bel warmed to him, and the rest of the luncheon passed pleasantly.

'I think you are a natural scholar,' she said to him with a smile, as the party stood up from the table to take coffee in the drawing room.

'It is most kind of you to say so, Izabela. Any compliment from you is worth a thousand from others. And you, too, are most knowledgeable on the subject of art.'

'I've always longed to travel to Europe, to see some of the works of the great masters,' she admitted to him with a sigh.

Half an hour later, the Bonifacios said their farewells.

As their car drew away from the house, Antonio turned and beamed at his wife and daughter sitting in the back seat. 'Well, I doubt that could have gone better.'

'Yes, my dear.' Carla, as usual, acquiescing to her husband's thoughts. 'The luncheon went well.'

'But the house . . . goodness! It needs razing to the ground and starting again. Or at least, a coffee fortune to restore it.' Antonio grinned smugly. 'And the food they served . . . I have eaten better at a beach-side shack. So, you will invite them to dinner next week, Carla, and we will show them how it should be done. Tell our cook to source the finest fish and beef and to spare no expense.'

'Yes, Antonio.'

When they arrived home, Antonio left immediately, saying he must spend a few hours at his office. Carla and Bel walked through the gardens towards the house.

'Gustavo seems sweet enough,' her mother ventured.

'Yes, he is,' Bel agreed.

'You know, Bel, don't you, that he is very taken with you?'

'No, Mãe, how can he be? Today is the first time we have ever properly spoken together.'

'I saw him watching you over luncheon, and I tell you now that he is already very fond of you.' Then Carla gave a long sigh. 'And that at least makes me happy.'

15

'Have you asked your father to speak to mine about Europe yet?' Bel said, when Maria Elisa came to see her a few days later. She could hear the desperation in her own voice.

'Yes, I have,' said Maria Elisa as they sat in their usual spot in the garden. 'He's happy for you to come with us if your father agrees. He's promised to speak to him when he arrives to collect me later.'

'*Meu Deus*,' breathed Bel. 'I can only pray that he'll do all he can to convince Pai that I should go.'

'But I worry, Bel, because from what you have just told me, it seems a proposal from Gustavo is closer than ever. Even if your father agrees, your fiancé will surely not let you out of his sight.' Maria Elisa paused and studied Bel's anxious face before continuing.

'Would it really be so terrible for you if you did marry him? After all, you've just said yourself that Gustavo is at least an intelligent, kind man. You would live in one of the most beautiful houses in Rio, which I'm sure your father would be only too happy to restore to your taste. And with your new surname added to your beauty, you would be the queen of Rio society. Many girls would long for this chance,' she pointed out.

'What are you saying?' Bel turned to her friend, her dark eyes flashing. 'I thought you were on my side?'

'I am, Bel, but you know me – I'm pragmatic and listen to my head rather than my heart. All I'm saying is that you could do worse.'

'Maria Elisa,' Bel wrung her hands, 'I don't love him! Surely, that's the most important thing of all?'

'In an ideal world, yes. But we both know the world is not ideal.'

'You sound like an old woman, Maria Elisa. Surely you wish to fall in love?'

'Maybe,' she agreed. 'But I also know that love is only one of many considerations when it comes to marriage. I'm just saying be careful, Bel, because if you refuse Gustavo, you know it will be a terrible snub to his family. They may not be rich any longer, but they hold so much power here in Rio. Life may become difficult for you and your parents.'

'Well then, you're telling me that if Gustavo proposes, I have no choice but to accept. So, shall I just climb up Corcovado Mountain and throw myself off the top of it?'

'Bel . . .' Maria Elisa shook her head and raised her eyebrows. 'Please calm yourself. I'm sure there are ways around it. But you may have to compromise a little between what *you* want and the wishes of others.'

Bel studied Maria Elisa as she sat watching a hummingbird dart through the trees. Her demeanour, as always, was serene, like a pool of calm water without a ripple on its surface. Whereas she herself was like a waterfall roaring down the mountains and crashing onto the rocks below.

'I wish I was more like you, Maria Elisa. You're so sensible.'

'No, just accepting. But then, Bel, I don't have your fire or your beauty.'

'Don't be silly. You are one of the most beautiful people I know, inside and out.' Bel reached spontaneously to hug her. 'Thank you for your advice and help. You are a true friend.'

An hour later, Heitor da Silva Costa, Maria Elisa's father, arrived at the front door of Mansão da Princesa. Gabriela opened it and Bel and Maria Elisa, secreted beside the door in the morning room, listened as he asked if Antonio was at home.

Bel had never exchanged more than a few pleasantries with Senhor da Silva Costa at various social gatherings, but she had liked what she had seen. She thought him a very handsome man, with his fine features and pale blue eyes that often seemed to drift away from his surroundings to another place. Perhaps, she thought, to the top of the Corcovado Mountain and the monumental figure of Christ he was constructing.

Bel breathed a sigh of relief as her father appeared from his study and greeted Heitor warmly, though with a little surprise, in the hall. What gave her hope was the fact that she knew Antonio respected Heitor, for not only was he from an old Portuguese family, but due to the *Cristo* project, he had recently become something of a celebrity in Rio.

The two girls heard their fathers walk into the drawing room and shut the door behind them.

'I can't bear it,' said Bel, sinking down into a chair. 'My whole future depends on this conversation.'

'You're so dramatic, Bel,' smiled Maria Elisa. 'Really, I'm sure everything will be fine.'

Twenty minutes later and still in an agony of suspense, Bel heard the drawing room door open and the two men emerge, chatting about the *Cristo*.

'Any time you wish to come up the mountain and see what I have planned for it, do let me know,' Heitor was saying. 'Now, I must find my daughter and take her home.'

'Of course.' Antonio signalled for Gabriela to find Maria Elisa. 'It is a pleasure to see you, senhor, and I thank you for your kind offer.'

'Not at all. Ah, there you are, Maria Elisa. We must hurry as I have a meeting scheduled at five in the city. *Adeus*, Senhor Bonifacio.'

As father and daughter turned to leave the house, Maria Elisa gave Bel, who was hovering at the end of the hallway, a shrug of uncertainty. Then she disappeared through the front door.

Bel watched her father pause for a few seconds then turn around to walk back to his study. Seeing her standing there, her face a picture of anxiety, he shook his head and sighed heavily.

'So, I can see from your face that you knew about this.'

'It was Maria Elisa's idea,' Bel said hastily. 'She asked me because she thought it would be better if she had a female companion to accompany her while she is in Europe. You know that she only has two younger brothers and—'

'As I told Senhor da Silva Costa and I will now tell you, Izabela, the idea is out of the question.'

'But why, Pai? Surely you can see how a tour of Europe would improve my education?'

'You need no more education, Izabela. I have spent thousands of reais on improving you and it has paid off. You have already netted a big fish. We both know that an offer of marriage from Senhor Gustavo is imminent. So tell me, why on earth would I agree at this crucial moment to send you far away across the sea to the Old World when you are about to be crowned queen of the New?'

'Pai, please, I—'

'Enough! I will hear no more about it. The matter is closed. I will see you at supper.'

With a sob, Bel turned away from him, ran through the kitchen at the back of the house, surprising the startled staff preparing the evening meal, and charged through the door which led outside. She raced across the garden and, not caring about her dress, began to scramble up the jungle-covered hillside, grabbing the plants and trees to aid her ascent.

Ten minutes later, satisfied she was now high enough for no one to hear her, she sank down onto the warm soil and howled like a wild animal. When her anger and frustration had finally subsided, Bel rolled over and brushed the soil from her muslin dress. She sat with her knees to her chin, her arms tightly folded around them. And as she looked out across Rio, the beautiful view began to calm her. She surveyed the scene below her, taking in the enclave of Cosme Velho. Then she turned to gaze above her at the soaring Corcovado Mountain, a grey cloud ringing its peak.

In the other direction, some distance away on a mountainside, was a *favela*, a slum village where the penniless inhabitants had built shelters from whatever they could find.

If she listened carefully, on the breeze she could hear the faint sounds of the surdo drums the slum-dwellers played night and day as they danced the samba, the music of the hills, to forget the misery of their lives. And the sight and sound of this desperate population brought her back to her senses.

I am nothing more than a spoilt, selfish rich girl, Bel berated herself. *How can I behave like this when I have everything and they have nothing?*

Bel lowered her head slowly onto her knees and asked for forgiveness. 'Please, blessed Virgin, strip out my passionate heart, and replace it with one like Maria Elisa's,' she prayed fervently, 'for mine does me no good at all. And I swear I will be grateful and obedient from now on and not fight against my father's wishes.'

Ten minutes later, Bel clambered back down the mountainside and walked through the kitchen, dirty and dishevelled, but with her head held high. Running upstairs, she asked Gabriela to fill her a bath, then she lay in it, thinking how in future she would be the perfect, submissive daughter . . . and *wife*.

The subject of the rejected trip to Europe was not brought up over dinner, and that night, Bel lay in bed knowing it would never be mentioned again.

16

Two weeks later, the three members of the Aires Cabral family attended a grand dinner at Mansão da Princesa. Antonio pulled out all the stops to impress, making much of how well his coffee business was growing, as the demand from America for Brazil's magical beans increased with each passing month.

'Our family once owned a number of coffee farms near Rio, but with the abolition of slavery, they quickly became uneconomical,' remarked Gustavo's father.

'Ah, yes. I am indeed fortunate that my farms are near São Paulo, where of course we never relied so heavily on slave labour,' replied Antonio. 'And of course the land around São Paulo is far better suited to growing coffee. I do believe that I produce some of the best. We shall taste it after dinner.'

'Yes, of course, we must all embrace the New World,' agreed Maurício stiffly.

'And strive to maintain the values and traditions of the Old,' Gustavo's mother added pointedly.

Bel watched Luiza Aires Cabral during dinner, her face rarely cracking a smile. There was no doubt that when she was younger she must have been a beauty, with her unusual blue eyes and fine bone structure. But it seemed as though bitterness had erased any outward charm, eating her away from the inside. Bel made a promise to herself that, no matter what turn her life took, the same fate would never befall her.

'I understand you know Heitor da Silva Costa's daughter, Maria Elisa,' Gustavo commented to Bel in his quiet voice. 'She is a good friend of yours?'

'Yes, she is.'

'Next week, I'm accompanying my father to meet Senhor da Silva Costa on Corcovado Mountain so that he can update us with his plans. Pai is part of the Catholic Circle that first dreamed up the idea of placing a monument to the *Cristo* there. I hear Senhor da Silva Costa's plans change regularly, and I don't envy him the task he has set himself. The mountain is more than seven hundred metres high.'

'I've never been up to the top, even though we live so near,' replied Bel. 'The mountain rises from the back of our garden.'

'Perhaps your father would allow me to take you.'

'I would like that, thank you,' she answered politely.

'Then we have a plan. I will ask him later.'

As Bel turned from Gustavo's gaze to eat the delicious dessert of *pudim de leite condensado*, made from condensed milk and caramel, she felt his eyes still on her.

Two hours later, as the maid closed the door on his guests, Antonio beamed at Carla and Bel. 'I think they were impressed, and I think you, my *princesa*' – he chucked Bel's chin – 'will have some news from Gustavo very soon. He asked me before he left if he could take you up Corcovado Mountain next week. It is a perfect place for a young man to propose, is it not?'

Bel opened her mouth to respond negatively to her father's suggestion, but then remembered her vow to adopt a more accepting demeanour. 'Yes, Pai,' she said, lowering her eyes demurely.

Later, as she climbed into bed, wishing yet again that Loen was here to chat to, she heard a knock on the door. 'Come in.'

'*Querida.*' Carla's face appeared. 'I didn't wake you, did I?'

'No, Mãe. Please, come in.' She patted the mattress and her mother sat down on the bed and reached for her hands.

'Izabela, please remember you are my beloved daughter and I know you well, so I must ask you now, as it seems Gustavo is bound to propose to you soon. Is this what you want?'

Again remembering her vow, Bel thought carefully about how she should reply. 'Mãe, in truth I don't love Gustavo. And neither do I like his mother or father. We both know they are patronising towards us and would prefer a Portuguese bride for their only son. But Gustavo is sweet and kind, and a good person, I think. I know how happy this will make you, and especially Pai. So' – Bel couldn't help releasing a small sigh before she said the words – 'if he proposes, I will be happy to accept.'

Carla stared hard at her daughter. 'Are you sure, Bel? Whatever your father wants, as a mother, I must know your true feelings. It would be a terrible sin to subject you to a life you don't wish for. Above all, I want you to be happy.'

'Thank you, Mãe, and I'm sure I will be.'

'Well,' Carla said after a pause, 'I believe that love can grow between a man and a woman over the years. Trust me, I know. I married your father.' She chuckled wryly. 'I too had doubts at the beginning, but now, for all his failings, I would not change him. And remember, it is always important for the man to be more in love with the woman than she is with him.'

'Why do you say that, Mãe?'

'Because, my dear, although women's hearts can be fickle, and love a number of times, men – although they are less outwardly emotional – once they love, they usually love forever. And I believe Gustavo does love you. I can see it in his eyes when he looks at you. And that will ensure your husband stays by your side and doesn't stray.' Carla kissed Bel. 'Sleep well, *querida*.'

Her mother left the room, and Bel lay thinking about what she had said. She only hoped that she was right.

'You are ready to go?'

'Yes.' Bel stood patiently in the drawing room as her mother and father inspected her.

'You look beautiful, my *princesa*,' said Antonio admiringly. 'What man could refuse you?'

'Are you nervous, *querida*?' asked Carla.

'I'm taking a train up Corcovado Mountain with Gustavo, that is all,' said Bel, trying hard to contain her rising irritation.

'Well,' said Antonio, visibly jumping as the doorbell rang, 'we shall see. He has arrived.'

'Good luck, and God bless you,' said Carla as she kissed her daughter on both cheeks.

'We'll be waiting here later for the news,' called Antonio,

as Bel left the room and found Gabriela outside, waiting to pin on her new silk cloche hat, purchased especially for the occasion.

Gustavo was standing on the doorstep, his thin, wiry frame looking unusually dapper in a cream linen suit, a jaunty straw hat perched on his head. 'Senhorita Izabela, you look beautiful. I have our driver waiting outside. Shall we go?'

As they walked to the car and both climbed into the back seat, Bel realised that Gustavo was far more nervous than she was. On the three-minute drive to the tiny station from where the train up to Corcovado Mountain left, he was silent. He escorted her from the car, and they climbed into one of the carriages, which in reality was one of two basic carts attached to the back of a miniature steam engine.

'I hope you will love the view, even though it is not a comfortable ride,' commented Gustavo.

The train began its ascent up the mountain, the incline so steep that Bel felt her neck straining to keep her head upright. As the train gave a lurch, instinctively Bel grabbed Gustavo's shoulder, and he immediately encircled her waist with his arm.

It was the most intimate physical gesture they had shared so far, and although Bel felt no stirring from it, neither did she feel revulsion. It was akin to the comforting touch of an older brother. The noise from the engine made any conversation impossible, so Bel relaxed and began to enjoy the ride as the little train chugged through the lush urban jungle, the roots of which lay at the back of her own garden.

Bel was almost disappointed when the train drew into the station at the top and the passengers climbed out.

'There is a vantage point here that affords an excellent

view of Rio, or we can climb the many steps right to the top and see how they are digging out the foundations for the *Cristo Redentor*,' said Gustavo.

'I want to go right to the top, of course,' smiled Bel, and she noted his approving look. They followed the braver souls up the steep steps, the burning sun testing their endurance as they grew warmer and warmer in their formal clothes.

I must not sweat, thought Bel, as she felt her undergarments damp against her skin. Finally, they arrived at the plateau at the top of the mountain. In front of them was a viewing pavilion. Further along the mountaintop, Bel could see mechanical diggers tearing out chunks of rock with their giant claws. Gustavo took her hand and pulled her into the shade of the pavilion.

'Senhor da Silva Costa explained that they must dig down many metres into the earth to make sure the statue doesn't topple over. Now' – he turned Bel around by her shoulders and led her to the edge of the pavilion – 'look over there.'

Bel followed his pointing finger and saw the glinting red roof of an elegant building.

'Is that not the Parque Lage?'

'Yes, and the botanical gardens are quite stunning. But do you know the story of the house that sits within them?'

'No, I don't.'

'Well, not so long ago, a Brazilian man fell in love with an Italian opera singer. He was desperate for her to marry him and join him in Rio, but she, used to Italy, did not want to move here. So he asked her what it would take for her to leave her beloved Rome behind. She told him that she wanted to live in a palazzo, just like the ones she loved in her own country. So,' Gustavo said, smiling, 'he built it for her. And she married him, and moved here to Rio, and she lives within the walls of her beautiful piece of homeland to this day.'

'What a romantic story,' Bel breathed before she could stop herself, then leant over as far as she could and looked down on the beautiful scene below her. Almost instantly, an arm came again about her waist.

'Careful. I wouldn't like to tell your parents that you fell off the top of Corcovado Mountain,' he said with a smile. 'You know, Izabela, that if I could, I would build you a house as beautiful as the one below us.'

Bel, still hanging over the edge, her face hidden from him, heard his words from behind her. 'That is sweet of you to say so, Gustavo.'

'It's also the truth. Izabela . . .' He gently turned her around to face him. 'You must know what I'm about to ask you.'

'I . . .'

Immediately a finger went to her mouth. 'I think it's better if you say nothing for the moment or maybe my courage will desert me.' He cleared his throat nervously. 'With your beauty, I understand that I am not physically what you deserve as your husband. We both know you could have any man you wished for. Every man in Rio is under your spell, just as I am. But I want to tell you that I appreciate more about you than your outer appearance.'

Gustavo paused, and Bel immediately felt she must answer him. She opened her mouth to reply, but again the finger came to her lips and he hushed her.

'Please, let me finish. From the first moment I saw you at your eighteenth birthday party, I knew that I wanted to be with you. I asked your father to introduce me, and well,' he shrugged, 'the rest we know. Of course, we must both be pragmatic and accept that on the surface the liaison between us is one of convenience, since your family has the money and mine has the breeding. But, Izabela, I have to tell you that for me, this wouldn't be a marriage built on those sad foundations. Because . . .' Gustavo hung his head for a moment, then looked up at her. 'I love you.'

Bel looked at him and saw the honesty in his eyes. Even though she'd known he would propose to her today, the words he'd spoken were more moving and genuine than any she'd expected. And she began to believe what her mother had said to her. She felt, ironically, a rush of sympathy for Gustavo, and guilt too, as she only wished to God she could share what he was feeling. It would make all the jigsaw pieces of her existence fit together.

'Gustavo, I . . .'

'Izabela, please,' he entreated. 'I promise I'm nearly done. I understand that at present you almost certainly don't feel the same way about me. But I believe I can give you the many things that you need to flourish in life. And I hope that one day you can grow to love me, at least a little.'

Bel looked beyond Gustavo and saw that the other recent occupants of the pavilion had retreated from it and that they were now alone.

'If it helps,' Gustavo continued, 'I saw Senhor da Silva Costa three days ago and he told me how much you wish to tour Europe with his family. Izabela, I wish you to go. If you agree that we will be engaged immediately and you will marry me after your return from Europe, then I will tell your father that I believe a cultural tour of the Old World would fit you out very well to be my wife.'

Bel stared at him, completely taken by surprise at his suggestion.

'You are very young, *querida*. You must remember that I am almost ten years your senior,' Gustavo said, as he touched her cheek. 'And I want you to broaden your horizons, just as I was allowed to do when I was younger. So, what do you say?'

Bel knew she must answer quickly. What Gustavo was offering her was a dream come true. One word from him could give her what she desired most – the freedom to travel beyond the narrow confines of Rio. It came with a heavy price, but one she'd already prepared herself to accept anyway.

'Gustavo, it's very generous of you to suggest such a thing.'

'Well, of course I'm not happy about it, Izabela. I will miss your presence every day, but I also understand that one cannot keep beautiful birds in a cage. If you love them, you must set them free to fly.' Gustavo reached for her hands. 'I would obviously prefer to show you the sights of Europe myself. In fact, I had considered taking you on a European tour as our honeymoon. But if truth be told, at this moment in time I simply don't have the finances to fund such an adventure. And besides, my parents depend on my presence here. So, what do you say?' He looked at her expectantly.

'Gustavo, surely your parents and Rio society will not approve of this idea? If I'm to be your fiancée, shouldn't I be here with you in Rio until we are married?'

'In the Old World from which my parents come, it's quite common for a young lady to undertake a cultural tour before she settles down to marriage. They will accept it. So, *querida*

Izabela, don't keep me waiting any longer. I can hardly bear the agony.'

'I think . . .' Bel took a deep breath. 'I think that I will say yes.'

'*Meu Deus*. Thank God,' he said in genuine relief. 'Then I can give you this.'

Gustavo reached into an inner jacket pocket and pulled out a battered leather-covered box. 'The ring inside is a part of the Aires Cabral heritage. Worn, so the story goes, by the cousin of Emperor Dom Pedro when she became engaged.'

Bel gazed at the flawless diamond, set between two sapphires. 'It's beautiful,' she replied honestly.

'The stone in the centre is very old, cut from the mines of Tejuco, and the gold is from Ouro Preto. May I place it on your finger? Just for size,' he added hastily. 'Because of course, I must accompany you back home and ask your father formally for your hand.'

'Of course.'

Gustavo slid the ring onto the fourth finger of her right hand. 'There,' he said. 'It will need to be altered slightly to fit your beautiful slim finger, but it looks well on you.' Gustavo took her hand in his and kissed the ring. 'Do you know, my sweet Izabela, that the first thing I noticed about you was your hands? They are,' he said as he kissed each fingertip, 'exquisite.'

'*Obrigada*.'

Gustavo gently removed the ring from her finger and placed it back in its box. 'Now, we had better make our way down before the train stops running for the night and we are stranded here. I can't imagine that would please your father,' he commented wryly.

'No,' she agreed as he drew her by the hand out of the pavilion and guided her back down the stairs towards the little station. But secretly, she knew that now she had netted her 'prince', her father would be pleased about absolutely everything.

When they arrived home, Bel disappeared immediately to her room while Gustavo spoke to her father. She sat tensely on the edge of her bed, shooing Gabriela away when she asked if she wished to change. She felt uncertain and ecstatic in equal measure.

She pondered the reason for Gustavo's decision to encourage her trip to Europe. Was it possible that he was secretly relieved to have an excuse to postpone their inevitable union, that he too felt unready for a hasty marriage? Perhaps, she mused, poor Gustavo had been subjected to the same pressure from his parents as she had from her father? But then, the look of affection in his eyes when he'd proposed had seemed so genuine . . .

Her thoughts were interrupted as Gabriela came into her bedroom, a beaming smile on her face. 'It seems your father wishes for your presence downstairs. I have been told to serve the best champagne. Congratulations, senhorita. I hope that you will be happy and that Our Lady will bless you with many children.'

'Thank you, Gabriela.' Bel smiled at her as she left the room, then stepped lightly down the stairs and followed the sound of voices into the drawing room.

'And here she is, the bride-to-be! Come, kiss your father,

my *princesa*, and know that I have just given my blessing to your match.'

'Thank you, Pai,' Bel replied as he kissed her on both cheeks.

'My Izabela, know that you have made me the happiest father in the world today.'

'And me, the happiest man in Rio,' Gustavo beamed.

'Ah, here is your mother to share the news,' Antonio added as Carla entered.

The mutual congratulations continued as the champagne arrived and the four of them toasted Bel and Gustavo's future health and happiness.

'Mind you, I am concerned that you wish to send her thousands of miles away from you before you marry, senhor,' said Antonio, a slight frown passing across his brow as he looked askance at Gustavo.

'As I explained, Bel is still very young, and I believe a visit to Europe will not only enhance her maturity, but what she sees there will make our conversations far more stimulating when we are old and have run out of endearments for each other.' Gustavo smiled and gave Bel gave a surreptitious wink.

'Well, I don't know about that,' said Antonio. 'But I suppose at least it means she will have access to the finest couturiers in Paris for the design of her wedding gown,' he conceded.

'Of course. And I'm sure she will look perfect in whatever she chooses. Now' – Gustavo drained his champagne glass – 'I must take my leave and tell my own parents the happy news. Not that they will be surprised,' he said with a smile.

'Of course. And before your fiancée leaves for Europe, we must throw an engagement party. Perhaps at the Copacabana

Palace, where you first laid eyes on your wife-to-be.' Antonio could hardly prevent himself from grinning from ear to ear. 'And we will need to make an announcement in the social columns of all the newspapers,' he added as he walked with Gustavo towards the front door.

'I am happy to leave the arrangements to my bride's family,' he agreed. Then he reached for Bel's hand and kissed it. 'Goodnight, Izabela, and thank you for making me a very happy man.'

Antonio waited until Gustavo's car had driven away from the house, then, with a whoop of joy, he picked Bel up in his strong arms and swung her around, just as he had done when she was a little girl. 'My *princesa*, you have done it! We have done it.' He put Bel down, and then went to his wife and hugged her to him. 'Are you not pleased too, Carla?'

'Of course. As long as Bel is happy, then it's wonderful news.'

Antonio studied Carla for a few seconds and frowned. 'Are you well, *querida*? You look pale.'

'I have a headache, that is all. Now' – Carla made an effort to smile – 'I will go and tell Cook to prepare something special for dinner.'

Bel followed her mother down the corridor to the kitchen, partly to escape from her father's overwhelming euphoria.

'Mãe, *are* you happy for me?'

'Of course I'm happy, Izabela.'

'And are you sure you're feeling well?'

'Yes, *querida*. Now you go up and put on a pretty gown for our celebration dinner.'

17

The next few weeks raced by as Bel and Gustavo's engagement was well and truly celebrated in Rio society. Everyone who was anyone wanted to be part of the fairy tale – the nearest thing they had left to a crown prince and his beautiful wife-to-be.

Antonio revelled in the invitations he and Carla began to receive to attend soirées and dinners at private houses, the doors of which had previously been closed to them.

Bel had little time to think about her forthcoming trip to Europe, although the steamer passage had been booked and Madame Duchaine had been summoned to fit Bel for a wardrobe suitable to visit the great fashion capital of the Old World.

Loen had at last returned from the *fazenda*, and Bel was anxious to know her opinion of Gustavo.

'I think that from what I have seen of him, Senhorita Bel,' she ventured as she helped Bel into her dress before dinner one evening, 'he is an honourable man who will make you a good husband. And certainly the family name will bring many advantages. But . . .' She stopped abruptly and shook her head. 'No, it is not my place to say.'

'Loen, please, you have known me since I was a child and there's no one I trust more. You must tell me what you're thinking.'

'Then forgive me for reminding you, *minha pequena*,' she replied, her expression softening, 'but you said in your letters that you were very unsure about this engagement. And now that I have seen you together . . . well, I can tell that you are not in love with him. Does this not worry you?'

'Mãe thinks that I will grow to love him. And besides, what choice do I have?' said Bel, her eyes pleading for reassurance.

'Then I'm sure your mother is right. Senhorita Bel, I . . .' Loen looked suddenly uncertain.

'What is it?'

'I want to tell you something. When I was staying at the *fazenda*, I met someone. A man, I mean.'

'Goodness, Loen!' Bel was surprised. 'Why have you said nothing before to me?'

'I was shy, I suppose, and you've been so busy with your engagement, there hasn't been the right moment.'

'Who is he?' Bel asked curiously.

'Bruno Canterino, Fabiana and Sandro's son,' she confessed.

Bel thought of the handsome young man who worked at the *fazenda* with his parents and smiled at Loen. 'He's very handsome and I can see you two will fit well together.'

'I've known him since we were very young and we've always been friends. But this time, it became something more,' Loen admitted.

'Do you love him?' questioned Bel.

'Yes, and I miss him very much now that I'm back here in

Rio. So, now we must finish getting you dressed or you will be late.'

Bel stood silently as Loen helped her, knowing exactly why she'd spoken so honestly to her of her own love, but equally aware that the wheels were already set in motion for her marriage to Gustavo and there was nothing to be done.

Bel was at least comforted by the fact that the more time she spent with Gustavo, the more he endeared himself to her. He was attentive to her slightest need and listened with interest to every sentence that dropped from her lips. His genuine happiness that she had agreed to marry him made it difficult not to warm to him.

'If he is no longer a ferret, then he is like a puppy dog,' laughed Maria Elisa when the two friends met at a charity gala in the Botanical Gardens. 'At least you don't dislike him any longer.'

'No, I like him very much,' said Bel, wanting to add that that was hardly the point. She was meant to *love* her intended.

'And I can hardly believe he's allowing you to come to Europe with my family. So many men in his position wouldn't countenance it.'

'It seems he wants the best for me,' said Bel guardedly.

'Yes, it seems he does. You're a very lucky girl. You will return to him, won't you?' Maria Elisa eyed her. 'This engagement isn't just an excuse to get your own way over going to Europe, is it?'

'What do you take me for?' exploded Bel. 'Of course I

will! As I've just told you, I've become extremely fond of Gustavo.'

'Good,' Maria Elisa said staunchly, 'because I don't want to be the one to come back here and tell him his bride has run off with an Italian painter.'

'Oh please, as if that would ever happen!' Bel rolled her eyes.

The day before Bel was due to leave on the steamer with the da Silva Costas and travel across the Atlantic to France, Gustavo came to Mansão da Princesa to say goodbye to her. For once, her parents discreetly left them alone in the drawing room.

'So, this is the last time we meet for many months.' He smiled at her sadly. 'I will miss you, Izabela.'

'And I you, Gustavo,' she replied. 'I cannot thank you enough for allowing me to go.'

'I simply want to make you happy. Now, I have something for you.' Gustavo dipped into his pocket and drew out a leather pouch. As he opened it, Bel saw it contained a necklace. 'This is for you,' he said, as he handed it to her. 'It's a moonstone, and it is meant to offer protection to the wearer, especially if they are travelling across the sea and away from loved ones.'

Bel looked at the delicate blueish-white stone, set in a circle of tiny diamonds. 'I love it,' she said with genuine enthusiasm. 'Thank you, Gustavo.'

'I chose it especially for you,' he said, looking pleased at her reaction. 'It's not of much value, but I'm glad you like it.'

'I do,' she said, touched by his thoughtfulness. 'Can you fasten it for me?'

Gustavo did so, then reached his lips to her neck and kissed it. '*Minha linda* Izabela,' he said admiringly. 'It suits you well.'

'I promise I'll wear it every day.'

'And write often?'

'Yes.'

'Izabela, I . . .' Suddenly his fingers tipped her chin to his and he kissed her on the lips for the very first time. Having never been kissed by any man before, Bel had long been curious as to what it would feel like. In the books she'd read, women normally went weak at the knees during the experience. Well, she thought as Gustavo's tongue made its way inside her mouth and she struggled to fathom what to do with her own, her knees certainly didn't feel weak. In fact, when he drew away from her, she decided it had not been unpleasant. It had simply been . . . nothing. Nothing at all.

'Goodbye, darling Loen. Keep safe, won't you?' said Bel as she prepared to leave her bedroom and join her parents on the journey to the port.

'And you, Senhorita Bel. I worry about you going across the sea without me. Please write to me often, won't you?'

'Of course,' Bel agreed. 'I'll tell you all the things I can't speak of to my parents,' she added with a conspiratorial smile. 'So make sure you keep my letters hidden. I must leave now, but please write to me and tell me everything that happens here. Take care, Loen.' She kissed her and left the room.

As Bel climbed into the car, she pondered on how even her maid seemed to be experiencing the one feeling she now knew for certain she'd be deprived of for the rest of her life: passion.

Both her parents accompanied her on board the ship in Rio's main port, Pier Mauá. Carla glanced round the comfortable suite in awe.

'Why, it's just like a room on land,' she said, walking to the bed and sitting down on it to test the mattress. 'There are electric lights and even pretty curtains,' she enthused.

'Don't tell me you expected Bel to travel by candlelight lying in a hammock on the deck?' joked Antonio. 'I can tell you that what this passage has cost warrants every modern convenience imaginable.'

For the thousandth time, Bel wished her father would desist from weighing everything by the amount of cash it had cost him. The ship's bell rang out to alert all remaining non-passengers to its imminent departure and Bel hugged her mother to her. 'Please take care, Mãe, until I'm back. You haven't seemed yourself lately.'

'Stop fussing, Bel. I'm just getting old, that is all,' Carla insisted. 'Now, look after yourself until you're home safe with us again.'

As Carla released her daughter, Bel could see the tears brimming in her mother's eyes.

Antonio then took her in his arms.

'Goodbye, my *princesa*, and I hope that once you have seen the beauty of the Old World, you will still wish to come back home to your loving mother and father and your fiancé.'

Bel went upstairs with them to the deck and waved them goodbye as they set off down the gangplank. As they shrank to specks from her high vantage point, for the first time Bel experienced a rush of anxiety. She was travelling across the world with a family she hardly knew. And as the ship's horn blasted the nerve endings in her ears, and the gap between vessel and shore began to widen, she waved frantically at them.

'*Adeus*, my sweet mother and father. Keep safe, and God bless you both.'

Bel enjoyed the voyage, with its endless stream of entertainments for the well-heeled guests. Maria Elisa and she whiled the hours away swimming in the pool – a pleasure far sweeter because it had always been denied to her in Rio – and playing croquet on the artificial grass on the upper deck. The two girls giggled over the admiring glances of the many young men aboard as they entered the dining room every evening.

As an engaged girl, Bel's large ring afforded protection from overly affectionate males emboldened by wine as they danced to the ship's band after dinner. But Maria Elisa enjoyed a number of innocent flirtations, which Bel supported and lived through vicariously.

During the voyage, she came to know Maria Elisa's family far better than she ever would have done in Rio, thrown together upon the ocean as they were. Maria Elisa's two younger brothers, Carlos and Paulo, were fourteen and sixteen respectively, at the awkward stage between childhood and adulthood, with rough growth beginning to sprout on their chins. They rarely plucked up the courage to speak to Bel. Maria Elisa's mother, Maria Georgiana, was an intelligent, sharp-eyed woman, who Bel soon learnt was prone to sudden bursts of anger if something didn't suit her. She spent much of the day playing bridge in the elegant salon, while her husband rarely surfaced from his cabin.

'What does your father do in there all day?' questioned Bel of Maria Elisa one evening as they were nearing the Cape Verde islands off the coast of Africa, where the boat was docking for a few hours to pick up supplies.

'He is working on his *Cristo*, of course,' Maria Elisa had answered. 'Mãe says she has lost the love of her husband to Our Lord, a person he has so often said he doesn't believe in! Ironic, isn't it?'

One afternoon, Bel knocked on the door of what she had thought was Maria Elisa's cabin. Receiving no reply, she opened the door and called out for her. She immediately realised that she'd made a mistake, as a surprised Heitor da Silva Costa looked up at her from a desk covered with sheets of complex architectural calculations. Not only had they taken over the desk, but the bed and the floor too.

'Senhorita Izabela, good afternoon. How can I help you?'

'I'm so sorry to disturb you, senhor. I was looking for Maria Elisa and I have simply come to the wrong cabin.'

'Please, don't worry. I myself become confused trying to find my way around. All the doors look the same,' said Heitor with a comforting smile. 'As to my daughter, you can try her cabin next door, but she could be anywhere on this ship – I confess to not keeping track of her whereabouts.' He gestured towards the desk. 'I have been distracted by other things.'

'May I . . . may I see your drawings?'

'You are interested?' Heitor's pale eyes lit up with pleasure.

'Why yes! Everyone in Rio says it is a miracle that this statue will be built on top of such a high mountain.'

'They are right. And as the *Cristo* cannot perform it Himself, I must.' He smiled wearily. 'Here,' he beckoned her. 'I will show you how I believe it can happen.'

Heitor indicated a chair for her to pull over, and for the next hour showed her how he would build a structure strong enough to support his Christ. 'Iron girders, and a new innovation from Europe called reinforced concrete will fill His innards. You see, Bel, the *Cristo* is not a statue, He is simply a building dressed as a human being. He must withstand the harsh winds that circle around Him, the rain that will pound on His head. Not to mention the bolts of lightning that His Father in heaven sends down to us mortals here on earth to remind us of His power.'

Bel sat there in awe. Listening to the poetic yet detailed way Heitor spoke of his project was a pleasure and she felt honoured to be trusted with the information.

'And now, when I reach Europe, I must find the sculptor who can breathe life into my outer vision of Him. The engineering of building His insides will not matter to a public who will only ever see His outer packaging.' He looked up at her thoughtfully. 'I think, senhorita, that is very common in life too. Do you not agree?'

'Yes,' Bel replied tentatively, having never thought of it before. 'I suppose I do.'

'For example,' he elaborated, 'you are a beautiful young woman, but do I know the soul inside you that fires you? And the answer is, of course, that no, I do not. So, I must find the right sculptor for the job, and return to Rio with the face, body and hands that His onlookers desire.'

That night, Bel climbed into bed feeling a little uncomfortable. Even though Heitor was old enough to be her father, she was embarrassed to admit she had developed a crush on Senhor da Silva Costa.

18

Six weeks after the steamer had left Rio, it docked gracefully at Le Havre. The da Silva Costa party duly boarded the train to Paris, where a car was waiting at the station to transfer them to an elegant apartment on the Avenue de Marigny just off the Champs-Élysées. The plan was to base the family there, near the office Heitor had rented in which to work and to meet the many experts he wished to consult with to finalise the structure of his Christ.

When he travelled to Italy and Germany to speak to two of the most renowned European sculptors of the day, the plan was for his family to travel with him.

But for the next week, Bel knew she could soak up Paris. After dinner that first night, she pulled up the sash window of the high-ceilinged room she shared with Maria Elisa and peered out, breathing in the new and very foreign smell, and shivering slightly in the cool evening air. It was early spring, which in Rio meant temperatures in the high seventies. Here in Paris, she surmised that it was barely in the fifties.

On the street below, she watched the Parisian women drifting along the pavement of the gracious boulevard, arm in arm with their beaux. They were all elegantly clad in the new, almost boyish fashion inspired by the house of Chanel, which featured simple, unstructured lines and knee-length skirts that were a world away from the formal corseted gowns Bel was used to.

She sighed and pulled her luxuriant hair out of its top-knot, wondering if she might dare to have it cut in the new short bobbed style. Her father, of course, would almost certainly disown her – he was always saying that her hair was her crowning glory. But here she was, thousands of miles away, and out of his grasp for the first time in her life.

A jolt of excitement shot through her and she craned her neck to the left where she could just see the twinkling lights of the Seine, the great river that flowed through Paris, and the Left Bank beyond. She had heard much talk of the Bohemian group of artists that populated the streets around Montmartre and Montparnasse; the models who were prepared to be painted naked by Picasso, and the poet Jean Cocteau, whose outrageous lifestyle, reputedly fuelled by opium, had even reached the gossip columns of Rio.

She knew from her art history lessons that the Left Bank had originally been the haunt of artists such as Degas, Cézanne and Monet. But these days, a new and far more daring set led by the Surrealists had taken over. Writers such as F. Scott Fitzgerald and his beautiful wife, Zelda, had been photographed at La Closerie des Lilas drinking absinthe with their famous Bohemian friends. From what she understood, the whole set ran fast and wild, drinking all day and dancing all night.

'Time for bed, Bel. I'm exhausted from all the travelling.' Maria Elisa broke into her thoughts as she entered the bedroom. 'Please can you shut that window? It's freezing in here.'

'Of course.' Bel pulled the sash down and went to the bathroom to put on her nightgown.

Ten minutes later, they lay side by side in their twin beds. 'Goodness, Paris is so cold,' said Maria Elisa, physically shivering as she pulled the sheets up to her chin. 'Do you not think so?'

'No, not really,' Bel replied as she reached to switch off the bedside lamp. 'Goodnight, Maria Elisa, sleep well.'

As Bel lay there in the dark, she was gripped by a restless anticipation of what this city, and the crowd across the river, whose lifestyles so excited her, could hold. And she felt very warm indeed.

Waking early the following morning, Bel was up and dressed by eight o'clock, so eager was she to go out and do nothing more than walk the streets of Paris, inhaling the atmosphere. Heitor was the only member of the family in the dining room when she arrived for breakfast.

'Good morning, Izabela.' He glanced up at her, pen in hand as he sipped his coffee. 'Are you well?'

'Yes, very well indeed. I'm not disturbing you, am I?'

'No, not at all. I'm glad of the company. I was expecting to breakfast alone as my wife is complaining of a sleepless night due to the cold.'

'Sadly, your daughter too,' reported Bel. 'She's asked for the maid to take her breakfast to her in bed. She thinks she might have a chill.'

'Well, from the look of you, it's good to see that you're not suffering from the same affliction,' Heitor commented.

'Oh, even if I had pneumonia this morning, I would still be up,' she assured him as the maid poured her some coffee. 'How can one feel sick in Paris?' she added as she reached for an unusual horn-shaped pastry from a basket in the centre of the table.

'That is a croissant,' Heitor informed her as he saw her studying it. 'Delicious eaten warm, with fruit *confiture*. I too love this city, although sadly I'll have little time to explore while I'm here. I have many meetings to attend.'

'With possible sculptors?'

'Yes, which of course I'm excited about. Also, I have an appointment with an expert on reinforced concrete, which may not sound so romantic, but for me, it may provide the key to my project.'

'Have you ever been to Montparnasse?' Bel ventured as she bit into the sweet pastry and her taste buds offered their approval.

'Yes, but not for many years. I went when I was a young man on my classical tour. So, the idea of the Left Bank and its . . . unusual inhabitants appeals to you?'

Bel saw Heitor's eyes were twinkling. 'Yes. I mean, it was the birthplace of some of the greatest artists of our generation. I like Picasso very much.'

'So, you're a Cubist?'

'No, and no expert either. I simply enjoy great works of art,' she clarified. 'Since my art history instruction in Rio, I've become interested in the artists who produce them.'

'Then no wonder you are eager to explore the Bohemian

quarter. I warn you, senhorita, it's very . . . decadent compared to Rio.'

'I imagine it's decadent compared to everywhere!' Bel agreed. 'They are living in a different way, trying out new ideas, pushing the world of art forwards . . .'

'Yes, they are. However, if I decided to make Picasso's style of painting my inspiration for the *Cristo*, I think I would have a problem,' he said with a chuckle. 'So, sadly, my search will not be leading me to Montparnasse. Now, I'm afraid I must be rude and leave you. I'm due at my first meeting in half an hour.'

'I shall be quite content by myself,' Bel replied, as she watched Heitor stand and gather up his papers and notebook.

'Thank you for your company. I enjoy our conversations very much.'

'As do I,' Bel said shyly, as he gave her a nod and left the room.

Maria Elisa's chill developed into a fever by lunchtime and the doctor was called. Her mother looked little better than her daughter, and both were prescribed aspirin and bed rest until the fever had passed. With all of Paris beckoning, Bel roamed the apartment like a caged animal, her frustration making her less sympathetic towards Maria Elisa than she knew she ought to be.

I am a terrible, selfish person, she scolded herself as she sat beside the window, longingly watching Paris living beneath her.

Finally, out of boredom, she agreed to play cards with

Maria Elisa's younger brothers, while the precious hours of her first day ticked by.

Due to the prolonged nature of Maria Georgiana's and Maria Elisa's illness, Bel's impatience to be out and about grew apace. Towards the end of her first week, during which she had not once set foot on a Parisian boulevard, she plucked up her courage and asked Maria Georgiana whether she would permit her to take a walk in the street to breathe some fresh air. The answer, as expected, was no.

'Certainly not unchaperoned, Izabela. And neither I nor Maria Elisa are currently well enough to accompany you. There'll be plenty of time to see the sights of Paris when we return from Florence,' Maria Georgiana said firmly.

Bel walked away from Maria Georgiana's room wondering how she would manage to contain herself until they left for Florence. She felt like a starving prisoner, gazing through the iron bars of her cell at a box of chocolate delights, tantalisingly placed only a few millimetres from her reach.

It was Heitor who finally saved the day. For the past week they had met at breakfast, and although he was preoccupied, even he had noticed her forlorn solitariness.

'Izabela, today I will visit Boulogne-Billancourt to meet the sculptor Professor Paul Landowski. We have already talked by letter and on the telephone, but I will go to his *atelier* for him to show me where and how he works. He is my current favourite for the commission, although I still have other sculptors to meet in Italy and Germany. Would you like to accompany me?'

'I . . . I would be honoured, senhor. But I worry that I might get in the way.'

'I am certain that you will not. I understand that you must be bored by your incarceration here, and while I speak to Professor Landowski, I'm sure we can find one of his assistants to show you round his *atelier*.'

'Senhor da Silva Costa, I can't think of anything I'd like more,' Bel said fervently.

'Well, don't think of it as too much of a favour,' responded Heitor. 'After all, your future father-in-law is a member of the Catholic Circle, instrumental in promoting the idea of a monument on the top of Corcovado and organising fundraising to build it. It would be a grave embarrassment to return you to Rio and tell him I have failed to introduce you to the cultural riches of the Old World. So,' Heitor said, smiling at her, 'we leave at eleven.'

As they drove over the Pont de l'Alma and onto the Left Bank, Bel peered eagerly out of the window, as though she expected Picasso himself to be sitting at a street café as they passed by.

'Landowski's *atelier* is some distance from here,' said Heitor. 'I think he's less interested in drinking with his cronies in the streets of Montparnasse and more inspired by his work. And, of course, he has a family, which is not something easily accommodated on the Left Bank.'

'His surname doesn't sound French,' said Bel, a little disappointed that Landowski was not part of the circle she craved to discover.

'No, he comes from Polish ancestors, although I believe his family has lived in France for seventy-five years. Perhaps his temperament doesn't suit the more outlandish vagaries of some of his contemporaries. However, he does embrace the new Art Deco style, which is becoming prominent in Europe. I think this may well prove very suitable for my Christ.'

'Art Deco?' questioned Bel. 'I don't know what that is.'

'Hmm . . . how can I explain the style?' Heitor murmured to himself. 'Well, it's as if anything you might see in the everyday world, like a table, or a gown, or even a human being, gets stripped down to its basic lines. It isn't fanciful or romantic in the classical style of many of the great artists and sculptors of the past. It is simple, raw . . . as I believe Christ Himself wished to be seen.'

As they drove on, the landscape became more rural, the built-up city giving way to occasional clusters of houses along the roadside. Bel couldn't help thinking how ironic it was that the moment she'd actually managed to escape the apartment, she was being driven away from the pulsating heart of the city she so longed to explore.

Having taken a number of wrong turns, finally their driver turned left into the entrance of a large, rambling house.

'This is it.' Heitor climbed out of the car immediately, his eyes alight with expectation. As Bel followed him through the gardens, she saw a wiry figure sporting a head of unruly grey hair and a long beard emerge from the side of the house, clad in a clay-spattered smock. She watched as the two men shook hands and began to talk earnestly together. She hovered some distance away, not wishing to interrupt their conversation, and it was a few minutes before Heitor seemed to remember she was there.

'Senhorita,' he said, turning to her. 'My apologies. It is always a great moment when you have the pleasure of meeting someone in person with whom you have only corresponded by letter previously. May I present Professor Paul Landowski. Professor, this is Senhorita Izabela Bonifacio.'

Landowski reached out his hand and raised her fingers to his lips. '*Enchanté*.' Then he looked down at her hand, and to Bel's surprise, began to gently trace its contours with his own fingertips. 'Mademoiselle, why, you have the most beautiful fingers. Does she not, Monsieur da Silva Costa?'

'I regret I've never noticed them before,' answered Heitor. 'But yes, senhor, you are right.'

'Now, down to business, monsieur,' said Landowski, letting go of Bel's hand. 'I will show you my *atelier*, and then we will discuss your vision of the Christ in more detail.'

Bel followed the two men through the garden, noting that the foliage seemed still asleep – green but with no flowers visible yet – whereas in her homeland, the vibrant colours of the native plants decorated the landscape all year round.

Landowski led them into a high, barn-like structure that sat at the end of the garden, the sides of it constructed from walls of glass to let in the light. A young man sat bent over a workbench in a corner of the airy space, working on a clay bust. He didn't even look up as they entered, so intently focused was he on his task.

'I'm working on a provisional sculpture of Sun Yat-sen and am struggling to perfect his eyes. They are, of course, a very different shape to our own western ones,' Landowski stated. 'My assistant is seeing if he can improve on my efforts.'

'You work mostly in clay or stone, Professor Landowski?' Heitor asked.

'Whichever the client desires. Have you any idea what you wish for your Christ?'

'I have thought of bronze, of course, but I'm concerned that Our Lord will wear a greenish hue as the bronze ages in the wind and the rain. And besides, I wish all of Rio to look up and see Him wearing light-coloured robes rather than dark ones.'

'I understand,' said Landowski. 'But if you are talking about thirty metres, I think that a stone statue of that height and size will be impossible to drag up a mountainside, let alone erect when you get there.'

'Of course,' Heitor agreed. 'Which is why, with the interior architectural structure I hope to finalise while I'm in Europe, I believe the *Cristo*'s outer shell must be cast in a mould, and then rebuilt piece by piece in Rio.'

'Well, if you've seen enough in here, we will retire to the house and study the sketches I have made. Mademoiselle,' Landowski said, turning his attention to Bel, 'are you content to amuse yourself in the *atelier* while we two men talk? Or would you be more comfortable in the drawing room with my wife?'

'I would be very happy here, thank you, monsieur,' said Bel. 'It's a privilege to see the workings of your *atelier*.'

'I'm sure if you ask him nicely, my assistant may rouse himself from Sun Yat-sen's eyeball and provide you with some refreshment.' Landowski nodded pointedly in the direction of the young man, then left the *atelier* with Heitor.

The assistant, however, seemed oblivious to her presence as she wandered around, wishing she could move closer to watch what he was doing, but not wanting to disturb him. On the far side of the main workspace was an enormous oven, presumably used for firing the clay. To her left were two partitioned-off rooms: one a very basic washroom, also containing a large sink with bags of clay stacked up the walls around it; the other a small windowless kitchen. She moved into the main *atelier* and glanced out of the back window, where she saw a number of enormous stone boulders of different shapes and sizes, presumably to be used by Landowski when he was sculpting in the future.

Having exhausted all immediate avenues of distraction, Bel spotted a rickety wooden chair and went to sit herself down on it. She watched the assistant, his head bent, working with total concentration. Ten minutes later, as the clock struck noon, he wiped his hands on his work shirt and abruptly looked up.

'Lunch,' he announced, and for the first time, he looked directly at Bel and smiled. '*Bonjour*, mademoiselle.'

Because his head had been lowered up until then, Bel had not been able to see his features. But as he smiled at her she felt a strange tipping in her stomach.

'*Bonjour.*' She smiled back at him shyly. He stood up and walked over to her and she too stood at his approach.

'Forgive me, mademoiselle, for ignoring you,' he said, speaking in French, 'but I was concentrating on an eyeball and it is very delicate work.' He stopped a metre away from her and studied her intently. 'Have we met before? You seem familiar.'

'No, I'm afraid that is impossible. I've only recently arrived from Rio de Janeiro.'

'Then I am mistaken.' He nodded thoughtfully. 'I will not shake your hand, as my own is covered in clay. Excuse me for a few moments while I go and clean myself up.'

'Of course,' said Bel, her voice seeming to come out as no more than a forced whisper. She had stood up perfectly easily as he'd walked over to greet her, but now, as he disappeared into the room with the sink, she sat down abruptly, feeling dizzy and breathless. She wondered if she was coming down with the chill that Maria Elisa and her mother had been suffering from.

Five minutes later, the young man reappeared, divested of his smock and clad in a clean shirt. Her fingers moved a few centimetres forward of their own volition, instinctively wishing to run themselves through his long, wavy chestnut hair, to stroke the pale skin of his cheek, trace the shape of his perfect aquiline nose, and the full pink lips concealing his even white teeth. The faraway expression in his green eyes reminded her of Heitor's: physically here, but with his inner thoughts elsewhere.

Bel suddenly realised that his lips were moving and a sound was coming out of his mouth. She realised he was asking her name. Shocked at her own reaction to his presence, she dragged herself out of her daydream, trying to pull herself together and speak lucidly in French.

'Mademoiselle, are you feeling well? You look as though you've seen a ghost.'

'My apologies, I was . . . elsewhere. My name is Izabela, Izabela Bonifacio.'

'Ah, like the old Queen of Spain,' the assistant nodded.

'And the late Princess of Brazil,' she interjected quickly.

'I regret to admit I know very little about your country

and its history. Apart from the fact they rival us here in believing they produce the best cup of coffee.'

'Certainly the best beans at least,' she said defensively. 'Obviously, I know a lot about your country,' she said, wondering if she was sounding as witless as she felt.

'Yes. Our art and culture have crossed the globe over many hundreds of years, whereas yours is still to emerge. And I have no doubt it will,' he added. 'Now, as you seem to have been abandoned by the professor and your friend the architect, perhaps I can offer you some lunch while you tell me more about Brazil.'

'I . . .' Bel glanced out of the window, vaguely nervous about the inappropriateness of the situation. She had never met this man in her life and she was alone with him. If her father or her fiancé could see her now . . .

The young man saw her concern and waved it away with a dismissive flick of his hand. 'I can guarantee they will forget all about you while they are deep in discussion. And they may be gone for hours. So, if you do not wish to starve, please, sit yourself down at that table over there and I will prepare our lunch.'

The young man turned from her and began to walk across the *atelier* towards the kitchen she had glimpsed earlier.

'Pardon me, monsieur, but what is *your* name?'

He stopped and turned. 'Forgive me, how rude I am. My name is Laurent, Laurent Brouilly.'

Bel sat down at the rough wooden bench placed in a small alcove in a corner of the room. A small chuckle escaped from her lips as she thought of the circumstances she found herself in. Alone with a young man, and not only that, one who was currently preparing lunch for them both. She had never seen Pai enter their kitchen, let alone prepare a meal.

A few minutes later, Laurent came towards her carrying a tray loaded with two sticks of the delicious freshly baked French bread she so loved, two hunks of strong-smelling French cheese, an earthenware jug and two glasses.

He set it down on the table, before drawing a piece of old curtain that ran on a track nailed to the ceiling. 'To keep the dust from the *atelier* off our food,' he explained as he emptied the contents of the tray onto the bare boards of the table. Then he poured a generous amount of a pale yellow liquid into the two glasses and passed one to her.

'You drink wine with bread and cheese alone?' she marvelled.

'Mademoiselle, we are French. We drink wine with anything, at *any* time.' He smiled as he lifted his glass towards her. '*Santé*,' he said, as he raised his glass to hers.

Laurent took a hearty gulp of the wine, and she too took a tentative sip. She watched as he tore a chunk off the baguette, prised it open with his fingers then proceeded to fill it with slices of cheese. Not wishing to ask where the plates were, she followed suit.

Never had such a plain menu tasted so delicious, she thought with pleasure. Although, instead of wolfing down the food in large bites as Laurent did, Bel took a more ladylike approach and tore off small pieces of bread and cheese with her fingers before placing them in her mouth. And all the time, his eyes seemed to be on her.

'What are you staring at?' she asked him eventually, uncomfortable under his constant gaze.

'You,' he answered, draining his wine glass and pouring himself more.

'Why?'

He took a further mouthful then shrugged in the uniquely Gallic way Bel had come to recognise from her study of Parisians on the street below her window. 'Because, Mademoiselle Izabela, you are quite glorious to look at.'

However inappropriate, her stomach somersaulted at his comment.

'Don't look so horrified, mademoiselle. I'm sure a woman such as you has been told this a thousand times? You must be used to people staring at you.'

Bel thought about this and supposed that yes, she did attract many admiring glances. But none had ever felt as intense as *his*.

'Have you ever been painted? Or maybe sculpted?' he asked.

'Once, when I was a child – my father commissioned my portrait.'

'I'm surprised. I would have thought they'd have been queuing up in Montparnasse to paint you.'

'I've been in Paris for less than a week, monsieur, and I haven't been out anywhere so far.'

'Well, having discovered you, I'm of the mind to keep you all to myself, and let none of those rogues and vagabonds near you,' he said with a wide grin.

'I would love to go and visit Montparnasse,' Bel sighed, 'but I doubt I would ever be allowed.'

'Of course,' he agreed. 'Parents across Paris would prefer their daughters to be drowned in the river rather than lose their virtue and their hearts on the Left Bank. Where are you staying?'

'In an apartment on Avenue de Marigny, just off the Champs-Élysées. I'm here as a guest of the da Silva Costa family. They are my guardians.'

'And are they not eager to embrace all Paris has to offer?'

'No.' Bel thought he was being serious, until she saw his playful expression.

'Well, as a true artist knows, every rule is there to be broken, every barrier to be pulled down. We have one life, mademoiselle, and we must live it as we choose.'

Bel remained silent, but the euphoria of finally finding someone who felt as she did was almost too much for her and tears pricked her eyes. Laurent noticed immediately.

'Why do you cry?'

'In Brazil, life is very different. We obey the rules.'

'I understand, mademoiselle,' he said softly. 'And I can see already that you have agreed to one of them.' Laurent indicated the engagement ring on her finger. 'You are due to be married?'

'Yes, when I return home from my time in Europe.'

'And you are happy about this match?'

Bel was taken aback by his direct approach. This man was a stranger who knew next to nothing about her, and yet they were sharing wine, bread and cheese – *and* intimacies – as though they had known each other all their lives. If this was the Bohemian way, Bel decided she wanted to embrace it wholeheartedly.

'Gustavo, my fiancé, will make a loyal and caring husband,' she replied carefully. 'And besides, I think that often marriage is not just about love,' she lied.

He looked at her for a while before he sighed and shook his head. 'Mademoiselle, a life without love is like a Frenchman without his wine, or a human being without oxygen. But,' he sighed, 'maybe you're right. Some people accept the lack of it and are prepared to settle for other things, such as wealth and status. But me, no.' Laurent shook his head. 'I could never sacrifice myself on the altar of materialism. If I'm to spend my life with another, I want to wake up every morning and stare into the eyes of the woman I love. I am surprised you are prepared to settle for less. Already I can see the passionate heart that beats inside you.'

'Please, monsieur . . .'

'Forgive me, mademoiselle, I go too far. So, enough! But I would very much like to have the honour of sculpting you. Would you object if I asked Monsieur da Silva Costa if I can practise my art using you as a model?'

'You can ask him, but I couldn't . . .' Bel, blushing from embarrassment, did not know how to phrase the sentence.

'No, mademoiselle,' said Laurent, reading her mind. 'Rest assured I will not be asking you to remove your clothes. At least, not yet,' he added.

Bel was rendered speechless at the intimate insinuation. It thrilled and frightened her in equal measure. 'Where do you live?' she asked, desperate to change the subject.

'Like any true artist, I rent an attic room, along with six others, situated in the alleyways of Montparnasse.'

'You work for Professor Landowski?'

'I wouldn't quite use that expression, because I'm paid only in food and wine,' Laurent corrected her. 'And if the attic I rent with the others in Montparnasse is too crowded, he allows me to sleep here sometimes on a pallet. I am learning my craft, and there is no finer teacher than Landowski. As the Surrealists are experimenting in painting, Landowski is doing the same in sculpture with Art Deco. He is moving forward from the busy, overly fussy works of the past. He was my professor at the École Nationale Supérieure des Beaux-Arts and when he chose me to be his assistant, I was delighted to take up his offer.'

'Where is your family from?' Bel asked.

'Why would that be of interest?' Laurent chuckled. 'Next you will ask me which social class I come from! You see, Mademoiselle Izabela, all of us artists here in Paris are simply who *we* are; we throw away our past and live only for the day. We are defined by our talent, not our heritage. But since you ask,' he said, taking a gulp of wine, 'I will tell you. My family comes from a noble lineage and has a chateau near Versailles. If I hadn't walked away from them and the life they wished for me as their oldest son, I would be Le Comte Quebedeaux Brouilly by now. However, since my father announced that he would cut me out of his will when I told him I wished to become a sculptor, as I said before, now I'm simply me. I have not a centime to my name, and anything I earn in the future will only come from these very hands.'

He eyed her, but she said nothing. What could she say when her entire life was based on all the values he'd just derided?

'Perhaps you're surprised? But I promise there are many of us who are the same in Paris. And at least my father didn't have to deal with the ignominy of his son being a homo-sexual, as several of my acquaintances' fathers have had to.'

Bel stared at him, horrified that he would even voice such a thought. 'But it's illegal!' she couldn't help exclaiming.

He tilted his head to one side and studied her. 'And because bigoted regimes make it so, does that mean it's wrong?'

'I . . . I don't know,' she floundered, falling silent and trying to regain her composure.

'Forgive me, mademoiselle, I fear I have shocked you.'

Bel saw the glint in his eye and could tell he was enjoying doing so.

Another sip of wine emboldened her. 'So, Monsieur Brouilly, you have made it clear that you don't care about money or material possessions? You are happy to live on thin air?'

'Yes, at least for now, while I'm young and fit and living in the centre of the world here in Paris. However, I accept that when I'm old and infirm, and have never earned money from my sculptures, then yes, I might regret my actions. Many of my artist friends have kind benefactors who help them while they are struggling. However, as many of these benefactors are ugly dowagers who expect the young artist they're supporting to gratify them in other ways, that is not the route for me. It's little better than whoring, and I will not be a part of it.'

Again, Bel was shocked at the openness with which he spoke such words. Of course she'd heard of the brothels at home in Lapa, where men would go to have their physical appetites quenched, but it would never be spoken of in open company. And certainly not by a man to a respectable woman.

'I think I *do* frighten you, mademoiselle.' Laurent smiled at her sympathetically.

'I think that perhaps I have a lot to learn about Paris, monsieur,' she replied.

'I'm sure that's true. So, maybe you can see me as your instructor in the ways of the avant-garde. Ah, I see the two wanderers have returned,' he said, glancing over her shoulder through the window. 'The professor is smiling – always a good sign.'

Bel watched as the two men entered the studio, still deep in conversation. Laurent busied himself collecting the remnants of lunch and piling them onto a tray, and Bel hurriedly added her wine glass to it, worrying that Heitor would disapprove.

'Senhorita,' Heitor said when he saw her. 'I apologise for keeping you so long, but Professor Landowski and I had much to talk about.'

'Not at all,' Bel replied quickly. 'Monsieur Brouilly has been explaining the . . . fundamentals of sculpture to me.'

'Good, good.' Bel could see Heitor was distracted as he immediately turned back to Landowski. 'So, I visit Florence next week and then travel on to Munich. I will be back in Paris on the twenty-fifth, after which I will be in contact.'

'Of course,' Landowski agreed. 'You may feel that my ideas and style are not suitable for your needs. But whatever you decide, I admire your bravery and determination to execute such a difficult project. And I would certainly enjoy the challenge of being a part of it.'

The two men shook hands, and Heitor turned to walk out of the *atelier*, with Bel following suit.

'Monsieur da Silva Costa, before you leave, I have a favour to ask of you,' said Laurent suddenly.

'And what might that be?' Heitor asked, turning towards him.

'I would like to sculpt your ward, Mademoiselle Izabela. She has the most exquisite features and I want to see if I can do them justice.'

Heitor paused uncertainly. 'I admit I'm not sure what to say. It is a very flattering offer, is it not, Izabela? And if you were my own daughter I would feel more able to answer in the affirmative. But . . .'

'You have heard the stories of the many disreputable Parisian artists, and what they expect from their models.' Professor Landowski smiled knowingly. 'But I can assure you, Monsieur da Silva Costa, that I can vouch for Brouilly. Not only is he a talented sculptor who I believe has the capacity to be a great one, but he is right under my roof. Therefore I can personally guarantee mademoiselle's safety.'

'Thank you, professor. I will talk to my wife and contact you when we're back from Munich,' agreed Heitor.

'Then I will wait to hear from you,' said Laurent. He turned to Bel. '*Au revoir*, mademoiselle.'

Both Bel and Heitor were silent on the journey home, lost in their own thoughts. As the car skirted Montparnasse, Bel felt a thrill running through her veins. Even though her impromptu lunch with Laurent Brouilly had unsettled her, on many different levels she felt truly alive for the first time in her life.

19

Contrary to her thoughts before she'd set sail for Europe –
when the idea of visiting Italy, the land of her forefathers, had
filled her with excitement – as she packed the following day
to travel to Florence, she was loath to leave.

Even when she arrived in the city she'd dreamed of visiting, and saw the spectacular domed roof of the great Duomo
from the window of her hotel suite, smelt the aroma of garlic
and fresh herbs wafting up from the picturesque restaurants
on the street below, her pulse did not rise in the way she'd
imagined.

And a few days later, when they took a train to Rome, and
she and Maria Elisa dropped coins in the Trevi Fountain, then
visited the Colosseum where the brave gladiators had fought
for their lives in the vast arena, she felt a vague air of dis-
interest.

She had left her heart behind in Paris.

That Sunday in Rome, she joined thousands of her fellow
Catholics in Saint Peter's Square for the Pope's weekly Mass.
She knelt down, her black lace mantilla covering her face,
looked up at the tiny figure dressed in white on the balcony
and gazed at the saints that stood on pedestals all around the

square. As she queued with the hundreds of others who were praying and reciting rosaries while waiting to receive the Host, Bel too asked God to bless her family and friends. And then sent up a fervent prayer of her own.

Please, please let Senhor Heitor not forget to ask about my sculpture, and please let me meet Laurent Brouilly again . . .

From Rome, having met with the sculptors he'd come to see and studied many of the famous works of art on display in the city, Heitor was leaving to go to Munich. His aim was to view the colossal *Bavaria* statue, fashioned entirely in bronze and innovatively constructed from four enormous sections of metal fused together.

'I feel it may provide inspiration for my current project, as the construction challenges bear many similarities to those I face with the *Cristo*,' he'd told Bel when she'd questioned him over dinner one night.

For reasons Bel did not know or understand, Heitor had now decided that the rest of the da Silva Costa family would not accompany him on the long journey to Munich. Instead, they were returning to Paris, where the two boys had a tutor waiting for them.

As they boarded the sleeper train at Roma Termini station to begin the overnight journey to Paris, Bel could only breathe a sigh of relief.

'You seem brighter tonight,' Maria Elisa commented as she climbed up into her red velvet-covered cot in their shared couchette. 'You were so quiet in Italy, it was like you were somewhere else.'

'I'm looking forward to returning to Paris,' Bel answered non-committally.

As Bel climbed into her own cot, Maria Elisa's head appeared over the edge of the bunk above. 'I'm just saying you seem different, Bel, that's all.'

'Do I? I don't believe I am. In what way?'

'Like you're . . . I don't know . . .' Maria Elisa sighed. 'As if you're daydreaming all the time. Anyway, I too am looking forward to seeing Paris properly this time. We'll enjoy it together, won't we?'

Bel reached for the hand that Maria Elisa had offered and squeezed it. 'Yes, of course we will.'

Apartment 4
48, Avenue de Marigny
Paris
France

9th April 1928

Dearest Mãe and Pai,

Well, here I am back in Paris after Italy. (I hope you received the letter I wrote to you from there.) Maria Elisa and her mother are feeling much better than they were when we were last here, so we have spent the past few days enjoying the sights of the city. We have been to the Louvre and seen the Mona Lisa, to the Sacré-Cœur in an area called Montmartre, where Monet, Cézanne and many other of the great French painters have lived and worked, and we have strolled in the magnificent Tuileries Garden and climbed to the top of the Arc de Triomphe. There are so many other sights still left to see – the Eiffel Tower being one of them – that I'm sure I will never become bored.

Just walking along the streets here is an experience, and Mãe, you would love the shops! The streets nearby contain the salons of many of the great French designers, and I have an appointment for my first wedding dress fitting, as Senhora Aires Cabral suggested, at the house of Lanvin in the Rue du Faubourg Saint-Honoré.

The women here are so chic, and even if they can only afford to buy from a department store, like Le Bon Marché, they are still turned out as stylishly as the rich. And the food . . . Pai, I must tell you that your daughter has eaten escargots, little snails cooked in garlic, butter and herbs. You must coax them out of their shells with tiny forks. I found them delicious, although I must admit the frogs' legs were not to my taste.

At night, the city does not seem to sleep, and from my window I can hear the sound of a jazz orchestra playing from the hotel across the street. This kind of music is played in many places in Paris, and Senhor da Silva Costa has said we can go and listen one night, in a respectable establishment, of course.

I am well and very happy, and am trying to make the most of this wonderful opportunity I've been

*given and not waste a second of it. The da Silva
Costas have been very kind, although Senhor da Silva
Costa has been in Germany for the past ten days, and
will return tonight.*

*I have also met a young Brazilian woman from
Rio, who came here for tea with her mother two days
ago. Her name is Margarida Lopes de Almeida and
you may recognise her mother's name, for she is Julia
Lopes de Almeida, who has earned great acclaim as a
writer in Brazil. Margarida is here on a scholarship,
granted by the Escola Nacional de Belas Artes in Rio,
and is presently in Paris learning the technique of
sculpture. She has told me there are courses that run
at the École Nationale Supérieure des Beaux-Arts and
I was thinking that I might try my hand at one. I
have become very interested in the subject, due to
Senhor da Silva Costa's influence.*

*I will write again next week, but for now, I send
you love and kisses across the sea.*

Your loving daughter,
Izabela

Bel put down her ink pen on the writing desk, stretched and
looked out of the window. In the past few days, the trees
below her had blossomed and were now covered in delicate
pink flowers. When a breeze blew, they fell like scented rain
onto the pavements, covering them in a layer of petals.

She looked at the clock on the desk and saw it was just
past four in the afternoon. She had already written to Loen
telling her of Italy and there was plenty of time to pen a third
letter to Gustavo before changing for dinner. But Bel was

disinclined to do so, for she found it so difficult to match the loving sentiments of the letters she received every few days from him.

Perhaps she would write later, she thought, as she stood up and wandered to the coffee table, absent-mindedly placing a bonbon in her mouth and chewing it. The apartment was quiet, although she could hear the hum of the boys' voices, busy with their lessons next door in the dining room. Maria Georgiana and Maria Elisa were both taking their afternoon naps.

Heitor, she'd been told, would be back from Munich in time for dinner with the family, and Bel would be glad of his presence. She knew she'd have to contain her eagerness to remind him about Laurent and his wish to sculpt her for a day or so, but at least the appearance of Margarida Lopes de Almeida in the apartment had cheered her up. As Margarida and Maria Elisa's mothers had chatted, the two girls had also talked. And in Margarida, Bel had sensed a kindred spirit.

'Have you been to Montparnasse?' Bel had asked quietly as they sat drinking tea.

'Yes, many times,' Margarida had whispered to her. 'But you mustn't tell anyone. We both know that Montparnasse is not the place for well-brought-up young ladies.'

Margarida had promised to come back and visit her again soon, and share details of the sculpture course she was taking at the Beaux-Arts school.

'Surely Senhor da Silva Costa cannot disapprove, given that Professor Landowski would be one of your tutors?' Margarida had added as she'd left. 'À bientôt, Izabela.'

Heitor duly arrived home later that evening, looking grey and exhausted from his long journey. Bel listened as he expanded on the delights of *Bavaria*, the statue he'd seen in Germany. But he also told them ominous tales of the rise of the National Socialist German Workers' party, under a man called Adolf Hitler.

'Have you decided on who you will choose to make your sculpture of the *Cristo*?' asked Bel, as the maid placed generous slices of tarte Tatin in front of each of them.

'I have thought of nothing else on my long journey back to Paris,' answered Heitor, 'and I am still leaning towards Landowski, since his work displays such perfect artistic balance. It is modern, but has a simplicity and a timeless quality that I think would work well for the project.'

'I am glad you feel that,' Bel ventured. 'Having met him and been to his *atelier*, I liked his realistic approach. And his technical skill is obvious to anyone.'

'Well, it's not obvious to someone who has never seen it,' grumbled Maria Georgiana, as she sat at Heitor's side. 'Perhaps you will allow me too to meet the man who will design the outer vision of your precious *Cristo*?'

'Of course, my dear,' Heitor agreed swiftly. 'If that is what I finally decide.'

'I thought his assistant was very accomplished too,' said Bel, desperately trying to prompt Heitor's memory.

'Yes,' he agreed. 'And now, you must excuse me, for I am truly exhausted from my travels.'

Disappointed, Bel watched Heitor as he left the room, and noted the grim expression on Maria Georgiana's face.

'Well, it seems your father, yet again, is retiring for the night with the *Cristo* rather than his family. No matter,' she said to the children as she picked up her spoon to finish her dessert, 'we will play a game of cards together after supper.'

Later that night in bed, Bel mused on the state of the da Silva Costas' marriage. And on that of her own parents. In a few short months, she would find herself wedded as they were. And it seemed more and more to her that marriage was simply about tolerance, and acceptance of the other's faults. Maria Georgiana clearly felt sidelined and ignored as her husband poured all his energy and attention into his project. And her own mother, against her wishes, had moved from her beloved *fazenda* to Rio to accommodate her husband's lust for upward social mobility.

Bel turned restlessly on her pillows, wondering whether this was all she too had ahead of her. And if it was, it made it all the more imperative that she should meet with Laurent Brouilly again as soon as possible.

By the time Bel awoke the following morning, Heitor had already left for a meeting. She sighed with frustration that she'd missed her opportunity to remind him of Laurent's request.

Her growing agitation over the situation didn't go unnoticed by Maria Elisa that day, as they took lunch at the Ritz with Maria Georgiana, strolled down the Champs-Élysées and later attended Bel's wedding dress fitting at the elegant salon of Jeanne Lanvin.

'What is wrong with you, Bel? You're acting as if you're a tiger trapped in a snare,' she complained. 'You barely even took an interest in the drawings or the fabrics for your beautiful wedding gown, when most young ladies would give their eye teeth to have Madame Lanvin herself designing for them! Aren't you enjoying Paris at all?'

'Yes, yes, but . . .'

'But what?' asked Maria Elisa.

'I just feel . . .' Bel walked to the window in the drawing room as she tried to explain. 'That there's a world out there we're not seeing.'

'But Bel, we've seen everything there is to see in Paris! What more is there?'

Bel did her best to stem her irritation. If Maria Elisa didn't know, then she couldn't tell her. With a sigh, she turned round. 'Nothing, nothing . . . As you said, we've seen everything in Paris. And you and your family have been most generous to me. I'm sorry. Perhaps I'm just missing home,' Bel lied, taking the easiest route for an explanation.

'Of course you are!' Immediately, Maria Elisa's sweet nature made her rush over to her friend. 'How selfish of me, here with all my family, when you're thousands of miles away from your own. And of course, Gustavo.'

Bel allowed herself to be taken into Maria Elisa's comforting embrace.

'I'm sure, if you wished, you could return home sooner,' she added.

Bel, leaning her chin on her friend's lace-covered shoulder, shook her head. 'Thank you for your understanding, dearest Maria Elisa, but I'm sure I'll be fine tomorrow.'

'Well, Mãe has suggested that she employs a French tutor to come in for me every morning while the boys are studying their lessons. My French is dreadful, and as Pai has indicated that we could potentially be here for another year, I'd like to improve it. Yours is so much better than mine, Bel, but perhaps you'd like to join me in my classes? It would at least while away a few hours every day.'

The thought of anyone believing that a second in Paris was boring and needed to be filled further depressed Bel.

'Thank you, Maria Elisa. I'll think about it.'

Having spent another restless night trying to accept that her time in Paris would continue as it was and that the delights it contained would never be hers to know, something happened the following day to restore Bel's spirits.

Margarida Lopes de Almeida arrived for tea that afternoon, accompanied by her mother. She talked avidly about her sculpture classes at the Beaux-Arts school, and told Bel that she had enquired whether she too could join them.

'Of course, having a fellow countrywoman at the lessons would make it so much more pleasant for me,' Margarida said to Maria Georgiana, giving Bel a subtle nudge under the table as she spoke.

'I didn't realise you were interested in making sculptures, Izabela? I thought appreciating them was more to your taste?' queried Maria Georgiana.

'Oh, I loved sculpting when I took a short course in Rio,' confirmed Bel, seeing the approving glance from Margarida. 'I would enjoy a chance to learn from some of the best teachers in the world.'

'Oh yes, Mãe,' interrupted Maria Elisa. 'Bel used to bore me senseless talking about her art lessons. And as her French is so superior to mine, perhaps it would benefit her more to take these sculpture classes Senhorita Margarida suggests than to sit with me while I massacre the language?'

Bel could have kissed her.

'And of course,' Margarida added, glancing at her mother, 'it would mean that you would no longer have to escort me to school and then collect me every afternoon. I would have a companion with me and our driver can take us. You would have far more time to write your book, Mãe,' she said encouragingly. 'We would look after each other, wouldn't we, Izabela?' Margarida turned to her.

'Yes, of course we would,' Bel agreed hastily.

'Well, as long as Senhora da Silva Costa is in agreement, I think that sounds like a very sensible idea,' said Margarida's mother.

Maria Georgiana, in awe of the woman who was so famous in Brazilian society, nodded in assent. 'If you think it suitable, senhora, then I will follow your lead.'

'So,' Margarida said, kissing Bel on both cheeks in the French way as she stood to take her leave of the apartment, 'I will arrive with the car next Monday and we will go together to the school.'

'Thank you,' Bel whispered gratefully to Margarida as mother and daughter made their way to the door.

'I promise, Izabela, it suits me very well too,' she whispered back. '*Ciao, chérie*,' Margarida called out, mixing up her languages in her farewell. Which, Bel thought, only added to her air of sophistication.

Heitor arrived home that evening triumphant.

'I have asked the maid to bring champagne to the drawing room. For I have great news which I wish to celebrate with my family.'

Once the champagne had been dispensed, Heitor stood with his glass poised.

'After discussions with Senhor Levy, Senhor Oswald and Senhor Caquot, I went today to see Professor Landowski. And I offered him the commission to sculpt the *Cristo*. I will sign the contract with him next week.'

'Pai, that is wonderful news!' Maria Elisa exclaimed. 'I'm happy that you've finally made your decision.'

'And I'm happy that I know in my heart that Landowski is the right choice. My dear' – Heitor turned to Maria Georgiana – 'we must invite him and his charming wife to dinner very soon so that you can meet him. He will feature very heavily in my life in the coming months.'

'Congratulations, Senhor da Silva Costa,' said Bel, wishing to voice her support. 'I think it is an excellent decision.'

'I appreciate your enthusiasm,' Heitor said, smiling at her.

20

On Monday morning at ten o'clock, Bel, who had already been in her coat for over an hour waiting at the drawing room window, saw the gleaming Delage drive up to the front entrance of the apartment building.

'Senhorita Margarida's here,' she announced to Maria Georgiana and the boys.

'Izabela, you are expected back at four o'clock sharp,' called Maria Georgiana to Bel's disappearing back as she walked swiftly from the room, barely able to contain her eagerness to escape.

'I promise I won't be late, Senhora da Silva Costa,' she called back, as Maria Elisa waylaid her in the hall.

'Enjoy your morning, and take care.'

'Of course I will, I have Margarida with me.'

'Yes, and from my impression, it is like releasing two hungry lions from their cages.' Maria Elisa raised her eyebrows. 'Have fun, dearest Bel.'

Bel took the lift to the ground floor and found Margarida waiting for her in the lobby.

'Come, we are already late. Tomorrow we must set off earlier. Professor Paquet will make an example of both of us if we arrive after he does,' Margarida said as they walked out to the Delage and clambered into the back.

As the car pulled away, Bel studied Margarida, who was wearing a plain navy skirt and a simple poplin blouse, whereas she herself was dressed as if she was taking tea at the Ritz.

'I apologise. I should have warned you,' said Margarida, noticing Bel's clothing too. 'The Beaux-Arts is full of starving artists who don't take kindly to rich girls such as us in the classes. Even though I'm sure we are among the few who pay the tutors' wages,' she added with a smile, flicking a stray lock of her brown, shiny bob behind her ear.

'I understand,' sighed Bel. 'Although it's important that I leave Senhora da Silva Costa under the impression that the class is only full of well-bred young ladies.'

At this, Margarida threw back her head and laughed. 'Bel, I'm warning you, apart from an elderly maiden aunt, and another . . . *person*, who I believe is female but has hair as short as a man's and, I swear, a moustache to match, we are the only girls in the class!'

'So your mother doesn't mind? Presumably she must know how it is there?'

'Perhaps not *completely* how it is,' Margarida answered honestly. 'But as you know, she's a great believer in female equality. And therefore she thinks it's healthy for me to learn to fight my battles in a male-dominated environment. Besides, I'm on an arts scholarship paid for by the Brazilian Government. I must attend the best school there is,' she said with a shrug.

As the car turned onto the Avenue Montaigne and began its journey towards the Pont de l'Alma, Margarida studied Bel. 'My mother tells me that you're engaged to marry Gustavo Aires Cabral. I'm surprised he let you loose in Paris.'

'Yes, I am engaged, but Gustavo wished me to see Europe for myself before I become his wife. He himself came here eight years ago.'

'So, we must make the short time you have here as exhilarating as possible. And Izabela, I am trusting you to repeat none of what you will see and hear today to anyone. My mother believes I have lessons at the Beaux-Arts until four this afternoon. This . . . is not quite the truth,' she admitted.

'I see. So, where do you go to instead?' Bel asked tentatively.

'To Montparnasse, to meet my friends for lunch, but you must swear you will never breathe a word.'

'Of course not,' Bel confirmed, almost beside herself with excitement at Margarida's confession.

'And the people I know . . . well,' she sighed, 'they are quite extreme. You may be shocked.'

'I've already been warned by someone who knows,' Bel confirmed, staring out of the window as they crossed the Seine.

'Surely not Senhora da Silva Costa?' They both shared a chuckle.

'No, it was a young sculptor I met at Professor Landowski's *atelier* when I visited with Senhor da Silva Costa.'

'What was his name?'

'Laurent Brouilly.'

'Really!' said Margarida, raising an eyebrow. 'I know him, or at least I've met him a few times in Montparnasse. He occasionally comes into the school to teach us when Professor Landowski is otherwise engaged. He's a beautiful man.'

Bel took a deep breath. 'He has asked to sculpt me,' she revealed, relieved to be able to share her inner excitement at the compliment.

'Has he really? Then you should feel honoured. I've heard our Monsieur Brouilly is extremely particular about his choice of sitters. He was the star pupil at the Beaux-Arts and he's tipped for big things in the future.' Margarida looked at Bel with new admiration. 'Well, Izabela, you are a dark horse,' she remarked as the car pulled up in a side street.

'Where is the school?' asked Bel, looking around.

'Two streets away, but I don't like the other students to see me arrive in such luxury, when many of them have walked several kilometres to get here and have probably eaten no breakfast,' she explained. 'Come on.'

The entrance to the Beaux-Arts school was set back behind the busts of the great French artists Pierre Paul Puget and Nicolas Poussin and accessed through an elaborate wrought-iron gate. The two of them stepped through it and crossed the symmetrical courtyard which was enclosed by elegant pale-stone buildings. The tall arched windows running along the ground floor were reminiscent of the holy cloisters which were rumoured to have originally stood there.

Once through the main door, they walked across the echoing entrance hall, full of the chatter of young people. A slim young woman brushed past them.

'Margarida, she's wearing trousers!' Bel exclaimed.

'Yes, many of the female students here do,' Margarida

said. 'Can you imagine either of us arriving to take tea at the Copacabana Palace *dans notre pantalon*! Now, we're in here today.'

The two of them walked into an airy classroom, the huge windows throwing shards of light onto the rows of wooden benches. Other students were filing in and sitting down with notebooks and pencils.

Bel was confused. 'Where do we sculpt? And no one is in a smock.'

'This is not a sculpting class, it is' – Margarida opened her notebook and checked the timetable – 'the technique of stone sculpting. In other words, we are learning the theory, but in the future we will have the chance to put it into practice.'

A middle-aged man – who, from the state of his wild, wiry hair, bloodshot eyes and a few days of stubble, looked as if he had simply climbed out of bed and walked straight into the classroom – arrived at the front of the room.

'*Bon matin, mesdames et messieurs*. Today, I will introduce you to the tools needed to create a sculpture from stone,' he announced to the class. 'So . . .' The man opened a wooden box and began to place what looked to Bel like instruments of torture upon the desk. 'This is a point chisel, which is used to rough out the stone by knocking off large portions. Once you are happy with the general shape, you will use something like this, a toothed chisel, also known as a claw chisel. You will see the many indentations which create grooved lines. We do this to add texture to the stone . . .'

As the tutor continued to talk through each tool and its function, Bel sat listening intently. But although her French was excellent, he spoke so fast that she had difficulty keeping up with him. Many of the words were also technical expressions that she struggled to understand.

In the end, she gave up and amused herself by studying her fellow classmates. A more raggle-taggle bunch of young men she had never seen, with their strange clothes, their over-long moustaches, and what must have been a current trend amongst artists: their beards and wild heads of hair. Bel chanced a glance towards her neighbour, and saw that underneath his facial hair, he was probably not much older than she. A rancid smell of unwashed bodies and clothes emanated from the room and Bel sat feeling conspicuous in her finery.

She mused on the irony that in Rio she had considered herself rather a rebel, with her discreet but passionate support for women's rights and her lack of interest in material possessions. And above all, her complete antipathy when it came to netting herself a good catch for a husband.

But here . . . Bel realised she felt like a prim princess from a bygone age, transplanted into a world that had left the rules of society far behind. It was obvious that no one in this room cared a fig for convention; in fact, she thought, perhaps they felt it their duty to do all in their power to fight against it.

As the teacher announced the end of the class, and the students gathered their notebooks and began to leave the room, Bel felt out of her depth.

'You look pale,' Margarida said, studying her. 'Are you feeling quite well, Izabela?'

'I think the room must be stuffy,' she lied as she followed Margarida out of the classroom.

'And smelly, yes?' Margarida giggled. 'Don't worry, you get used to it. I'm sorry if that class was not a good introduction for you. I promise the practical lessons are far more exciting. Now, we shall take a walk together and find some lunch?'

Bel was glad to be out on the streets, and as they walked along the Rue Bonaparte in the direction of Montparnasse, she listened as Margarida chatted about her time in Europe.

'I've only been here in Paris for six months, but it already feels like home. I was away in Italy for three years, and will be here for another two. I think it will be hard to go back to Brazil after more than five years in Europe.'

'I'm sure,' agreed Bel with feeling, as the streets began to narrow and they passed cafés teeming with customers sitting at small wooden tables outside, shaded from the midday sun by colourful parasols. The air was heavy with the rich aromas of tobacco, coffee and alcohol.

'What is that liquid in small glasses that everybody seems to be drinking?' she asked Margarida.

'Oh, it's called absinthe. All the artists drink it because it's cheap and very strong. Personally, I think it tastes disgusting.'

While a few men glanced appreciatively in their direction, here their status as two unaccompanied ladies without an older chaperone did not raise so much as an eyebrow of disapproval. *Nobody cares*, Bel thought, her mood lifting at the heady reality of being in Montparnasse for the first time.

'We'll go to La Closerie des Lilas,' Margarida announced, 'and if we're lucky, you may see some familiar faces there.'

Margarida indicated a café that looked similar to the ones they had just passed and, after weaving a path between the heaving outdoor tables that were crammed together on the wide pavement in front of it, she led Bel inside. Speaking in rapid French to the waiter, Margarida was shown to a table in the front corner of the room by the window.

'Now,' she said as they sat down on the leather-covered banquette, 'this is the best vantage point from which to watch as the residents of Montparnasse go about their business. And we will see how long it takes them to spot you,' Margarida added.

'Why me?' Bel asked.

'Because, *chérie,* you are astoundingly beautiful. And as a woman, there is no better currency to trade with in Montparnasse than that. I give them ten minutes before they are over here, eager to know who you are.'

'You know many of them?' Bel asked in awe.

'Oh yes. It's a surprisingly small community here, and everyone knows everybody else.'

Their attention was caught by a man with swept-back grey hair who was moving towards a grand piano, cheered on by the table he had arisen from. He sat down and began to play. The entire café fell silent and Bel too listened spellbound, as the wonderful piece of music slowly, tantalisingly, built to a crescendo. As the final note hovered in the air, a roar of appreciation went up and the man was cheered and stamped back to his table.

'I've never heard anything quite like that,' said Bel, breathless with enjoyment. 'And who was the pianist? He is truly inspired.'

'*Querida,* that was Ravel himself, and the piece he was playing is called *Boléro.* It hasn't even had its official premiere yet, so we're honoured indeed to hear it. Now, what shall we order for lunch?'

Margarida had been correct in her assumption that they would not be left alone for long. A stream of men, ranging from young to very old, came to their table and greeted her, then promptly enquired who her beautiful companion was.

'Ah, another dark-eyed and hot-blooded woman from that exotic land of yours,' commented one gentleman, who Bel was sure was wearing lipstick.

The men would pause and stare at her face until she knew she was blushing as pink as the radishes in her untouched chef's salad. She was far too exhilarated to eat.

'Yes, I can paint you,' some would say languidly, 'and I will immortalise your beauty forever. Margarida knows where my studio is.' Then the artist concerned would give a small bow and leave the table. Every few minutes, a waiter would appear with a glass of strange-coloured liquid, and announce 'with the compliments of the gentleman at table six . . .'

'Of course, you will pose for none of them,' said Margarida pragmatically. 'They are all Surrealists, which means they will only capture the *essence* of you and not your physical form. In all likelihood, your image would turn out to be a red flame of passion, with your breast in one corner and your eye in the other!' she giggled. 'Try this one, it's grenadine. I like it.' Margarida proffered a glass full of scarlet-coloured liquid, then said suddenly, 'Izabela, quickly! Look over there by the door.'

Bel drew her uncertain gaze from the glass in front of her and turned it towards the entrance of the café. 'You know who it is?' asked Margarida.

'Yes,' she breathed as she took in the slight figure and dark wavy hair of the man Margarida was indicating. 'It's Jean Cocteau.'

'Indeed, the prince of the avant-garde. He's a fascinating, albeit sensitive, man.'

'You *know* him?' said Bel.

'A little, I suppose,' shrugged Margarida. 'Sometimes he's asked me to play the piano in here.'

As Bel focused her attention on Monsieur Cocteau, she didn't notice a young man emerge from the melee in the café and make his way over to their table.

'Mademoiselle Margarida, I have missed your presence for too long. And Mademoiselle Izabela, is it not?'

Bel dragged her gaze back from the Cocteau table and looked up, straight into the eyes of Laurent Brouilly. Her heart began to beat hard against her chest at the sight of him.

'Yes. My apologies, Monsieur Brouilly, I was miles away.'

'Mademoiselle Izabela, you were feasting your eyes on a far more fascinating personage than myself,' he said as he smiled at her. 'I didn't realise that you two ladies knew each other.'

'We've only recently begun to,' explained Margarida. 'I am helping to introduce Izabela to the delights of Montparnasse.'

'Which I'm sure she appreciates very well.' Laurent cast Bel a glance that said he clearly remembered every word of their last conversation.

'As you can imagine, every artist in the café has begged to paint her,' continued Margarida. 'But of course, I've told her to beware.'

'Well, for that I must thank you. Because as Mademoiselle Izabela knows, she was promised to me first. I'm happy that you have preserved her artistic virtue for me,' Laurent said with a smile.

Perhaps it was the alcohol, or the excitement of simply being a part of this incredible new world, but Bel shivered in pleasure at his words.

A deeply tanned young man had appeared simultaneously with Laurent and now stepped forward to make a request.

'Mademoiselle Margarida, we at Monsieur Cocteau's table are asking for you to entertain us with your marvellous skill on the piano. He is asking for his favourite. You know the one?'

'Yes.' With a quick glance at the clock that hung over the central bar, Margarida acquiesced. 'I would be honoured, although I could never match up to the superb keystrokes of Monsieur Ravel,' she announced as she stood and bowed her head in the direction of Ravel's table.

Bel watched Margarida as she swept through the crowd and sat down on the stool which Ravel himself had only recently vacated. A cheer went up from around the room.

'May I sit down so I can enjoy her playing?' Laurent asked Bel.

'Of course,' she replied, and Laurent joined her on the narrow seat, his hip pressed against hers as he squeezed in beside her on the banquette. Bel once again marvelled at the easy physical intimacy these people took for granted.

As the resonant opening chords of Gershwin's *Rhapsody in Blue* filled the café, its occupants quietened. Bel watched as Laurent surveyed the many glasses, most still sitting untouched on the table, chose one and clasped his lean, strong fingers around it.

Under the table, Laurent placed his other hand casually on his thigh as any man would. But as the minutes passed, he moved it so that it came to rest in the crevice that was formed where their thighs touched. Bel held her breath, half convinced that the touch must be accidental, but she was sure she could feel his fingers gently caressing her thigh through her dress . . .

Her entire body tingled, and the blood began to rush wildly through her veins as the music rose to its own climax.

'Mademoiselle Margarida is truly gifted, is she not?' Bel felt Laurent's warm breath on her ear and she nodded dumbly in agreement.

'I had no idea of her musical talent,' she said as the room once again erupted in applause. 'She seems to have so many different gifts.' Her own voice sounded strange to her – muffled, as though she was swimming under water.

'I'm a great believer that when one is born creative,' commented Laurent, 'it's as if your soul is a sky filled with shooting stars; a globe that is constantly turning towards whichever muse captures your imagination. Many of the people in this room can not only draw and sculpt, but they can write poetry, encourage beautiful sounds out of instruments, make audiences weep with their acting skills and sing like the birds in the trees. Ah, mademoiselle.' Laurent stood up and bowed in admiration as Margarida returned to their table. 'You were a *virtuoso*.'

'Monsieur, you are too kind,' Margarida said modestly as she sat down.

'And I believe we will be sharing an *atelier* soon. Professor Landowski tells me you are to take up an internship with us in the next few weeks.'

'He has suggested it, but I wasn't intending to tell anyone until it's confirmed,' said Margarida, signalling the waiter to bring her the bill. 'I will be honoured if he will have me there.'

'He thinks you show great ability. For a woman, that is,' Laurent teased.

'I will take that as a compliment.' Margarida smiled at him as the bill arrived and she laid a few notes on top of it.

'And perhaps if you are there in the studio, you could act as chaperone while I take time to sculpt Mademoiselle Izabela?' suggested Laurent.

'It may be possible to arrange, but we shall have to see,' said Margarida, her eyes again darting between Laurent and Bel and the clock behind the bar. 'We must take our leave. *À bientôt*, Monsieur Brouilly.' She kissed him on both cheeks, as Bel too rose.

'And Mademoiselle Izabela, it seems that fate has conspired to bring us together. I hope the next time it can be for longer.' Laurent kissed her hand, shooting her a glance from under his lashes as he did so. Naive as she was, she instantly understood what his look contained.

Luckily, when Bel arrived back at the apartment, Maria Georgiana was taking her afternoon nap. Maria Elisa, however, was reading a book in the drawing room.

'How was it?' she asked as Bel came in.

'It was wonderful!' Bel threw herself down in a chair, exhausted from nervous excitement, but still elated from her encounter with Laurent.

'Good. So, what did you learn?'

'Oh, all about the tools needed for stone sculpting,' she said airily, her alcohol-infused brain preventing her lips from moving in the way they usually did.

'For six hours, you were learning about the tools needed

for sculpting?' questioned Maria Elisa, glancing at her suspiciously.

'Yes, for most of it, and then we went for lunch and . . .' Bel stood up abruptly. 'I think the day has exhausted me. I will go and take a nap before dinner.'

'Bel?'

'Yes?'

'Have you been drinking?'

'No . . . well, only a glass of wine with lunch. After all, everyone in Paris does the same.'

Bel walked towards the door, vowing that in future she would refrain from whatever she was offered on the rustic tables of La Closerie des Lilas.

21

Apartment 4
48, Avenue de Marigny
Paris
France

27th June 1928

Dearest Pai and Mãe,

I can hardly believe that I have been away from
Rio for four months; the time has flown by so fast. I
am still loving the lessons I take with Margarida de
Lopes Almeida at the Beaux-Arts school. Although I
know I will never be a great artist like some of my
classmates, my lessons have given me a far deeper
appreciation of painting and sculpture and I feel this
will benefit me greatly in my future life as Gustavo's
wife.

Summer has really arrived in Paris now, and
the city has become even more alive with the turn
of the season. I am beginning to feel like a true
Parisienne!

I hope that some day you can both see for

*yourselves the magic I'm lucky enough to behold
every day.*
  My dearest love to both of you,
  Izabela

Bel folded the page neatly and placed it in the envelope to be posted. She sat back in the chair, wishing she could share with her parents her true feelings about the city she was growing to love, about the new freedoms she was enjoying and the people she was meeting. But she knew they would not understand. More than that, they would worry that they had made the wrong decision in allowing her to go.

The only person she felt she could truly confide in was Loen. Taking a sheet of paper, she penned a very different letter, pouring out her true emotions, telling her of Montparnasse and, of course, of Laurent Brouilly, the young assistant who wished to sculpt her . . .

Thanks to Margarida, Bel woke up with a wonderful sense of anticipation every morning. The classes she attended were indeed informative, but it was the lunches at La Closerie des Lilas afterwards that she looked forward to most.

Every day was different there, a feast for the creative senses, as artists, musicians and writers filled its tables. Only last week, she'd seen the author James Joyce sitting at a table outside drinking wine and poring over a huge stack of typewritten pages.

'I glanced over his shoulder,' said Arnaud, a would-be writer acquaintance of Margarida's, breathless with excitement. 'The manuscript was entitled *Finnegans Wake*. It's the book he's been writing for six years!'

Even though Bel knew she should be content with the fact that she was brushing shoulders and breathing the same air as these luminaries each day, Margarida and she still spent most of their walk from the school to Montparnasse hatching fruitless plots to escape during the evening, which was the time when the Left Bank really came to life.

'Of course it's impossible, but I can dream,' Bel would remark.

'Well, I suppose we must count our blessings that we have freedom during the day at least,' sighed Margarida.

Bel looked at her watch, realising that Margarida's car would be here to collect her at any moment. Dressing in a navy blue gabardine sailor dress, which she'd taken to wearing as it was the plainest item of clothing she possessed, she combed her hair, added a dash of lipstick and shouted a goodbye from the hall as she closed the door behind her.

'You're well this morning?' Margarida asked her as she climbed inside the car.

'Yes, very well, thank you.'

'Izabela, I'm afraid I have bad news for you. Professor Landowski has confirmed that he's prepared to offer me an internship in his *atelier* in Boulogne-Billancourt. So I will no longer be attending classes at the Beaux-Arts.'

'Congratulations, you must be thrilled.' Bel did her best to raise a smile at her friend's good fortune.

'Yes, I'm delighted of course,' said Margarida. 'But I do

understand that this puts you in a difficult position. I'm not sure that Senhora da Silva Costa will allow you to continue attending lessons at the school alone.'

'She won't. It's as simple as that.' Bel's eyes filled with involuntary tears.

'Bel, don't despair.' Margarida patted her hand comfortingly. 'We will find a solution, I promise.'

Ironically, their tutor for the morning session was Landowski himself, whose rare lessons Bel was normally enthralled by, as he expanded his theory of simple lines and discussed the technical difficulty of achieving perfection. But today, Bel didn't hear him.

The worst thing was that since the very first lunch at La Closerie des Lilas, over a month ago now, she hadn't set eyes on Laurent Brouilly. When she'd asked Margarida as casually as she could where he was, she had said he was heavily employed assisting Landowski in producing the first prototype for Heitor's *Cristo*.

'I believe Monsieur Brouilly has been sleeping in the *atelier* every night. Senhor da Silva Costa is eager to be given something that he can begin to work with for his mathematical calculations.'

After the class, Landowski beckoned Margarida over.

'So, mademoiselle, you will join us at my *atelier* next week?'

'Yes, Professor Landowski, and I'm honoured to be given the opportunity.'

'And I see you are with your compatriot, the girl with the

beautiful hands,' Landowski said, nodding at Bel. 'Brouilly still talks of wishing to sculpt you. When this week is over and my first sculpture goes to your guardian, perhaps you can accompany Mademoiselle Lopes de Almeida to my *atelier* and Brouilly can have his wish? Your presence will be a prize for the long hours he has spent on the *Cristo* these past three weeks. It will be healthy for him to study a woman's form, after looking so long at Our Lord.'

'I'm sure Izabela would be delighted to do so,' Margarida answered quickly for her. Landowski nodded at both of them and left the classroom.

'So, you see, Izabela?' Margarida crowed as they walked from the school and commenced their daily walk to Montparnasse. 'God, or in fact the *Cristo*, seems to be on your side!'

'Yes,' agreed Bel, her heart lifting with renewed hope. 'It seems He is.'

'Bel, I have something I wish to talk to you about,' said Maria Elisa suddenly that evening as they readied themselves for bed. 'And I want to know your opinion.'

'Yes, of course.' Bel sat down, glad of a chance to be a sounding board for her friend, with whom she felt she had been spending far less time than she should. 'What is it?'

'I've decided that I'd like to begin training as a nurse.'

'Why, that's wonderful news,' Bel said with a delighted smile.

'Do you think so? I'm worried that Mãe may not agree. None of the women in our family have ever had a career before. But it's something I've thought about for a long time, and I need to pluck up the courage to tell her.' Maria Elisa bit her lip. 'What do you think she will say?'

'I hope she will say how proud she is that her daughter wishes to do something useful with her life. And I'm sure your father will be very happy with your decision.'

'Well, I hope you're right,' said Maria Elisa fervently. 'And I was thinking that while I'm in Paris, rather than waste my time here, I might volunteer at a hospital. There is one only a few minutes' walk away from the apartment.'

Bel reached for Maria Elisa's hands and squeezed them tightly. 'You're such a good person, Maria Elisa, always thinking of others. I think you have the perfect qualities to be a nurse. The world is changing for women, and there's no reason why we shouldn't make something of our lives.'

'Well, since I have no thought of marriage at present, why not? Of course, Bel, it's very different for you. When you sail home in six weeks' time, you'll become Gustavo's wife, run his household, and soon after that you'll be the mother of his children. But for me, I need some other purpose in my life. Thank you for your support. I'll speak to Mãe tomorrow.'

Once they had climbed into bed and Maria Elisa had switched off the lamp, Bel lay there sleepless once again.

Six weeks. That was all she had left in Paris, before she returned to the life her friend had so succinctly described.

Try as she might to think positive thoughts about her future, not a single one came to mind.

Margarida had promised she would contact Bel once she had completed a few days in Landowski's *atelier* to let her know when the professor deemed it suitable for Bel to join her. But so far there had been no word.

Yet again, Bel was confined to the apartment alone, as now it was Maria Elisa who was out every morning at nine, having gained the reluctant permission of her mother and secured a volunteer position at the nearby hospital. Maria Georgiana spent most of her morning attending to household tasks or writing letters.

'It's my mother's birthday next month and I'd very much like to buy her something from Paris and send it to her. Would it be all right if I took a walk, senhora?' she asked Maria Georgiana one morning at breakfast.

'No, Izabela, I'm sure your parents would not approve of you gadding around Paris unaccompanied. And I have much to do today.'

'Well then,' said Heitor, overhearing, 'why doesn't Izabela accompany me as I walk down the Champs-Élysées to my office? Perhaps she can choose something at one of the galleries on her way? I'm sure she would come to no harm walking the few hundred metres back, my dear.'

'As you wish,' said Maria Georgiana with a sigh of irritation at being overruled.

'The weather these days is what even a Brazilian would call warm,' Heitor commented as the two of them set off from the apartment twenty minutes later and walked in the direction of the Champs-Élysées. 'So, are you still enjoying Paris?' he asked her.

'I love it,' Bel replied with feeling.

'And I hear that you have been investigating the more, shall we say, Bohemian haunts of the city?'

Bel shot Heitor a guilty glance. 'I . . .'

'I saw your friend Margarida at Landowski's *atelier* yesterday and overheard her chatting to his young assistant about your mutual lunches at La Closerie des Lilas.'

Bel quailed at his remark, but Heitor saw her expression and gave her a comforting pat on the arm. 'Don't worry, your secret is safe with me. And besides, Margarida is a very sensible young woman. She knows her way around Paris. She also asked me to tell you she will collect you tomorrow at ten o'clock on the way to the *atelier*. As you know, Monsieur Brouilly wishes to sculpt you. At least that will keep you out of trouble and we will all know where you are.'

Bel watched Heitor raise an eyebrow, but knew he was teasing her.

'Thank you for relaying the news,' she replied demurely, not wishing to express the full extent of her delight. She swiftly changed the subject. 'Are you happy with Professor Landowski's work on your *Cristo*?'

'So far, I'm absolutely certain that I made the right decision and Landowski's vision seems to be very much the same as mine. However, I have a long way to go before I can safely say we have the final design. And there are a number of problems that I'm pondering over at the moment. The first and major one being what material to clad our *Cristo* in. I have thought through so many options, but none of them sit well with me aesthetically or practically. Now, how about we try this arcade for a present for your mother? I bought Maria Georgiana a rather beautiful silk scarf from a boutique in here.'

The two of them turned into an elegant gallery and Heitor pointed to the boutique he had spoken of.

'I shall wait for you here,' he indicated as she went inside.

Bel picked out a soft peach scarf and a matching handkerchief that she knew would go well with her mother's complexion. After paying for her purchases, she left the shop to find Heitor leaning over a small fountain that played in the centre of the gallery. He was staring at the bottom of it intently.

She went to stand next to him, and, sensing her presence, he pointed to the mosaic tiles that decorated the bottom of the fountain.

'What about that?' he asked her.

'Forgive me, senhor, but what do you mean?'

'What about cladding the *Cristo* in mosaic? Then the outer shell will not be subject to cracking, as each tile will be individual. I would have to source which stone to use, something porous, hardwearing . . . yes, like the soapstone that is found in Minas Gerais, perhaps. It is a light colour and may work well. I must bring Senhor Levy here to see this immediately. He leaves for Rio tomorrow and we must make a decision.'

Bel looked at Heitor's exhilarated expression and followed in his wake as he walked swiftly out of the gallery.

'You are happy to make your way home from here alone, Izabela?'

'Of course,' she replied. Heitor nodded at her, then walked off at a brisk pace away from her.

22

'*Bienvenue,* Mademoiselle Izabela.' Laurent walked towards her and kissed her on both cheeks as she entered the *atelier* with Margarida. 'First we shall brew some coffee together. And Mademoiselle Margarida,' he said as she walked past them to don her smock, 'the professor says that the left elbow of your sculpture needs work, but overall, it was a good attempt.'

'Thank you,' Margarida called back. 'From the professor, that is a compliment indeed.'

'Now, Izabela,' said Laurent, 'come with me and show me how you would brew coffee in your own country. Strong and dark, I'm sure,' he said as he grabbed her hand and pulled her through to the tiny kitchen. Taking a brown paper bag from one of the shelves, he opened it and smelt its contents. 'Brazilian beans freshly ground this morning from a shop I know in Montparnasse. I bought it especially to help relax you and remind you of home.'

Bel inhaled the aroma, and was sent flying over five thousand miles back across the seas.

'So, show me how you like it,' he insisted as he handed her a teaspoon and stood back so that she could continue.

Bel waited for the water to boil on the small hob, not wanting to admit she had never made a cup of coffee in her life. The servants performed this task at home.

'Do you have cups?' she ventured.

'Of course,' he said, reaching into a cupboard and pulling out two enamel mugs. 'My apologies that they are not made of delicate china. But the coffee will taste the same anyway.'

'Yes,' she agreed nervously, as she spooned some coffee into the mugs.

'Actually, mademoiselle,' he said with a gentle smile, as he reached up to a shelf and pulled down a small silver pot, 'we use this to make coffee here.'

Bel blushed in embarrassment at her mistake as he transferred the coffee grounds from the mugs to the pot and added hot water. 'So, once this has brewed, we will sit together and talk.'

A few minutes later Laurent led her back into the studio, where Margarida was already sitting at a bench, working on her sculpture. Picking up a sketch pad, he guided her to the trestle table and benches where they had sat for lunch before, and pulled the curtain closed behind them.

'Please, sit there.' He indicated that she should sit opposite him. So' – he lifted his mug – 'you will talk to me of your life in Brazil.'

Bel stared at him in surprise. 'Why would you wish me to talk of Brazil?'

'Because, mademoiselle, currently you sit facing me like a beam of wood stiff with the tension of holding up a roof for one hundred years. I want you to relax, so that I can see the muscles in your face soften, your lips lose their tension and your eyes light up. If I cannot, then the sculpture will be the worse for it. Do you understand?'

'I . . . I think so,' Bel replied.

'You don't seem convinced. So I will try to explain,' he said. 'Many people think that the art of sculpture is only about the outer, physical shell of a human being. And indeed on a technical level, they would be right. But any great sculptor knows the art of producing a good likeness relies on interpreting the essence of the object they are portraying.'

Bel looked at him uncertainly. 'I see.'

'To use a simple example,' he continued, 'if I was sculpting a young girl, and I saw in her eyes that she had a soft heart that bled for others, perhaps I would place an animal, such as a dove, in her hands. I would have her cupping it tenderly. However, if I noticed another woman's greed, perhaps I would place a showy bracelet on her wrist, or a large ring on her finger. So' – Laurent opened the sketch pad, his pencil poised – 'you will talk to me and I will sketch you as you do. Tell me, where did you grow up?'

'For most of my childhood, on a farm in the mountains,' Bel answered, and the image of the *fazenda* she loved immediately brought a smile to her lips. 'We kept horses, and in the mornings I would ride across the hills, or take a swim in the lake.'

'It sounds idyllic,' Laurent interjected as his pencil danced across the sheet of paper.

'It was,' Bel agreed. 'But then we moved to Rio, into a house at the bottom of Corcovado Mountain. The *Cristo* will one day be erected at the top of it. Although it is beautiful, and far grander than our *fazenda*, the mountain which rises up behind it means it is dark. Sometimes when I'm there, I feel' – she paused as she tried to find the right words – 'as if I can't breathe.'

'And how do you feel being here in Paris?' he queried. 'It too is a big city. Trapped, like in Rio?'

'Oh no.' Bel shook her head, the frown that had appeared on her forehead disappearing immediately. 'I love this city, especially the streets of Montparnasse.'

'Hmm, then I would surmise that it is not your location that affects you, but more your state of mind. Paris too can be very claustrophobic, yet you say you love it here.'

'You're right, of course,' she admitted. 'It is more to do with the life I live in Rio than the city itself.'

Laurent continued with his sketching as he observed her expression. 'And what is wrong with that life?'

'Nothing. I mean . . .' Bel struggled to find the words to explain. 'I am very fortunate. I have an extremely privileged life. This time next year, I will be married. I will live in a beautiful house and have all a woman could want.'

'Then why do I see unhappiness in your eyes as you talk of your future? Could it be – as you hinted the first time we met – because your marriage is an arrangement of the head and not of the heart?'

Bel was silent as the heat rose to her cheeks, betraying the truth Laurent had just spoken.

'Monsieur Brouilly, you don't understand,' she said eventually. 'Things are different in Rio. It is my father's wish that I make a good marriage. My fiancé is from one of the highest-placed families in Brazil. And besides,' she added despairingly, 'I have no talent like you with which to earn a living. I am completely dependent on my father and, soon, on my husband for everything I have.'

'Yes, mademoiselle, I understand and sympathise with your plight. But sadly,' he sighed, 'it is only you who can do anything to change it.' He put his pencil down and contemplated his sketches for several minutes while Bel sat tensely, unsettled and frustrated by their conversation.

Finally, Laurent looked up. 'Well, seeing these, I can assure you that you could earn your own living as an artist's model in Montparnasse. Not only do you have a beautiful face, but underneath the layers you wear on your body, I'm sure you are the very epitome of womanhood.'

As his eyes swept over her, Bel felt once more a strange heat spreading up from her chest and into her face.

'Why so embarrassed?' he asked her. 'Here in Paris, we celebrate the beauty of the female form. After all, we are all born naked, and it's only society that dictates we wear clothes. And of course, the weather in Paris in the winter,' he chuckled, looking up at the clock. 'And don't worry,' he added, appraising her once more, 'I will be sculpting you in exactly what you are wearing today. It is perfect.'

Bel nodded silently in relief.

'So, now that I have forced you to reveal your inner soul, it is already noon. I will prepare some bread and cheese and bring you some wine as your reward.'

Laurent collected the coffee cups and walked across the studio in the direction of the kitchen, pausing to ask Margarida if she would join them for lunch too.

'Thank you,' she answered, and left her sculpture to wash the clay from her hands. Bel sat alone, gazing out of the window at the beds of lavender, feeling shaken and vulnerable. Somehow, Laurent had coaxed her to reveal her true feelings about the future.

'Are you all right, Izabela?' Margarida came to sit next to her and placed a hand on her shoulder, her expression one of concern. 'I heard snippets of your conversation. I hope Monsieur Brouilly didn't push you too far in his quest to portray you honestly. And I hope,' she said, lowering her voice, 'that it really was out of professional motives.'

'What do you mean?'

But Margarida had no time to reply as Laurent arrived with the tray.

Bel sat quietly during lunch, listening to Margarida and Laurent chat about their mutual acquaintances and gossip about the latest antics of the colourful crowd they knew.

'Cocteau has set up a back room in a building on the Rue de Châteaudun, and invites his cronies there to drink cocktails that he has made and named himself. I hear they are lethal,' said Laurent as he took a large gulp of wine. 'They say his new fad is holding séances.'

'What are they?' Bel asked, fascinated.

'It's when you try to contact the dead,' clarified Margarida. 'Not something that would ever appeal to me,' she said with a shudder.

'He's also indulging in group hypnosis sessions, to see if it's possible to reach the subconscious mind. Now that I would be interested in. The human psyche fascinates me almost as much as its physical form.' Laurent glanced at Bel. 'As you might have realised this morning, mademoiselle. Now, it is time to return to work. While I place a chair in the corner of the *atelier* where the light is best, I suggest you take a short walk in the gardens. For once I begin, I shall insist you are still, like the stone I will work from.'

'I shall accompany her, Monsieur Brouilly. I too need to breathe some fresh air,' said Margarida. 'Come, Izabela.'

The two women stood up, left the *atelier* and went into the gardens, where they stood by the voluptuously scented beds of lavender.

'The only sound I can hear is the buzzing of the bees that are stealing the nectar.' Margarida sighed in pleasure as she took Bel's arm and crooked her own into it. 'Are you sure you are all right, Izabela?' she asked.

'Yes,' Bel confirmed, her tension calmed by the lunchtime wine.

'Well, just promise me you won't allow him to make you feel uncomfortable.'

'I won't,' Bel reassured her. 'Isn't it strange?' she said as they walked slowly along the edge of the garden, enclosed by a neatly clipped cypress hedge. 'Even though, with its wealth of flora and fauna, Brazil has the same beauty, the energy and atmosphere in France is so different. At home, I find it difficult to be contemplative, to be at peace with myself. And yet here, even in the heart of Montparnasse, I am somehow able to do so. To see myself clearly.' Margarida shrugged. 'Now, we must return to the *atelier* so that Monsieur Brouilly can begin his masterpiece.'

Three hours later, in the car on the way home, Bel found she was exhausted. For what had felt like an eternity, she had sat on a chair, her hands on her knees, her fingers displayed exactly as Laurent had placed them.

Rather than feeling sensuous, she had felt like a maiden

aunt, whose likeness was to be captured in sepia tones with a camera. Now her back ached from sitting upright for so long and her neck felt stiff. And if she'd dared to even twitch one of her fingers to move it to a more comfortable position, Laurent noticed. He would stand up from behind the chunk of stone he was working with, and move towards her to replace the hand exactly as he'd originally positioned it.

'Izabela, wake up, *querida*. We've arrived at your apartment.'

She jumped, embarrassed that Margarida had caught her dozing.

'I'm sorry,' she said, as she roused herself and the chauffeur opened the car door. 'I didn't realise it would be so tiring.'

'It's been a long, hard day for you, in all senses. Everything is new to you, and that in itself is exhausting. Are you up to coming to the *atelier* tomorrow?'

'Of course,' said Bel staunchly as she climbed out of the car. 'Goodnight, Margarida. See you at ten.'

That night, as she excused herself from the usual round of cards that ensued after dinner, and laid her head thankfully on the pillow, Bel decided Laurent's suggestion of her earning her crust as an artist's model would not be as easy an option as she'd first presumed.

23

For the next three weeks, Bel accompanied Margarida every morning to Landowski's *atelier* in Boulogne-Billancourt. On a couple of occasions, Heitor da Silva Costa came with them, hitching a lift with a new set of designs and drawings for his Christ.

'Landowski is making yet another model for me as we try to refine it,' he'd say, and then hurry out of the car the minute they arrived, in anticipation of seeing whether Landowski had completed the new version.

Landowski, issued with a further list of small alterations which required him to make a further model, would sit mumbling under his breath at his workbench.

'That crazy Brazilian. How I wish I'd never agreed to be a part of his impossible dream.'

But it was said affectionately, and with implicit admiration for the scale of the project.

And slowly, Bel's own project began to progress as her likeness took shape under the sensitive fingers of Laurent. She became adept at disappearing into her own imagination while she sat motionless. Most of her thoughts centred around Laurent, whom she watched constantly out of the corner of her eye, deep in concentration as he chipped away at the stone with a claw hammer and riffler.

One particularly hot July morning, Landowski's hand fell on Laurent's shoulder as he worked.

'I have just returned from delivering my latest version of the Christ to Monsieur da Silva Costa's office in Paris,' Landowski growled. 'And now, the mad Brazilian has asked me to make a four-metre scale model of it, which he wishes me to begin immediately. I will need your help, Brouilly, so no more playing with your sculpture of the beautiful lady. You have one more day to finish her.'

'Yes, professor, of course,' he answered, throwing Bel a look of resignation.

Bel tried not to show the utter despair she felt at his words. Then Landowski moved towards her and Bel felt his appraising eyes upon her.

'So,' he said eventually, 'you can start by casting mademoiselle's beautiful, long fingers. I will need a model to work from for Christ's hands, and they must be as sensitive and as elegant as hers. They will embrace and protect all His children beneath Him and cannot be the calloused, clumsy hands of a man.'

'Yes, professor,' Laurent replied obediently.

Landowski took Bel's hand and drew her up from the chair. He walked her over to the bench and placed her hand sideways upon its surface, so that her little finger rested against it. He then stretched her fingers out and closed them together, placing her thumb along the edge of her palm.

'There, you will cast mademoiselle's hands like this. You know how the model looks, Brouilly. Try to make it as close to that as you can. And also, cast Mademoiselle Margarida's hands at the same time. She too has elegant fingers. I shall compare how they will look on our Christ.'

'Of course,' said Laurent. 'But may we begin tomorrow morning? Mademoiselle Izabela must be weary after a long day sitting for me.'

'If mademoiselle can bear it, I wish it to be done now. Then the casts will be dry by tomorrow morning and I will have something to work with. I'm sure you don't mind, mademoiselle?' Landowski glanced at her as if her reply was irrelevant anyway.

She shook her head. 'I would be honoured, professor.'

'Now,' Laurent said, once he'd coated her hands in the white plaster of Paris paste. 'You have to swear to me you will not move even a cuticle until this has set. Otherwise we will have to start all over again.'

Bel sat, trying to ignore an irritating itch on her left palm, and watched Laurent go through the same process with Margarida. When he'd finished with her too, he checked the clock and gently tapped the plaster that was setting around Bel's hands.

'Another fifteen minutes will do it,' he said, and then he chuckled. 'If only I had a camera to take a photograph of the two of you sitting there with your hands coated in white plaster. It is a strange sight indeed. Now, please excuse me while I leave you to find a drink of water. Don't worry, mesdemoiselles, I shall be back eventually . . . before nightfall.' He winked at them and walked in the direction of the kitchen.

The two girls looked at each other, their lips twitching to

giggle at how ridiculous they both must look, but desperately refraining, knowing that any physical movement might reverberate through their hands.

'Perhaps one day, we'll look up at Corcovado and remember this moment,' mused Margarida with a smile.

'I certainly will do so,' replied Bel wistfully.

It took only a few minutes of delicate and, as Bel thought afterwards, dangerous work for Laurent to make tiny slits along her hands with a sharp knife, then gently ease the cast away from her pre-greased fingers. When he had finished, he looked at the casts laid on the table in satisfaction. 'Perfect,' he said. 'The professor will be pleased. How do you think your hands look in plaster?' he asked her as he began the same process of removal on Margarida.

'Not at all like mine,' said Bel as she studied the white shapes. 'May I now go and wash them?'

'Yes. The soap and the scrubbing brush are beside the sink,' he advised her.

When Bel returned, feeling better now she'd cleared the grease and plaster dust from her hands, Laurent was frowning at a finger which had broken off as he'd removed Margarida's cast.

'I'm sure it's salvageable,' he said. 'There will be a slight hairline crack on the joint, but it should be good enough.'

Margarida then disappeared to wash her hands and Laurent began to clear up the *atelier* for the night. 'It is a pity the professor needs my help urgently. I still have a lot to do on your sculpture, but at least I have your fingers now,' he added wryly.

'We must leave,' said Margarida as she reappeared. 'My

driver has been waiting for hours and Mademoiselle Bel's guardian will wonder where she's got to.'

'Tell her that I've kidnapped their ward and I don't wish to return her until my sculpture is finished,' Laurent joked as the girls collected their hats and made towards the door. 'Izabela, are you not forgetting something?' Laurent called to her just as she'd stepped outside. He dangled her engagement ring on the end of his little finger. 'Perhaps we should replace this where it belongs, lest others suspect you removed it on purpose,' he said as she walked back into the *atelier* towards him. 'Here, I shall put it on for you.' Laurent took her hand in his and slid the ring back into place, staring intently into her eyes. 'There, you are reunited. *À bientôt,* mademoiselle. And do not worry, I will find a way for us to continue with your sculpture.'

The girls left the *atelier*, climbed into the car and set off on their journey back to central Paris. Bel gazed out of the window, feeling miserable.

'Izabela?'

She turned and saw that Margarida was watching her thoughtfully.

'May I ask you a personal question?'

'I think so,' she said cautiously.

'Well, it's in two parts really. You remember I overheard you talking with Laurent when he was sketching you, and you voiced your fears about returning to Rio and marrying your fiancé?'

'Yes. But please, Margarida, that is for no other ears but Laurent's and yours,' she added hastily, terrified that word might get back via the Brazilian grapevine.

'I understand what you meant. But of course, I couldn't

help wondering whether your reluctance to marry your fiancé has increased over the past few weeks?'

Bel stretched out her finger and absent-mindedly surveyed the engagement ring upon it as she thought about Margarida's question. 'When I left Rio, I felt grateful to Gustavo for allowing me come to Europe with the da Silva Costas before I married him. I never expected that he'd let me go and I felt he'd given me a gift. But now that the gift is nearly spent, and I must return home in less than three weeks, the truth is . . . that I find myself feeling differently about him. Yes, Paris has changed my perspective on many things,' she sighed.

'I understand that you love the freedom that Paris offers you,' replied Margarida. 'As do I.'

'Yes,' Bel said fervently, a catch in her voice. 'And the worst thing is, now that I've tasted a different way of life, it's made thoughts of the future even more difficult. Part of me wishes I'd never come here and experienced what I could have had and now never can.'

'And so, I come to the second part of my question,' Margarida continued softly. 'I've been observing you and Laurent together as he's sculpted you. I will be honest and say that at first I thought his flattery and innuendo were no more than he'd give to any pretty woman he chose as his model. But in the past few days, I've noticed the way he gazes at you sometimes, the tender way he touches the stone as he works, as if he is dreaming that it's really you he's caressing. Forgive me, Izabela,' Margarida said, shaking her head. 'I'm usually pragmatic when it comes to the subject of love. I understand well what men are, especially here in Paris, but I feel I must warn you. I fear he may, in his undoubted passion for you, and the fact that your time together is running out, forget that you are spoken for.'

'A fact that I would of course immediately remind him of,' replied Bel, giving Margarida the only appropriate reply.

'Would you? I wonder,' she said thoughtfully. 'For as I see the way Laurent feels about you, I also see the way you are with him. In fact, I knew it from the minute he walked over to our table at La Closerie des Lilas on our very first lunch together in Montparnasse. And I will be honest, it worried me from the start. I thought back then that perhaps he was playing a game with you, sensing your naivety. There are many unscrupulous men amongst the creative fraternity in Paris. They see love as an amusement, the woman's heart no more than a toy to be played with. And when they have seduced their prey with their golden tongues, and she is ripe for the plucking, they take what they desire. And then of course, having achieved their aim, the game no longer holds any novelty and they move on, looking for a fresh challenge.'

Bel watched Margarida's features tighten with pain as she delivered her speech, and noticed her eyes were moist.

'Yes, Izabela.' Margarida shot her a glance. 'What you're thinking is right. When I was in Italy, I fell in love with just the kind of man I've described. And of course, having come straight from the protective cloak of Rio, I was as innocent as you. And yes, he seduced me. In *all* senses of the word. But when I left for Paris, I heard from him no longer.'

Bel computed in silent shock exactly what Margarida was telling her.

'There. I have shared my biggest secret with you,' Margarida breathed. 'And I do it simply because I hope something positive can emerge from the terrible blackness and despair I suffered afterwards. I'm a little older than you, and sadly, after what happened to me, wiser. And I can't help seeing in you what I was then: a young woman in love for the first time.'

Bel was fit to burst with her feelings for Laurent. Up to now, she'd only been able to pen them in heartfelt outpourings to Loen. She decided to trust Margarida, given the secret she herself had shared.

'Yes,' she said. 'I love him. I love him with all my heart. And I can't even bear to think how I will live the rest of my life without him.'

She burst into tears, the relief of sharing her true feelings face to face with Margarida cutting through her reserve.

'Bel, I'm so sorry, I didn't mean to distress you. Listen' – Margarida glanced out of the window – 'we're near to your apartment now and you can't arrive home like this. Let's go and sit somewhere quiet. We're so late anyway, a few more minutes won't make any difference.'

Margarida spoke to the driver and gave him directions. A few seconds later, the car pulled up on the Avenue de Marigny beside a small park surrounded by iron railings.

They climbed out of the Delage and Margarida led her to a bench and sat her down. Bel watched the setting sun dip gracefully beyond the plane trees that bordered the park and graced every boulevard she'd seen in Paris.

'Please, you must forgive me for speaking so bluntly,' Margarida apologised. 'The affairs of your heart are none of my business, I know. But seeing both of you so filled with passion for each other made me feel I must say something.'

'But surely my circumstances are different to yours in Italy?' Bel insisted. 'You yourself said in the car that you thought Laurent had feelings for me. That maybe he loved me.'

'At the time, I was sure that Marcello loved *me*. Or at least, I wanted to believe that he did. But whatever Laurent says to you, Izabela, however he persuades you, please remember that although you think there may be a future together, there is not. Laurent can offer you nothing: no home, no security, and believe me, the last thing he wishes for is to ever be tied down with a wife and a brood of children. The problem with creatives is that they are simply in love with the idea of being in love. But it can never lead anywhere, no matter what heights your joint passions reach. Do you understand me?'

Bel stared blankly at a nursemaid with her two young charges, the only other residents of the gardens. 'Yes. But I will also be honest and say that even though my ears hear you and my brain understands your warning, my heart is not so easy to convince.'

'No, of course not,' Margarida conceded. 'But please, Bel, at the very least, think about what I've said. I would hate for you to ruin the rest of your life by allowing your heart to rule your head for a few short minutes. Given that your fiancé allowed you to come here, if he discovered your secret, it would be a betrayal that he could never forgive.'

'I know.' Bel bit her lip guiltily. 'Thank you, Margarida. I'm grateful for your advice. But now, we really must go, or Maria Georgiana will never allow me out of her sight again.'

Sweetly, Margarida came up to the da Silva Costas' apartment with Bel and explained to a stony-faced Maria Georgiana how Landowski himself had kept both of them behind while his assistant cast their hands in a mould.

'Well, as you can imagine, my mind was full of all sorts of terrible occurrences that might have befallen you. Just make sure it doesn't happen again.'

'I will, I promise,' Bel agreed, then left the drawing room to show Margarida to the door. The two women hugged affectionately.

'Goodnight, Izabela, and I'll see you tomorrow.'

In bed, rather than contemplating Margarida's descriptions of the dreadful fate she might suffer if she succumbed to Laurent's infinite charms, all Bel could feel was exhilaration.

She thinks Laurent loves me . . . He loves me . . .

And that night she drifted off to sleep easily, a beatific smile on her slumbering face.

24

'I've spoken to the professor,' said Laurent when Bel and Margarida arrived at the *atelier* the next morning, 'And I simply explained that I could not complete the sculpture within one day. We agreed that from now on you can come here in the early evenings, when we have finished working on the Christ. I can speak to Senhor da Silva Costa and explain the circumstances if it helps.'

Bel, having arrived at the *atelier* in a state of agonised tension, was so relieved by his words that she nodded eagerly.

'But, Monsieur Brouilly,' interjected Margarida with a concerned frown. 'I will not be able to accompany Mademoiselle Izabela here at that hour of the day. I must return home every night at six for dinner with my mother.'.

'Surely, mademoiselle, there is nothing inappropriate about the situation?' said Laurent. 'The professor himself will be present, and his wife and children are a stone's throw away in the house.'

In that moment, as she threw a pleading glance at Margarida, Bel saw the surrender in her friend's eyes. 'No, of course not,' she said abruptly. 'Excuse me, but I must go and change.'

'So, now we set to work,' said Laurent, smiling at Bel in triumph.

That evening, Heitor announced at dinner that Laurent Brouilly had called him at his office and had explained the circumstances that required Bel's presence at the *atelier* in the evenings.

'Given that it is the urgency of my project that has forced yours to be sidelined, I feel I must agree,' Heitor concluded. 'Izabela, my driver will take you to the *atelier* for five o'clock each day and return you home here for nine.'

'But surely there must be a bus that can take me? I don't want to put you to any trouble, Senhor da Silva Costa,' Bel suggested.

'Bus?' Maria Georgiana looked horrified. 'I hardly think that your parents would wish for you to be using public transport alone in Paris in the evening. You must of course be driven there and back.'

'Thank you. I will pay for any expenses incurred,' said Bel quietly, disguising the true extent of her relief and joy.

'As a matter of fact, Izabela,' continued Heitor, 'it rather suits me to have you in Landowski's *atelier*. You can be the spy in the camp, and report back to me on the progress of the new four-metre model of my *Cristo*,' he smiled.

'Perhaps one evening I could accompany you to the *atelier* and watch as you are sculpted?' asked Maria Elisa as they climbed into bed later that evening.

'I will ask Monsieur Brouilly if he would mind,' said Bel. 'Are you still enjoying the hospital?' she asked, changing the subject and hoping Maria Elisa would forget about her request.

'Very much,' Maria Elisa replied. 'And a few days ago, I spoke to my parents about making nursing my career in the future. Mãe wasn't happy, as you can imagine, but Pai was very supportive and told Mãe off for being so old-fashioned.' Maria Elisa smiled. 'It isn't her fault,' she equivocated hastily, always ready to forgive. 'She was brought up in a different era. So now I'm eager to return to Rio and embark on my chosen course. Sadly, Pai thinks it will be another year before he'll have finished his work here. You're so lucky to be returning home in two weeks, Bel. Sleep well.'

'And you,' Bel responded.

She lay in bed thinking about what Maria Elisa had just said. *If only we could change places*, she thought sleepily, knowing that she would sell her soul to be in her friend's position and spend another year in Paris.

Two days later, Bel found herself sitting in the *atelier* as dusk fell. Out of the corner of her eye, she could see the vast emerging structure of the four-metre *Cristo*, dominating the studio. Margarida had already departed for the day, and as Bel had arrived, Landowski had been leaving to take supper with his wife and children next door. Without the usual human hum of the studio, Bel listened to the silence.

'What are you thinking?' Laurent asked her suddenly.

Bel saw his hands were working on her upper torso, currently engaged in shaping the outline of her breasts beneath the high-necked muslin blouse she was wearing.

'Just how different it is here at night,' she answered.

'Yes, it certainly has a serenity as the sun sets. I often work here alone in the evenings as I enjoy the peace. Landowski must attend to his family, and besides, he says he cannot sculpt after the light fades.'

'Can you?'

'Izabela, even if you were no longer sitting in front of me, I would be able to sculpt you perfectly. Having gazed at you for so long, the exact details of your form are engrained on my memory.'

'So, perhaps you do not need me here after all?'

'No, perhaps you're right.' He smiled lazily at her. 'But it's the perfect excuse to have your company. Don't you agree?'

It was the first time Laurent had made a direct comment that confirmed he desired her presence for more than artistic reasons.

She lowered her eyes. 'Yes,' she answered.

Laurent said no more, and worked on silently for the next hour. Then he stretched and suggested it was time for a break.

As he went to the kitchen, Bel stood up and walked around the *atelier* to ease her stiff back. She glanced at her unfinished sculpture and admired its simple lines.

'Would you recognise yourself?' Laurent asked as he brought through a jug of wine and a bowl of olives and she followed him to the trestle table.

'Not really,' she replied honestly, studying the sculpture as he poured the wine into two glasses. 'Perhaps when you have finished my face I might. I look so young at present, almost like a little girl from the way you have had me pose.'

'Excellent!' said Laurent. 'I have had in my mind the image of a closed rosebud, just before it begins to open and blossom into a perfect flower. The moment between childhood and womanhood; on the threshold of the latter and contemplating the delights it might hold.'

'I'm not a child,' Bel retorted, feeling patronised by Laurent's explanation.

'But neither are you a woman yet,' he said, eyeing her as he drank his wine.

Bel did not know how to reply. She took another sip of wine from her glass as her heart rate increased.

'So, back to work,' he said briskly, 'before the light fades completely.'

Two hours later, Bel rose to take her leave. Laurent followed her to the *atelier* door. 'Safe return home, Izabela. And you must forgive me if you felt what I said earlier was inappropriate. You've hardly spoken to me since.'

'I . . .'

'Hush.' Laurent put a gentle finger to her lips. 'I understand. I know your circumstances, but I can't help wishing that things were different. Goodnight, my sweet Bel.'

As she was driven home, Bel knew that in his own way, Laurent had been telling her that if she was free, he would want to be with her. But that he also understood her situation and, as a gentleman, would never cross the line.

'Even though he wishes to . . .' she murmured to herself in rapture.

Over the course of the next few evenings at the *atelier*, there was no further innuendo from Laurent. If he spoke, it was to do with the sculpture, or idle gossip about Montparnasse and its inhabitants. Ironically, the more neutral his conversation, the higher the emotional and physical tension rose within Bel. It was *she* who began to make the odd comment to him, noticing a new shirt he was wearing and how it suited him, or praising his talent as a sculptor.

With each passing day, Bel's frustration escalated to greater heights. Given that Laurent had ceased to flirt with her completely, she had nowhere to go. And besides, she asked herself over and over again, where did she *want* to go?

But no matter how often she posed this question to herself, and her head told her that the sooner she was on the boat back to Brazil the better, it made no difference. As she sat for hours in his presence, the fact he was so near yet so far was a delicious torture to her soul.

One evening, as she said a chaste goodnight to Laurent and paused in the garden to compose herself before climbing into the waiting car and making the journey home, she noticed a bundle of rags lying under the cypress hedge. She was sure that it had not been there when she'd taken a walk outside during an earlier break. Moving tentatively forwards, she put a foot out towards it and poked it with the toe of her shoe. The bundle of rags moved and Bel jumped back in fright.

Warily maintaining her distance, she watched as a small, filthy human foot emerged from the edge of the rags, and then, from the other end of the bundle, a head of dirt-matted hair. As the figure began to reveal itself, Bel saw it was a young boy of perhaps seven or eight years of age. A pair of eyes, which Bel saw were dazed with exhaustion, opened for a few seconds. Then they closed again and she realised the child had fallen back to sleep.

'*Meu Deus*,' she whispered to herself, moved to tears by the sight of him. Debating what to do, she walked tentatively towards the boy and quietly knelt down next to him, not wishing to startle him. Her fingers reached out towards him, but this time, her touch woke the boy and he sat up in alarm, immediately on full alert.

'Please, have no fear, I will not hurt you. *Tu parles français?*' The boy, his grimy face a picture of terror, put his emaciated arms up protectively in front of himself and backed away from her under the hedge.

'Where are you from?' she tried again, this time in English. Again, he merely stared at her in fear, like a trapped animal, as she noticed the deep gash on his shin, caked with dried blood. As the boy cowered in front of her, his huge frightened eyes bringing further tears to her own, she slowly reached out a hand and placed it gently on his cheek. She smiled at him, knowing she mustn't frighten him, but instead try to gain his trust. As her fingers gently cupped the side of his face, she felt the boy relax.

'What has happened to you?' she murmured, studying his eyes. 'Whatever you have seen, you are too young to know such pain.'

Suddenly the boy's head fell heavily against her palm, but jerked upwards in alarm a few seconds later. Eventually, when he realised that her comforting caress had not been withdrawn, he returned to sleep.

Leaving her hand where it was so as not to disturb him, Bel managed to crawl nearer to him, whispering endearments in the three different languages she knew, and placing her other arm around him. Finally, she pulled him gently from the bushes towards her. He was whimpering now, but no longer seemed frightened of her, only jumping in pain when she moved his right leg with the terrible gash so that she could cradle his bony body upon her knee.

Once there, the boy gave a sigh and turned his head to nestle against her. Doing her best to swallow down the bile that rose to her mouth at the terrible stench of him, Bel sat rocking him in her arms, hugging him to her breast.

'Izabela,' a voice came from behind her. 'What on earth are you doing sitting in the grass?'

'Shh!' she hushed Laurent as she stroked the boy's sleeping face to reassure him. 'You'll wake him.'

'Where did you find him?' Laurent returned the whisper.

'Under the hedge. He can be no more than seven or eight, but he's so thin he weighs less than a toddler. What do we do?' She looked up at him, her eyes agonised. 'We can't leave him here. He has a bad injury to his leg which needs attending to. It could turn septic and the poison might seep into his blood and kill him.'

Laurent looked down at Bel and the filthy child, and shook his head.

'Izabela, surely you understand that there are many such children on the streets of France. Most of them come illegally across the borders from Russia or Poland.'

'Yes,' she hissed. 'And it happens in Brazil too. But this boy is here with us now, and it is *I* who have found him. How could I possibly leave him, dump him on the roadside outside Landowski's land and let him perish? It would be on my conscience for the rest of my life.'

Laurent watched as tears coursed down Bel's face, her eyes

alight with pain and passion. He bent down next to her, then reached a hand to tentatively stroke the sleeping boy's matted hair.

'Forgive me,' he whispered. 'Perhaps the sights I see on the streets of Paris every day have made me immune to suffering. God has put this child in your path and of course you must do what you can to help him,' Laurent agreed. 'It is too late now to disturb the Landowskis. For tonight, he can sleep on a pallet in the kitchen. I have a key to the door and I can lock him in, safely away from Landowski's precious Christ. Sadly, one never knows the state of mind of a stray like him. I'll sleep here tonight in the *atelier* and keep guard. So, can you carry him inside?

'Yes,' said Bel, gratefully. 'Thank you, Laurent.'

'I'll go and warn your driver you may be some time yet.' Laurent helped Bel to her feet, the boy still sleeping in her arms.

'He's as light as a feather,' Bel whispered, as she looked down at his innocent young face, trusting her to take care of him, simply because he had no alternative.

Laurent watched her as she carried the child carefully, tenderly, into the *atelier* so as not to wake him. And as he went to speak with Bel's driver, his own eyes brimmed momentarily with tears.

She was waiting for him on the chair where she sat every day as he sculpted her, the child still in her arms.

'I'll prepare a pallet for him in the kitchen,' said Laurent, wondering what on earth Landowski would say when he arrived to find a filthy street child in his *atelier* at sunrise tomorrow. But nevertheless, he wished to help.

A few minutes later, Bel carried the child through to the

kitchen and gently laid him down. 'At least I should wash his face and perhaps try to clean his wound. Have you some cloth and antiseptic?'

'Somewhere,' Laurent said, and he began searching in the cupboards until he found the antiseptic. Disappearing from the room, he arrived back with a piece of white cotton netting, more commonly employed in the studio for plaster of Paris moulds, so Bel could use it to clean the child's wound.

'Have you a bandage?' she asked, and when Laurent said there were none in the cupboards, he watched as she gently bound the wound with the netting to protect it. The boy flinched, but remained asleep.

'Even though the night is warm, he is shivering with fever. We need a blanket,' she ordered and Laurent duly brought the one that he would have wrapped around his own shoulders that night.

'I will sit here for a while, bathe him in cold water to bring down his fever and make sure he feels safe,' she said, as Laurent stood above her in the tiny kitchen. Nodding, he left and went to prepare his own pallet in the *atelier* next door.

'Sweet child,' she whispered as she wiped a water-soaked rag across his forehead and stroked his hair. 'When you wake up tomorrow, I won't be here, but don't be afraid. I promise when I return, I will make sure you are safe. But now I must leave you. Sleep well.'

As Bel began to rise, a hand suddenly reached out from beneath the blanket and grabbed at her skirt. The boy's eyes were open wide as he stared at her.

And in perfect French, he said, 'I will never forget what you have done for me tonight, mademoiselle.' And then, with a sigh of contentment, the child rolled over and once again closed his eyes.

'I must go,' Bel said to Laurent as she emerged from the kitchen. 'Where is the key to lock the prison door?' she added, sarcasm in her voice.

'Izabela, you know I only do it to protect the professor and his family. This is their house, and his great work of art,' he reminded her as he indicated the half-formed sculpture of Christ.

'Of course,' she agreed. 'But you must promise me that when the boy wakes tomorrow, you will tell him he is safe here? And I myself will speak to the professor and explain, as it was me who has caused this trouble. Now, I must leave. God knows what wrath I'll face from Senhora da Silva Costa in the morning.'

'Izabela . . . Bel . . .' Laurent grabbed her arm as she made to walk to the door. He pulled her towards him suddenly and wrapped her in his arms. 'You are truly beautiful, inside and out. And I can't bear any longer to continue with this masquerade, this pretence between us. Please feel free to tell me to release you from my arms, but God help me, seeing your compassion tonight . . .' He shook his head. 'At the very least, I want to feel the touch of your lips on mine.'

Bel stared at him, knowing she was on the precipice and that not a single part of her cared if she leapt off it.

'I am yours,' she murmured. And his lips fell upon hers.

And in the kitchen next door, the young boy slept peacefully for the first time in months.

25

When Bel arrived back at the *atelier* at five the following evening, she was full of trepidation. Not only for the fate of the young boy, but also to discover whether Laurent's declaration and kiss had merely been a reaction to the high emotion of last night.

'Aha!' said Landowski, who was cleaning himself up after a day's work. 'It's Saint Izabela herself!'

'How is he, professor?' she asked, blushing at his comment.

'Your foundling is currently sitting down to supper with my children,' said Landowski. 'Like you, when I called my wife in to see him sleeping like an emaciated rat on the kitchen floor, she immediately took pity on him. She insisted he have a good hosing-down outside in the garden and scrubbed him from head to toe with carbolic soap for fear of lice. Then she wrapped him in a blanket and put him to bed in our house.'

'Thank you, professor. I'm sorry to put this trouble on your household.'

'Well, if it was me, I'd have kicked him out on the street where he belongs, but you women, you all have soft hearts. And us men are thankful for them,' he added gently.

'Has he said yet where he's from?'

'No, because he hasn't uttered a word since my wife took charge of him. She thinks he is mute.'

'Monsieur, I know he isn't. He spoke to me just before I left him last night.'

'Did he? How interesting.' Landowski nodded thoughtfully. 'Well, so far he has not chosen to share his gift of speech with anyone else. He also carries a leather pouch slung around his body, which my wife discovered when she stripped off his filthy rags. He growled like a mad dog when she tried to remove it from him to wash him, and refused to let her take it. Well, we shall see. My guess is, from looking at him, that he is from Poland. It takes one to know one,' he added soberly. 'Goodnight.'

When Landowski left the *atelier*, Bel turned and saw Laurent smiling at her, his arms folded.

'Are you happy, now that your little waif is being taken care of?'

'Yes, and I must thank you for your part in helping him too.'

'How are you today, my Bel?'

'I am well, monsieur,' she whispered, averting her eyes.

'Not regretting what passed between us yesterday evening?' He held out his hands to her. And shyly, she lifted her own to meet them.

'No, not even for a moment.'

'Thank God for that,' he breathed, pulling her into the kitchen so they could not be seen from the windows, and kissing her equally passionately again.

And so their love affair began, innocent apart from the touch of their lips, both of them knowing the risk they were running if they were caught by Landowski, who had taken to returning to the *atelier* at odd hours to study his half-finished Christ. Laurent's hands worked faster on her sculpture than ever before, as he hurried to shape her face so there would be more snatched minutes together afterwards.

'My God, my Izabela, we have so little time left. This time next week, you will be sailing out of my life,' he said to her one night as she stood in his arms, her head resting on his shoulder as he held her. 'How will I be able to bear it?'

'How will I?'

'When I first saw you, of course I admired your beauty, and I admit to flirting with you,' he said as he tipped her chin up so he could see her eyes. 'And then, as you sat for me day after day, and began to reveal your soul, I found myself thinking of you long after you had left. And finally that night, when I saw your compassion for the boy, I knew that I loved you.' Laurent sighed and shook his head. 'This has never happened to me before. I never believed I'd feel this way about a woman. And as fate would have it, it has to be a woman who is promised to another and whom I'll never see again. It's a tragic situation that many of my writer friends would put in their books and poems. But sadly, for me it's real.'

'Yes, it is,' Bel sighed despairingly.

'Then, *ma chérie*, we must make the most of the time we have left.'

Bel floated through her last week in Paris in an ecstatic trance, unable to contemplate her imminent departure. She watched the maid bring her trunk into her bedroom and begin to fill it as if it belonged to someone else. Talk of her passage home and Maria Georgiana's fears that Bel would be travelling on the ship unaccompanied merely passed her by.

'Of course, it cannot be helped. You must return in order to prepare for your marriage, but you must swear that you will not disembark from the boat when it docks at any of the ports, especially not in Africa.'

'Of course,' Bel replied automatically. 'I'm sure I will be perfectly safe.'

'I have contacted the shipping company's office, and they have replied saying that the purser will find a suitable older woman who can chaperone you during your voyage.'

'Thank you, senhora,' Bel responded distractedly, hardly hearing as she pinned on her hat ready to leave for the *atelier*, her thoughts already with Laurent.

'Heitor tells me your sculpture is almost finished. So, tonight will be your last night at Landowski's studio. Tomorrow, our family wish to hold a farewell dinner in honour of you.' Maria Georgiana smiled at her.

Bel looked at her in barely disguised horror, then realised how churlish she must seem. 'Thank you, senhora. It is most kind of you.'

In the car on the drive to the *atelier*, the awful realisation that this was the last night she would ever see Laurent hit her with a jolt of terror.

When she arrived, Laurent was looking pleased and proud.

'After you left last night, I stayed up until dawn to finish it,' he said, indicating the sculpture which currently sat shielded from view under a dust sheet. 'Would you like to see it?'

'Yes, very much,' she muttered, not wishing to let her misery spoil Laurent's obvious excitement. He whipped off the protective sheet with a flourish to reveal it.

Bel stared at her image; as with any subject of a visual study, she was not immediately sure of her reaction. She could see he had caught her shape perfectly and the face that stared back was her own. But what struck her most about the sculpture was the stillness it evoked, as though she'd been captured in a moment of deep contemplation.

'I look . . . so alone. And sad,' she added. 'It's . . . stark, there's nothing frivolous about it.'

'No, which is, as you know, the style Landowski teaches and why I'm here in his *atelier*. He saw it before he left this evening, and told me it was the best piece of work I've ever produced.'

'Then I'm happy for you, Laurent,' Bel replied.

'Well, perhaps one day in the future, you will see it in an exhibition of my work and know that it is of you. And it will always remind you of me, and the beautiful interlude we spent together in Paris, once, long ago.'

'Don't! Please don't!' she moaned as her control left her and she placed her head in her hands. 'I can't bear it.'

'Izabela, please don't cry.' He was by her side immediately, an arm around her shoulder, comforting her. 'If I could change things, then I would, I swear. Remember, I'm free to love you; it's *you* who are not free to love me.'

'I know,' she said. 'And tonight will be our last night together, for just as I left the apartment, Maria Georgiana told me the da Silva Costa family are throwing a dinner for me tomorrow night. The following day, I board the ship to return to Rio. Besides, you have finished with me now.' Bel indicated her sculpture miserably.

'Bel, I can assure you, I have only just begun.'

She buried her head back into his shoulder. 'What can we do? What can be done?'

There was a pause before Laurent said, 'Don't go back to Brazil, Izabela. Stay in Paris with me.'

Bel drew in her breath, hardly believing the words she was hearing.

'Listen,' he said as he took her by the hand and dragged her over to the bench before sitting down next to her. 'You know I can offer you nothing compared to what your rich fiancé can give you. I have only an attic room in Montparnasse, which is like ice in the winter and a furnace in the summer. And only these hands with which to change my circumstances. But I swear I could love you, Izabela, like no other man could.'

Bel, nestled against him, listened to his words as if they were drops of water pouring into her parched mouth. As she sat there with his arm around her, she glimpsed a future with him for the first time . . . and it was so tantalisingly perfect that, despite all he'd said, she knew she must blank out the image from her mind.

'Laurent, you know that I cannot. It would destroy my parents; my marriage to Gustavo is the pinnacle of my father's dreams, what he has spent his life working towards. How could I do this to him, and to my sweet mother?'

'I understand that you can't, but I need you to understand before you leave how much I want you too.'

'I'm not like you.' Bel shook her head. 'Perhaps it's because our worlds are so different, or more simply that you are a man and I am a woman. But in my country, family means everything.'

'I respect that,' he said. 'Although it seems to me there is a point at which a person must stop thinking of others and think of themselves. Marrying a man you don't love and being thrown into a life you don't desire – in essence, sacrificing your own happiness – seems to me a step too far, even for the most devoted daughter.'

'I have no choice,' Bel replied despairingly.

'I understand why you think that, but as you know, every human being has free will; it's what differentiates us from the animals. And' – Laurent paused as he thought about his next sentence – 'what about your fiancé? You've told me he's in love with you?'

'Yes, I believe he is.'

'So how will he cope with being married to a woman who can never have the same feelings for him? Will your indifference, the fact that he is aware that you're marrying him out of duty, eventually eat into his soul?'

'My mother says I will grow to love him, and I have to believe her.'

'Well then.' Laurent's arm dropped from around her shoulder. 'I must wish you luck and a happy life. I think we're finished here.' He stood up abruptly and moved away from her back into the main space of the *atelier*.

'Please, Laurent, don't be like this. These are the last few moments we will ever spend together,' she begged him.

'Izabela, I have said all I can. I have declared my love and my devotion to you. I have asked you not to return home, but to stay here with me.' He shrugged sadly. 'I can do no more. Forgive me if I can't bear to hear you telling me that one day you may love your husband.'

Bel's mind was a blur of powerful contradictions. Her heart was pounding and she felt physically sick. She watched Laurent placing the dust sheet over her sculpture, hiding her from view as one would place a cover over a beloved relative who had just passed from the world. Whether the gesture was symbolic or practical, Bel did not know or care, but it roused her from the bench and she walked towards him.

'Laurent, please, you must give me time to think . . . I must think,' she sobbed, as she put her fingers to her temples.

Laurent paused, seeming to waver for a second before he spoke. 'I know you can't come here to the *atelier* again. But please, if it's the last thing I ever ask of you, will you meet me tomorrow afternoon in Paris?'

'Is there any point?'

'I beg you, Izabela. Just tell me where and when.'

She looked into his eyes and knew she was powerless to resist. 'By the south entrance to the park on Avenue de Marigny and Avenue Gabriel. Meet me there at three.'

He looked at her and nodded. 'I'll be there. Goodnight, my Bel.'

Bel left the *atelier*, for there was simply no more she could say now. Walking through the gardens, she spied the young boy standing alone, looking up at the stars. She walked over to him, and when he saw her, he smiled.

'Hello,' she said. 'You look much better. How are you feeling?'

He nodded at her, and she knew he understood.

'I'm leaving France the day after tomorrow, to return to

my home in Brazil.' Bel pulled a small notebook and a pencil from the purse she carried with her, and scribbled in it. 'If you ever need anything, please contact me. Here is my name and my parents' address.' She ripped the sheet of paper from the notebook and handed it to the boy, watching as he read it, mouthing the words carefully. Digging once more into her purse, she brought out a twenty-franc note. Pressing it into his small hands, she leaned forward and kissed him on the top of his head.

'Goodbye, *querido*, and good luck.'

Later, when Bel looked back on her time in Paris, one of the things she would remember vividly was the long, sleepless nights. As Maria Elisa slumbered contentedly in her bed, Bel would tweak the curtains open a fraction and sit on the window seat watching the Paris streets below her, dreaming of the delights outside.

This particular night, as she sat with her hot forehead pressed against the cool glass, was the longest of them all. And the questions she asked herself were ones that would determine her future.

When the dark night ended and her decision was made, she crept desolately back to bed as a grey dawn seeped through the gap in the curtains, echoing her mood.

'I have come to say goodbye,' she said as Laurent's look of hope disintegrated and fell like dust into the stony ground below him. 'I cannot betray my parents. You must understand why.'

He looked down at his feet. With effort, he said, 'I understand.'

'And now, it's best that I go. Thank you for coming to meet me, and I wish you all the joy and happiness that life can offer. I'm sure that one day I will hear of you and your sculptures again. And I am sure they will be talked about with reverence.'

Bel stood up, every single muscle in her body taut with the tension of holding her emotions in check, and reached up to kiss him on the cheek. 'Goodbye, Laurent, and God bless you.'

Then she began to walk away from him.

A few seconds later, she felt a hand on her shoulder.
'Bel, please, if you ever change your mind, know that I am waiting for you. *Au revoir*, my love.' And then he turned and ran swiftly across the grass in the opposite direction.

26

Somehow Bel got through the following twenty-four hours and the special dinner that had been prepared for her by the da Silva Costas.

'Sadly, we won't be there to celebrate with you on your wedding day,' Heitor said as the family toasted her with champagne. 'But we want to wish you and your fiancé all the happiness in the world.'

After dinner, they presented her with a beautiful Limoges china coffee pot and a set of cups, to remind her of the time she had spent in France. And as the family dispersed from the table, Heitor smiled at Bel.

'Are you happy to be going home, Izabela?'

'I am looking forward to seeing my family. And my fiancé, of course,' she added quickly. 'But I will miss Paris very much.'

'Perhaps one day, when you see the *Cristo* monument on the top of Corcovado Mountain, you will tell your children how you came to be present as it was created.'

'Yes, I feel honoured that I have been,' Bel agreed. 'How are you progressing with it?'

'As you know, Landowski has almost finished the

four-metre model, and now I must find somewhere to go which has room for me and my draftsmen to enlarge the scale to thirty metres. Landowski will begin work next week on the full-sized head and the hands. He told me when I last saw him that he had had Senhor Brouilly take casts of both your and Senhorita Lopes de Almeida's hands as possible proto-types. Who knows,' Heitor said, 'one day, those elegant fingers of yours may end up casting benediction on Rio from the top of Corcovado Mountain.'

Maria Georgiana insisted on coming with Maria Elisa to see Bel safely aboard her ship home. Thankfully, as soon as Bel had been installed in her cabin, she left the two girls alone for a few minutes as she bustled off to check arrangements with the purser. 'Be happy, dearest Izabela,' Maria Elisa said, kissing Bel goodbye.

'I will try,' she agreed, as her friend watched her face carefully.

'Is something wrong?'

'No, I . . . suppose I'm simply nervous about my wedding,' she replied.

'Well, write to me, and tell me all about it, and I will see you when I too am home in Rio. Bel, I . . .'

'What is it?'

The ship's bell rang out to give a thirty-minute warning.

'Remember this time in Paris, but please, try to embrace your future with Gustavo too.'

Bel stared at Maria Elisa and knew instinctively what she was saying to her.

'I will, I promise.'

Maria Georgiana reappeared in the cabin. 'The purser had a crowd of guests around him so I could not speak to him in person, but make sure that you introduce yourself to him. He already knows you're a woman travelling alone, and I'm sure he will provide someone suitable as a chaperone.'

'I will, I assure you. Goodbye, Senhora da Silva Costa. Thank you for all your kindness.'

'And you must swear to me that you won't set foot off this ship until you dock safely at Pier Mauá,' she added. 'The moment you're delivered safely to your parents, I would appreciate a telegram.'

'I assure you I will do so the second I arrive home.'

Bel followed them up onto the deck to say her final goodbyes. Once they had left, she went to lean on the railings. She looked out over the port of Le Havre, knowing it was her last glimpse of France.

Somewhere to the south lay Paris, and somewhere in it was Laurent. The ship began to move smoothly out of its berth, and Bel stood there gazing at the shoreline until it finally melted into the horizon.

'Goodbye, my love, goodbye,' she whispered. And, consumed by utter misery, she walked down to her cabin.

Bel took her supper in her room that evening, unable to face the jolly atmosphere of the dining room, full of happy occupants looking forward to the voyage. She lay on her bed, feeling the gentle rocking of the ship, and, as night fell, watched her porthole become as black as her heart.

She'd wondered whether, when she left terra firma, and the ship and her life were pointed towards home, the dreadful pain in her heart would begin to ease. After all, she would see her beloved mother and father and be back in the familiarity of her own country.

Plans were already well underway for the wedding day itself and Antonio had written in a state of high excitement, saying they were to be married in Rio's beautiful cathedral, an honour only rarely bestowed.

But try as she might, as the ship moved further and further away from Laurent, her heart felt as heavy as the stone boulders that sat at the back of Landowski's *atelier*.

'Blessed Virgin,' she prayed, as tears spilled down her face and onto her pillow. 'Give me the strength to live without him, for at this very moment, I don't know how I can bear it.'

Maia

June 2007

Full Moon

13; 49; 44

27

When I'd finished reading the last letter, I saw that it was past midnight. Izabela Bonifacio was on board the steamer, facing the return to a man she did not love and leaving Laurent Brouilly behind.

L a u . . .

With excitement coursing through my veins, I realised I now knew the origin of the first three letters on the back of the soapstone tile; Laurent, Bel's secret love. And the sculpture of the woman on the chair in the garden of the Casa must surely be the very one that Bel had sat for during those heady days in Paris? Though how it had made its way across the sea to Brazil, I had no idea.

Tomorrow, I would not only reread the letters – I'd been so eager to discover the story I knew I hadn't taken in the detail – but also look up Monsieur Laurent Brouilly on the internet. His name certainly rang a bell. But for now, exhausted, I removed my clothes, pulled the sheet around me and fell asleep with my hand still resting on my history.

I was awoken by a harsh jangling noise, and it took my disoriented senses a few seconds to compute that it was the telephone by the bed making the discordant sound. Reaching over to the side table, I put the receiver to my ear and muttered, 'Hello?'

'Maia, it's Floriano. How are you feeling?'

'I'm . . . better,' I said, immediately feeling guilty for the lie I'd told him the night before.

'Good. Are you up to meeting today? I have a lot to tell you.'

And I you, I thought, but didn't say. 'Of course I am.'

'The weather is beautiful, so let's take a walk along the beach. Shall I see you at eleven in the lobby downstairs?'

'Yes, but please, Floriano, if you have other things to do, I—'

'Maia, I'm a novelist, and any diversion that gives me an excuse not to sit down at my desk and write is always a welcome one. See you in an hour.'

Ordering breakfast from room service, I reread the first few letters in order to have them clearer in my mind. Then, seeing the time, took a fast shower and presented myself in the lobby promptly at eleven.

Floriano was already waiting for me, sitting reading a page from a bulging plastic wallet that sat on his lap.

'Morning,' I greeted him.

'Morning,' he replied, glancing up at me. 'You look well.'

'Yes, I'm fine,' I said, sitting down next to him and deciding to tell him the truth immediately. 'Floriano, it wasn't just my stomach that kept me in my room last night. Yara, the elderly maid, handed me a package just before we left the Casa yesterday,' I confessed. 'And swore me to secrecy.'

'I see.' Floriano raised an eyebrow at my news. 'And what did this package contain?'

'Letters, written by Izabela Bonifacio to her maid at the time. A woman called Loen Fagundes. She was Yara's mother.'

'Right.'

'I'm sorry I didn't tell you about the letters yesterday. I just wanted to read them through before I did. And swear to me you won't breathe a word about them to anyone else. Yara was terrified of Senhora Carvalho finding out that she'd given the letters to me.'

'Of course. No problem. I understand.' He nodded sagely. 'After all, it's your family history, not mine. And I think you're someone who always finds it difficult to trust. I'm sure you have many other secrets you keep to yourself. So, do you want to share the content of the letters with me or not? It is up to you and I won't be at all offended if you say no.'

'Yes, of course I'm happy to share them,' I confirmed, discomfited by his incisive assessment of me, which mirrored the essence of what Pa had said in his letter.

'Then we walk and talk at the same time.'

I followed Floriano out of the lobby and together we crossed the road onto the wide promenade that fronted the beach. Its many kiosks, which sold fresh coconut water, beer and snacks to beach-goers, were already busy with customers.

'We will walk up to Copacabana and I shall show you where your great-grandmother had her grand wedding.'

'And her eighteenth birthday party,' I added.

'Yes, I have some photos of that too taken from the newspaper archives in the *biblioteca*. So,' he suggested, 'if you're comfortable doing so, Maia, tell me all you have discovered.'

As we strolled along Ipanema Beach, I told him in as much detail as I could what I had learned from the letters.

When we arrived at what Floriano told me was Copacabana Beach, we walked as far as the famous Copacabana Palace Hotel. Newly refurbished and completely unmissable, it gleamed bright white in the sunshine, one of the most iconic jewels in Rio's architectural crown.

'It's certainly impressive,' I said, gazing up at the facade. 'I can see why this would have been the obvious choice for Bel and Gustavo's wedding. I can just imagine her standing there in her beautiful wedding dress, being feted by the great and the good of Rio.'

The morning sun was very strong now, so we took two stools under a shady umbrella at one of the beach kiosks. He ordered a beer for himself and a coconut water for me.

'The first thing to tell you is that my friend in the UV imaging department of the Museu da República has confirmed the two names on the back of the soapstone tile. He's still working on the date and the inscription, but the names are definitely "Izabela Aires Cabral" and "Laurent Brouilly". Of course, thanks to the letters, we both now know irrefutably who Bel's amour in Paris was. He went on to become a very well-known sculptor back in France. Here.' Floriano pulled some pages out of his plastic wallet and handed them to me. 'These are some of his works.'

I looked at the grainy images of Laurent Brouilly's sculptures. They were mostly simple human shapes, similar to the one I'd seen in the garden of A Casa das Orquídeas. And a large number of men clad in old-fashioned soldiers' uniforms.

'He made his name as a sculptor during the Second World War, in which he also fought as part of the Resistance,' Floriano clarified. 'His page on Wikipedia says he was honoured for bravery. Definitely a very interesting man. Here, this is a photograph of him. You might notice that he was certainly not unattractive,' he added.

I studied Laurent's handsome face. With his strong features, chiselled jaw and razor-sharp cheekbones, he looked distinctly Gallic.

'And here are Gustavo and Izabela on their wedding day.'

I stared at the photograph, bypassing Izabela to look at Gustavo first. The contrast with Laurent could not have been more marked. His insubstantial physique, coupled with his small and pointed features, made me understand why Bel and Maria Elisa had likened him to a ferret. But I could see there was kindness in his eyes.

Then I glanced at Izabela, her features so like my own. And was about to put the photo down, when I noticed the necklace she was wearing.

'Oh my God!'

'What?'

'Look.' I indicated what Floriano should concentrate on in the photograph, my fingers instinctively clasping the moonstone around my own neck.

He studied both the picture and me carefully. 'Yes, Maia. It seems they are one and the same.'

'That was the reason Yara gave me the letters. She said she recognised the necklace.'

'So now you finally believe you are related to the Aires Cabrals?' He smiled at me.

'Yes, I do,' I said, genuinely convinced for the first time. 'It's irrefutable proof,' I agreed.

'You must be happy.'

'I am, but . . .' I put the pages down and sighed. Floriano lit a cigarette and stared at me.

'What is it?'

'She left the man she loved in France to marry Gustavo Aires Cabral, whom she didn't. It's very sad.'

'You are a romantic, Maia?'

'No, but if you'd read the letters Izabela wrote to her maid about her love for Laurent Brouilly, you couldn't help but be moved by the story.'

'Well, I hope you'll allow me to do that very soon.'

'Of course,' I said. 'Although, perhaps Izabela's feelings for Laurent were just a crush and nothing more.'

'True,' he agreed. 'But if so, why did your father give you that soapstone tile as a clue to your history? It would have been far simpler to have included a photograph of Izabela and her husband.'

'I don't know,' I sighed. 'And maybe I never will. I mean, I have no more letters after October 1928, when she left Paris and returned to Rio. So, I have to presume that she married Gustavo and settled down with him here.'

'Actually, I don't think that *was* the whole story,' Floriano said, producing another photocopied picture and passing it across to me. 'That was taken in January 1929. It shows the plaster mould of the *Cristo*'s head just after it had been taken off the ship that had brought it across from France. That strange-looking object next to it is actually a giant-sized palm of a hand. There are two men in this picture. One of them I recognise as Heitor Levy, the project manager for the construction of the *Cristo*. Now look closely at the other man.' Floriano indicated the figure with his finger.

I stared at the features of the man leaning against the

Cristo's hand. I double checked it against the image Floriano had handed me only minutes earlier.

'My God, it's Laurent Brouilly!'

'Yes, it is.'

'So he was here in Rio?'

'So it seems. I suppose it doesn't take a genius to surmise that he was over here from France because of the *Cristo* project.'

'And perhaps to see Izabela?' I queried.

'As an historian, one should never make such assumptions, especially as you've only read about Izabela's feelings towards Laurent. We can't be sure of how he felt about her,' Floriano reminded me.

'True. But in her letters, she talks about sitting in Paul Landowski's studio for the sculpture that now stands in the gardens of A Casa das Orquídeas. She also tells Loen, her maid, that Laurent begged her to stay in France and not to return to Brazil. I wonder if he followed her here . . . But how do we discover whether they *did* meet again after he arrived in Rio?'

'We ask your friend Yara, the maid,' shrugged Floriano. 'If she gave you those letters, I think it's safe to say that, for whatever reason, she wants you to know the truth.'

'But she's terrified of her mistress. Giving me the letters is one thing, but speaking to me about what else she knows about my own heritage is another.'

'Maia,' Floriano said firmly, 'stop being so defeatist. She's already trusted you enough to hand over the letters. Now, how about we walk back to your hotel and I read them?'

'Okay,' I agreed.

While Floriano sat in my suite and began to read Bel's letters, I crossed back over the road to Ipanema Beach and went for an exhilarating swim in the fierce waves of the Atlantic Ocean. Drying myself in the sun, I decided that Floriano was right and I mustn't be frightened of pursuing the story I had travelled halfway across the world to discover.

As I lay there on the warm sand, I wondered whether my reluctance was something to do with the fact that every step would take me closer to discovering the truth about my real parents. I had no idea if they were alive or dead, or, in fact, why Pa Salt had given me a clue that had led me much further back into the past than logically I needed to go.

And why was Senhora Carvalho so intent on refusing to admit that her daughter had even *had* a child? A young woman who had definitely been the right age to be my mother . . .

Yet again, I remembered Pa Salt's words engraved on the armillary sphere.

I couldn't and shouldn't run away.

'Are you happy to take a trip back up to the Casa with me to see if Yara will tell us more?' I asked Floriano as I arrived back in the hotel suite.

'Sure,' he said, not looking up from the letter he was reading. 'I've only a couple more letters to go.'

'I'll take a shower while you finish.'

'Okay.'

After I'd closed the bathroom door behind me and removed my clothes, I stepped into the shower, feeling acutely aware of Floriano's presence in the next room. Given that he'd been a total stranger to me only two days ago, his easy-going attitude and relaxed manner made me feel as if I'd known him for far longer.

And yet, his book I'd translated was philosophical, moving and full of human angst. So I supposed I'd expected someone who took himself far more seriously than the man currently sitting only a few feet away from me next door. Emerging from the bathroom, I saw that Floriano had placed the letters neatly in a pile and was staring out of the window towards the beach.

'Do you want to put these in the safe?' he asked me.

'Yes.'

He handed them to me and I moved to open it.

'Thank you, Maia,' he said suddenly.

'What for?' I asked, as I tapped in my security code.

'For allowing me to be privy to those letters. I'm sure there are many of my colleagues who would love to have had the privilege of reading them. The fact that your great-grandmother was actually there at the time our *Cristo* was being constructed, staying under the same roof as Heitor da Silva Costa and his family and actually sitting in Landowski's *atelier* while he was making the moulds, is really astonishing. I'm honoured, truly,' he said, offering me a small mock bow.

'It's you who deserves thanks. You've already helped me so much in putting some of the pieces of the jigsaw puzzle together.'

'Well, let's drive up to the Casa and see if we can add a few more.'

'You would have to wait outside, Floriano. I promised

Yara I wouldn't tell anyone about the letters. I don't want to break her trust.'

'Then I will simply provide a chauffeur service for the senhorita.' He grinned at me. 'Shall we go?'

We left the suite to walk in the direction of the lift and Floriano pressed the button to call it. As it opened and we stepped inside, I saw he was studying my reflection in the mirrored walls.

'You have a tan. It suits you. Now,' he added as the doors opened onto the lobby and he marched through it purposefully, 'onwards and upwards.'

Twenty minutes later, we were parked on the opposite side of the road from the Casa. The two of us had driven past the rusting iron gates and seen that they had been heavily padlocked since our visit the day before.

'What's happened?' I said, as we both climbed out of the car. 'Do you think it's because Senhora Carvalho thought we'd be back?'

'Your guess is as good as mine,' replied Floriano, walking away from me along the length of the overgrown hedge. 'I'm going to investigate if there's another way in, legal or illegal.'

I stared through the iron bars at the house beyond, disappointment and frustration coursing through my veins. Perhaps our visit had simply been coincidence and there had already been a plan for the old woman and Yara to leave the house – to visit relatives perhaps. But it was in this moment that I realised how desperately I wanted to know the past I was now convinced belonged to me.

Floriano appeared by my side. 'The place is like a fortress. I've walked all the way around the perimeter and, short of slashing our way through the hedge with a chainsaw, there's no way in. When I peered through the hedge at the back of the house, I saw that even the rear window shutters are closed. It looks like the place has been shut up completely and there's no one at home.'

'What if they don't come back?' I asked, hearing the frustration in my voice.

'There's no saying they won't, Maia. It could simply be a case of bad timing. Look, at least there's a post box for the house, so I suggest you leave Yara a note with the address of your hotel and a contact number.'

'But what if the old woman is the one to find it?'

'I can absolutely guarantee that Senhora Carvalho will not arrive back and rifle through the contents of her post box. She's a woman from a different era and that's her maid's job. It's probably handed to her on a silver salver,' he said with a grin.

'All right,' I agreed reluctantly, as I dug my notebook and pen out from my handbag before scribbling a note to Yara as Floriano had suggested.

'There's nothing more we can do here. Come on,' he said as I opened the rusty metal flap and dropped the note inside.

I was initially silent on the twenty-minute journey back to downtown Rio, deflated after the excitement of reading the letters and wanting to know more.

'I hope you're not thinking of giving up.' Floriano read my thoughts as we drove along Ipanema Beach.

'Of course not. But I really don't know where I should go from here.'

'Patience is the key, Maia. We will simply have to wait and see if Yara responds to your note. And of course we must continue to check on the Casa to see whether they reappear. Normally under these circumstances there's no great mystery, just a perfectly rational reason. So, in the meantime, I suggest we think of what the explanation could be.'

'They've gone away to visit relatives?' I voiced my earlier thought.

'A possibility, but given how frail the old woman seemed, I doubt she was up to long journeys. Or any pleasant small talk once she'd arrived.'

'Then maybe they've left because they're scared we'll return?'

'Again, a possibility, but unlikely. Senhora Carvalho has lived in that house for all of her life, and even though she didn't seem keen to discuss your possible relationship to her, we were hardly wielding guns and knives,' he mused as he drove. 'Personally, I think there's only one reason that neither mistress nor servant are at home at present.'

'And what's that?'

'That Senhora Carvalho has been taken ill, and has had to be moved to a hospital. So, I think I shall call the local ones and see if my dear "great-aunt" has been admitted to any of them in the past twenty-four hours.'

I looked at Floriano in admiration. 'You could well be right.'

'We'll go back to my apartment and I'll look up the local hospital numbers, then call around them,' he said, taking a right turn off the Avenida Vieira Souto instead of continuing along the seafront to my hotel.

'Please, Floriano, I don't want to bother you. I can do it on my laptop.'

'Maia, will you please shut up. The letters I read this morning are some of the most interesting I've ever laid eyes on as an historian. There's also something else in them that I haven't told you about yet, which makes them still more fascinating. And perhaps even solves a long-standing mystery about the *Cristo*. So please believe that we are helping each other. I'm warning you, though, my home isn't exactly the Copacabana Palace,' he cautioned as we continued to head away from Ipanema Beach.

Shortly afterwards, Floriano made a sharp right turn and pulled his car up on a small concrete strip in front of a crumbling apartment building. It was probably only five or ten minutes' walk from the hotel, yet it felt like a different world.

'So,' he said, as we got out of the car and climbed up the steps to the front door. 'Welcome to *chez moi*. There's no lift, I'm afraid.' He opened the front door and began to bound up the narrow staircase two steps at a time.

I followed him up and up, and up again, until we arrived on a small landing and unlocked the door.

'I'm not the world's greatest domestic, but it's home,' he warned me again. 'Please come in.'

Floriano walked through the door as I stood on the threshold, experiencing a fleeting moment of trepidation that I was entering the apartment of a man who was, to all intents and purposes, a stranger. I pushed the thought away, remembering the first night we'd met, when he'd had to return home to let in the girl he lived with, and followed him inside.

The sitting room we entered was as Floriano had described: a jumbled melange of objects used and never returned to their rightful place. A battered leather sofa and armchair formed a seating arrangement and a coffee table overflowed with books, papers, a food-encrusted bowl and a brimming ashtray.

'I'll take you upstairs. It's far more pleasant up there, I swear,' he said, walking along the corridor.

Climbing another flight of stairs, we arrived on a tiny landing which had two doors. Floriano opened one of them to reveal a terrace, the majority of which was protected by a sloping roof. Beneath it was a sofa, a table and chairs and a desk in the corner which held a laptop, above which was a shelf of books. The front of the terrace beyond the overhang of the roof was open to the elements, and all along the balcony edge pots full of flowers added vibrancy and colour to the atmosphere.

'This is where I live and work. Make yourself comfortable,' he said, strolling to his desk, opening his laptop and sitting down.

I walked to the edge of the terrace and immediately felt the burning sun on my face. Leaning on my elbows, I looked upwards to see a small city of buildings tumbling haphazardly down the hill only a few hundred metres away. From the tops of the buildings, I could see kites flying in the breeze and hear the muffled thrum of what sounded like drums.

After the sterility of my hotel room, I suddenly felt I had a finger on the real, throbbing pulse of the city. 'It's beautiful here,' I breathed. 'Is that a *favela*?' I pointed into the air at the houses on the mountainside beyond us.

'Yes, and until a few years ago, a very dangerous one. Drugs and murders were commonplace, and even though it backs onto Ipanema, one of the most exclusive areas in Rio, no one would live in the streets nearby,' Floriano explained. 'But now it's been cleaned up and the government has even provided a lift for its residents. Some said the money would have been better used for some kind of basic healthcare provision for them, but at least it's a start.'

'But Brazil is becoming very prosperous, isn't it?' I queried.

'Yes, but as with any fast-growing economy, to begin with it's a tiny percentage of the population that gains from the new-found wealth, and little changes for the vast majority who are poor. It's the same in India and Russia at present. Anyway,' Floriano sighed, 'let's not get onto the topic of social injustice here in Brazil. It's my favourite hobby horse, and we have other things to discuss.' He turned his attention back to the computer. 'Now, I'm assuming that Senhora Carvalho is one of the lucky few who can afford to avoid the appalling public hospitals here in Rio. So I'm looking for a list of the private ones and then we can call them. Here we are.' I walked back towards him and leant over his shoulder to study the screen. 'So, we have approximately ten. I'll print off their telephone numbers.'

'Why don't we take half each?' I suggested.

'Okay,' he agreed. 'But just make sure you announce yourself as a close relative to the switchboard, maybe a granddaughter' – Floriano shot me an ironic glance – 'otherwise they won't give you any information.'

For the next fifteen minutes, Floriano disappeared downstairs with his mobile and I remained up on the terrace with mine, working through the list of numbers. None of them brought any joy, with everyone we spoke to confirming that a Senhora Carvalho had not been admitted in the past twenty-four hours. When Floriano eventually reappeared carrying a tray, his face told a similar story.

'Don't look so downhearted, Maia,' he said as he placed a platter of different kinds of cheeses, salamis and a fresh baguette onto the table. 'Let's eat and think.'

I ate hungrily, realising it was now past six in the evening and I hadn't eaten since breakfast. 'What was the mystery you thought might be solved by something you'd read in Bel's letters?' I prompted him, as he finished eating and wandered across to the open part of the terrace to light a cigarette.

'Well,' he said, leaning over the balcony and gazing out into the descending dusk. 'The young woman whom Bel mentions in her letters, Margarida Lopes de Almeida, was always thought to have been the model that Landowski used for the *Cristo*'s hands. In the letters, Bel confirms that Margarida was indeed in Landowski's *atelier* and was also a gifted pianist. For her entire life, Margarida never denied the rumour that they were indeed her hands that graced the sculpture. And then, on her deathbed a few years ago, she retracted, saying that they were not her hands Landowski had used.'

Floriano watched me to see if I could follow where he was leading.

'Bel writes that she also had her hands cast by Landowski at the same time as Margarida,' I answered.

'Exactly. Of course, it may be that neither of the moulds Landowski took were used in his final sculpture, but perhaps Margarida always knew there was some doubt. Who knows? Maybe instead the hands were those of Izabela, the young woman who was with her at the *atelier* at the time.'

'My God,' I breathed, hardly able to compute the enormity of what Floriano was suggesting. That it might actually be my great-grandmother's hands that reached out so iconically, loving and protecting the world beneath them.

'To be honest, I doubt we will ever be able to ascertain the truth of the matter, but you can understand why the letters have excited me so much,' said Floriano. 'And would excite many others too, if Yara ever agrees to you sharing their contents with the world. So, not just for the sake of discovering your own heritage, Maia, but for that of Brazil's too, we must not give up on trying to find out more.'

'No, we mustn't,' I agreed. 'But surely now we've come to a dead end?'

'Which we have simply to reverse out of before planning another route forward.'

'Well, there was one other thing I was thinking earlier,' I said.

'And what would that be?' Floriano encouraged.

'Yara made it very clear that her mistress was seriously ill. That Senhora Carvalho was dying. At the time, I thought that Yara was perhaps using this as an excuse to get rid of us. But Senhora Carvalho certainly looked frail and the table next to her was full of pill bottles. What I'm trying to say is that in Switzerland, if someone was reaching the end of their life and they were in terrible pain, they would go into a hospice. Do you have those here in Brazil?'

'For the rich, yes, we do. As a matter of fact, there's one just outside Rio which is run by nuns. And certainly the Aires Cabrals were a devout Catholic family. You know, Maia, you could be right.' Floriano stood up and was just making his way across to his computer when the door burst open. A small, dark-eyed child in a Hello Kitty T-shirt and pink shorts hurtled across the room and threw herself into his arms.

'Papai!'

'Hello, *minha pequena*. How was your day?' he asked, smiling down at her.

'It was good, but I missed you.'

My eyes then turned to the open door where a young, willowy female was standing. Her eyes fell on me briefly and she smiled a 'hello', then turned back to the child. 'Come now, Valentina, your father is busy and you need a shower. We went to the beach after school as the weather was so warm,' the woman added to neither of us in particular.

'Can't I stay up here with you for a while, Papai?' Valentina pouted as her father set her back down on the floor.

'You go and take a shower and when you're ready for bed, bring up your book and I'll read the next chapter to you.' He kissed her tenderly on the top of her dark head before nudging her gently towards the young woman. 'See you later, *querida*.'

'I must go too,' I said, standing up as the door closed behind them. 'I've taken up enough of your time already.'

'Not until we've contacted the convent hospice I'm thinking of,' said Floriano, sitting down at his laptop.

'Your daughter is beautiful. She looks like you,' I commented. 'How old is she?'

'Six,' he replied as he tapped away on the keyboard. 'Right, here we are. There's a telephone number, although I doubt they'd have a manned reception at this time of night. However, I'll try it.'

I watched him as he dialled the number from the screen into his mobile and put it to his ear. A few seconds later, he tapped it off. 'As I thought, there's an emergency out-of-hours number, but I think it would alert too much suspicion for us to use it. A worried relative calling a hospital when they can't locate their nearest and dearest is one thing, but it's pretty unlikely that close family members wouldn't be aware that their relative had entered a hospice. So, I suggest we simply present ourselves in person there tomorrow.'

'It may well be another blind alley.'

'Yes, it might be, but my instinct tells me it's the only thing that makes sense. Well done, Maia,' he said, giving me a warm smile of approval. 'I'll turn you into an historical detective yet.'

'We will see tomorrow. And for now, I'll leave you in peace,' I said, standing up.

'I'll give you a lift back to the hotel.' Floriano rose too.

'Really, I can walk,' I said firmly.

'Okay. Can we say twelve o'clock tomorrow? I have a parent–teacher meeting at nine thirty. They think Valentina might be dyslexic,' he said with a sigh.

'Of course. And I'm sorry to hear that. Although Electra, one of my sisters, is dyslexic. And she's one of the smartest people I know,' I said to comfort him. 'Goodnight, Floriano.'

28

When I woke up the next morning, I took Yara's letters out of the safe and reread the ones that Bel had sent to Loen from Paris. This time, instead of desperately searching for clues to my own heritage, I revisited them as Floriano – the historian – had. And I understood why he was so excited about them. I put the letters down and lay back on my pillows, thinking about him and his pretty daughter, and the mother, who, to my eyes, had seemed at the very most to be in her early twenties.

For some reason, I was surprised that Floriano had chosen such a young woman as his partner. And if I was honest, I'd felt the tiniest prick of jealousy when mother and daughter had appeared in the apartment last night. Sometimes it seemed the whole world was in love except for me.

I showered, dressed and went downstairs to the lobby to meet Floriano. For the first time, he wasn't there, so I sat down to wait for him. He arrived fifteen minutes later, look-ing uncharacteristically harassed.

'My apologies, Maia. My meeting at the school went on longer than I'd anticipated.'

'No problem at all,' I assured him as we climbed into the Fiat. 'Did it go well?'

'If being told your precious child has a problem can ever go "well",' he sighed. 'At least the dyslexia's been identified at an early stage, so I hope that Valentina will be able to get the help and support she needs. But obviously, as I'm a writer, it's sad and ironic that my child will have a lifelong struggle with words.'

'I can see that must hurt. I'm sorry,' I offered, not sure what else to say.

'She's such a good girl and she hasn't had an easy life.'

'Well, from what I saw last night, she certainly has two loving parents at least.'

'*One* loving parent,' Floriano contradicted me. 'Sadly, my wife died when Valentina was a baby. She went into hospital for a simple operation, returned from it two days later and the wound became infected. Of course we sought immediate medical help and were told it would heal in time. Two weeks later, Andrea was dead of septicaemia. So you can understand why I have so little regard for the Brazilian health service.'

'I'm so sorry, Floriano. I thought last night that . . .'

'That Petra was her mother?' Floriano shot me a grin as his features relaxed a little. 'Maia, she's not even twenty, but I'm flattered that you think an old man like me could attract such a young and beautiful woman.'

'Oh,' I said, blushing. 'Sorry.'

'Petra is a university student and she has a bedroom in my apartment in return for some childcare, especially during the school holidays. Thankfully, Valentina's grandparents live not far away and have her to stay often, especially when I'm writing. They offered to have her live with them permanently when my wife died, but I refused. It can get complicated sometimes, but we seem to get through somehow. And it helps that she's such an easy child.'

I looked at Floriano again through new eyes, and realised this man never ceased to surprise me. It also made me ponder how empty my own life was in comparison to the complexity of his.

'Do you have children, Maia?' he asked me.

'No,' I said abruptly.

'Any plans for them in the future?'

'I doubt it. I don't have anyone special to provide me with any.'

'So, have you even been in love, Maia?'

'Once, yes, but it didn't work out.'

'I'm sure someone will come along. It's hard being alone. Even though I have Valentina, I still struggle sometimes.'

'At least it's safe,' I murmured before I could stop myself.

'Safe?' he said as he shot me an odd glance. '*Meu Deus*, Maia! My life has had considerable moments of deep pain, especially when my wife died. But "safe" is something I've never aspired to.'

'I didn't mean it like that,' I backtracked wildly, blushing with embarrassment.

'You know, I think you *did* and I find it very sad. Besides, hiding away from the world never works, because you still have to meet yourself in the mirror every morning. You'd make a terrible gambler.' He smiled suddenly, sensing my tension and wanting to ease it. 'Now, what is the plan when we get to the convent?'

'What do you suggest?' I asked, shaken from our previous exchange.

'We ask if your grandmother has been admitted, I suppose. And take it from there.'

'Okay.'

The rest of the journey passed in silence, with me still regretting my instinctive comment and smarting from Floriano's reaction to it. I glanced out of the window at the view as we drove away from the city and the road began to climb upwards.

Eventually, we turned along a winding gravel track and arrived in front of a large, austere grey stone building. The convent of *São Sebastião*, the patron saint of Rio, had been built two hundred years ago and, from the look of it, not modernised much since.

'Shall we?' he asked me, then gave my hand a reassuring squeeze.

'Yes,' I replied, as we both climbed out of the car and walked towards the entrance.

We went inside and found ourselves in a large, echoing hallway. It was completely deserted, and I looked at Floriano askance.

'As this is a functioning convent, rather than just a hospice, it probably has a hospital wing on the side of it. Ah, here we are,' he said as we came to halt in front of an old-fashioned Bakelite buzzer mounted on the wall near the door. He pressed it and a loud ringing emanated from somewhere inside the building. A few seconds later, a nun appeared in the entrance hall and walked towards us.

'Can I help you?'

'Yes, we believe that my wife's grandmother has admitted herself to the convent,' said Floriano. 'We weren't expecting her to come here so soon and we're obviously concerned for her state of health.'

'What is the name of the patient?'

'Senhora Beatriz Carvalho,' Floriano replied. 'She may well have come here with her maid, Yara.'

The nun surveyed us, then finally nodded. 'Yes, she and her maid are here. But it isn't visiting hours for relatives at present and Senhora Carvalho has requested that she be left in peace. You will obviously know how sick she is.'

'Of course,' Floriano agreed calmly. 'We do not wish to disturb Senhora Carvalho, but perhaps it's possible for us to speak to Yara, her maid, to ask if there's anything she needs from her home? We would be happy to go and get it for her.'

'Wait here, and I'll see if I can find Senhora Canterino.'

The nun turned and walked away from us and I looked at Floriano in admiration. 'Well done,' I said.

'Well, let's see if Yara will talk to us, because I'm telling you now, I'd prefer to face a gang of armed bandits than I would a group of nuns who are protecting one of their flock in her last days on earth.'

'At least we now know where she is.'

'Yes. You see, Maia?' he encouraged me. 'When you trust your instincts, they're often proved right.'

To distract myself while we waited, I walked outside and sat down on a bench which was placed at a vantage point giving a beautiful view of Rio below. Its hectic streets seemed like a distant dream up here, I mused, as the Angelus bell struck noon, calling the nuns to prayer. I felt the peaceful atmosphere calm me and thought that I too would be happy to spend my last days here. It was as if the convent was suspended somewhere between the earth below and heaven above.

A hand tapped me on the shoulder, making me jump out of my reverie. I turned round and saw Floriano with Yara next to him, looking distinctly agitated.

'I'll leave you two ladies alone for a while,' Floriano said diplomatically, and walked away through the gardens.

I stood up. 'Hello. Thank you for coming out to see me.'

'How did you find us?' Yara hissed, as if her mistress, far away inside the thick walls of the convent, might hear. 'Senhora Carvalho would be very distressed if she knew you were here.'

'Won't you sit down?' I gestured to the bench.

'I can only stay a few minutes, for if Senhora Carvalho found out I was talking to you . . .'

'I promise that I will leave you both in peace as soon as I can. But Yara, having read the letters you gave me, surely you can understand why I was desperate to speak to you again?'

Finally, she sank down onto the bench. 'Yes,' she said with a sigh. 'I've regretted giving them to you ever since.'

'Then why did you?'

'Because . . .' Yara shrugged her bony shoulders. 'Something told me I should. What you must understand is that Senhora Carvalho knows very little of her mother's past. Her father protected her from it after . . .' She nervously smoothed her skirt with her thin hands.

'After what?' I persisted.

She shook her head. 'I can't speak to you here. Please, you don't understand anything. Senhora Carvalho has come here to die. She is very sick and only has a short time left. She must be left in peace.'

'I understand. But senhora, please tell me if you know what happened when Izabela Bonifacio returned from Paris?'

329

'She married your great-grandfather, Gustavo Aires Cabral.'

'I know that much, but what about Laurent Brouilly? I know for a fact he was here in Brazil. I've seen a photograph of him in Rio with the *Cristo*. I—'

'Hush!' said Yara, glancing about her anxiously. 'Please! We must not talk of these things here.'

'Then where, and when?' I urged her, seeing she was torn between loyalty to her mistress and her desire to speak further. 'Please, Yara, I swear I'm not here to make trouble, I just want to know where I came from. Surely that's the right of every human being? And if you do know, I beg you to tell me. Then I promise I'll go away.'

I watched as she stared into the distance, her eyes falling on the *Cristo*, his head and hands currently masked by a cloud.

'All right. But not here. Tomorrow I must return to the Casa to collect some possessions Senhora Carvalho has asked me for. I will meet you there at two o'clock. Now please, leave!'

Yara was already standing and I followed suit.

'Thank you,' I called to her as she walked quickly away from me and disappeared inside the entrance to the convent. I saw Floriano leaning against his car and made my way towards him.

'Success?' he asked me.

'She'll meet me at the Casa tomorrow afternoon,' I replied as he opened the passenger door for me and I climbed in.

'That's fantastic news, Maia,' he said as he started the engine and we sped off.

As we approached the city, I realised I was on the verge of tears.

'Are you okay?' Floriano asked me as we came to a halt outside the hotel.

'Yes, thank you,' I replied abruptly, not trusting myself to say any more because I could hear the wobble in my own voice.

'Would you like to come round later this evening? Apparently, Valentina is cooking me supper tonight. You'd be welcome to join us.'

'No, I wouldn't want to intrude.'

'You won't be, really. Actually, it's my birthday today,' he said with a shrug. 'Anyway, as I said, you're very welcome.'

'Happy birthday,' I said, feeling either irrationally guilty for not knowing, or hurt that he hadn't told me this sooner. And I wasn't sure which.

'Thanks. Well, if you won't join us this evening, shall I collect you tomorrow and drive you up to the Casa?'

'Really, Floriano, you've done enough. I can take a cab.'

'Maia, please, it would be my pleasure,' he reassured me. 'I can see that you're upset. Do you want to talk about it?'

'No. I'll be fine tomorrow after a good night's sleep.' I made to open the passenger door, but as I did so, he placed a gentle hand on my wrist.

'Remember that you're grieving. You only lost your father a couple of weeks ago and this . . . odyssey back into your past must be emotionally unsettling on top of it. Try to be kind to yourself, Maia,' he added softly. 'If you need me, you know where I am.'

'Thank you.' I climbed out of the car, walked swiftly through the hotel lobby and took the lift to my floor. Once in the sanctuary of my room, I let the tears flow. Though precisely *what* I was crying about, I had no idea.

Eventually, I fell asleep, and awoke feeling calmer. It was past four o'clock, so I took myself off to the beach and had a swim in the bracing Atlantic waves. As I wandered back to the hotel, I thought about Floriano and the fact that it was his birthday. He'd been so very kind to me, perhaps the least I could do was to take round a bottle of wine as a gift.

As I showered the beach from my body, I imagined Valentina, Floriano's six-year-old daughter, making him supper on his birthday. The image was so poignant I could hardly bear it. Floriano had brought her up almost entirely single-handedly, even though he could easily have handed her over to her grandparents.

I knew that witnessing father and daughter together and the obvious love they shared was what had destabilised me earlier. Not to mention Floriano's incisive comments about me on the drive up to the convent.

Maia, you have to get over yourself, I told myself firmly, aware that all that had happened and was happening to me was making me feel as though my protective outer shell was slowly being peeled away, revealing my vulnerable inner self. And I *had* to start dealing with it.

Having dressed, I listened to my phone messages for the first time in three days. Both Tiggy and Ally had obviously heard from Ma about my abrupt departure and were request-ing a call back to find out where on earth I was. I decided I'd contact them once I'd met with Yara tomorrow and perhaps then I could tell them exactly why I was here.

I texted them both to say I was fine and I'd email them all with my news soon, then, mirroring my earlier thoughts with decisive action, I left the hotel and walked into the heart of Ipanema. I found a supermarket and bought two bottles of the best red wine they had and some chocolates for Valentina. I walked through the bustling square, where a night market was attracting the locals, and made my way to the street where Floriano lived.

Climbing the steps, I was faced with the choice of five buzzers. I pressed the first one and got no reply, then the second and the third. Pressing the last one and receiving silence, I was just about to turn tail and retrace my footsteps back to the hotel when I heard a shout from high above me.

'Hey, Maia! Press the top buzzer and I'll let you in.'

'Okay,' I called out to him. And a few seconds later, I was at the already open door to his apartment.

'We're in the kitchen,' he shouted as I entered. 'Go up to the roof terrace and I'll see you there.'

I did as I was told, noticing a definite smell of burnt food pervading the downstairs rooms. I stood looking out over the terrace at the sun setting behind the hillside which housed the *favela*. Finally, Floriano appeared, sweating slightly.

'Sorry about that. Valentina insisted she wanted no help heating up the pasta dish that Petra had helped her make earlier for her to serve to me tonight. Sadly, she turned the gas onto full power and I'm afraid it's a burnt offering for my birthday supper. I've left her in the kitchen to plate it up, but she wants to know if you would like some too. I think I could do with some help to chew my way through it,' he admitted.

'If you're sure there's enough, then yes, I'd love to stay.'

'Oh yes, there's plenty,' he said as he noticed the bottles of wine and the chocolates.

'To wish you a happy birthday,' I said. 'And also to say thank you for all the help you've given me.'

'That's sweet of you, Maia, I appreciate it. I'll go and get another wine glass and see how the cook's getting on downstairs. And tell her that we have another guest for supper. Please, sit down.'

He indicated the table as he left and I saw that it had been spread with a white lace tablecloth and carefully set for two. In the centre of the table, taking pride of place, was a big homemade birthday card, depicting a man with stick arms and legs, and bearing the caption, '*Feliz Aniversário Papai!*'

Floriano eventually returned, carrying a tray with a wine glass, extra cutlery and two bowls of food. 'Valentina has ordered us to begin eating,' he said as he set the contents of the tray on the table and proceeded to open a bottle of the wine I'd brought.

'Thank you,' I said as he carried an extra chair to the table and set another place for himself. 'I really hope I'm not disturbing you. And that Valentina doesn't mind me gatecrashing her special supper with her father.'

'Quite the opposite – she's absolutely thrilled. Although I warn you, she keeps calling you my girlfriend. Just ignore her; she's forever trying to matchmake her poor old Papai! *Saúde!*' he said as he lifted his glass to mine.

'*Saúde*. And happy birthday,' I toasted him.

Valentina appeared through the door and brought another bowl to the table, placing it shyly in front of me.

'Hello,' she said. 'Papai said your name was Maia; it's a

pretty name. And you are pretty too, don't you think so?' she added, turning to her father as she sat down between us at the table.

'I think that Maia is very pretty indeed,' Floriano agreed gallantly. 'And this supper looks delicious. Thank you, *querida*.'

'Papai, we both know it's burnt and will taste horrible and I don't at all mind if you want to put it in the dustbin and we have chocolate instead,' Valentina replied pragmatically, eyeing the gift I had brought with me. 'I'm not a very good cook yet,' she shrugged as her dark eyes turned to me. 'Are you married?' she asked me as we all lifted our forks tentatively to start eating.

'No, I'm not, Valentina.' I suppressed a smile at her blatant interrogation tactic.

'Do you have a boyfriend?' she continued.

'No, not at the moment.'

'Then perhaps Papai can be your boyfriend?' she suggested, as she put a forkful of food to her mouth, chewed it for a few seconds then unceremoniously spat it out into her bowl.

'Valentina! That was disgusting!' Floriano chided her harshly.

'Like this is.' She indicated her bowl.

'Well, I rather like it. I've always been fond of barbeques,' I winked at her.

'I'm really sorry. You don't have to eat it, either of you. But at least there's a very good thing for pudding. Why are you here, Maia?' she asked me, changing the subject without even pausing for breath. 'Are you helping Papai with his work?'

'Yes. I've translated your father's book into French.'

'You don't sound French and you look Brazilian. Doesn't she, Papai?'

'Yes, you're right, she does,' Floriano agreed.

'So do you live in Paris?' Valentina asked.

'No, I live in Switzerland, on the shores of a very big lake.'

Valentina rested the palms of her hands under her chin. 'I've never been away from Brazil. Can you tell me about the place you live?'

I did my best to describe Switzerland to her. When I mentioned the snow that fell so heavily in the winter, Valentina's eyes lit up.

'I've never seen snow, except in pictures. Perhaps I can come and stay with you one time and make the snow angels you said you used to make with your sisters when you were a little girl?'

'Valentina, it's very rude to invite yourself to someone else's house. Now, I think it's time we cleared away the plates.' Floriano indicated the half-finished bowls of food.

'Yes, Papai. Don't worry, I will do it. You stay here and talk to your girlfriend.'

She winked cheekily at both of us as she collected the three bowls onto the tray and made off with it perilously rattling down the stairs.

'My apologies,' said Floriano, as he moved away from the table and leant against the terrace wall to light a cigarette. 'She can be a little precocious, I'm afraid. Perhaps it comes from being an only child.'

'There's no need to apologise for her at all. She asks questions because she's bright and interested in the world around her. And besides,' I added, 'I know from experience that it's not just "only" children who can be precocious. I'm one of six sisters and the youngest certainly fits the bill. I think your daughter's delightful.'

'I always worry that I spoil her, give her too much attention to make up for the fact she doesn't have a mother,' Floriano sighed. 'And whatever the modern ethos is on these things, men are simply not born with the same maternal instinct as women. Although I've done my best to learn,' he added.

'Personally, I don't think it matters who brings you up, be it male or female, natural parent or adoptive, as long as the child is loved. But then I would say that, wouldn't I?' I shrugged.

'Yes, I suppose so. You've certainly had a very unusual upbringing, Maia, from the sound of what you were telling Valentina just now. It must have had its complications as well as its privileges.'

'You can say that again,' I smiled ruefully.

'At some point, I'd like to know more. Especially about your father. He sounds like a very interesting man.'

'He was.'

'So, tell me, are you feeling a little calmer than you seemed this morning?' he asked me gently.

'I am. And you're right, of course, that the shock of losing the person I loved most in the world is only just beginning to dawn on me. It's easier here because I can still imagine Pa at home. But to be honest, the thought of returning to the reality of him not being there when I leave Rio turns my stomach.'

'Then stay a while longer,' he encouraged me.

'Well, I'll see what happens tomorrow when I meet with Yara,' I answered, batting away his comment. 'But if that leads nowhere, I've decided that I'm not going to battle to find out the truth any more. After all, Senhora Carvalho has made it perfectly obvious that she doesn't wish to know me, whether I'm her granddaughter or not.'

'I can understand how you would see it like that. But Maia, you don't yet know what happened in the past to provoke her reaction to you,' Floriano urged me. 'Or what her *own* childhood was like.'

'Maia' – Valentina's head poked round the door – 'can you come and help me, please?' she said in a loud whisper.

'Of course,' I said, as I rose from the table and followed her down the stairs to the kitchen. Where, amidst the chaos of burnt saucepans, stood a cake with candles on the top. Valentina picked it up carefully.

'Can you light them for me? Papai won't let me use matches. I've put twenty-two candles on it because I'm not sure how old he is.'

'I think twenty-two will be fine,' I smiled. 'Let's light them at the top of the stairs so they don't blow out on the way up.'

On the top landing, we crouched outside the door to the roof terrace and I lit the candles carefully, feeling Valentina's eyes upon me. They held the same perceptive gaze as her father's.

'Thank you, Maia,' she said when I'd lit the last one. As she prepared to parade through the door with the cake, she smiled up at me. 'I'm glad you're here.'

'So am I,' I said. And I realised it was true.

I left the two of them half an hour later, having noticed that Valentina was yawning and angling for a story from Floriano.

'So, am I taking you tomorrow, or would you prefer to go to the Casa alone?' he asked me as he opened the door to the apartment.

'I'd really like you to come,' I admitted honestly. 'I think I need some support.'

'Good. Then I'll see you at one o'clock tomorrow.' Floriano kissed me formally on both cheeks. 'Goodnight, Maia.'

29

I slept well and peacefully that night, my body having finally adjusted to the new time zone. I woke at nine, and crossed the road to Ipanema Beach for what was becoming a habitual daily swim. Then I returned to my suite to reread the letters, making notes of any questions I wanted to ask Yara. Upstairs on the hotel roof terrace, I drank a glass of wine with lunch in an attempt to steady my nerves. I knew that if Yara refused to elaborate, or, in fact, didn't know herself how I'd ended up being adopted by Pa Salt, I'd have nowhere else to go.

'Feeling hopeful?' Floriano asked me as I climbed into the Fiat.

'Yes. Or at least, I'm trying to.'

'Good girl. You have to believe that Yara can help you until you know differently.'

'The problem is,' I said, 'I've suddenly realised how much this matters to me.'

'I know,' he agreed. 'I can see it.'

When we arrived outside the Casa, we saw with relief

that, although the gates were still drawn shut, the padlock had been removed.

'So far so good,' said Floriano. 'I shall wait here for you until you've finished.'

'Are you sure? I don't mind at all if you come in with me.'

'Absolutely sure. I feel this is something that would be better done woman to woman. Good luck,' he said, squeezing my hand as I climbed out of the car.

'Thank you.' And, taking a deep breath, I crossed the road and stood outside the high gates. I pushed one and it swung open with a groan of neglect. Once behind it, I glanced across to Floriano, who was staring at me from inside his car. With a wave, I turned, walked up the drive and mounted the steps to the front door.

It was opened immediately by Yara, who had obviously been waiting by it. She ushered me inside, then shut and bolted the door behind us.

'I haven't got long,' she said tensely, as she led me down the dark corridor and into the same room in which Floriano and I had previously seen Senhora Carvalho.

This time, though, the shutters remained tightly closed, and there was only a dim standard lamp throwing a ghostly light into the room.

'Please, sit down,' she said.

'Thank you.' I did so, then looked at Yara as she perched herself nervously on a chair opposite me. 'I'm so sorry if my sudden appearance has caused you and Senhora Carvalho worry,' I began. 'But I have to believe that you gave me those letters for a reason. And you must have known that once I'd read them, I would want to know more.'

'Yes, yes . . .' Yara rubbed her brow. 'Senhorita, you must

understand that your grandmother is dying. Once she has gone, I have no idea what will become of me. Whether she has even left me anything to live on.'

Immediately, I wondered if Yara was wanting to offer me information in return for payment. And if so, whether that information was reliable. Yara must have seen my frown and was quick to reassure me.

'No, I'm not asking for money. What I'm saying is that if she found out I was speaking to you now, she might decide that any pension she was thinking of giving me should be withdrawn.'

'But why? What is it that she doesn't wish for me to know?'

'Senhorita Maia, it is to do with your mother, Cristina. She left this house over thirty-four years ago. I do not wish for Senhora Carvalho to be distressed during her final days on earth. Do you understand?'

'No, not really,' I replied, every nerve ending tingling at the first mention of my *mother* . . . 'Then why did you give me those letters? They were written eighty years ago by my great-grandmother, three generations before I was even born!'

'Because to understand what happened to you, you have to know what came before,' Yara explained. 'Although I can only repeat what my mother, Loen, told me, as I too was only just born when Senhora Izabela gave birth to Senhora Carvalho.'

'Please, I beg you, Yara, tell me everything you know,' I urged, intuiting that before Yara's courage left her, every second was precious. 'I swear that I would never compromise you by telling Senhora Carvalho you have spoken to me.'

'Not even if you knew that you stood to inherit this house?' Yara eyed me.

'I assure you that I was adopted by an extremely wealthy man and I want for nothing financially. *Please*, Yara.'

She stared at me for a few seconds, then gave a small sigh of surrender.

'The letters you read that were written to my mother ended when Senhora Izabela returned to Rio, yes?'

'Yes. The last one was posted from the ship when it docked in Africa on its way back from France,' I confirmed. 'I know Bel returned home to Rio. I've seen the photos of her wedding to Gustavo Aires Cabral in the archives.'

'Yes. So, I will tell you what my mother said happened to Izabela in the eighteen months that followed . . .'

Izabela

Rio de Janeiro

October 1928

30

'Izabela! My beloved daughter, you are returned home safe to us!' Antonio cried as Bel walked off the gangplank and into his open arms. He clasped her in his strong embrace then stood back to look at her. 'Why, what is this? You feel like a sparrow to hold. Have you not been eating? And you are so pale, *princesa,* but I suppose that is the Northern European weather for you. You need the hot sun of your own country to put some colour in your cheeks. Come, they are already loading your trunk into the car and it is parked not far along the quay.'

'Where is Mãe?' Bel asked, as she walked by his side. The sky was unusually grey and gloomy for October and she only wished the sun had been out; that at least might have lightened her mood.

'She's resting at home,' her father replied. 'She has not been well.'

'You said nothing in your letters to me,' Bel said with a worried frown.

'I'm sure your presence will speed her recovery.' Her father stopped beside an impressive silver car and the chauffeur opened the door to the back seat so Bel could climb inside.

'What do you think?' asked Antonio as he joined her on the soft grey calf-leather seat. 'I had it shipped from America. It is a Rolls-Royce, a "Phantom", and I believe the first one in Rio. I will be proud to take my *princesa* in it to the cathedral on her wedding day.'

'It is beautiful,' said Bel automatically, her thoughts still with her mother.

'We will take the scenic route along the beach, to remind my daughter of what she has missed,' Antonio instructed the driver. 'We have so much to tell each other, it will be hard to know where to begin,' he said. 'But business-wise, all is very good here. The price of coffee rises daily, thanks to the demand from America, and I have purchased two further farms. My name has also been put forward as a possible candidate for the Federal Senate,' he said proudly. 'Gustavo's father, Maurício, nominated me. They have just completed a new and marvellous building in Rua Moncorvo Filho, where even the floor and the cornices are decorated with coffee beans. That is the power of our simple bean here in Brazil.'

'I'm happy for you, Pai,' Bel replied flatly as they drove through the familiar streets.

'And I've no doubt that yours will be the greatest wedding Rio has ever seen. I have been talking to Gustavo and Maurício about the need to restore their family home, as it will be where you live too once you are married. As you know, it is a gracious old building, but the fabric and interior are ageing. We have agreed, as part of your dowry, that I will finance its restoration, and the renovations have already begun. My *princesa*, by the time it is finished, you will live in a palace!'

'Thank you, Pai,' answered Bel with a smile, wanting to

convince him, and, more importantly, herself, that she was grateful.

'We are planning the wedding for after the New Year, just before the Carnival. You and your new home will have three months to prepare yourselves. So you will be kept busy, *querida*.'

Bel had been half expecting to be marched up the aisle as soon as she'd returned to Rio. So at least a small delay was something, she thought, as they drove past the Copacabana Palace Hotel and she stared out at the roaring grey sea, crashing its white foam onto the sand.

'When you have recovered from your journey, we will hold a dinner so that you can share all the wonderful new sights and culture you have gleaned from the Old World and impress our friends with your knowledge.'

'I loved Paris,' she ventured. 'It's such a beautiful city, and Professor Landowski, who is making the outer shell of the *Cristo* figure for Senhor da Silva Costa, had an assistant who made a sculpture of me also.'

'Well, if it is good, we must contact him. I will buy it and bring it to Brazil,' commented Antonio.

'I doubt that it would be for sale,' she said wistfully.

'*Querida*, anything is for sale at the right price,' Antonio stated flatly. 'Now, we're almost home and I'm sure your mother will have risen from her bed to greet you.'

If Antonio had expressed concern at the pale, waif-like appearance of his daughter, it was nothing compared to Bel's shock when her mother appeared to greet her. Carla, always voluptuous, seemed to have shed half her bodyweight in the eight and a half months since Bel had last seen her.

'Mãe!' Bel exclaimed as she ran into her arms and hugged

her. 'What have you done to yourself? You must have been on a diet!'

Carla did her best to smile and Bel saw how huge her brown eyes looked in her gaunt face. 'I wish to look modish for my daughter's wedding,' she joked. 'Do you not think the weight loss suits me?'

Used to her comfortingly large breasts, which had cushioned Bel on many occasions as a child, Bel looked at Carla and thought her new figure had aged her by years.

'Yes, Mãe, I think it does,' she lied.

'Good, good. Now,' she said, tucking her arm into her daughter's as they walked inside, 'I have so much to tell you, but I'm sure that you wish to rest first.'

Given that Bel had just spent many days aboard ship with little to do but rest, she didn't feel in the least bit weary. But as her mother winced suddenly, Bel realised it was her need, not her daughter's, that had prompted the suggestion.

'Of course, we can both take a nap and then talk later,' she said, seeing a flash of relief pass across her mother's face. 'It's you who seems weary, Mãe,' Bel said, as they reached her parents' bedroom door. 'Shall I come and help you back to bed?'

'No,' Carla replied firmly. 'Gabriela is already inside and she will attend to me. I will see you later.' She nodded as she opened the bedroom door and then shut it behind her.

Bel sought out her father immediately and found him in his study. 'Pai, please tell me, how ill is Mãe?'

Antonio, who had begun wearing glasses since she'd last seen him, looked up from his papers and took them off his nose.

'*Querida*, your mother did not want you to worry while

you were away, but she had an operation a month ago to remove a growth from her breast. The operation was a success and the surgeons are full of positivity for a complete recovery. The procedure has taken its toll on her, that is all. Once she has recovered her strength, she will be well again.'

'Pai, she looks dreadful! Please tell me the truth. Don't hide the extent of her sickness from me.'

'I swear, Izabela, that I am not hiding anything. Ask her doctors if you don't believe me. All she needs is rest and good food. Her appetite has been very limited since the operation.'

'You are sure she will recover?'

'I am sure.'

'Then now I am home, I will nurse her.'

Ironically, the fact that Bel had her mother's well-being to think of helped her greatly in the next few days. It gave her a focus, something to concentrate on other than her own misery. She oversaw the preparation of Carla's food herself, making sure the kitchen staff prepared nourishing dishes that were easy for her mother to swallow and digest. She sat with her in the mornings, talking brightly about what she'd seen in the Old World, about Landowski and the Beaux-Arts school and Senhor da Silva Costa's wonderful *Cristo* project.

'They have started digging the foundations up on the top of Corcovado Mountain,' Carla had remarked one day. 'I would love to go up and see it sometime.'

'And I will take you there,' Bel had replied, willing her mother to get well again so that it would be possible.

'And we must, of course, talk about the plans for your

wedding,' said Carla, having pronounced herself well enough to sit in a chair on the terrace that led from her bedroom. 'There is so much to discuss.'

'All in good time, Mãe, when you are stronger,' Bel had insisted adamantly.

Over supper together, three nights after Bel had arrived home, Antonio told her that he had just taken a call from Gustavo.

'He wishes to know when he can come and see you.'

'Perhaps when Mãe is a little better,' she suggested.

'Izabela, you have been out of his sight for nine months. So I have suggested he calls tomorrow afternoon. Gabriela can sit with your mother while you entertain Gustavo. I wouldn't wish him to think you don't want to see him.'

'Yes, Pai,' Bel agreed meekly.

'And surely you must be eager to see him too?'

'Of course.'

Gustavo duly arrived at three the following afternoon. Carla insisted Bel change into one of the new dresses she'd had fitted in Paris.

'You must look even more beautiful than he remembers you,' Carla emphasised. 'After so long apart, we wouldn't wish that he changes his mind. Especially as you are as scrawny as me these days,' she teased her daughter.

Loen helped her into the dress and then styled her hair into an elegant chignon.

'How do you feel about seeing Gustavo again?' Loen asked her tentatively.

'I don't know,' Bel replied honestly. 'Nervous, I suppose.'

'And the . . . other man you wrote to me of in Paris? You can forget him?'

Bel stared at her reflection in the mirror. 'Never, Loen, never.'

Downstairs, ready and waiting for Gustavo in the drawing room, she heard the doorbell ring with trepidation and Gabriela walk down the hall to answer it. Hearing Gustavo's voice, and enjoying the few seconds' hiatus before he entered the room and she saw him, Bel asked for heavenly help, praying that Gustavo would never see the turmoil in her heart.

'Izabela,' he said as he walked in and moved towards her, his arms outstretched.

'Gustavo.' She lifted her hands to his and he clasped them, surveying her as he did so.

'My goodness, I think Europe must have suited you, as you look even more radiant than I remember. You've grown into a beautiful woman,' he said, as she felt him drink in every centimetre of her. 'Was it wonderful?'

'Truly,' she replied, signalling to Gabriela to bring in a jug of fresh mango juice and gesturing to Gustavo to sit down. 'Paris especially.'

'Ah, yes, the city of love,' he commented. 'And I'm so sad I was not there to enjoy it with you. Perhaps someday, if God is kind, we will go together. So, tell me all about your travels.'

As Bel spoke to him of all that she had seen in the past few months, she decided that Gustavo seemed even more insubstantial than she remembered. But she forced herself to focus instead on his warm brown eyes, and the kindness within them.

'Well,' he said, as he sipped his juice, 'it indeed sounds like you had a marvellous time. You gave so few details in your letters that I wasn't sure if it had been a success or not. For example, you didn't mention that a sculptor had asked you to sit for him while you were in Paris.'

'Who told you?' asked Bel, shaken that he had heard about this.

'Your father, of course, when I spoke to him on the telephone yesterday. That must have been an interesting experience.'

'It was,' Bel agreed weakly.

'You know,' he said, smiling at her, 'six weeks or so ago, just as you were preparing to leave Paris, I had the strangest feeling that you weren't going to return to me. I actually contacted your father to make sure you had boarded the ship as planned. But of course, it was simply my own fear getting the better of me. Because here you are, Izabela.' He reached his hand to hers. 'Have you missed me as I have missed you?'

'Yes, very much.'

'It's a shame we can't marry sooner, but of course we must give your mother time to recover. How is she?'

'Weak, but improving slowly,' said Bel. 'I'm still very angry that neither she nor my father told me of her illness when I was away. I would of course have returned earlier.'

'Well, Izabela, perhaps there are some things it's best not to share in a letter, don't you agree?'

Bel felt herself blushing under his gaze, as every word that dropped from his mouth seemed to suggest he knew the secret she was hiding.

'Even if they meant well by trying to protect me, they should have told me,' she replied brusquely.

'Well.' Gustavo dropped her hand. 'You're safe home with

me, and your mother is on the mend. And that's all that matters, isn't it? Now,' he said, 'my mother is eager to see you too and to start discussing some of the arrangements for the wedding. Obviously, she hasn't wanted to disturb Senhora Carla, but there are some details that need to be finalised very soon. For example, the date. Have you any particular preference as to when in January?'

'I would prefer it towards the end of the month, to give my mother as much time to recover as possible.'

'Of course. Perhaps in the next few days, you would like to visit my mother at the Casa and discuss the wedding plans? And also review those your father and I have for the renovation of our house. The structural work is already underway and your father has found an architect who has some very modern ideas. He has suggested we remodel the upper floors so that we can add bathrooms to the main bedrooms. And I'm sure you wish to have a hand in the interior design of our own private suite of rooms. I know you ladies have much better ideas on decor than us men.'

The mere thought of a future room – and a *bed* – shared with Gustavo sent a shiver of fear up her spine. 'I would be happy to come up whenever it is suitable for your mother,' she answered.

'Well, shall I suggest next Wednesday?'

'I'm sure that will be fine.'

'Good. And I hope you will allow me to enjoy your company in the meantime. Perhaps I can call on you tomorrow afternoon?'

'I will be here,' said Bel as Gustavo stood and she did too.

'Until tomorrow, Izabela,' he murmured, kissing her hand.

'And I long for the day when I no longer have to book an appointment to see you.'

When Gustavo had left the house, Bel walked upstairs to her bedroom to gather herself together before she went to check on her mother. Standing by the window, she gave herself a thorough talking-to. Gustavo was sweet, kind and gentle, and she must remember that it wasn't his fault that she could never love him the way he loved her. Or that she already loved another . . .

Remembering with a shudder Laurent's words of warning – that one day her true feelings would reveal themselves – Bel splashed her face with cold water before making her way to her mother's room.

A week later, Bel was pleased to see that Carla, although still weak and thin, was most definitely improving.

'Oh,' Carla sighed one afternoon, after listening to Bel read *Madame Bovary* by Gustave Flaubert, translating it from French into Portuguese so her mother could understand the words. 'I have such a clever daughter! Who would have thought it?' Carla looked at Bel fondly and stroked her cheek. 'You make me very proud.'

'And you will make me proud if you eat every bit of your supper,' Bel replied.

Carla glanced out of the window at the sunny afternoon, watching shadows dance across the lush flora and fauna in the gardens. 'The brightness makes me long to be at my beloved *fazenda*,' she said. 'I always find the mountain air there so restorative and the atmosphere so tranquil.'

'Would you like to go, Mãe?'

'You know how I love it there, Izabela. But of course, your father is so busy at his office that he would not wish to leave Rio.'

'What's important is what's best for your health. You leave it to me,' replied Bel firmly.

Over dinner that evening with her father, Bel broached the idea of her accompanying Carla to the *fazenda*.

'I think it would lift her spirits, and therefore benefit her health immensely. Would you let us go, Pai, just for a couple of weeks or so? It's so very hot in Rio just now.'

'Izabela,' Antonio said with a frown, 'you have only just arrived back and now you talk of leaving again. Anyone would think you disliked being here.'

'You know that isn't true, Pai. But until we both feel Mãe is on the mend, I'm not comfortable with finalising a date for the wedding. And you know how eager I am to do that. So if some time spent at the *fazenda* would hasten her recovery, I'm happy to accompany her.'

'And leave me all alone here, with no wife or child to come home to?' Antonio complained.

'I'm sure it would be possible to visit us at the weekends when you're not working, Pai.'

'Perhaps. But it isn't me you have to convince; it's your fiancé, who may not wish you to disappear from his sight again.'

'I will talk to Gustavo,' Bel agreed.

'Of course,' Gustavo nodded, as Bel explained her plan the following afternoon. 'I'm in favour of anything that will hasten our walk to the altar. And,' he added quickly, 'it will be the best thing for your mother's health. However, before you go, we must make a few decisions.'

Bel told a delighted Carla that they were to leave for the *fazenda* the following week. She wasn't the only member of the Bonifacio household who was happy at the thought. Loen's face lit up when Bel asked her to accompany mother and daughter up to the mountains. Even though her presence wasn't technically necessary, as Fabiana and Sandro who ran the *fazenda* were capable of caring for their needs, Bel knew it would give her a chance to spend time with her young man.

'Oh, Senhorita Bel,' Loen had said, her eyes glowing with pleasure. 'I cannot believe I will see him again! Because he can't read or write, we haven't spoken since we last saw each other. *Obrigada! Obrigada!*'

Giving her mistress a spontaneous hug, Loen had virtually skipped from the room. And Bel decided that even if she herself could never be reunited with the one she loved, she'd live vicariously through Loen's joy.

The following day, Bel duly went to meet with both Gustavo and his mother to discuss the wedding plans.

'It is most unfortunate that your mother's illness means she is unable to contribute to the organisation at this crucial time,' said Luiza Aires Cabral. 'But we must do as much as we can to plan the event in the meantime.'

Bel had an urge to reach out and slap Luiza's arrogant face, but she managed to restrain herself. 'I'm sure she will be better very soon, especially with a dose of fresh mountain air,' she answered.

'Well, if we can at least set the date, Rio will not feel as though there is further procrastination, given that you have already spent so long abroad. Now . . .' Luiza put on her glasses and studied her diary. 'The archbishop has already informed me of the dates he has available. As you can imagine, his schedule is booked up months in advance. Gustavo has told me that you wish the marriage to take place towards the end of January. On a Friday, of course. Weekend weddings are so vulgar.'

'Whatever you think best,' Bel agreed demurely.

'As for the reception afterwards, your father has a notion that we should hold the wedding breakfast at the Copacabana Palace Hotel. Personally, I find it's rather a common crowd that rate it and would have favoured a smaller, more select event here at the house, following in the family tradition. But as your father has decided to renovate what I think are already adequate facilities here, that is not possible. The house is crawling with tradesmen and I can't run the risk of them not being finished by January. So we must select another venue.'

'I'm happy with whatever you decide,' Bel repeated.

'As for bridesmaids and pages, your mother has put forward a number of names of your cousins from São Paulo. Eight in all,' Luiza clarified. 'We too have at least twelve from our side whom I must consider, as they are godchildren and would of course expect to take a leading role in the ceremony. Eight is the maximum number of attendants we could allow without it looking showy. Do you have anyone you especially wish to be included on the shortlist?'

Bel named two young daughters of her mother's cousin and one boy from her father's side. 'Please, I am happy to accept the rest of my attendants from Gustavo's side of the family.'

She glanced at her fiancé, and he gave her a sweet, sympathetic smile.

For the next two hours, Luiza questioned Bel on every tiny detail of the wedding. But each time Bel ventured a suggestion, her ideas were just as quickly rebuffed, due to her future mother-in-law's determination to have things her own way.

However, there was one point on which Bel was determined not to budge: that after the marriage, Loen would accompany her to her new home as her personal maid.

When she dared to raise the subject, Luiza fixed her with an icy stare before waving her hand dismissively. 'That is quite ridiculous,' she said. 'We already have servants here who are more than capable of taking care of your needs.'

'But—'

'Mãe,' Gustavo interrupted, finally rising to Bel's defence. 'If Izabela wishes to bring her maid, whom she has known since childhood, then I cannot see why it should pose a problem.'

Luiza looked at him with an irritated raise of her eyebrows. 'I see. Well then, so be it,' she said, nodding at her son curtly before turning back to Bel and continuing. 'At least what we've discussed today gives me some detail to work with while you scurry off to the mountains next week. Given you have been so long apart from my son, anyone would think that you didn't wish for your intended's company.'

Again, Gustavo intervened. 'Come now, Mãe, that is not fair. Izabela simply wishes for her mother's health to improve.'

'Of course, and I will mention her in my prayers when I

attend Mass tomorrow. In the meantime, I will do my duty and take control of arrangements until you and Senhora Bonifacio are back in Rio to share the burden. Now' – Luiza glanced at the clock on the mantelpiece – 'if you'll excuse me, I have a committee meeting with the Sisters of Mercy orphanage in less than half an hour. Gustavo, I am sure you can escort Izabela around the gardens to take some air, and show her the renovations in progress. Good day to you.'

Bel watched Luiza leave the room, feeling akin to a kettle left too long on the stove and near to boiling over.

'Don't mind her.' Gustavo walked over to her and put a comforting hand on her shoulder, sensing her irritation. 'Mãe might complain, but she loves every second of it. She's talked of nothing else for the past nine months. Now, allow me to accompany you into the garden.'

'Gustavo,' Bel said as they left the house, 'where will your parents live after we are married and I am living here with you?'

He raised an eyebrow in surprise at her question. 'Well, of course they will continue to live here with us. Where else would they go?'

The following morning, Bel made Carla comfortable in the back of the Rolls-Royce and climbed in next to her. Loen sat with their driver in the front as they embarked on the five-hour journey up to the cool air of the mountainous region of Paty do Alferes. For two hundred years Fazenda Santa Tereza had belonged to the family of the Baron Paty do Alferes, a Portuguese nobleman and also, as Antonio had pointed out before they'd left that morning, a distant cousin of the Aires Cabral family.

The roads up to the region were surprisingly good, due to the fact that the wealthy landowners had once needed to transport their coffee beans and themselves back and forth to Rio and had financed the construction. Carla was able to sleep most of the way without disturbance.

Bel gazed out of the window as they began to climb up through the mountains, the gentle slopes falling into the valleys beneath, the streams that carried pure, fresh spring water cutting narrow crevices into them.

'Mãe, we are here,' said Bel, as the car bumped along the dusty drive which led to the main house.

Carla stirred as the car came to a halt and Bel jumped out to breathe in the wonderful clean air the area was renowned for. As it was almost dusk, the cicadas chirruped at full force and Vanila and Donna – the two strays that Bel had begged her parents to keep when they'd arrived as hungry puppies at the kitchen door seven years ago – yelped excitedly around their mistress's legs.

'Home,' Bel sighed in pleasure as she saw Fabiana and Sandro, who took care of the *fazenda*, following behind the dogs.

'Senhorita Izabela!' Fabiana wrapped her in a comforting embrace. 'Why, I think you have grown more beautiful since the last time I saw you. Are you well?'

'Yes, I am, thank you. But,' she said, lowering her voice, 'I think you will be shocked when you see my mother. Try not to show her,' she warned.

Fabiana nodded and watched as the driver helped Carla out of the car. She patted Bel's arm and then walked over to greet her mistress. If anyone could restore her mother to health, thought Bel, it was Fabiana. Not only would she offer up prayers in the tiny chapel which sat in an alcove just off the drawing room, she would also ply Carla with all types of traditional remedies: mixtures of the different plants and flowers that grew in abundance here and were renowned for their medicinal qualities.

Out of the corner of her eye, she saw Bruno – Fabiana and Sandro's dark-eyed son – hovering in the background. As they all approached the entrance to the house, she saw Loen throw him a coy smile. And watched as Bruno returned it.

Bel followed Fabiana and Carla inside the house, seeing how the housekeeper had a maternal arm around Carla's shoulder, and breathed a sigh of relief. Having borne the worry of her mother's care alone, she knew that Fabiana would now assume the responsibility. As Fabiana took Carla to her bedroom to unpack and get her settled, Bel walked across the wide-planked wooden floor of the drawing room, filled with heavy mahogany and rosewood furniture, and opened the door to her own childhood bedroom.

The sash windows were drawn up and the exterior shutters thrown open. A wonderful cool breeze blew in as she leant her elbows upon the sill and gazed at her favourite view. Below her in the paddock were Loty, her pony, and Luppa, her father's stallion, grazing peacefully. Beyond rose a gentle hill, still dotted with old coffee bushes that had somehow managed to survive despite years of being untended. A herd of white oxen peppered the hillside, the odd barren patch revealing the deep red soil beneath the wiry grass.

She walked back through the drawing room and stood at the front door, flanked by two of the majestic, ancient palm trees from which the area took its name. Sitting down on the stone bench outside on the terrace, and smelling the sweet scent of the hibiscus that grew abundantly here, she gazed across the gardens to the freshwater lake in which she had swum every day as a child. As she listened to the steady drone of dragonflies hovering over the flower beds and watched two yellow butterflies dance playfully in front of her eyes, Bel felt some of her inner tension fall away.

Laurent would love it here, she thought to herself wistfully, and despite her determination not to think of him, tears sprang to her eyes. Even though she'd known when she took the decision to walk away from him in Paris that it signalled the end, the girlish, imaginative part of her had wondered if he'd attempt to make contact. Every morning, when she'd seen the post on its silver tray at the breakfast table, she'd imagined receiving a letter from him, begging her to return to him, telling her he couldn't live without her.

But of course, that hadn't happened. And as the weeks had passed, she'd begun to ponder whether his declarations of love had been as Margarida had suggested: simply part of a plan to seduce her. She wondered if Laurent ever thought of her now, or whether the short time they'd spent together had passed through his mind like flotsam and was now forgotten.

Whichever the true answer, what did it matter? She was the one who had drawn the line in the sand, chosen to return to Brazil and her forthcoming marriage. The atmosphere of La Closerie des Lilas and the sensation of Laurent's lips on hers were now a memory, a brief dance with another world that she had chosen to end. And no amount of wishing and hoping could change the course of the life which she herself had decided on.

31

Paris, November 1928

'So, at last the statue is finished.' Professor Landowski thumped his workbench in relief. 'But now the crazy Brazilian needs me to make a scale model of his Christ's head and hands. The head will be nearly four metres high, so it will only just fit into the studio. The fingers too will almost reach the rafters. All of us here in the *atelier* will, in the most literal sense, experience Christ's hand upon us,' Landowski joked. 'Then, so da Silva Costa tells me, once I have finished this, he will carve my creations up like joints of beef in order to ship them over to Rio de Janeiro. Never before have I worked liked this. But,' he sighed, 'perhaps I should trust to his madness.'

'Perhaps you have no choice,' agreed Laurent.

'Well, it pays the bills, Brouilly, although I can accept no more commissions until Our Lord's head and hands are gone from my *atelier*. There would simply be no room. So, we begin. Bring me the casts you made of the two ladies' hands some weeks ago. I must have something to work with.'

Laurent went to retrieve the casts from the storeroom and

placed them in front of Landowski. The two men studied them intently.

'They both have beautiful, sensitive fingers, but I must think how they will look when each hand stretches for more than three metres,' Landowski commented. 'Now, Brouilly, don't you have a home to go to?'

This was the signal that Landowski wished to be left alone. 'Of course, professor. I will see you tomorrow.'

On his way out of the *atelier*, Laurent found the young boy sitting on the stone bench on the terrace outside. The evening was chilly but clear, and the stars formed a perfect canopy above them. Laurent sat down next to him, watching him gazing up to the heavens.

'You like stars?' Laurent ventured, although he had long ago accepted he would never receive a reply.

The boy gave a short smile and nodded.

'There is the belt of Orion.' Laurent pointed to it. 'And close by are The Seven Sisters in a cluster together. With their parents, Atlas and Pleione, watching over them.'

Laurent saw the boy was following his finger and listening intently. 'My father was interested in astronomy, and kept a telescope in one of the attic rooms on the top floor of our chateau. Sometimes, he would take it up to the roof on clear nights and teach me about the stars. I once saw a shooting star, and thought it the most magical thing I had ever seen.' He looked at the young boy. 'Do you have parents?'

The boy pretended not to hear him, and simply continued to gaze upwards.

'Ah well, I must be going.' He patted the boy on the head. 'Goodnight.'

Laurent managed to hitch a lift on the back of a motorcycle for part of the journey back to Montparnasse. When he arrived in his attic room, he saw a shape huddled in his bed. Another body lay asleep on a mattress on the floor. This wasn't unusual, especially as these days he so often stayed at Landowski's *atelier*.

Normally, he would leave the sleeper alone for a few hours longer while he joined his friends in the bars of Montparnasse, returning later to remove the body from his bed and climb into it himself. But tonight he felt unusually tired and not in the mood for socialising.

In fact, his general *joie de vivre* seemed to have deserted him completely since the moment Izabela Bonifacio boarded her ship back to Brazil.

Even Landowski had noticed that he was quieter than usual and had commented on it.

'Are you sick, Brouilly? Or perhaps pining?' he'd asked him with a knowing glint in his eye.

'Neither,' Laurent had replied defensively.

'Well, whichever kind of sickness it is, remember that these things always pass.'

Laurent had taken comfort from Landowski's perceptive and sympathetic words. Often he thought the professor lived so much in his own world he hardly noticed Laurent's presence, let alone his mood. Currently, he felt as though someone had gouged his heart out and then trampled it underfoot for good measure.

Walking towards his bed he shook the body in it, but the man simply groaned, opened his mouth and let out a whistle of stale alcohol before rolling over. Laurent knew there'd be no rousing him, so with a heavy sigh, he decided to give him a couple of further hours to sleep off his drunkenness while he went in search of supper.

The narrow streets of Montparnasse were as vibrant as usual, with the sound of the gay chatter of people glad to be alive. Even though it was a cold night, the pavement cafés were overflowing and a cacophony of different music from inside the bars assaulted Laurent's senses. Normally Montparnasse and its vivacity exhilarated him, but lately it had irritated him. How could everyone be so happy when he himself seemed unable to rise from the torpor and misery of his affliction?

Avoiding La Closerie des Lilas, as there would be too many acquaintances who would drag him into witless conversation, Laurent made his way to a quieter establishment, sat down on a stool at the bar and ordered himself an absinthe, knocking it back in one. He looked around at the tables, and immediately noticed a dusky brunette who reminded him of Izabela. Of course, when he looked closer, he saw the girl's features were not as fine, and that her eyes were hard. But these days, it seemed that everywhere he went, he saw her.

Ordering another absinthe, Laurent pondered his situation. In the past, he'd been known as a Casanova, a charming, attractive man envied by his friends, as it seemed that with the merest blink of an eye he could have any woman he chose to warm his bed. And yes, he'd made the most of it, for he enjoyed women. Not only for their bodies, but for their minds.

As for love . . . he had thought on a couple of occasions in the past that he was perhaps experiencing what all the great writers and artists spent their lives describing. But both times the feeling had passed quickly enough and Laurent had begun to convince himself that he would never truly know how it felt.

Until Izabela . . .

When he'd first met her, he'd used all his usual tricks to seduce her, and had enjoyed watching her blush as she slowly fell under his spell. Sure enough, it had been a game he'd excelled at playing many times in the past. But usually, once the fish was hooked and was dangling on his line to do with as he wished, the novelty would wear off and he'd become bored and move on.

And then, when he'd realised Izabela was leaving, and that, perhaps for the first time, what he felt for her was genuine, he'd made his first and only heartfelt declaration of love and asked her to stay on in Paris.

And she had refused him.

In those first few days after she'd left France, he'd put his misery down to the fact that it was the first time a woman had not succumbed to him. Perhaps the fact she was unattainable made the idea of her even more provocative, and the thought that she was sailing across the sea to be chained to a man she didn't love for the rest of her life heightened the drama of the situation.

But no . . . it seemed it had been none of these things. Because eight weeks on, despite taking other women to his bed to see if that helped – which it hadn't – and getting so drunk that he'd managed to sleep through the entire following day – which had incurred the wrath of Landowski – he felt no different.

He still thought of Izabela every waking moment. At the *atelier*, he found himself staring into space, remembering when she had sat so serenely in front of him and he'd been able to feast his eyes on her day after day, for hours at a time . . . *why* had he not appreciated it more? She was unlike any woman he had ever met, so innocent, so good . . . Yet, as he'd discovered when he'd questioned her that first day as he sketched her, she was also so full of passion and eagerness to discover all that life could hold. And her kindness that night, when she'd so tenderly carried the young boy in her arms, brooking no discussion about the rights and wrongs of her actions . . .

As Laurent drained his glass and ordered another, he decided she was truly a goddess.

At night in bed, he'd often go over their conversations, mentally kicking himself for ever playing with her emotions, wishing he could take back any of the outrageous *doubles entendres* he'd embarrassed her with in the beginning. She hadn't deserved them.

And now she was gone forever. And it was too late.

Besides, he thought morosely, what had he to offer a woman like her? A dirty shared attic where even the bed was rented out by the hour, no form of steady income and a reputation with women that she must surely have heard of any time she had visited Montparnasse. He had seen Margarida Lopes de Almeida watching him knowingly, and Laurent was sure she'd have commented to Izabela on what she thought of him.

Calling for some soup before the absinthe overwhelmed his brain cells and he fell off the bar stool, Laurent pondered for the thousandth time whether he should send the letter he'd written in his head every hour since she'd left. But of course, he knew that if he did, it might fall into the wrong hands and compromise her.

He tortured himself constantly about whether she was already married and all was lost. He wanted to ask Margarida, but she was no longer at the *atelier*, her two-month internship there now at an end. He'd heard on the Montparnasse grapevine that she and her mother had gone to Saint-Paul de Vence for the warmer weather.

'Brouilly.'

He felt a hand on his shoulder and turned his bloodshot eyes towards the voice.

'How are you?'

'I'm well, Marius,' he replied. 'You?'

'The same as always: poor, drunk and in need of a woman. But instead, you will have to do. Drink?'

Laurent watched as Marius pulled up a bar stool next to him. Just another unknown artist in Montparnasse getting through his life on cheap alcohol, sex and the dream of a glittering future. He thought of the body in his bed in the filthy attic and decided in favour of rolling out of the bar at dawn and sleeping where he fell in the street.

'Yes,' he agreed. 'Another absinthe.'

That night was the start of a weekend during which Laurent drowned his sorrows. And of which, as he staggered bleary-eyed into Landowski's *atelier*, he had little recollection.

'Look what the cat dragged in,' remarked Landowski to the young boy, who sat on a stool, avidly watching the professor working.

'*Mon Dieu*, professor, you've done so much already!' Laurent stared at the enormous hand of Christ and could only believe Landowski had spent the past forty-eight hours working continuously on the structure.

'Well, you have been away from us for five days, so someone had to continue the work. The boy and I were about to send out a search party to trawl the gutters of Montparnasse to find you,' he added.

'Are you saying it's Wednesday?' queried Laurent in shock.

'Correct,' said Landowski, turning his attention back to the vast white shape and taking a scalpel to the still wet plaster of Paris. 'Now, I will shape the fingernails of Our Lord,' he said, addressing the boy and pointedly ignoring Laurent.

When Laurent returned from the kitchen, having splashed his face with water and gulped down two glasses of it in an attempt to relieve his aching head, Landowski glanced at him.

'As you can see, I've found myself a new assistant.' He winked at the boy. 'At least *he* doesn't disappear for five days and arrive back still drunk from the night before.'

'My apologies, professor, I—'

'Enough! Understand I won't tolerate any further behaviour such as this, Brouilly. I needed you to help me with this and you weren't here. Now, before you dare to touch my Christ's hands, you will go to my wife in the house and tell her I have ordered you to sleep off your hangover.'

'Yes, professor.'

Red-faced, Laurent left the *atelier*, berating himself for allowing this to happen, and was put to bed by Landowski's ever-understanding wife, Amélie.

He woke four hours later, took a cold shower and ate a bowl of soup that Amélie offered him, arriving back at the *atelier* much restored.

'That is better,' nodded the professor, sweeping his eyes over Laurent. 'Now you are fit to work.'

The giant hand now had an index finger, and the boy still sat where Laurent had last seen him on the stool, intently watching Landowski work.

'So, we start now on the ring finger. There is the model I'm working from.' Landowski pointed to one of the moulds Laurent had taken of Izabela's and Margarida's hands.

Walking towards it, Laurent asked, 'Which set of hands did you choose in the end?'

'I have no idea, for they were unnamed. And perhaps that is how it should be. After all, they are Christ's hands and only His.'

Laurent studied the mould, looking for the telltale crack in the little finger that he'd glued carefully back together when he'd removed it from Mademoiselle Margarida's hand. There was no such fissure.

With a jolt of pleasure, Laurent knew without doubt that Landowski had chosen Izabela's hands to be those of the Rio Christ.

32

In the two weeks that Bel had been up in the mountains at the *fazenda*, she had watched her mother's strength begin to return. Whether it was the clean mountain air, the beauty and serenity of the setting, or Fabiana's nursing, Bel didn't know. But Carla had put on a little weight and was able to find the energy to take short walks around the glorious gardens unsupported.

Everything they ate was grown either on the farm itself, or sourced from the surrounding district: meat from their cattle, cheese and milk from the goats on the lower land, and vegetables and fruit from the local farms. The region was famous for the production of tomatoes and Fabiana swore by their healing qualities, chopping, mincing and sieving them into all manner of foodstuffs.

And Bel began to feel that she too was healing. Waking up every morning, donning her bathing costume and taking a refreshing dip in the lake before sitting down to a breakfast of the delicious pound cake Fabiana made was therapeutic. There was a waterfall on their land, where the fresh water fell in a cascade from the mountains above. Bel would often sit under it, staring out at the mountains, feeling the icy-cold ripples massage her back.

During the day, if her mother was resting, she would lie on the cool veranda and read, preferring books on philosophy and the art of being at peace with oneself, rather than the romantic stories she'd once favoured when she was younger. She understood now that they were fiction, and that in real life love did not always have a happy ending.

Most afternoons, she would saddle Loty and ride up the rough tracks and across the slopes, coming to rest on a hilltop, where horse and rider would pause and take a moment to enjoy the marvellous view.

Evenings were spent playing cards with her mother and Bel would retire to her room peaceful and sleepy. Before she closed her eyes, she'd say her prayers, asking God to restore her mother to good health, to grant her father success in his business dealings and to ensure that Laurent – so far away from her physically, yet still nurtured in her heart – found happiness in the future.

It was the only gift she could give him. And she tried to offer it freely and without remorse.

It didn't help that she'd often find Loen and Bruno out together for an evening stroll, completely wrapped up in each other. She once saw them sneaking a surreptitious kiss by the lake and her heart had burned with envy.

Up here, Bel thought one night as she lay in her bed yet again remembering Laurent's touch, life outside the *fazenda* felt far removed. It was the same feeling she'd experienced in Paris, when her marriage to Gustavo and the life she would live in Rio had seemed distant, as the maze of alleyways that made up Montparnasse – where she so often imagined Laurent walking – did now . . .

When they had been at the *fazenda* for three weeks, Antonio arrived to spend the weekend with them. Immediately, the atmosphere changed, as Fabiana went into a frenzy of cleaning and had her husband clip the already immaculate grass and polish the perpetually gleaming copper ornaments that hung on the wall in the dining room.

'How is she?' Antonio asked when he arrived mid-afternoon while Carla was taking a rest.

'She's much improved, Pai. I think in another few weeks, she will be strong enough to return to Rio. Fabiana is taking such good care of her.'

'Well, I will see for myself when she wakes. But Izabela, it is almost December,' said Antonio. 'Your marriage takes place at the end of January, and there is still much to do. If, as you say, your mother is recovering under the care of Fabiana, then I feel that you must leave her here and return to Rio with me.'

'But Pai, I'm sure Mãe would prefer her daughter near to her.'

'And I'm sure your mother would understand that the bride needs to be in Rio to organise her wedding,' countered Antonio. 'Not to mention showing your face to your fiancé. I think Gustavo has been extremely patient under the circumstances. He must feel his intended runs away from him at any given opportunity. And I know his parents are becoming most anxious about the arrangements. As am I. So, you will return to Rio with me and that's my final word on the matter.'

As her father left the room to see his wife, Bel knew she was beaten.

'Mãe,' she said as she kissed Carla goodbye two days later, 'please, if you need me, know that I am happy to return. Fabiana will use the telephone in the village to let me know how you are.'

'Don't worry about me, *piccolina*,' Carla said as she stroked her daughter's cheek tenderly. 'I promise I am on the road to recovery. Send my apologies to Senhora Aires Cabral, and tell her I hope to be back in Rio very shortly. Come, give your mother a hug.'

Bel did so and Carla stood at the front door, waving her husband and daughter goodbye. Antonio blew his wife a kiss and the car inched along the stony drive.

'I am very relieved that she is on the mend,' he said suddenly. 'Because I really don't know what I would do without her.'

Bel was surprised to see a rare look of vulnerability in her father's eyes. For much of the time, it seemed to her that Antonio barely noticed his wife.

The following month was filled with endless trips to A Casa das Orquídeas to meet with Luiza and finalise the details for the wedding. Even though Bel was determined not to let the woman rile her, her patronising, arrogant manner had her biting her tongue on many occasions.

Initially, she'd made suggestions for her preferred hymns, the design of her bridesmaids' dresses to complement her own magnificent gown, and a possible menu for the wedding breakfast. But every time she did so, Luiza would find a reason why Bel's ideas were inappropriate. Eventually, seeing it was by far the least painful course of action, she'd simply agreed to everything Luiza suggested.

Gustavo, who sometimes joined them in the drawing room during their meetings, would give her hand a squeeze as she left. 'Thank you for being so good with my mother. I understand she can be domineering.'

Bel would arrive home exhausted, with a headache from the stress of having to comply with everything Luiza said and wondering how on earth she would control herself when she was actually living under the same roof.

As high summer arrived in Rio, Bel found that without her mother at home, and with her father at the office from dawn until dusk, she had far more freedom than usual. Loen, who had entered a slough of despondency since leaving Bruno behind to return to Rio, would accompany Bel to the little station and take the train up the mountain to see how the *Cristo* project was progressing. They could see from the viewing platform the hive of activity the site was becoming; great iron bars were being hoisted into place and it was now possible to make out the shape of the cross.

Watching its progress comforted Bel. Since her time at the *fazenda*, she felt more at peace with the fact that no matter what Laurent thought of her, or whether he loved her, she would always love him. She'd understood that trying to fight it was simply impossible. So, she had surrendered and accepted, knowing she'd harbour her love for Laurent secretly in her heart for the rest of her life.

33

Paris, December 1928

'So, they are finished and ready to be chopped into pieces and shipped off to that great coffee factory of a country across the seas,' declared Landowski as he studied the head and hands of Christ, which now took up every spare inch of space in the *atelier*.

Landowski wandered about the head, studying it thoughtfully. 'The chin still concerns me. From this distance it sticks out from the rest of his face like a giant slide, but the crazy Brazilian tells me this is how he wishes it.'

'It will be seen from a great distance, remember, professor,' commented Laurent.

'His Father in heaven only knows if my masterpiece will make it safely to Rio de Janeiro,' Landowski grumbled. 'The Brazilian is arranging a passage on a cargo ship for it. Let us hope that the seas are calm and another container in the hold does not smash into my creation. I would go with it if I could, to oversee the shipping and to observe the early stages of construction, but I simply cannot spare the time. This project has already taken up twice the time it was meant to and I still have the commission of Sun Yat-sen to complete, which is already considerably behind schedule. Well,' he sighed, 'I have done what I can and now it is out of my control.'

As Laurent listened to Landowski, the tiniest seed of an idea sprouted in his mind. He kept it to himself, wanting to think it through before he suggested it.

The following day, Heitor da Silva Costa came to the *atelier*, and the two men decided where and how the head should be cut into pieces. Laurent listened as Landowski again voiced his concerns about the safety of the sculpture moulds on their journey.

'You're right,' agreed Heitor. 'There should be someone to check them regularly in the hold, but I simply cannot spare any of my team to make the journey. My draftsmen here are not yet finished.'

'I could go,' said Laurent suddenly, voicing the idea that had been growing in his mind since the previous day.

Both men turned to him in surprise. 'You, Brouilly? But I thought you were wedded to the streets of Montparnasse and your hectic social life here,' said Landowski.

'Sadly, I've never had the opportunity to travel outside of France before, professor. Perhaps a few months abroad in such an exotic country would expand my artistic horizons and inspire me.'

'Then you will return to make a great sculpture of a coffee bean, no doubt,' Landowski quipped.

'Senhor Brouilly,' said Heitor, 'if you are serious, then I think it would be an excellent idea. You have been present since the inception of the structure. In fact, your own hands have contributed to parts of it. If the professor can spare you, you could be his eyes in Rio as we construct it.'

'And ensure that a finger does not end up stuck on Our Lord's nose as they fit the pieces together,' Landowski mumbled under his breath.

'I'm happy to go if you wish it, professor,' Laurent reiterated. 'When would we sail, Monsieur da Silva Costa?'

'I have a passage booked for next week, which should give us time to cut and then wrap the moulds securely in their crates. The sooner they reach Rio, and we have all the parts safely delivered, the happier I will be. Are you able to travel at such short notice, Monsieur Brouilly?' asked Heitor.

'I am sure he will have to consult his diary to see if he can move some of his upcoming commissions back,' said Landowski, throwing Laurent a glance which told him to be silent. 'Presumably, there will be some financial recompense for his travels and the loss of his time? For example, bed and board?'

'Of course,' agreed Heitor quickly. 'And in fact, that reminds me, I had a telephone call a few days ago from Gustavo Aires Cabral, Izabela Bonifacio's fiancé. He's heard about the sculpture you did of her, Senhor Brouilly, and would like to present it to his wife-to-be as a wedding gift. I said I would ask you whether you were willing to sell?'

'I . . .'

Laurent was just about to say that under no circumstances would he ever sell the sculpture of his precious Izabela to her fiancé, when Landowski cut in on him.

'What a shame, and just as you had found a wealthy buyer here, Brouilly. Have you accepted his offer?'

Confused, Laurent replied, 'No, I . . .'

'Well then, perhaps Mademoiselle Bonifacio's fiancé would like to make a better one, and you can decide. You said you'd been offered two thousand francs, is that correct?'

Landowski shot a further glance at Laurent, willing him to play along.

'Yes.'

'So, Heitor, tell this Monsieur Aires Cabral that if he is prepared to offer more, and cover the shipping costs to Rio, then the sculpture can be his.'

'I will,' said Heitor, his expression showing that he wasn't remotely interested in haggling over the price of someone else's sculpture when he had his own to think about. 'I'm sure that won't be a problem. So, I will come tomorrow and see how you are progressing with our giant jigsaw puzzle. Good day to you both.' Heitor nodded at them and left the *atelier*.

'Professor, what was that all about?' Laurent asked. 'I have no buyer for Mademoiselle Izabela's sculpture. And in fact, had no thought of selling it.'

'Brouilly, can't you see I was doing you a favour by acting as your agent?' Landowski chided him. 'You should thank me for it. Don't think that the real reason for your sudden eagerness to travel halfway around the world with pieces of the Christ is lost on me. And if you decide to stay in Brazil, you will need some money behind you to help you. What need will you have there of your precious sculpture when you will be close to the living, breathing person who inspired it? Let the fiancé have her immortalised in stone and worship her outer beauty. My guess is that he will never reach her soul, as you so obviously did. Personally, I think it's rather a good swap,' Landowski chuckled. 'So, now we set to work.'

That night, as Laurent settled down on his pallet in the *atelier*, wedged between the head and an enormous finger of the Lord, he wondered what on earth he was doing.

Izabela had made it clear where her future lay. Her

marriage must be imminent and would, in all likelihood, have taken place by the time he arrived in Rio. What exactly he hoped to achieve by travelling there, he wasn't sure.

But Laurent, like all those in love, was a great believer in fate. And, as he glanced at the giant palm before shutting his eyes, he only hoped that it would take a hand.

34

The morning of the wedding of Gustavo Maurício Aires Cabral to Izabela Rosa Bonifacio dawned hot and bright, with barely a cloud in the sky. Reluctantly, Bel climbed out of her maiden bed for the last time. It was early, and as she walked out of her bedroom, the only sound she could hear was the distant clatter of pans from the kitchen.

Tripping downstairs barefooted, she went to the drawing room and then into the small alcove which housed the chapel. Lighting a candle on the altar, she knelt down on the red velvet-covered prie-dieu, closed her eyes and clasped her hands together.

'Please, Blessed Virgin, on this my wedding day, give me the strength and fortitude to go into my marriage with an open heart and be a good and loving wife to my husband. And a patient and caring daughter-in-law to his parents,' she added with feeling. 'Grant me healthy children and that I may count my blessings rather than dwell on my problems. Bring continued wealth to my father and restored health to my dearest mother. Amen.'

Opening her eyes, Bel glanced up at the faded face of the Madonna and blinked away tears.

'You are a woman, so I hope you will forgive the thoughts I still carry in my heart,' she whispered.

A few minutes later, Bel genuflected, rose and, with a deep intake of breath, left the chapel to begin what was supposed to be the happiest day of her life.

Technically, nothing could have gone better on the day than it did. Crowds lined the streets to watch Izabela and her father arrive at the cathedral, and cheered when she stepped out of the Rolls-Royce in the stunning Chantilly lace wedding dress that Jeanne Lanvin had designed in Paris. The magnificent cathedral was packed and as her father walked her proudly down the aisle towards Gustavo, she glanced surreptitiously through her gauzy white veil and saw many familiar faces from among the highest in the land.

An hour later, the bells rang out as Gustavo led his bride back down the aisle and outside onto the steps of the cathedral. The crowd cheered again as he handed her into the horse-drawn carriage so they could ride through the streets to the Copacabana Palace. Bel stood beside her new husband and received the three hundred guests as they filed into the huge salon.

After the many courses of the wedding breakfast, Bel and Gustavo retired to their suite to rest before the grand ball later that evening.

Once the door was shut behind them, Gustavo took her in his arms.

'At last,' he murmured as he burrowed his face into her neck. 'I'm free to kiss you. Come here.' He pulled her head towards him and kissed her ferociously, like a starving man. His hands moved to touch the thin layer of lace covering her breasts and fondled them roughly.

'Ouch,' she gasped. 'You're hurting me.'

'Forgive me, Bel,' Gustavo said, releasing her and regaining his composure with visible effort. 'But you must understand how long I've waited. No matter,' he said with a wink. 'Only a few hours more until I can finally hold you naked in my arms. Can I get you a drink?' he asked as he turned away from her and Bel shuddered involuntarily.

She watched as Gustavo went to the decanter on the side table and poured himself a large measure of brandy.

'No thank you.'

'Perhaps that's wise. I wouldn't want your senses dulled for tonight.' He grinned at her and raised his glass. 'To my wife, my beautiful wife,' he added as he drained the brandy in one gulp.

Bel had noticed on the few times she had accompanied Gustavo to social events that he seemed to enjoy alcohol. On occasion, she had thought him a little drunk by the time the evening was finished.

'And I must tell you that I've bought you a very special wedding gift,' he continued. 'Sadly, it hasn't arrived yet, but it is due to be here by the time we return from our honeymoon. So,' he asked her, 'would you like me to help you out of that gown so you can take a rest?'

Bel glanced longingly at the enormous double bed in the suite. Her feet, stuck as they were in a pair of high-heeled satin shoes – which had meant that with her tiara and hair piled up

on her head she had stood three inches taller than her bride-
groom at the altar – were hurting her. Not to mention the
uncomfortable corset, which she'd been tightly strapped into
this morning by Loen, underneath the lace. But the thought of
Gustavo releasing her from it with his pale, thin fingers was
not an appealing option.

'I'm going to the bathroom,' she announced, blushing with
embarrassment.

Gustavo nodded, having just poured himself another
brandy.

Bel walked into the opulent mirrored room and sat down
gratefully in a chair. She closed her eyes, and pondered on the
ridiculousness of the fact that a ring on her finger and a few
short sentences could change her life so profoundly.

The contrast between her unmarried feminine self, whose
virtue must be protected at all costs from any predatory male,
and the woman who now, only hours later, was supposed to
enter a bedroom alone with a man and perform the most intimate acts, verged on the ridiculous. She looked up at her
reflection in the mirror and sighed.

'He's a stranger,' she whispered to it, thinking back to the
conversation she'd had with her mother last night.

Carla, looking much restored after her time at the *fazenda*,
had come into her bedroom just before Bel had turned off the
light, and had taken her daughter's hands in hers.

'*Querida*, I am now going to tell you what will happen to
you tomorrow night,' she'd begun.

'Mãe,' Bel had said, as horribly embarrassed as Carla, 'I
think I know.'

Her mother had looked vaguely relieved, but had still
persisted.

'So you are aware that the first time may be a little . . . uncomfortable? And that you might bleed? Though some say if you have ridden horses, the delicate tissue that marks a woman out as pure could already have broken. And you rode such a lot at the *fazenda*.'

'I didn't know any of that,' said Bel truthfully.

'The . . . process takes some getting used to, but I imagine Gustavo is experienced in the ways of it and I'm sure he will be gentle with you.'

'Mãe, is it . . . is it ladylike to enjoy it?' asked Bel tentatively.

Carla let out a peal of laughter. 'Of course, *querida*. You will be a married woman, and there is nothing a husband wishes for more than a wife who is happy to explore the pleasures of the bedroom. It's how you keep your husband, and how I have kept mine.' A faint tinge of colour rose to her cheeks. 'And remember, it's for God's purpose: to beget babies. It is a holy state between a husband and wife. Goodnight, Izabela. Sleep well and do not fear for tomorrow. It will be better than you expect, I promise.'

As Bel remembered this conversation, she also thought of her automatic revulsion at the thought of Gustavo touching her in the ways her mother had subtly described. Rising from the chair to return to him, she only hoped that it was first-time nerves and that after tonight, it would be as her mother had told her.

An awed hush fell on the grand ballroom as Izabela entered in her spectacular Patou ballgown of shimmering white, which hugged her curves and cascaded into a fishtail train behind her.

As Gustavo embraced her, the guests applauded.

'You look beautiful, my darling, and every man in the room is jealous that it will be me sharing your bed tonight,' he whispered in her ear.

Apart from the first dance, for the next three hours she hardly saw Gustavo. They each entertained their own family, and Bel danced with numerous nameless men who all told her how lucky Gustavo was to have caught her on his hook. She drank very little, already sick with tension about what would happen afterwards, a feeling that resurfaced with a vengeance as the guests began to gather near the main staircase to cheer them both on their way upstairs.

'It is time,' Gustavo said, appearing beside her, and they walked together through to the front of the crowd.

Gustavo called for silence. '*Meus senhores, senhoras e amigos*. May I thank you for coming and celebrating this great day with us. But now, it is time for me to take my wife's hand and lead her upstairs.'

A round of whistles and lewd catcalls followed his remark.

'So, I bid you good evening and goodnight. Come, Izabela.' He offered his arm to her and she took it. And turning, they walked up the stairs.

This time, once the door to their suite was shut, Gustavo's approach was not so subtle. Without further ado, he pushed her onto the bed and pinned her wrists against the mattress, covering her face and neck with frenzied kisses and pawing at her beautiful gown.

'One moment,' she whispered. 'Let me turn over and you can undo the buttons,' she said, relieved that she could roll away from the stench of the alcohol on his breath.

She felt his hands clumsily picking at the tiny seed pearls that held her dress together and felt his frustration as he finally grabbed the material and tore it open.

Pulling the dress away from her body, he undid her brassiere then turned her over, his lips diving straight to her nipples. A hand travelled up her stockinged inner thigh and then ventured beneath the triangle of silk that covered her innermost part.

After a few seconds of further fumbling, he ripped the silk away, then knelt up to undo his own trouser buttons and release himself. Still fully dressed, he pushed his hardness against her tender skin, moaning in frustration when it could not find entry. Finally, using his own hand, he manoeuvred himself to the opening he sought and thrust himself into her.

Bel lay beneath him biting her lip from the pain. The world was black above her as she closed her eyes and took deep breaths to stop the panic. Thankfully, after only a few seconds, he gave a strangely feminine high-pitched scream, and collapsed on top of her.

Bel lay still, listening to the heavy breathing in her ear. His head was next to hers, face down on the counterpane, his entire weight upon her so that she was pinned beneath him, her knees bent over the edge of the bed. Finally, when she made a move to disentangle herself, he raised his head and looked at her.

'At last, you're truly mine.' He smiled as he touched her cheek. 'Now, you must go and clean yourself up. You understand that the first time—'

'I know,' she said quickly, making swiftly for the bathroom before he had a chance to elaborate.

Bel was glad that she and her mother had had the conversation the night before the wedding. For even though her insides ached, when she wiped herself, the tissue remained clear. Taking down her hair, she changed into the nightdress and *peignoir* that a hotel chambermaid had thoughtfully hung on the back of the door earlier. When she returned to the bedroom, Gustavo was already lying naked in bed. His face wore a puzzled expression.

'I checked, but there was no blood on the counterpane.' He looked at her. 'How can that be?'

'My mother said that if there wasn't, it would be because I rode so frequently at the *fazenda* as a child,' she said, embarrassed by his blatant enquiry.

'Ah. Then that, perhaps, explains it. But of course, you were a virgin?'

'Gustavo, you insult me!' Bel felt her anger rise.

'Of course, of course.' He patted the space on the mattress next to him. 'Then come and join your husband in bed.'

Bel did as she was told, still smarting from his insinuation.

An arm went around her, pulling her towards him, and he reached to turn off the light. 'I think we can agree that we are now well and truly married.'

'Yes.'

'I love you, Izabela. This is the happiest night of my life.'

'And mine.' She managed to dredge up the expected words, despite the unspoken protest that echoed from the depths of her soul.

And as Bel lay sleepless next to her husband of only a few hours, the cargo ship carrying the head and hands of the *Cristo*, and Laurent Brouilly, docked at a pier on the outskirts of Rio de Janeiro.

35

As Laurent woke from his first night on dry land in six weeks, he found himself and the sheets he lay in drenched with sweat. Even on the hottest days in Montparnasse, he'd never known anything like the intensity of the heat here in Rio.

Staggering over to the table where the maid had left him a flagon of water, he picked it up and gulped it down gratefully, feeling his thirst abate. Walking into the tiny bathroom next door, he ran the tap in the sink and put his head beneath it. Wrapping a towel around his nakedness, and feeling at least a little restored, Laurent padded back into the bedroom and went to draw open the shutters.

Last night, when he'd arrived at the hotel which Heitor had suggested he stay in while he found more permanent accommodation, it had been past midnight and too dark to see where he was. But as he'd lain on his bed, he'd heard the sound of the waves crashing onto the shore and had known he must be somewhere near the sea.

And this morning . . . what a sight greeted him! However far his gaze stretched, spread out beneath him on the other side of the road was the most magnificent beach he'd ever seen. Miles of pure white sand, deserted now as the hour was early, and waves that must be two metres high, rolling in relentlessly in a dramatic climax of white foamy spray.

Even the sight of it cooled his blood; Laurent had always loved swimming in the Mediterranean when his family had gone to their summer house near Saint-Raphaël, and he longed to run out of the hotel, over the road and into the water. But first he must ask whether the sea here was safe; for all he knew, it might contain sharks, or other man-eating fish. He'd been warned before he left Paris that one could never be too careful in the tropics.

Even the very smell of the air was new and exotic. Like many of his French compatriots, the fact that their home country provided them with every form of season – from the exhilarating snow-covered slopes of the Alps to the glorious south of the country with its beautiful scenery and climate – meant that Laurent had never been tempted to travel abroad before.

But now, standing here, he felt ashamed he could ever have thought that no other country had anything more to offer him.

He wanted to explore Rio, but before he did so, he had to meet Monsieur da Silva Costa's construction manager, Heitor Levy, who had left him a note at the hotel saying he would collect him at eleven that morning. The head and hands of Christ had been taken off the ship yesterday before it docked in the main port, and had been placed on some open land close to the port, where Monsieur Levy owned a small farm. Laurent only hoped that the delicate pieces of the moulds had made the journey intact. He'd carried out a check on them four times a day down in the hold, and now he could only pray that they had survived the unloading.

He began to dress, noticing that his legs were covered in small, circular welts. Laurent scratched them and pulled on his trousers, knowing that some hungry Brazilian mosquito must have done its worst drinking his blood in the night.

Walking downstairs for breakfast, he entered the dining room and saw a feast of exotic fruits laid out on a long table for the guests. He had no idea what they were, but took a sample of each, determined to embrace this new culture; he also took a slice of some kind of delicious-smelling cake, still warm from the oven. A waitress served him some hot, strong coffee and he drank it in relief, feeling comforted that some things were the same here as at home.

At eleven o'clock, he made his way to the reception area, and saw a man standing beside the desk, checking his watch. Surmising correctly that it must be Monsieur Levy, he walked over and introduced himself.

'Welcome to Rio, Senhor Brouilly. How was your passage?' the man asked him in decent French.

'Extremely comfortable, thank you. I learnt all manner of card games and lewd jokes from my fellow sailors,' said Laurent with a smile.

'Good. Now, my car is outside and we shall drive to my *fazenda*.'

As they drove through the streets of the city, Laurent was surprised to see how very modern it was. Landowski had obviously been teasing him when he said that the residents were all natives, running around the streets naked, throwing spears and eating babies, as this city seemed as civilised and western as many in France itself.

He did, however, find it strange to see the deeply tanned skin of the locals clad in carbon copies of his own country's modern fashions. As they drove through the outskirts, Laurent saw a large slum town appear on his right.

'We call it a *favela*,' Levy said as he saw Laurent staring at it. 'And sadly, it has far too many residents.'

Laurent thought of Paris, where the poor seemed almost invisible. Here, wealth and poverty seemed to have separated themselves totally from each other.

'Yes, Senhor Brouilly,' Levy echoed his thoughts. 'Here in Brazil, the rich are very rich and the poor are . . . starving,' he shrugged.

'Are you Portuguese, monsieur?'

'No. My mother is Italian and my father German. And I am a Jew. Here in Brazil, you will find a very large melting pot of different nationalities, although it is the Portuguese who consider themselves the true Brazilians. We have immigrants from Italy, Spain, and, of course, the Africans, who were brought over as slaves by the Portuguese to work on the coffee farms. And nowadays, Rio is experiencing a huge influx of Japanese. Everyone comes here seeking their pot of gold. Some find it, but others sadly do not, and end up in the *favelas*.'

'It's very different from France. Most of our residents are French born and bred,' commented Laurent.

'But this is the New World, Senhor Brouilly,' Levy said, 'and we will all make it what it is, whatever our original place of birth.'

For the rest of his life, Laurent would never forget the bizarre spectacle of Christ's enormous head sitting in a field, while chickens pecked at the soil around it and a large cockerel preened itself as it sat atop His nose.

'Senhor da Silva Costa called me at five this morning, anxious to know his precious *Cristo* had made the journey safely. So I decided to reconstruct the pieces here and make sure there is no damage. And so far, all is well,' Levy confirmed.

The sight of the head, last seen as a whole in Landowski's *atelier* and now here in Rio thousands of miles away, almost brought a lump to Laurent's throat.

'It looks to me as if He was kept safe on His journey. Maybe watched over by heaven,' said Levy, also moved by the sight. 'I won't endeavour to put the hands together yet, but I had a look and they too seem to have escaped without a scratch. One of my workers will take a photograph to mark the occasion for all of us. I will also send it to Senhor da Silva Costa, and Landowski of course.'

The photograph duly taken, and having closely surveyed the head and hands so he too could write to Landowski and reassure him, Laurent hoped the same good luck had befallen his sculpture of Bel, currently sitting in a crate on the dock somewhere inside the main port.

After agonising over the sale, Laurent had taken Landowski's advice and decided to accept Senhor Aires Cabral's offer of two and a half thousand francs. Landowski had been right: he could always sculpt another and it was a windfall that was impossible to refuse, whatever the future held.

'So, your initial mission has been completed successfully, although I am sure you are eager to see the construction site at Corcovado Mountain,' Levy continued. 'It is truly some-thing to behold. I am living up there with the workers, as we only have a relatively short time in which to complete the project.'

'I would love to see it,' Laurent said eagerly. 'I've struggled to imagine how it is possible to build such a monument on the top of a mountain.'

'So have we all,' Levy agreed phlegmatically. 'But rest assured, it is happening. Now, Senhor da Silva Costa tells me that you are in need of accommodation while you are here. He asked me if I would help you find some, given that I'm sure you don't speak a word of Portuguese.'

'No, monsieur, I do not.'

'Well, it just so happens that I have an apartment going spare. It's in an area called Ipanema, not far from Copa-cabana Beach where you are staying presently. I bought it in my bachelor days before my marriage, and have never had the heart to part with it. I would be happy to let you have the use of it for the time you are here. Senhor da Silva Costa, of course, will pick up any bills, just as you agreed in France. I think you will like it as it has a spectacular view and is full of light. Perfect for a sculptor like yourself,' he added.

'Thank you, Monsieur Levy. I am overwhelmed by your generosity.'

'Well, we shall go and visit it. And if it suits you, you can move in later today.'

By late afternoon, Laurent was the proud tenant of a spacious, airy third-floor apartment in a beautiful block near Ipanema Beach. The graceful high-ceilinged rooms were elegantly furnished and when he opened the door to the shady balcony, he could see the beach in the distance. The warm wind brought with it the unmistakeable smell of the ocean.

Levy had left him there to settle in after they'd retrieved his suitcase from the hotel, telling him he'd be back later to introduce him to the maid who would cook and clean for him during his stay.

Laurent wandered wide-eyed from room to room, the luxury of having such space all to himself after his squalid attic room in Montparnasse, let alone the thought of a maid to wait on him, almost too much to comprehend. He sat on the enormous mahogany bed and lay back, enjoying the breeze from the ceiling fan that brushed his face like tiny wings. Breathing a sigh of contentment, he promptly fell asleep.

That evening, as promised, Levy brought Monica, a middle-aged African woman, to see him.

'I've warned her that you don't speak any Portuguese, but if you agree, Monsieur Brouilly, she will clean the apartment, shop for provisions in the local market and prepare your evening meal. Anything else you need, there is a telephone in the drawing room. Please, call me at any time.'

'I really can't thank you enough for your kindness, Monsieur Levy,' Laurent replied gratefully.

'You are our honoured guest here in Brazil, and we can't have you reporting back to Senhor Landowski and the rest of Paris that we live like heathens,' Levy smiled, raising a knowing eyebrow.

'Indeed not, monsieur. From what I've seen so far, I think you are more civilised than us in Paris.'

'By the way, did your own sculpture arrive safely?' Levy enquired.

'Yes, it is at the dock, and the authorities said they will notify the buyer and arrange for it to be delivered to him.'

'The Aires Cabrals are doubtless away on honeymoon. They married only yesterday.'

Laurent stared at Levy in shock. 'Mademoiselle Izabela was married yesterday?'

'Yes. Their photograph is on the front of all the newspapers here today. She looked most beautiful. It was a high-society wedding indeed. It seems the subject of your sculpture has done well for herself.'

Laurent felt physically sick at the news. The irony of arriving in Rio on the very day Izabela had married was almost too much for him to bear.

'Well, I must be off. Goodnight, Senhor Brouilly.'

Levy left him for the evening, reminding him that he would collect him at two o'clock on Monday afternoon to take him up to the construction site at the top of Corcovado Mountain. Monica was clattering pans in the kitchen and a wonderful smell was emanating from it.

In need of a drink, Laurent pulled a bottle of French wine out of his suitcase, uncorked it, and took it out onto the terrace. Hoisting his feet up onto the table, he poured it into a glass and sipped it, the flavour reminding him immediately of home. He watched the sun setting behind the mountains, his heart heavy.

'Izabela,' he whispered to the air, 'I'm here, in your beautiful country. I came all this way to find you, but now it seems it's too late.'

36

A week after her marriage, Bel arrived back from her honeymoon tense and exhausted. They'd spent it in the region of
Minas Gerais, in an old and once-beautiful house belonging
to Gustavo's great-aunt and uncle. The weather had been
stifling, and without a sea breeze or altitude to lower the temperature, the air had been so hot it had felt as if it was
burning her nostrils when she inhaled it.

There had been endless dinners to endure as she was
introduced to elderly members of Gustavo's family who'd
been too frail to attend the wedding. All of these things she
could have coped with, if it hadn't been for the nights.

One thing her mother had not told her was how often the
bedroom loving was meant to happen. She had presumed
perhaps once a week, but Gustavo's appetite seemed to be
insatiable. Even though she had done her best to relax and try
to enjoy some of the intimate things he liked to do to her –
things that no one had ever explained to her and still made
her blush just to think of them – she had not succeeded.

Every night, once the bedroom door was shut, he would
pounce on her, tearing at her clothes to remove them – and on
a couple of occasions, not even bothering to do that. She'd

lain beneath him as he pounded against her sore, bruised inner flesh, just waiting for it to be over.

At least when it was, he'd fall asleep immediately, but sometimes she'd wake in the morning and feel him reach for her, and within seconds the weight of his body would again be on top of hers.

Last night, he'd tried to push himself into her unwilling mouth. She'd gagged as he did so, and he'd laughed, telling her she'd become used to it, that it was something all wives did for their husbands to give them pleasure and she mustn't be ashamed.

Bel was desperate to ask someone for advice, someone who could tell her whether this really *was* normal and something she'd simply have to endure for the rest of her life. Where was the tenderness, the gentle loving her mother had talked of? she asked herself as she entered her newly refurbished marital bedroom at A Casa das Orquídeas. Currently, she thought, sitting down abruptly in a chair, she felt like a rag doll, pushed and pulled at her husband's bidding.

At home, her father had a dressing room with a bed in it where he would often sleep. There was no such luxury here, she thought desperately as she walked into the newly added bathroom next door. Perhaps if she managed to conceive a child, surely he'd leave her alone then?

Bel tried to comfort herself that in daylight hours Gustavo could not be more loving towards her. He'd constantly reach for her hand, put an arm around her shoulder as they walked together, and tell anyone who would listen how happy he was. If only the nightly horror would cease, she felt she could at least cope with her new circumstances. But until that day came, she knew she would wake up each morning with dread in her heart.

'You look pale, my dear,' said Luiza over dinner that night. 'Perhaps a child is already on the way?' She looked proudly at Gustavo.

'Maybe, Mãe. We will see,' he said.

'I was thinking that I might go and visit my mother in Cosme Velho tomorrow,' Bel ventured into the silence. 'I would like to see how she is.'

'Of course, Izabela,' agreed Gustavo. 'I was thinking I would visit my club, so I can have the car drop you off and then come to collect you later.'

'Thank you,' she said, as they walked through to the drawing room to take coffee. As she conversed with Maurício, she saw her husband pouring himself a further large brandy.

'Tomorrow morning, Izabela,' interrupted Luiza, 'I would like you to come and see me in the library and we will go over the household accounts. I'm sure there was no need for a budget at your parents' home, but here at the Casa we don't like waste.'

'Yes, Luiza.'

Bel refrained from pointing out that her father was paying for their family home to be renovated. And had, she knew, granted a very generous sum of cash to Gustavo on their marriage, which was meant to cover such things as their living expenses and her wardrobe.

'Time for bed, my love,' Gustavo said, and Bel's heart began to beat uncomfortably fast at the prospect. The heavy, salty meal which the ageing cook had prepared sat uneasily in her stomach as Gustavo signalled for her to rise.

'Goodnight, Mãe and Pai.' He bowed slightly to them. 'We will see you in the morning.'

With Gustavo leading her by the hand up the stairs, Bel took a deep breath and followed her husband into their bedroom.

'*Querida*,' said Carla as she greeted Bel at the front door. 'I have missed you. Come inside and tell me all about your honeymoon. Was it wonderful?'

The comforting sight of her mother made Bel want to throw herself into her arms and weep on her shoulder.

'Yes,' she agreed quietly as Carla led her through to the drawing room. 'Gustavo's relatives were most kind to me.'

'Good, good,' she said as Gabriela brought them some coffee. 'And Gustavo? He is well and happy?'

'Yes, he has gone to his club this afternoon. To be quite honest, I've no idea what it is he does there.'

'Gentlemen's business,' Carla replied. 'Probably checking his stocks and shares. Which, if they are anything like your father's, are doing very well at present. The coffee trade continues to boom. Only last week your father bought another two farms. Which one day you, and therefore Gustavo, will inherit. So, tell me, how is married life?'

'I'm . . . adjusting.'

'"Adjusting"?' Carla frowned. 'Izabela, what does that word mean? You're not happy with your new state?'

'Mama,' Bel said, reverting to her childhood word, 'I . . .'

'Please, Izabela, continue with what you wish to say.'

'I . . . need to know if, well, Gustavo will always wish to have . . . activity . . . in the bedroom every night?'

Carla studied her daughter, then chuckled.

'Now I understand. You have a husband who is hot-blooded and wishes to enjoy his beautiful new wife. Izabela, this is a good thing. It means he loves you and wants you. Surely you must understand that?'

Bel was desperate to ask her about the other things Gustavo did and wished her to do, but she could not voice the words. 'But Mãe, I am very tired.'

'You are not getting much sleep, that is to be expected,' said Carla, either stubbornly refusing to acknowledge her daughter's tension or being genuinely blind to it. 'I remember it is how your father and I were in the days after we married. It is natural, *querida*, and yes, after a time, of course it will calm down. Perhaps when you are pregnant, which from the sounds of things, you soon will be,' she added with a smile. 'I have always longed to be a grandmother.'

'And I a mother.'

'How is it living in your beautiful new home? Is Senhora Aires Cabral being kind to you?'

'She has been welcoming,' said Bel shortly. 'Although this morning we talked about the household accounts. They live far more frugally than we do.'

'Surely now, with your father giving Gustavo such a handsome sum, that will change? And in fact, we have something to tell you. But I will wait until your father is here with me before we do,' said Carla secretively.

'You are well, Mãe?' Bel changed the subject, realising that Carla simply did not wish to know or hear about any problems her daughter was experiencing. She also thought Carla still looked far too thin and pale.

'I am feeling very well indeed,' her mother replied brightly. 'Although it's very strange in the house without you. When you were away in the Old World, I always knew that you were returning home here. I know now that you never will. Still, you are not far away and I hope we will see each other often.'

'Of course we will.' Bel was depressed by the odd feeling of distance that seemed to have suddenly emerged between them. It was as though Carla had accepted that her daughter no longer belonged to her, but to Bel's husband and *his* family.

'Ah, here is your father. I told him you were coming to visit and he promised he would return early from the office to see you.'

Antonio arrived, full of his usual bonhomie. Once he'd hugged his daughter, he sat down next to her and took her hands in his.

'I wanted to wait until you were returned from honeymoon to tell you of our gift to you on the occasion of your marriage. Yesterday, Izabela, I transferred the deeds of Fazenda Santa Tereza to you.'

'Pai!' Bel stared at her father in genuine delight. 'You are telling me the *fazenda* is mine? Just mine alone?'

'Yes, Izabela. However,' her father continued, 'there is a slight complication that you should be aware of.' Antonio paused and rubbed his chin in contemplation for a moment. 'You may not know that currently in Brazil a husband normally acquires the legal rights to any property that his wife owns. So, since your mother insisted that the *fazenda* should be yours alone, I had to be a little . . . creative. I have set up a trust in your name, to be administered by my lawyer, which includes the *fazenda* within it and your right to any income that the farm earns. Plus the right to live in it until your death. We must hope that before that happens, our outdated laws will be changed and you will own the *fazenda* outright. There is also a clause which allows the trust to be passed on automatically to any children you may have.'

'I understand. Thank you, both of you,' Bel whispered, so moved she could barely speak. 'Nothing you could have done could have made me happier.' Bel rose to embrace her mother, who she now knew was primarily responsible for this wonderful gift.

'I felt that your father has been more than generous to your husband's family,' Carla said. 'Even if Gustavo knew about this – which he does not – he could hardly complain that Antonio wishes to be equally generous to his daughter. Especially when he has worked so hard all his life to be able to provide for her.'

Bel saw the hint of disapproval in her mother's eyes, and realised that there was part of Carla that resented Antonio's financial benevolence to a family who had never worked a single day in their lives.

'Now . . .' Antonio retrieved a sheaf of documents from an envelope he had brought in with him. 'Come here and sign these along with me. Witnessed by your mother and Gabriela.'

Bel put her name to the documents underneath her father's, then Carla and Gabriela signed as witnesses. Her spirits had lifted enormously at the thought of a home that was truly hers. Given her current misgivings about her marriage, it gave her a much needed sense of security.

'There,' smiled Antonio, never happier than when he was being munificent. 'I will get these to my lawyer as soon as possible,' he said, stowing the documents away in his desk drawer.

Gustavo arrived an hour later to take her home. After the formal greetings from his new in-laws, he announced that they must leave to be in time for dinner with his parents.

'I'll be back to see you as soon as possible, Mãe. And perhaps we can take that ride up Corcovado Mountain in the train and see how the *Cristo* statue is coming along?' said Bel.

'I would like that very much, Izabela,' agreed Carla. 'Maybe on Thursday?'

'Yes, I will see you then,' she said and followed Gustavo dutifully out to the car.

As the driver began the journey home, Bel decided not to mention to her husband the gift her parents had just made her. It was her beautiful secret and she wished to keep it to herself. As they passed the Estação do Corcovado, she saw the train emptying its passengers onto the tiny platform. And there, walking towards her along the narrow path, was . . . Bel's heart skipped a beat as she stared at him, but he turned away down the street too quickly for her to be absolutely sure.

Bel closed her eyes and shook her head. Of course it wasn't Laurent, just someone who looked very like him. After all, what would he be doing in Brazil?

'My wedding gift is to be delivered to the Casa tomorrow,' said Gustavo, pulling Bel out of her reverie and putting his hand on hers. 'I have seen it and I think it's very beautiful. I hope you will too.'

'Then I will look forward to it,' she said, with as much enthusiasm as she could muster.

Later that evening after dinner, Bel felt exhausted. The image of the phantom Laurent had unsettled her and her stomach was cramping painfully. When Gustavo and she arrived in their bedroom, she moved swiftly into the bathroom and locked it behind her. Changing into her nightgown, she cleaned her teeth and brushed her hair. She unlocked the door and went into the bedroom where Gustavo was already undressed and in bed waiting for her. As he reached for her, she backed away and shook her head.

'I am sorry, but tonight we cannot. I have the curse.'

At that, Gustavo nodded briskly, climbed off the bed and donned his robe. 'Then I will sleep in my old room and let you rest. Goodnight, my dear.'

As the door closed behind him, Bel sat down on the bed and let out a small chuckle at Gustavo's swift exit. At least, she thought, she'd have a few days every month when she would sleep alone and in peace.

Two days later, as agreed with Carla, Bel arrived at her old house to collect her mother and take her on the train up to the top of Corcovado Mountain. As they climbed into one of the carriages and began to ascend, Carla grasped her daughter's arm in fear.

'Is this safe? The incline is so steep, how can it reach the top?'

'Don't be frightened, Mãe. It is worth it when we get there and you can see the beautiful view of Rio.'

At the top, they climbed the steps slowly together, Carla needing to pause every so often to catch her breath. Bel guided her mother to the viewing pavilion. 'Isn't it beautiful?' she smiled. 'And of course, they are building the structure for the *Cristo* over there. It is so strange to think that I saw the sculpture being designed and made with my very own eyes in Professor Landowski's studio. He actually took a mould of my hands to perhaps use as models for the *Cristo*'s . . .'

As Bel turned from the view below her to the *Cristo* structure, she saw two men walking from it, deep in conversation. She stared in disbelief, her heart almost stopping as he glanced upwards and saw her.

They gazed at each other for a few seconds, then he smiled at her and turned his attention to the steps. And following his companion down them, he disappeared from view.

'Who was that?'

Carla was watching her daughter with interest.

'I . . . it was Senhor Levy, Heitor da Silva Costa's project manager.'

'Yes, I recognise him from his photograph in the newspaper. But what about the other man?'

'Oh, I couldn't tell for definite, but I believe it was an assistant of Professor Landowski's.'

'I see. Well, he certainly seemed to know who you were.'

'We did meet in Paris, yes,' Bel said as she tried desperately to compose herself. Every nerve ending in her body was telling her to run from the pavilion, hurtle down the steps and fall into Laurent's arms. And it took every ounce of restraint to prevent herself from doing so.

Fifteen minutes later, when Carla had said she'd had enough of the blistering heat and they walked slowly back down the steps and onto the platform to wait for the train, the two men were nowhere to be seen.

When they arrived back at the house, Carla asked her if she wanted to come in for some refreshment, but Bel declined and told her driver she must go straight home. She needed some time alone to collect herself, and she knew if she stayed with her mother, she might give herself away.

How can he be here? Why has he come?

But of course, Laurent had been with Senhor Levy, so she could only presume he'd been sent by Landowski as his envoy to oversee the *Cristo* project for him.

Yes, thought Bel, climbing out of the car and walking reluctantly up the front steps, that was it. Laurent's presence in Rio was nothing more mysterious than that. She made her way straight upstairs to her bedroom, knowing that Gustavo wouldn't be home from his club for at least a couple of hours and feeling relieved at the prospect.

Lying on the bed, Bel breathed deeply and tried to think rationally. The chances were that she would never set eyes on him here. It was unlikely their paths would cross in Rio, as the engineer Senhor Levy was not part of their social circle and Heitor da Silva Costa was still in Paris. It was simply a cruel twist of fate that she'd seen him today. And with all her heart, as she remembered the sweet smile he'd given her as they'd stared at each other for that split second, she wished she hadn't.

The following evening, Gustavo arrived home early from his club and told her she was not to enter the drawing room until he gave the word. She could see from his expression that whatever it was he'd bought her as a wedding gift had pleased him. She prepared to show her appreciation for whatever it might be.

'Your parents are joining us for dinner tonight, as well as another surprise guest, so put on your most beautiful gown,' her husband suggested.

Laurent too had been moved and unsettled by his glimpse of Izabela standing in the viewing pavilion. The sun had been behind her as he had looked up, which had made her appear almost angelic; her whole being lit up. In the days since he'd heard from Levy of her wedding, the excitement he'd felt when he first arrived in Rio had been tempered with misery. He'd decided the best thing he could do was to view the construction project as soon as possible, so at least he could tell Landowski all was looking well for his sculpture. Then he would also see a little more of the land he'd travelled so far to reach, and afterwards, return home to France. Now he knew for certain Izabela could never be his, there was nothing here for him. He'd berated himself for his impetuous decision to board the ship in the first place. However, he had stayed for the past month, fuelled by the knowledge that at some point Izabela would return to Rio from her honeymoon, and by a blind belief that they would meet by chance.

And then yesterday, Monsieur Levy had told him that Monsieur da Silva Costa had contacted him, asking for Laurent's telephone number.

'It seems Gustavo Aires Cabral would like to meet the sculptor of his wife in person. He's invited you to dinner at their beautiful house tomorrow evening. I believe he also wishes to pay you,' Levy had added. 'He will call you to make the arrangements in due course.'

'Thank you.'

Laurent had decided initially that he would of course refuse the dinner offer, and arrange to meet the man at his club in Rio to receive payment for the sculpture. Izabela's husband was hardly a person with whom he wished to become acquainted.

But then yesterday afternoon he'd seen her . . .

Now, after endless debates with himself, he'd decided – whether the husband was there or not – that he'd allow himself an evening when he would have the pleasure of gazing at her beautiful face once more. So when Monsieur Aires Cabral had called him, he accepted the invitation to attend the dinner.

As the taxi drove through the streets of Ipanema and out of the hecticness of the city into the suburbs, Laurent wondered now what on earth had possessed him. Surely, spending hours in her presence was suicide for his heart? It would only reignite his passion further. However, he thought, as the car turned into the long drive of an elegant colonial-style house, he was here now and would simply have to make the best of it.

Laurent climbed out of the taxi, paid the driver and stood staring up in wonder at the facade of the building, which was certainly one of the most impressive he'd seen in Rio so far. He mounted the wide marble steps to the gracious front door and rang the bell.

It was opened by a maid, and he was ushered into a drawing room, already occupied by two middle-aged couples. In the corner of the room, draped with a tablecloth to hide it from view, was what he recognised from the shape as his sculpture.

'Ah, you have arrived!' said a thin man with features that reminded him of a rodent as he entered the room behind him. 'The sculptor himself!' He smiled and held out his pale hand. 'Gustavo Aires Cabral. And you must be Senhor Laurent Brouilly.'

'Yes. I'm pleased to make your acquaintance, senhor,' he replied, noticing that the man's handshake was rather weak and that he stood at least four inches below Laurent in height. Surely, he thought, as Gustavo guided him over to introduce him to the other occupants of the room, this scrawny, unattractive man could not be Izabela's new husband?

'Champagne, senhor?' asked a maid, offering him a glass from a tray.

'*Merci*,' he said as he shook hands with Gustavo's parents, and was then introduced to Izabela's mother and father.

Antonio Bonifacio, a tall, attractive man, with flecks of grey appearing in his black hair, shook his hand heartily, and Carla gave him a warm smile. She was a beautiful woman and Laurent could see where Izabela had inherited her dark, sultry looks from. Neither of them could speak French, so Gustavo translated for them both.

'Senhor Bonifacio says that Izabela has told him so much

about Professor Landowski and the time she spent in the *atelier* while you sculpted her. He waits to see if you have captured her beauty well enough,' said Gustavo.

'I can only hope you think I've done your daughter justice, senhor,' Laurent replied, feeling the mother's eyes upon him, assessing him as he spoke. He recognised her as the woman who'd been with Izabela yesterday on the top of Corcovado Mountain.

'Senhora Carla says that of course, Izabela doesn't know anything about either the sculpture being here, or you,' said Gustavo, 'and that it will be a big surprise for her when she comes down to join us.'

'It certainly will,' Laurent replied with feeling.

'Are you ready?' said Gustavo, entering the bedroom and finding Bel sitting on the bed looking pensive.

She turned and smiled at him. 'Yes.'

Gustavo surveyed his wife in a beautiful gown of green silk, the emeralds her father had presented her with for her eighteenth birthday in her ears and around her neck.

'You look radiant, *querida*,' he said offering her his arm. 'Shall we go?'

'I can't imagine what it might be that warrants such an audience,' said Bel as she walked with him down the stairs.

'Well, you shall soon see.' Gustavo tapped his nose and then opened the drawing room door. 'Here she is,' he said to the assembled company, and Bel smiled as her mother and father came over to greet her. Gustavo steered Bel away from them towards his own parents, who were talking to another guest.

'This is the first part of your surprise, which may help you guess what your gift is. May I present Senhor Laurent Brouilly, all the way from Paris.'

Bel watched as Laurent turned towards her, Gustavo smiling gaily between the two of them, so happy with his surprise plan.

She gazed at Laurent witlessly, knowing that all eyes in the room had turned towards the two of them to watch for her reaction. She could not think of a thing to say to him, so deep was her shock. She felt her silence lasting forever as the seconds ticked by.

'Madame Aires Cabral,' said Laurent, taking her hand in his and saving the day. 'It is such a pleasure to make your acquaintance again.' He kissed her hand, and then studied her. 'Your father was asking a few minutes ago whether I felt I had done you justice, but seeing you again, I fear I have not.'

'I . . .' Bel forced her brain to make her mouth open and speak to him in French. 'Senhor Brouilly, what a pleasant surprise. I did not expect to see you in Rio.'

'Well,' said Gustavo, 'it was a happy coincidence that Senhor Brouilly was here in Brazil for the *Cristo* project. Surely you must have guessed what my gift is by now?'

Bel's mind was so full of Laurent, she hadn't even begun to contemplate the correlation between his presence and the gift from her husband. Luckily, before she could answer, Gustavo steered her towards an object that stood draped under a tablecloth, as everyone gathered round.

'Shall I remove it?' Gustavo asked her.

'Yes,' said Bel with a gulp, finally understanding what the gift was.

There were gasps of delight as Laurent's sculpture was revealed. And Bel could only thank God Laurent had captured her as a chaste young woman. No one gazing at her image could possibly suggest the sculpture was in any way inappropriate.

'So?' Gustavo's eyes swept around the room, gauging the onlookers' opinions.

Antonio was the first to speak. 'Why, it is the most incredible likeness. You have captured her well, Senhor Brouilly.'

'Yes indeed, that is the image of my daughter,' said Carla approvingly.

Gustavo translated both the positive responses to Laurent and he gave them a bow of appreciation.

'I'm not sure that you have quite caught her lips,' said Luiza in French, always eager to find something negative to say. 'They are not as full as they could be.'

'Well, senhora,' replied Laurent, 'studying your daughter-in-law after her marriage, she has definitely flowered since I last saw her in person. It must be that being a wife, with all its pleasures, suits her.'

Bel almost gasped at Laurent's response to Luiza's criticism, ostensibly gracious yet so soaked with innuendo that no one in the room could miss it. Luiza had the grace to blush.

'And what do you think of my gift to you, Izabela?' enquired Gustavo, placing a proprietorial arm around her waist.

'I don't think I can judge the merits of a sculpture of myself without sounding arrogant, but it is a very thoughtful wedding gift, Gustavo. And you have made me very happy.'

As robotically as she had spoken those words, Bel planted a kiss on her husband's cheek. And during every second of this exchange, she felt – or imagined she felt – Laurent's eyes burning into her.

The elderly butler entered the room and announced that dinner was served. At the table, Bel was grateful that Laurent had been placed between Luiza and Carla; she was between her father and her father-in-law, with Gustavo holding court at the top of the table. Unfortunately, Laurent was seated directly opposite her, so every time she looked up, there he was. She thought how the table arrangement was a dreadful parody of the hours they had sat facing each other in the *atelier* in France.

Taking a large gulp of the wine the butler had poured her to calm her nerves, Bel turned to her right and began an in-depth conversation about anything that sprang to mind with Maurício. Antonio, hearing that they had begun discussing coffee prices, soon joined in and the two men spoke of their concerns that the amount currently being produced in Brazil was creating a surplus which was driving the price down.

'My friends in the senate are talking about the idea of stockpiling,' commented Maurício.

'Yes, and I'm planning to follow their lead on my farms,' confirmed Antonio. 'The price has already dropped in the space of a month and the profits are not as healthy as they were.'

While the conversation was lost on her, Bel had no choice but to sit slightly back in her chair as the two men conversed across her. Which meant she often found herself staring straight ahead at Laurent.

And as their eyes locked for a few seconds, they both knew that nothing had changed.

Over coffee in the drawing room, Bel found herself in a three-way conversation with Gustavo and Laurent.

'When will you return to Paris?' Gustavo enquired of him.

'I haven't made a decision yet,' he said. 'It depends on how things turn out, and what opportunities I find here,' Laurent replied, glancing at Bel. 'Your mother, monsieur, has kindly promised to introduce me to some possible clients who may wish members of their family to be sculpted. Who knows?' he said with a smile. 'I may fall in love with your beautiful country and decide to stay here forever.'

'Well, if you have secured my mother as your champion and patron, then that may well be an option,' Gustavo said. 'More brandy?' he asked, rising from the sofa where he'd been sitting next to Bel.

'Not for me, thank you, senhor,' said Laurent.

Gustavo walked away, and the two of them were left alone together for the first time.

'How are you, Izabela?' he asked her.

Bel gazed down at the table, at the floorboards, anywhere so that her eyes did not have to meet Laurent's. There was a world she wanted to say to him, but could not. 'I am . . . married,' she managed eventually.

She glanced up for his response and saw him furtively checking the room to see if any eyes were upon them.

'Bel,' he whispered, as he leant towards her as close as he dared from his chair. 'You must know that I came here to find you. You *must* know it,' he reiterated. 'If you wish me to turn around and catch the next boat back to France, I will. But I want to hear it from your lips. Now,' he urged her as he saw

Gustavo pouring the brandy into his glass from the decanter. 'Tell me, are you happy with your husband?'

She could not find the words to reply. She saw Gustavo replacing the crystal stopper on the decanter. 'I cannot,' she finally managed, knowing the seconds were running out.

'Then do you still love me?'

'Yes.' She watched Gustavo bend down to his mother and whisper something in her ear.

'Then meet me tomorrow afternoon. My address is seventeen Rua Visconde de Pirajá. It's an apartment block in Ipanema and I am number six on the top floor.'

Bel consigned it to memory as Gustavo swayed back towards them both. She saw Laurent noticing how drunk he was, and she shuddered as Gustavo sat down next to her, put a fierce arm around her and pulled her to him to kiss her.

'Isn't my wife beautiful?' he said to Laurent.

'Indeed she is, monsieur.'

'Sometimes I feel I don't deserve her,' Gustavo said as he took another slug of his brandy. 'As you can imagine, I'm enjoying my first few weeks of married life.'

'Oh yes, I can imagine,' said Laurent. 'And now, forgive me, but I must take my leave.' He stood up abruptly, and walked away to say his goodbyes to the assembled company.

'Are you healthy again?' Gustavo whispered in Bel's ear as she saw Laurent kissing Carla's hand.

'Sadly not, but maybe tomorrow.'

'A shame,' Gustavo commented. 'Tonight I wanted to love my beautiful wife.'

Laurent came back and stood in front of them. 'I will say goodnight and thank you to both of you.'

Gustavo and Bel rose, Laurent shaking his hand and then taking hers briefly and kissing it.

'*À bientôt*, Madame Aires Cabral.'

'*Bonne nuit*, Senhor Brouilly.'

Once Laurent had left, the rest of the party began to disperse.

'Goodnight, *querida*,' said Carla on the doorstep. 'Come and visit me soon,' she said, giving her daughter a quizzical glance before walking down the steps behind Antonio.

Upstairs on the landing outside their bedroom, Gustavo kissed Bel passionately. 'I can't wait until tomorrow evening,' he said.

Bel shut the door, disrobed and climbed into bed, thanking God she was alone tonight.

37

Bel woke the following morning knowing she must have drunk too much the night before. Or had at least experienced a rush of blood to her head. Why else would she have agreed to meet Laurent this afternoon at his apartment?

She rolled over and groaned. Last night, she'd lain in bed joyfully reliving every heated glance and word that had passed between them, but now she played out the dreadful consequences of Laurent's presence here in Rio.

She had been married to Gustavo for less than a month. And yet she had confessed to Laurent that not only was she unhappy in her marriage, but that she still loved *him* . . .

What madness had possessed her?

The madness of love . . .

Whatever affliction it was, the consequences of Gustavo finding out about the relationship they'd had in France, let alone if it was continued now, were too awful even to contemplate.

Bel stood up and went to the bathroom. She looked at her reflection in the mirror, asking it what she should do. The safest option was simply not to visit Laurent at his apartment this afternoon. If she stayed away, she was sure he would accept it and not bother her again.

Laurent's eyes immediately took the place of her own in the glass, full of love, promise and fulfilment, and she shuddered with pleasure despite herself.

Loen was in her bedroom when she came out of the bathroom.

'How are you, Senhora Bel?' Loen asked as she hung up the beautiful silk dress Bel had discarded in a heap on the floor last night.

'I am . . . a little tired,' she admitted.

'He was here last night, wasn't he? Your sculptor?' Loen said as she continued to tidy the room.

'Yes, he was. I . . . Oh Loen.' Bel sank onto the bed, put her head in her hands and wept. Loen came to sit next to her and put an arm round her mistress.

'Please don't cry. Surely you must be a little happy he has come to Brazil?'

'Yes . . . no . . .' Bel looked up at Loen. 'I've done something very silly,' she admitted. 'I told him I'd meet him at his apartment in Ipanema this afternoon.'

'I see.' Loen nodded calmly. 'Will you go?'

'How can I? I am married and I have agreed to meet another man! What would you do, Loen? Please, tell me.'

'I don't know,' Loen sighed. 'I want to tell you that of course it would be wrong to meet with him. But if it was Bruno, I doubt I could stop myself. Especially if I knew he might only be here temporarily.'

'You're encouraging me, Loen,' Bel said as she eyed her maid, 'when I need to be told that it's madness.'

'It is,' Loen agreed, 'but you know that anyway. Perhaps it would be best if you met him just this once and told him that you can't ever see him again. And said a final goodbye.'

'And how would I do that? Senhora Aires Cabral watches my every move.'

'You have a fitting in Ipanema with Madame Duchaine at two o'clock this afternoon for your new season's wardrobe,' Loen replied. 'We can attend, then perhaps you could say you felt unwell and leave your fitting, giving you enough time to meet with your sculptor. It would give you at least a couple of hours together.'

'Loen, what are you doing to me?' Bel said despairingly, knowing her maid's plan was all too easy to execute.

'I'm being your friend, Bel, as you have been mine. I've seen the misery in your eyes every day since your marriage. I want you to be happy. Life is very short, and marriage to one you don't love is very long. So,' Loen said, rising from the bed, 'you make your decision and I will do whatever you wish to help you.'

'Thank you. I will think,' Bel agreed.

'Good morning,' Luiza greeted her as she arrived at the table. 'Did you sleep well, my dear?'

'Yes, I did, thank you.'

'I've had a note this morning from a friend of mine. They are looking for young ladies to assemble at Igreja de Nossa Senhora da Glória do Outeiro, the church not far from your parents' house, Senhor da Silva Costa, the engineer on the *Cristo* project, has decided he will decorate the statue with a soapstone mosaic. He's looking for a large number of willing hands to stick the soapstone on the netting, triangle by triangle. It will be a long job, but from what my friend tells me, it will be performed by women from the best backgrounds. I have noticed you don't seem to have many suitable female acquaintances in Rio. This would be the perfect way for you to make more friends.'

'Yes, of course, I'd be glad to help,' Bel agreed. 'Especially as it's for such a worthy cause and a project close to my heart.'

'Then I will reply to her and say that you have volunteered. Perhaps you can begin tomorrow.'

'Yes,' said Bel as the maid served her coffee.

After breakfast, Bel took a walk around the gardens, deep in thought. At least the mosaic would give her something positive to spend her time doing, because here, it was obvious she was never going to be mistress of her own household. Even though Luiza had thrown her a bone by telling her how the household accounts ran, she continued to organise everything herself. If Bel made a suggestion for the dinner menu, it would be rejected, and when she'd attempted to ask yesterday if they could use the Limoges dinner service rather than the Wedgwood, she was told that it only came out for family celebrations such as birthdays and anniversaries.

Every day, Gustavo would disappear off to his club straight after lunch, which meant she spent endless hours of the afternoon alone. Her stomach gave a sudden lurch – so what was she going to do about *this* afternoon?

By lunchtime, Bel was in a state of frenzy. At half past one, she called for the car.

'Luiza,' she said, when she found her writing letters in the drawing room, 'I am off to see Madame Duchaine in the city. Loen will accompany me. I may be some time as she's fitting me for my winter wardrobe.'

'Well, I hear she's very costly and her stitching can sometimes be clumsy. I can give you the name of another dressmaker who is far less expensive and very reliable.'

'As a matter of fact, Madame Duchaine has always done an excellent job for me,' Bel retorted. 'I will see you at dinner, Luiza.'

Without waiting for her mother-in-law's look of surprise that Bel had actually dared question her judgement, she walked towards the door and pinned on her hat.

Loen was already waiting there for her. 'Well?' she whispered as they walked towards the car.

'I don't know,' she groaned.

'Then we shall go to Madame Duchaine's and if you decide to feign a headache, I will follow your lead,' Loen said as they climbed into the car. The driver set off, Bel staring sightlessly out of the window, her heart pounding so hard against her chest she felt it might burst open.

When they arrived at Madame Duchaine's, Bel and Loen climbed out of the car.

'There's no need for you to wait, Jorge,' Bel told the driver. 'I will be some time. Please return and collect me at six.'

'Yes, senhora.'

She watched him pull away from the kerb, then entered the salon with Loen.

Ten minutes later, Bel found herself staring blankly at her

reflection in the full-length mirror, her mind in turmoil, while Madame Duchaine fussed around her with a tape measure and pins. She was still in an agony of indecision, her stomach churning. If she didn't make her mind up soon, it would be too late anyway.

Madame Duchaine stood up and moved behind Bel, surveying her handiwork in the mirror over Bel's shoulder. As her beady eyes reached Bel's face, she frowned.

'Why, you do not look well at all, senhora. You are very pale. Are you perhaps sickening for something?'

'I am feeling a little faint,' Bel agreed.

'Well, perhaps we should continue the fitting on another day? I think it may be best if you leave and take some rest,' she said, surreptitiously eyeing her client's stomach in the mirror.

In that split second, Bel caught Loen's eye, and knew her decision had been made for her.

'Yes, perhaps you're right. I will telephone tomorrow to make another appointment. Come, Loen,' she added to her maid. 'We shall leave now.'

As the two women left the salon and emerged onto the street, Bel turned to Loen. 'Well, this is it. I must be out of my mind, but I'm going to meet him. Wish me luck.'

'Of course. Just be sure to meet me back here in time for the car to pick us up. And Senhora Bel,' she added softly, 'even if you decide you can never be with him again after today, I think you are making the right decision to see him.'

'Thank you.'

Bel walked swiftly through the streets of Ipanema towards Rua Visconde de Pirajá. Twice she turned back in uncertainty, but then retraced her footsteps forward, until she found herself in front of Laurent's apartment block.

Yes, she told herself. *I will go inside, tell him in person that I can't ever see him again, just as I did in Paris. And then I will leave.*

Darting inside the entrance, she moved towards the stairs and began to climb them, noting the numbers on the apartment doors.

When she reached number six, she hesitated, then, closing her eyes and sending up a silent prayer, she knocked on the door.

She heard footsteps crossing the wooden boards, and when the door opened, Laurent stood in front of her.

'*Bonjour*, Madame Aires Cabral. Please, come in.'

He smiled at her, holding the door open so she could walk through it. Closing it behind him, he double-locked it, just in case Monica the maid should make an unexpected appearance. Having finally got Bel alone, he wanted no disturbances.

'What a wonderful view,' she said nervously as she stood in the drawing room and gazed out over the ocean.

'Yes, it is, isn't it?'

'Laurent . . .'

'Izabela . . .'

They smiled at each other as they spoke at the same time.

'Shall we sit down?' she asked him, walking to a chair and seating herself, trying in vain to calm her rapid breathing.

Laurent pulled up another chair so that it was facing hers and sat down. 'So, what would you like to talk about?'

'I . . .' She shook her head and sighed. 'It's no good. I shouldn't be here.'

'Neither should I,' he agreed, 'But it seems that in spite of our determination not to be, here we both are.'

'Yes.' Bel took a deep breath. 'I've come to tell you that we can't possibly meet again.'

'That's what you said in the park in Paris. And look where it got us.'

'I didn't ask you to come here to Rio.'

'No, you didn't. Are you sorry I have?'

'Yes . . . No . . .' Bel sighed in desperation.

'You're married,' he said flatly.

'Yes. I know that the situation is impossible.'

'Bel . . .' He stood up from his chair and walked swiftly towards her, kneeling down in front of her and taking her hands in his. 'Last night, I asked if you were happy and you replied that you weren't.'

'But—'

'And then I asked you if you still loved me, and you said you did.'

'I—'

'Hush, let me speak. I understand your circumstances and how inappropriate and badly timed my arrival here is. And I promise you, if you tell me now to my face to go away, as you did in Paris, I swear I will leave Rio as soon as I can book my passage. You have to tell me what it is you want. Because I think I've made it obvious what I want.'

'To be my lover?' She glanced down at him. 'Because that is the most I can ever offer you. And it's not what you deserve,' she added.

'What I deserve has no bearing on the situation. Fate has decreed that you're the woman I want. And try as I might, I can't seem to live without you. Ideally, yes, I'd like to kidnap you right now, put you in my suitcase and drag you off to France so we could live together for the rest of our lives. But I'm prepared to compromise. Are you?' His soulful eyes were darting across her face, searching it for clues, drinking in her features.

Bel looked down at him, wondering how she could ever have doubted his feelings for her. He had walked away from his life in France and followed her across the world to Rio, even though he had no guarantee that he would even find her here. And unwittingly, her poor husband had played a part in their reunion. Thinking of Gustavo brought her to her senses.

'What's past is past,' she said as firmly as she could manage. 'And it's not fair for you to simply arrive here, making me remember, when I had done all I could to tell you goodbye, to try to forget you. I . . .' Tears came to her eyes and her voice trailed off.

'*Ma chérie*, forgive me, the last thing I want to do is to make you cry. And yes, you are right,' he agreed. 'You told me to go away and I didn't take any notice. So any fault lies with me and not you.'

'But tell me how I can find the strength to say goodbye to you again?' She wept despairingly as his arms went around her. 'You don't know what it took last time. And to do it again . . .'

'Then *don't* do it. Just tell me you want me to stay and I will.'

'I . . .'

Laurent slowly bent his head and began to kiss her neck, so gently that it felt as though a butterfly's wing was caressing her skin. She groaned. 'Please, please, don't make it any harder than it is.'

'Bel, stop torturing yourself. Let's just be together while we have the chance. I love you, *chérie*, so very much,' he murmured, as his fingertips smoothed the tears from her cheeks.

She reached for his hand and clasped it in her own. 'You have no idea how much I've longed for you,' she wept.

'As I have for you.' He leant towards her and put his lips to hers.

Bel melted against him, her resolve broken, knowing she could fight no longer.

'*Chérie*,' he said as their lips finally broke apart, 'let me take you to bed. I will accept if you simply want to lie next to me, but I just want to hold you.'

Without waiting for a response, Laurent swept Bel up from the chair and carried her through to the bedroom, placing her gently on the mattress.

Bel braced herself for a frenzied onslaught, as she'd come to expect with Gustavo, but it didn't happen. Instead, Laurent lay down next to her and enfolded her in his arms. As he kissed her again, his fingertips tenderly traced the contours of her breasts and her waist through her clothes, until she herself could think of nothing else but the promise of his naked body on hers.

'Shall I set you free, or will you?' he whispered into her ear.

She rolled over willingly to allow him to undo the buttons at the back of her dress. Slowly he did so, taking his time to kiss the area of bare flesh that each button revealed, then he slid the sleeves of her dress down her arms. Next came her brassiere, and once that was free of her body and discarded on the floor, he gently rolled her towards him and looked at her.

'You are so, so beautiful,' he whispered, as she arched herself towards him, her body aching for his touch. As his lips sought out her nipples, a moan escaped her.

His hand moved slowly across her perfect, flat stomach as he raised his head from her breast and looked at her, his eyes seeking permission to go further. She gave it with her own, and he carefully undid her suspenders and rolled down her stockings, each brush of his fingers against her flesh sending electric currents of longing through her. Finally, she lay completely naked in front of him.

Breathing heavily, he paused for a moment, surveying her body.

'Forgive me, but I want to sculpt you now.'

'No, I . . .'

He silenced her with a kiss. 'I'm teasing you, my beautiful Bel. All I wish to do is make love to you.'

Soon, he was also naked and as she chanced a shy glance at him, she saw how beautiful he was too. His body covered hers, and finally, after making sure she was ready, he entered her. As her own body accepted him willingly, ecstatically, she suddenly understood what it was that her mother had been describing.

Afterwards, as they lay languidly in each other's arms, she gave in to the urge to touch him, to caress every centimetre of him, to discover his physical being. And she was eager for him to do the same to her.

Although she tried not to, as Laurent dozed next to her later, Bel could not help thinking of the contrast to the couplings she'd endured with Gustavo. How could the same act elicit such a startlingly different response from her mind and her body?

She understood then with sudden clarity that Laurent had been right when he'd said she shouldn't marry Gustavo. For nothing could ever change the fact that she didn't, and wouldn't ever, love her husband the way he loved her.

The revulsion she felt towards him physically was not his fault – he was not a bad man, a tyrant who didn't care for her. If anything, he cared too much and wanted to show her in the only way available to him.

'What is it?'

Laurent had woken, and was gazing intently at her.

'I was thinking about Gustavo.'

'Try not to, Bel. No good can come of it.'

'No, you don't understand,' she sighed, and rolled away from him onto her side. She felt his hand caress the soft contour of her hip, then slide into the valley of her waist. He pulled her towards him, so that they lay curved into each other's bodies as one.

'I know, *ma chérie*, I know. It's a terrible, terrible mess. And we must both do all we can to shield your husband from it.'

As his hand moved upwards to cup her breast, she sighed with pleasure and wriggled luxuriantly against him. All thoughts of Gustavo were forgotten as Laurent made love to her again, and she was transported to realms of pleasure that she'd never visited before.

Afterwards, Bel too dozed contentedly until she jumped awake and saw the time.

'*Meu Deus!* I must leave. My driver will be waiting for me

at Madame Duchaine's,' she gasped in panic, scrambling out of the bed. She collected her clothes, which were either twisted in the sheets or strewn on the floor, and dressed as fast as she could. All the time, Laurent watched her quietly from the mattress.

'When will I see you again?' he asked.

'Not tomorrow, for I must make an appearance at the church where I'm helping with the making of the mosaic for the *Cristo*'s outer-self. But maybe on Monday?' she said as she hurriedly tidied her hair, then pinned on her hat and moved towards the door.

Laurent was immediately by her side, encircling her in his arms.

'I shall miss you, every second.'

Bel shivered as she felt his nakedness press against her. 'And I you.'

'Until then, *ma chérie*. I love you.'

Bel glanced at him one last time before walking out of the door.

38

Over the next few months, Bel floated through the days on a wave of heightened emotion. It was as if her life before that afternoon in February at Laurent's apartment had been no more than a dull, grey existence without meaning. Now, when she woke up in the morning and lay thinking of Laurent, every part of her body tingled with adrenaline. The blue of the sky beyond her bedroom window seemed almost dazzling in its brightness and the flowers in the garden exploded before her eyes in an exotic kaleidoscope of colour.

As she walked down the stairs each morning to breakfast and took her place opposite the pinched, disapproving face of Luiza, she'd think of Laurent and allow a secret smile to form on her lips. Nothing could touch her, nobody could hurt her any longer. She was protected and inviolate, simply through the love the two of them shared.

However, when she was unable to visit him at his apartment for a few days, Bel would plummet down to the depths of despair, torturing herself with visions of where Laurent was, what he was doing and who he was with. An icy fear would beset her, freezing the blood in her veins and making her shiver, even though the burning sun still forced sweat onto her brow. The truth was that he was free to love anyone he chose. And she was not.

'*Mon Dieu, chérie*,' Laurent had sighed as they had lain together in his big mahogany bed a few days ago, 'I admit I'm finding it harder and harder to share you. The thought of *him* touching you at all sends shudders through me. Let alone in the way I just have,' he'd added as his fingers lightly brushed her naked breast. 'Run away with me, Bel. We'll return to Paris. No more hiding, just endless hours filled with good wine, good food, talking, making love . . .' His voice had trailed off in a whisper as his lips had covered hers.

Thankfully, at least, her mother-in-law had unwittingly played a part in keeping her lover near her for the time being. As she'd promised to, Luiza had introduced Laurent to many of her rich friends in Rio, who were shown Bel's sculpture and wanted to immortalise their own family members in a similar fashion. Laurent was currently working on a commission of a chihuahua, beloved by its wealthy owners. In essence, her mother-in-law had become Laurent's patron, and the irony was not lost on Bel.

'Not exactly the kind of work I want to be doing,' he'd admitted to her, 'but it keeps me out of trouble when you're not here.'

So, on the afternoons when Bel was unable to steal away, Laurent would chip away at the block of soapstone that Luiza had acquired for him from a mine-owning relative of hers. Luiza's suggestion that Bel should volunteer to help clad the *Cristo* in the thousands of mesh sheets of soapstone at the Igreja da Glória had provided a perfect alibi for her absence from the Casa. And as her own hands closed around the smooth, cool triangles of the same material that Laurent was working on, the feel of it would comfort her.

It was only Luiza who noticed her comings and goings to and from the Casa, as Gustavo was spending more and more time at his club and arriving home before dinner stinking of alcohol. Bel's husband rarely enquired about her daily routine.

In fact, thought Bel as she put on her hat and Loen went to call Jorge, the family's driver, these days Gustavo hardly noticed her at all. In the past four months since her affair with Laurent had begun, the attentiveness he'd shown her at the start of their marriage had disappeared completely. Although at night, as she joined Gustavo with trepidation in the bed they shared, he'd still attempt to make love to her, more often than not the process ended with him being unable to perform. Bel had deduced that this must be due to the fact that most of the time he could hardly stand upright before he climbed into bed. And on more than one occasion, he had passed out cold in the very act of trying to enter her. She'd roll him off her and would lie next to him, listening to his drunken snores and smelling the sourness of his breath, which seemed to permeate the bedroom. Most mornings, she'd be up, dressed and breakfasted before Gustavo had even woken.

If his parents noticed their son's drinking problem, they did not allude to it. The only time Luiza probed her daughter-in-law about their marriage was to ask if there was any news of a grandchild yet. She would then sniff in displeasure when Bel assured her there was not.

Given her passionate physical relationship with Laurent, Bel was continually anxious that her body – which had not responded to Gustavo's initial frenzied attempts to produce an heir – might succumb to Laurent's gentle touch. And in fact, it had been her lover who had seen the worried frown creasing her forehead one afternoon and had explained to Bel how it was possible for her to attempt to avoid conceiving a child. He'd described to her the workings of her body in a way her mother never had, and told her how to watch and feel for the times when she was most likely to conceive.

'It's not fail-safe, *chérie*, which is why so many of us Catholics continue to have such large families.' Laurent had smiled at her ruefully. 'But there are ways that I can play my part too when you are in the danger time.'

Bel had looked at him in wonder. 'How do you know all this?'

'There are many artists like myself in Montparnasse who have wished to indulge in a little fun, but not end up being pursued by a woman claiming she is carrying our child.' Laurent had seen her stricken face and moved quickly to put his arms around her and pull her to his chest. '*Chérie*, sadly, things are as they are for the present, and I would not like to see you compromised. *Or* any child of mine brought up by that excuse for a man that is your husband,' he'd added. 'So for now, we must take care.'

Bel left the Casa and climbed into the car, staring out of the window as Jorge drove her the short distance to her parents' house in Cosme Velho. Due to the fact that any spare moments she could steal from the time she was away from the house were spent with Laurent, Bel had not seen her parents for over a month. And yesterday, Loen had asked her when she might next be visiting her mother.

'Soon, soon,' Bel had replied with a jolt of guilt.

'I know you are . . . busy, but perhaps you should go and

see her,' Loen had said pointedly as she'd helped Bel into her dress. 'My mother is worried about her.'

'Is she sick?'

'I don't . . . know,' Loen had replied warily.

'Then of course I will go tomorrow and see her for myself.'

As the car arrived in the drive of Mansão da Princesa, Bel instructed Jorge to collect her from the Copacabana Palace at six thirty that evening.

She'd told Luiza earlier this morning that after she had called on her mother, she was meeting her new friend Heloise, whom she sat next to at the Igreja da Glória, for tea at the Copacabana Palace. Bel had known Luiza would approve, as she had been the one to encourage her daughter-in-law to befriend suitable young ladies that matched her new status, and Heloise came from a very old aristocratic family. More-over, knowing that Luiza found the flamboyant grandeur of the hotel distasteful, Bel had deduced correctly that she would not suggest she join them there.

As she walked towards the front door of her old home, Bel's stomach churned at the thought of being caught out in her deception, but she knew she had little choice. Sadly, in the past two months she had become a reluctant but adept liar.

Gabriela opened the front door and her face lit up when she saw Bel. 'Senhora, it is a pleasure to see you. Your mother is resting at present, but she asked me to wake her when you arrived.'

'Is she unwell?' Bel frowned as she followed Gabriela into the drawing room. 'Loen said you were concerned about her.'

'I . . .' Gabriela hesitated. 'I don't know if she is sick, but she is certainly very tired.'

'You don't think' – Bel steeled herself to say the words – 'that her problem has returned, do you?'

'Senhora, I do not know. Perhaps you must ask her yourself. And persuade her to see a doctor. Now, what can I get you to drink?'

As Gabriela left to fetch some orange juice and wake her mother, Bel stood up and paced the familiar room anxiously. Eventually, Carla arrived to join her and Bel noticed that her mother not only looked pale and tired, but had also developed a strange yellow tinge to her skin since the last time she'd seen her.

'Mãe, forgive me for not seeing you for so long. How are you?' she said, trying to quell her fear and her guilt for not visiting sooner, as she walked towards Carla to greet her with a kiss.

'I am well. And you?'

'Yes, Mãe . . .'

'Shall we sit down?' said Carla, slumping heavily onto a chair as if her legs could hold her upright no longer.

'Mãe, it is obvious you are not well. Are you in pain?'

'Only a little, I'm sure it is nothing. I . . .'

'Please, you know it is *something*. Surely Pai must have noticed you're not yourself?'

'Your father has other things to concern him at the moment,' sighed Carla. 'The coffee farms are not making the yield they once did, and the stockpiling plan the government has suggested does not seem to be helping.'

'I hardly think that Pai's business concerns are more important than his wife's health,' Bel shot back.

'*Querida*, with your father so strained, I don't wish to burden him further.'

Tears brimmed in Bel's eyes. 'It might be inconvenient timing, but don't you see that nothing is as important as your health? Besides, you may be fearing the worst.'

'It is my body and I live in it, and I understand and can feel what is happening to it,' Carla interrupted firmly. 'I do not want to put myself, or you and your father, through a distressing process that will only lead to the same end.'

'Mãe,' Bel uttered, her throat constricted with the hard lump of emotion that had formed there. 'Please, at the very least, let me book an appointment with the doctor who treated you last time. You trust him, don't you?'

'Yes, I think he is the best that there is in Rio. But I promise you, Bel, I am beyond his help.'

'Don't say that! I need you here, and so does Pai.'

'Maybe,' Carla agreed with a grim smile. 'But Izabela, I am not a coffee bean or a *real* note. And I can assure you that they are his first true loves.'

'You are wrong, Mãe! Please, even though you may not see it, your daughter does. You are everything to him and without you, his life would be nothing.'

The two women sat in silence for a few minutes.

'If it makes you happy, Izabela, you can book an appointment with my doctor and accompany me to see him. Then you will hear, I am sure, that every word I have spoken to you is true. I have only one request if I agree to see the doctor.'

'What is that?'

'For the present, do not tell your father. I couldn't bear to make him suffer for any longer than he has to.'

Bel left the house with her parents' driver half an hour later, after Carla had admitted that she needed to lie down, and asked him to take her to Ipanema. She was reeling from shock. Surely, she thought, her mother was exaggerating through fear?

Bel left the car two blocks away from Laurent's apartment and began to pick up speed, running mentally and physically to the one person who she believed could give her comfort.

'*Chérie!* I thought you were not coming. *Mon Dieu!* What is wrong? What has happened?' Laurent appeared at the door and embraced her.

'My mother,' Bel managed to utter between gasps. 'She thinks she is dying!' she cried into his shoulder.

'What? Has she been told this by a doctor?'

'No, but she was sick with cancer a year ago and is certain it has returned. She is convinced that it is the end for her. But she doesn't want to worry my father, who has business problems. I've told her, of course, that she must see a doctor, but . . . in the month since I last saw her, she has deteriorated so much. And' – Bel looked up into Laurent's eyes – 'I am so very fearful that her instincts may be right.'

'Bel,' Laurent said, taking her shaking hands and gently pulling her down onto the sofa next to him, 'of course you and she must go and get a professional opinion. It is easy to imagine these things are back if you have suffered them before, but it may not be what it seems. Your maman tells you that your papa has business problems?' Laurent clarified. 'I thought he was as rich as Croesus.'

'He is, and I'm sure that if he does have concerns, they are overexaggerated,' Bel agreed. 'So,' she said, struggling to pull herself together, 'are you well, Laurent?'

'Yes, *chérie*, I am well, but I think that we are past those kinds of formalities. I have missed you terribly in the past few days,' he admitted.

'And I you,' she replied, turning her head into his chest as if to block out the pain of the past two hours.

Laurent stroked her hair gently and tried to think of something to distract Bel temporarily from her misery. 'I was here this morning wondering what I would do with myself in a few days' time when the sculpture of the dreaded dog is finished, when who should come to call but Madame Silveira and her daughter, Alessandra. The mother wishes for me to sculpt Alessandra as a gift for her twenty-first birthday.'

'Alessandra Silveira? I know her,' said Bel uneasily. 'Her family are distant cousins of the Aires Cabrals and she came to my wedding. I remember her being very beautiful.'

'Well, she is certainly more attractive than the chihuahua,' Laurent agreed equably. 'And inevitably there will be better conversation. She spoke to me today in good French,' he added.

'And she is unmarried, I believe,' said Bel dully, a further clutch of fear tugging at her heart.

'Indeed she is.' Laurent continued to stroke Bel's hair. 'Perhaps her parents are hoping my sculpture can advertise her beauty and sophistication to a suitable husband.'

'Or perhaps they might see a talented young French sculptor as an appropriate suitor,' Bel shot back as she pulled away from him, her arms instinctively crossing protectively around herself.

'Izabela!' Laurent chided, watching her intently. 'Please don't tell me that you're jealous?'

'No, of course I'm not.' Bel bit her lip. The thought of

another woman sitting in front of Laurent day after day, just as *she* had once done in Boulogne-Billancourt, sent hot ripples of envy coursing through her. 'But you can't deny that you've been invited to many society soirées recently and have become quite the man about town?'

'Yes, but I hardly think that I'm seen as a suitable match for any of the young ladies present. I am more of a novelty.'

'Laurent, I can assure you that the very fact you are French and from the Old World in a town such as Rio, let alone with my mother-in-law's patronage of your sculpture, makes you far more than a novelty,' Bel countered firmly.

At this, Laurent threw back his head and laughed. 'Well, if you are right, I am happy for it,' he responded eventually. 'For as you know, in France, I and my band of artists are considered the bottom of the barrel. As I said to you once before, French mothers would prefer their daughters dead rather than shackled to a struggling artist.'

'Well, I think you should understand that you are viewed differently here.' Bel knew she was sounding churlish, but couldn't help herself.

Laurent tipped his head to one side and surveyed her. 'I understand that you are upset, *chérie*, especially given the bad news about your mother. But surely you can see that you're being ridiculous? It is not *I* who has to run off back to a husband on the afternoons we do manage to meet. It is not *I* who still shares a bed every night with another. And it is not *I* who refuses to countenance any thought of changing the situation we currently find ourselves in. No, but it *is* I who must endure these things. *I* whose stomach churns every time I think of your husband making love to you. *I* who has to be available any time you click your fingers to say you might come to visit me. And *I* who must find something to fill the lonely hours I spend thinking of you without losing my mind!'

Bel put her head onto her knees. It was the first time Laurent had ever spoken of their situation with such bluntness and anger, and she wished she could block out the words from her heart and her mind. For she knew every one of them was true.

The two of them sat in silence for a while until eventually Bel felt a hand on her shoulder.

'*Chérie*, I understand that now is not the time to discuss such matters. But please, accept that I am still here in Brazil marking time as best I can for one reason only. And that reason is you.'

'Forgive me, Laurent,' she murmured into her knees. 'As you say, today I feel desolate. What are we to do?'

'Now is not the time to discuss it. You must concentrate on your mother and her health. And although I hate to say it, you must take a cab immediately to the Copacabana Palace so you can emerge as if you have been there taking tea with your friend,' he reminded her. 'It is already past six.'

'*Meu Deus!*' Bel stood up and immediately turned towards the door. Laurent caught her arm and dragged her back towards him.

'Bel,' he said as he stroked her cheek, 'please remember it is you I love and you I want.' He kissed her tenderly and her eyes filled with tears. 'Now, hurry away before I kidnap you and lock you up here in my apartment to keep you all to myself.'

39

Two days later, Bel walked out of the hospital entrance alone. The doctor they had just seen had insisted that Carla admit herself immediately for tests and Bel was to collect her at six that evening.

Even though Luiza and Gustavo were aware she was at the hospital and it would have been possible for her to spend the afternoon in Laurent's arms while she waited for Carla, Bel could not bring herself to do so. Guilt that she had selfishly neglected her mother for Laurent ate into her. While Carla underwent the necessary tests, Bel sat numbly watching the trail of human tragedy enter and exit the hospital doors.

At six o'clock, she reported as requested to the ward to which her mother had been taken.

'The doctor has asked to see you when you arrive,' said the nurse. 'Follow me.'

'How is she?' Bel asked as she followed the nurse along a corridor.

'Sitting up in a chair and drinking tea,' said the nurse briskly as she knocked on an office door.

Bel entered and the doctor ushered her to a chair in front of his desk.

Fifteen minutes later, Bel left the doctor and walked shakily along the corridor to collect her mother. The doctor had confirmed that the cancer had spread to Carla's liver, and almost certainly further. Her mother's instincts had been right. There was no hope.

In the car on the way home, Carla seemed simply relieved to be leaving the hospital. She made jokes that Bel found impossible to respond to and talked about the fact she hoped that the cook had remembered that Antonio had asked for fish that evening. When they arrived at the house, Carla turned to her daughter and clasped her hands in her own.

'Don't worry about coming in, *querida*. I know that you saw the doctor and I know also what he said to you, because he had already spoken to me before he called you in to see him. I only went with you today because I knew that I must convince you. And now that I have, we will speak no more about it to anyone. Especially not to your father.'

Bel felt the heat of her mother's glance and the desperation contained within it. 'But surely—'

'When it is necessary, we will tell him,' Carla said, and Bel knew it was her final word on the subject.

Bel returned that night to the Casa, feeling her world had tipped on its axis. For the first time, she was being forced to face her mother's mortality. And, through that, her own. She sat down to dinner that evening and glanced at Gustavo next to her, before gazing across the table at Maurício and then Luiza. Both her husband and her mother-in-law had known where she was this afternoon. And yet neither of them cared enough to ask after Carla's health, enquire of her what had happened at the hospital. Gustavo was already inebriated and incapable of lucid conversation, while Luiza probably considered that touching on a distressing subject would upset her digestion of the beef, the texture of which would challenge the most cannibalistic of incisors.

After dinner, and the endless rounds of cards, matched in numbers by the glasses of brandy downed by her husband, she accompanied him upstairs.

'Coming to bed, *querida*?' Gustavo asked her as he divested himself of his clothes and fell back onto the mattress.

'Yes,' she replied, walking towards the bathroom. 'I will be there in a few minutes.'

Shutting the door behind her, Bel slumped onto the edge of the bath and put her head in her hands, hoping that by the time she emerged, Gustavo would be fast asleep and snoring. As she sat there desolately, she remembered Carla talking to her before her marriage of the fact that she had needed to grow used to Antonio and learn to love him.

However much Bel had inwardly derided what she had seen as her mother's subservience to her father in the past, and wondered how she could tolerate his arrogance and never-ending desire for social acceptance, for the first time she understood the strength of the love her mother had for her husband.

And Bel had never admired her more.

'How is she?'

Laurent's concerned face greeted her at the door of his apartment as he ushered Bel inside a few days later.

'She's dying, as she told me she was.'

'I'm so sorry, *chérie*. So what will happen now?' Laurent asked as he led her into the drawing room.

'I . . . I don't know. My mother is still refusing to tell my father,' she murmured as she sat down abruptly in a chair.

'Oh my Bel, how difficult things are for you just now. You're still so young – not even at your twentieth birthday – and yet you have the weight of the world on your shoulders. This bad news has almost certainly made you look at your own life too.'

Bel wasn't sure whether she felt patronised or comforted by his comment. 'Yes,' she admitted. 'It has.'

'I'm guessing that you must also be in a quandary of guilt because of the news you've just had. Deciding whether this means that you should do your duty as a faithful wife and daughter and forget me. Or whether your sudden realisation of how short life really is means you should take advantage of the time you've been granted and live your life following your heart.'

Bel stared at him in surprise. 'How could you know that is exactly what I have been thinking?'

'Because I am a human being too,' Laurent shrugged. 'And I believe that the powers up above often throw us such dilemmas to make us fully aware of our situations. But it is only *we* who can ever make the decision as to what we should do.'

'You are very wise,' Bel commented quietly.

'As I said, I am simply human. I am also a few years older than you and have been forced to make decisions in my past that have involved asking myself the same questions. I understand, and don't wish to prejudice you either way. And I want to reassure you that if you wish me to stay with you here in

Brazil during this difficult time, I will. Because I love you and I want to be here for you. I also understand that my love for you has made me a better person. There, I have learned a lesson too!' Laurent smiled at her wryly. 'But . . . I am still not *completely* selfless. So if I stay, you would have to promise me that when the . . . situation with your mother is resolved, you and I will come to a decision on our future. But that is not for now. Come, let me hold you.' Laurent opened his arms to her and she rose slowly and went into them.

'I love you, my Bel,' he said, as he stroked her hair tenderly. 'And I am here if you need me.'

'Thank you,' she replied as she clung to him. 'Thank you.'

As June turned to July, Bel returned home from an afternoon working on the soapstone mosaic at the Igreja da Glória to be informed by Loen that her father was waiting for her in the drawing room.

'How does he seem?' she asked Loen as she removed her hat and handed it to her.

'He appears to have lost some weight,' said Loen cautiously. 'But you must see for yourself.'

Taking a deep breath, Bel opened the door to the drawing room and saw her father pacing the room. He turned as she walked in, and Bel saw that Antonio had indeed shed some pounds. But more than that, his handsome face was gaunt and tiny trails of lines had etched themselves onto his skin. His black wavy hair, which had previously contained only a sprinkling of silver around the temples, was now almost uniformly grey. Bel felt he had aged ten years since she had last set eyes upon him.

'*Princesa*,' he said, walking towards her and embracing her. 'It seems so long since we last saw each other.'

'Yes, it must be three months or so,' Bel agreed.

'Of course, you are a married woman with your own life now, and have no time for your old Pai,' he joked lamely.

'I have been at the house visiting Mãe many times in the past few weeks,' countered Bel. 'You have never been there. It seems it is you who is unavailable, Pai.'

'Yes, I agree, I have been busy. As I'm sure your father-in-law has told you, the coffee business is very difficult at the moment.'

'Well, I'm glad to see you today at least. Please' – Bel gestured to a chair – 'sit down and I will send for some refreshments.'

'No, I don't need anything,' said Antonio, sitting down as his daughter had requested. 'Izabela, what is wrong with your mother? On Sunday, she spent most of the day in bed. She said she had a migraine, as she has said many times before in the past few months.'

'Pai, I . . .'

'She's ill again, isn't she? I noticed over breakfast this morning that her skin has a terrible colour to it and that she ate nothing.'

Bel stared at her father for a while. 'Pai, you're saying that you haven't seen these signs before now?'

'I have been so busy at the office that often I leave before your mother rises and am not home until after she is in bed. But yes . . .' Antonio hung his head. 'Perhaps I *should* have seen, but didn't wish to. So,' he said with a sigh of despairing resignation, 'do you know how sick she is?'

'Yes, Pai. I do.'

'Is it . . . ? Is it . . . ?' Antonio couldn't bring himself to utter the words.

'Yes, it is,' Bel confirmed.

Antonio stood up and hit his temple with his palm in anguish. '*Meu Deus!* Of course I should have seen! What kind of man am I? What kind of husband am I to my wife?'

'Pai, I understand that you feel guilty, but Mãe was determined that she must not worry you, given that you have so many problems at the office. She has played her part in this too.'

'As if work matters compared to the health of my wife! She must truly believe that I am a monster for her to have hidden what she has from me! Why have you not said anything to me before, Izabela?' he shouted, rounding on her angrily.

'Because I promised Mãe I would not,' Bel replied firmly. 'She was adamant she didn't wish you to know until you had to.'

'Well, at least now I do,' said Antonio, rallying a little. 'We can find the best doctors, surgeons, whatever she needs to recover.'

'As I said, Mãe has seen her doctor and I was there with her. He told me there was no hope. I'm sorry, Pai, but you must finally face the truth.'

Antonio stared at her as a mixture of expressions – from disbelief, to anger, to devastation – crossed his features.

'You are telling me she is dying?' he managed to whisper eventually.

'Yes. I am so very sorry.'

Antonio slumped into a chair, put his head in his hands and began to weep noisily. 'No, no . . . not my Carla, *please*, not my Carla.'

Bel stood up and went to comfort him. She put an arm around his hunched shoulders as they shook with emotion.

'To think that she has carried this burden alone for all this time and didn't trust me enough to tell me.'

'Pai, I swear to you that even if she had, nothing could have been done,' Bel reiterated. 'It is Mãe's wish that she is not put through any further treatment. She says she is at peace, has accepted it and I believe her. Please,' Bel entreated, 'for her sake, you must respect her wishes. You have finally seen for yourself how sick she is. Now all she needs is love and support from both of us.'

Antonio's shoulders sagged suddenly as all his energy left him. Despite her horror that it had taken him so long to notice her mother's deteriorating health, she felt a wave of sympathy for him.

He looked up at her, the pain evident in his eyes. 'Whatever you or she may think, she is everything to me and I simply can't imagine a life without her.'

Bel watched helplessly as he stood up, turned and left the room.

40

'What's wrong with you these days?' slurred Gustavo as Bel emerged from the bathroom in her nightgown. 'You hardly say a word over dinner any longer. And you rarely speak to me when we are alone.' He eyed her as she climbed into bed next to him.

It had been a week since Antonio had appeared at the Casa and left devastated by the dreadful news. Bel had visited her mother the following day, and had found Antonio sitting in a chair at her bedside, holding her hand and weeping silently.

Carla had given her daughter a wan smile as she'd entered and indicated her husband. 'I've told him to go to the office, that there's nothing he can do for me that Gabriela can't. But he refuses and continues to cluck around me like a mother hen.'

Bel had seen that, despite her words, Carla was comforted and gratified by Antonio's presence. And from the dreadful way her mother had looked that afternoon, Bel knew it was just in time. When her father had finally been persuaded to leave them alone and go off to the office for a few hours, Carla had spoken quietly to Bel.

'Now that he knows, I would like to tell you of what I wish to do in the time I have left . . .'

Since then, Bel had been plucking up the courage to tell Gustavo where her mother would like to spend her final days. For of course, Bel must accompany her, and she knew her absence wouldn't please her husband.

She sat down slowly on the edge of the bed and looked at him, taking in his red eyes and the enlarged, drink-sodden pupils. 'Gustavo,' she began, 'my mother is dying.'

'What?' He turned his head towards her. 'This is the first that I've heard about it. How long have you known?'

'A few weeks, but my mother insisted that I tell no one.'

'Not even your husband?'

'Not until she'd told her own, no.'

'I see. The cancer is back, I presume?'

'Yes.'

'How long does she have left?' he asked her.

'Not long . . .' Bel's voice quavered with emotion at his coldness. She steeled herself to ask Gustavo what she needed to. 'She has requested that she be taken to the mountains to spend her last days at her beloved *fazenda*. Gustavo, would you let me accompany her?'

He stared at her with glazed eyes. 'How long for?'

'I don't know. It could be weeks, or perhaps, God willing, two months.'

'Would you be back by the beginning of the season?'

'I . . .' It was impossible for Bel to put a timescale on the final time she would spend with her mother merely to suit her husband. 'I would think so, yes,' she managed.

'Well, I can hardly say no, can I? But of course, I would prefer you here by my side. Especially as there seems to be no heir so far, and this will delay the production of one further. My mother is getting most perturbed that you seem infertile,' he said cruelly.

'I apologise.' Bel lowered her eyes, wanting to retort that the situation was hardly *her* fault. It was at least two months since Gustavo had managed to successfully make love to her, although she accepted that he probably couldn't remember the full extent of his ineptitude.

'We will try tonight,' he said, grabbing her suddenly and throwing her back onto the bed. With one movement, he was on top of her and clumsily pulling her nightgown up, then she felt his hardness poking and prodding to find where it needed to be, but failing to hit its target. His mouth descended on hers and she felt him moving against her, as though he thought he was inside her. As usual, she felt Gustavo's weight fall more heavily on top of her as he finally moaned with relief before rolling off her. Bel felt the stickiness already congealing on her thighs and looked at him with a mixture of revulsion and pity.

'Perhaps tonight we will finally have made a child,' he said, before his breath was consumed by drunken snores.

Bel stood up and went to the bathroom to clean Gustavo from her skin. How he could possibly believe that the apology which had been their coupling could result in the miracle of a baby, Bel did not dare to question. Any slight aptitude he had once shown as a lover was lost – along with his memory of such events – in the mire of drunkenness.

However, she thought, as she made her way back to the bedroom, if what she had just endured was the price for leaving Rio to be with her mother until the end, then she was content to have paid it.

The following morning, Bel left Gustavo sleeping and went down for breakfast. Both Luiza and Maurício were at the table.

'Good morning, Izabela,' said Luiza.

'Good morning, Luiza,' Bel replied politely as she sat down.

'Gustavo is not joining us?'

'He will be down very soon, I'm sure,' said Bel, wondering at her need to protect her husband from his mother.

'Did you sleep well?'

'Very well, thank you.'

Every morning, this was the beginning and end of the conversation, the rest of breakfast only punctuated by the odd grunt of pleasure or disapproval emanating from behind Maurício's newspaper.

'Luiza, I must tell you that my mother is extremely unwell,' said Bel as she stirred her coffee. 'In fact, it is very doubtful she will live to see another summer.'

'I am sorry to hear that, Izabela,' replied Luiza, a subtle raise of an eyebrow her only physical reaction to the news. 'This is very sudden. Are you quite sure?'

'Sadly, yes. I've known for some time, but my mother wished me to say nothing to anyone until she had to. That time has now come and she has requested that she spends her last days at our *fazenda*. Which, as you know, is five hours' journey from here. She has asked me to go with her and help nurse her to . . . the end. I spoke to Gustavo last night and he has agreed that I should go.'

'Really?' Luiza's thin lips puckered in displeasure. 'That is indeed generous of him. For exactly how long will you be away?' she asked, voicing the same question as her son.

'I . . .' Bel could feel the tears beginning to rise in her eyes.

'Surely, my dear, for as long as it takes,' said a sudden voice from over his newspaper. Maurício gave her a nod of sympathy. 'Please send my best wishes to your dear mother.'

'Thank you,' Bel whispered, feeling touched by her father-in-law's sudden show of empathy and support. She took out a handkerchief and surreptitiously dabbed at her eyes.

'Perhaps you can at least say when you will leave?' Luiza demanded of her.

'At the end of this week,' Bel confirmed. 'My father will accompany us and stay for a few days, but then, of course, he must return to his office in Rio.'

'Yes,' said Maurício gravely. 'I can understand that things must be difficult for him at the moment. They are difficult for us all.'

Two afternoons later, as Bel sat at a table with the other women in the Igreja da Glória sticking the small triangles of soapstone onto the mesh netting, she thought how the hours she spent in the cool church had provided her with much-needed moments of quiet contemplation. The women – even though they *were* women and well practised at chatter amongst themselves – did not speak more than they needed to, simply concentrating instead on their joint task. There was a mutual feeling of harmony and peace.

Heloise, the friend she had once used as an alibi when she'd visited Laurent, was sitting next to her at the trestle table. Bel noticed she was busy writing something on the back of her soapstone triangle. Bel leant over and studied it.

'What are you doing?' she asked.

'I am writing down the names of my family. And also that of my sweetheart. Then they will be up on Corcovado Mountain and part of the *Cristo* forever. Many of the women do this, Izabela.'

'What a beautiful idea,' sighed Bel, looking sadly at the names of Heloise's mother, her father, her brothers and sisters . . . and then the name of her sweetheart. Bel looked down at her own tile – just about to be covered in glue – and knew that one precious member of her family would not be on this earth for much longer, and would never see the *Cristo* finished. Her eyes filled with involuntary tears.

'When you are done with it, may I borrow your pen?' she asked Heloise.

'Of course.'

When Heloise handed the pen to her, Bel wrote out the name of her beloved mother, then her father and then her own name. Her pen hovered below the names, but try as she might, she could not bring herself to write the name of her husband.

Testing the ink to see if it was dry, Bel applied the thick glue to the tile and placed it on the netting. As she did so, the woman in charge told them it was time for their break, and she watched as the other volunteers stood up from the trestle benches. Instinctively, she grabbed a soapstone triangle from the pile in the centre of the table and secreted it surreptitiously in her small handbag, which lay at her feet under the table. Standing up, she made her way over to the group of women who were drinking coffee at the back of the church.

Refusing the cup of coffee offered to her by the maid, she turned to the woman in charge.

'Senhora, forgive me, but I'm afraid I must leave now.'

'Of course. The committee is only grateful for any help you can offer, Senhora Aires Cabral. Please write your name down on the rota as usual, to tell us when you are free to come back.'

'Senhora, that will not be possible for some time, I'm afraid. My mother is seriously ill and I must be there for her in her final days,' Bel explained.

'I understand. Please accept my sympathy.' The woman reached out a hand to touch her shoulder.

'Thank you.'

Bel left the church and hurried to Jorge, who was waiting for her in the car outside. Climbing into the back, she directed him to Madame Duchaine's in Ipanema.

Fifteen minutes later they arrived, and she asked him to return for her at six o'clock. She walked towards the front door of the salon and pretended to press the bell, until, with her head surreptitiously cocked to the left, she saw Jorge move the car off along the road. She waited on the doorstep for two or three minutes before leaving it, and then hurried as fast as she could along the street to Laurent's apartment.

Today, given it was the last time she would see him for perhaps two months, she did not wish to waste any time discussing new-season gowns with her dressmaker. She knew her actions would mean there was no alibi for her lost hours, but as Bel mounted the many steps to Laurent's apartment, for the first time, neither did she care.

'*Chérie*, you are so pale! Come in quickly and let me make you something to drink,' Laurent said as she arrived at his front door, panting from exertion and shaky with nerves. She allowed him to lead her inside and sit her down.

'Water, please,' she murmured, feeling suddenly faint. As Laurent went to fetch some, Bel lowered her head onto her knees to try and relieve the dizziness.

'Are you unwell?'

'No . . . I will be fine,' she said as she took the water from him and drank it quickly.

'Bel, what has happened?' He sat down next to her and took her hands in his.

'I . . . have something to tell you.'

'What is it?'

'My mother has asked to go to our farm in the mountains for her final days and I must go with her,' she blurted out. Then as all the tension of the past few weeks gathered within her, she began to sob. 'I'm sorry, Laurent, but I have no choice. My mother needs me. I hope you can forgive me and understand why I must leave Rio for a time.'

'Bel, what do you take me for? Of *course* you must go to be with your mother. Why did you think I would be angry?' he asked her gently.

'Because . . . because you've told me you're only in Rio for me and now I'm leaving.' She looked at him despairingly.

'Well, it is not ideal, I agree. But if you want to know the truth, the fact that you will no longer be sharing a bed with your husband, even if *I* am unable to set eyes on you for a while, is actually preferable,' he comforted her. 'I can feel for that time at least that you are truly mine. Surely we can write? I can send letters to the farm, perhaps addressed to your maid?'

'Yes,' agreed Bel as she blew her nose on a handkerchief

he passed her. 'Forgive me, Laurent, but Gustavo and Luiza were so cold when I told them that I thought you would be too,' she confessed.

'I'll refrain from comment on your husband and mother-in-law, but I can assure you there is only sympathy for you in my heart. Besides' – his eyes twinkled suddenly and a smile came to his lips – 'I have the luscious Alessandra Silveira to keep me company until you come back.'

'Laurent—'

'Izabela, you know I am only teasing you. She might be attractive to look at from the outside, but she has the personality of the rock I am fashioning her from,' he chuckled.

'I saw the photograph in the newspaper the other day of you at Parque Lage, attending a charity gala hosted by the famous Gabriella Besanzoni,' Bel commented morosely.

'Yes, it seems I'm quite the toast of Rio presently. But you know it means nothing without you, *chérie*. Just as I hope your life is as empty without me.'

'It is,' she answered vehemently.

'And your father? How is he?'

'Broken,' Bel shrugged sadly. 'Part of the reason Mãe wants to go to the *fazenda* is to spare him the pain of watching her slowly die. He will visit when he can. If I were in her shoes, I would wish for the same. Men are not good with illness.'

'Most men, I agree. But please don't tar us all with the same brush,' Laurent chided her. 'If it were you dying, I'd like to think that I'd be there for you. Will I see you again before you leave?'

'No, forgive me but I cannot, Laurent. I have many things I must do, including an appointment with my mother's doctor so that he can give me the necessary pills and some morphine for her when the time comes.'

'Then let us waste no more time, and spend the last few hours we have only thinking of each other.' Laurent stood and pulled her up, then led her in the direction of the bedroom.

41

Bel felt a terrible air of finality as her father helped a weak Carla into the back of the Rolls-Royce. As Antonio climbed into the driver's seat and Loen sat in front with him, Bel settled her mother next to her with pillows to support her fragile body. When Antonio started the engine and began to pull out of the drive, Bel watched her mother strain her neck to look back at her home. Bel understood Carla knew that this was the last time she would ever see it.

On arrival at the *fazenda*, Fabiana struggled to drag a bright smile to her lips as she greeted her frail mistress. Exhausted after the journey, Carla staggered as Antonio helped her from the car. Immediately, he swept his wife into his arms and carried her inside.

During the next few days, Bel felt redundant, as Antonio, knowing he must soon leave to attend to his worsening business situation in Rio, spent every waking moment with Carla. His devotion to her brought tears to both Fabiana's and Bel's eyes as they sat in the kitchen together, currently unwanted either by the patient or her unlikely nurse.

'I wouldn't have thought your father had it in him,' said

Fabiana for the hundredth time as she mopped her eyes. 'Such love for a woman . . . it breaks my heart.'

'Yes,' sighed Bel. 'And mine too.'

The only member of the household who was happy – but was doing her best to hide it given the circumstances – was Loen, who was reunited with Bruno. Bel had granted her maid an initial few days off, knowing there was little for her to do with Antonio so devoted to caring for his wife. But equally, how she would be needed as Carla's time drew nearer.

Bel watched again in envy as Loen and Bruno spent every hour they could together, their love prompting thoughts of how much had changed since she was last at the *fazenda*. At least the time she had gave her the chance to write long letters of love to Laurent, which she handed surreptitiously to Loen to post when she and Bruno took a walk into the nearby village. Laurent replied regularly, addressing his letters to Loen as they had discussed. Reading them over and over, Bel felt she had never missed him more.

As for her husband, Bel thought about him as little as she could. Despite the dreadful circumstances, she was simply relieved to be away from the claustrophobic and miserable atmosphere of the Casa and the realisation that she was married to a man she now actively despised.

Ten days after they'd arrived at the *fazenda*, Antonio, looking grey and drawn, took his leave. Clasping Bel to him and on the verge of tears, he kissed her on both cheeks.

'I will be back next Friday evening, but for God's sake, Izabela, please call me every day to let me know how she is. And if I need to come sooner, you must let me know. No secrets any more, please?'

'I will do as you ask, Pai, but Mãe at least seems settled for now.'

With a nod of despair, Antonio climbed into the Rolls-Royce and drove off at a pace down the drive, sending a shower of dust and gravel into the air from beneath the tyres.

Gustavo sat in his club reading the newspaper and noticed that the library was empty this afternoon. Apparently, President Washington Luís had called the major coffee producers together for an emergency meeting on the tumbling bean prices, and at lunchtime the restaurant had been deserted too.

As he drained his third whisky, Gustavo thought about his wife and her pale, drawn features when she had said goodbye to him three weeks ago. Since she'd been away, he'd missed her terribly. The household seemed to have contracted without her presence, reverting to how it had been before Izabela had married him.

The fact that his mother continued to treat him as a naughty little boy, patronising him constantly, seemed even more obvious with his wife missing from his side. And his father still assumed he was equally inept on the financial side of things, brushing away his tentative enquiries into the running of the family coffers as if he was an irritating fly.

Ordering another whisky, Gustavo grimaced at the thought of his initial cold response to his wife's news about her mother. He'd always prided himself on his sympathetic nature, which his mother had sniffed at when he'd been a child, if he'd cried over a dead bird in the garden or a beating from his father.

'You're far too sensitive,' his mother would say. 'You are a boy, Gustavo, and you must not show your emotions.'

And certainly, he confessed to himself, when he drank, he found it far easier *not* to feel as sensitive. Since his marriage to Izabela – a change that he'd believed would make him feel so much more worthy – if anything, his self-esteem had dissipated, not grown. Which had subsequently made him turn to drink even more regularly.

Gustavo sighed heavily. Even though he'd known Izabela didn't love him as he loved her, he had hoped that her affection for him would grow once they were married. But he'd felt her reticence towards him – especially when they made love – from the start. And these days, every time she glanced at him, he saw something akin to pity in her eyes, which turned occasionally to blatant dislike. The thought that he might be a disappointment to his wife, as well as his parents, had added to his self-loathing.

And the fact that Izabela had not yet conceived a child exacerbated his feeling of failure. The look in his mother's eyes told him that he'd not even been able to perform his duties as a man. And even though since his marriage *he* was the official master of their household, and Izabela its mistress, Gustavo knew he had done little to stamp his authority on it, or curb his mother's need to control it.

The waiter passed with a tray and picked up his empty glass. 'The same again, sir?' he asked automatically, and expecting the usual nod, was almost walking away before Gustavo said with effort, 'No, thank you. Can you bring me a coffee?'

'Of course, sir.'

As he drank the hot, bitter liquid, Gustavo mused on the

short time he and Izabela had been married, and, for the first time, confessed to himself honestly how their relationship had deteriorated. It had reached the point where he felt that, only six months on, they led separate lives. He also admitted brutally to himself that much of this was to do with him and the fact that he'd been spending too much time here at the club, drowning his feelings of inadequacy in alcohol.

Gustavo could suddenly see clearly how it was that he had failed his wife.

No wonder she seemed so unhappy. Between the coldness of his mother and his own descent into drunkenness and self-pity, Izabela must feel as though she had made a dreadful mistake.

'But I love her,' Gustavo whispered desperately into the bottom of the coffee cup.

Surely, he thought, it wasn't too late to mend their relationship? To return to the level of affection and communication they had shared before they'd married? Gustavo remembered that at least Izabela had seemed to like him back then.

I will take control, he vowed, as he signed his bill and went outside to his waiting car, determined to speak to his parents on his arrival back at the Casa. For he knew if he did not, he was bound to lose his wife for good.

In the last two weeks of Carla's life, Fabiana, Bel and Loen took it in turns to sit with her so that she was never alone. One evening, in a rare lucid moment, Carla had reached weakly for her daughter's hand.

'*Querida*, there is something I must say to you while I still can,' she said, her voice barely more than a whisper, so that Bel had to lean in close to hear her words. 'I understand that married life has not been easy for you so far and I feel it is my duty to offer some guidance—'

'Mãe, please,' Bel interrupted desperately. 'Gustavo and I have had our problems, like all married couples, but really, there is nothing for you to concern yourself with now.'

'Maybe not,' Carla continued doggedly. 'But you are my daughter and I know you better than you can imagine. It has not been lost on me that you may have developed an . . . attachment to a certain person who is not your husband. I saw it that night at the Casa when he came to unveil his sculpture.'

'Mãe, really, it is nothing. He is . . . was only a friend,' Bel said, shocked to the core that her mother had noticed.

'I doubt it,' Carla replied with a grim smile. 'Remember that I also saw the look that passed between you that day on Corcovado Mountain. You pretended you did not know him, but I could see you did, very well indeed. And I should warn you that following that path can only result in heartache for all concerned. I beg you, Izabela, you have been married for such a short time. Give Gustavo a chance to make you happy.'

Not wishing to distress her mother further, Bel nodded her acquiescence. 'I will, I promise.'

Two days later, Fabiana came to Bel's room at sunrise.

'Senhora, I think it is time to call for your father.'

Antonio came immediately, and for the last hours of his

wife's life, barely left her side. The end came peacefully and Antonio and Bel stood together at the end of the bed, their arms around each other, weeping silently.

They travelled back to Rio together after the funeral – Carla had insisted on being buried in the small cemetery in Paty do Alferes – both of them desolate.

'Pai, please,' Bel said as they arrived at Mansão da Princesa and she prepared to return to the Casa. 'Anything you need, you must tell me. Shall I come and visit you here tomorrow? See how you are? I'm sure Gustavo wouldn't mind if I stayed with you for the next few days.'

'No, no, *querida*. You have your own life to lead. Me?' Antonio looked around the drawing room in which he'd spent so many hours with his wife. 'I have nothing left.'

'Pai, please don't say that. You know Mãe's last wish was for you to try to find some happiness in the rest of the time you have here on earth.'

'I know, my *princesa*, and I promise I will try. But forgive me; at this moment, arriving here to this emptiness, it is impossible.'

Seeing that Jorge had just pulled the car up into the drive to collect her, Bel went to her father and hugged him tightly to her. 'Try to remember that you still have me. I love you, Pai.'

As she left the drawing room and walked into the hall, she saw Loen and Gabriela whispering together.

'Jorge is here, Loen, and we must leave,' she said, then turned to Gabriela. 'You can see how my father is,' she said helplessly.

'Senhora, I will do my best to comfort him. And perhaps,

with God's blessing, he will recover. Please remember that time is a great healer.'

'Thank you. I'll be back to see him tomorrow. Come, Loen.'

Bel watched as mother and daughter said a fond goodbye, which only served to underline her own terrible loss.

On the short drive to the Casa, Bel wondered what she would encounter when she arrived. She'd ignored Gustavo's frequent telephone calls as often as she dared, asking Fabiana to tell him she was with her mother, and only speaking to him when she had to. Although to her surprise, when she'd told him of her mother's death, his response had been unusually sympathetic. And he'd sounded sober. When she'd assured him there was no need to attend the funeral, which Carla had requested to be for close family only, Gustavo had said that he understood and would look forward very much to seeing her on her return.

In the strange hinterland of approaching death, Bel had spent little time contemplating her future, but as they neared her marital home, she realised she must begin to face it. Especially one particular part of it, which she'd discussed with Loen only last week, who'd reassured her that these things could be brought on by stress. She'd allowed herself to be comforted by her maid's theory, unable to begin to contemplate the complexity of the alternative while her heart was so full of grief.

Bel entered the house, noticing as she always did the change from the warmth of the air outside to the chilly atmosphere within. She shivered involuntarily as Loen helped her remove her hat, wondering if she should simply climb the stairs straight up to her bedroom, or go in search of her husband or his parents. There was certainly no sympathetic welcome committee waiting for her here.

'I will take your suitcase upstairs to your room, unpack and draw you a bath, Senhora Bel,' said Loen, sensing her discomfort and giving her shoulder a light pat of understanding as she moved to walk upstairs.

'Hello?' Bel called into the empty hallway.

There was no reply. She called again, to no response, and finally decided to follow Loen up the stairs.

Suddenly, a figure emerged from the drawing room. 'I see you are home at last.'

'Yes, Luiza.'

'I am sorry for your loss, and so is my husband.'

'Thank you.'

'Dinner is at the usual time.'

'Then I will go upstairs and prepare for it.'

Receiving only a brusque nod in response, Bel walked up the stairs, her feet treading automatically, one after the other. Entering her bedroom, she thought that at least Loen was a comforting, familiar presence. Bel let her maid help her undress, a task she hadn't asked her to perform at the *fazenda* as the usual rituals had been forgotten amidst the need to focus entirely on Carla. But now she watched Loen's surprised expression as she stood naked in front of her.

'What is it?'

Loen's eyes had moved to her stomach. 'Nothing, I . . . nothing, Senhora Bel. The bath is run. Why don't you get in while the water is warm?'

Bel did as she was told, and lay in the bath. And as she gazed down at herself, she became fully aware of the change in the familiar contours of her body. There were no baths at the *fazenda*, only pails of water warmed by the sun and thrown over oneself, and she'd barely glanced at herself in the mirror for weeks.

'*Meu Deus!*' said Bel as her fingers tentatively touched the barely visible but newly rounded shape of her normally flat belly, which now appeared like a half-risen soufflé from the water that surrounded it. Her breasts too seemed fuller and heavier.

'I am with child,' she whispered, her heart beginning to pound.

There was no further time to contemplate what she had just seen, or berate herself for taking Loen's advice on the 'monthly' she'd missed being merely due to stress as gospel, for she heard Gustavo's reedy voice talking to Loen next door. Washing herself quickly, she stepped out of the bath, donned her robe, making sure that she tied it loosely in case her husband noticed the subtle change in her shape, and walked into the bedroom.

Gustavo stood there, his expression wary and a little shy.

'Thank you, Loen. You may go,' he said.

Loen left the room and Bel stayed where she was, waiting for Gustavo to speak first.

'I am so sorry for your loss, Izabela,' he said, parroting the words of his mother.

'Thank you. I admit it has not been easy.'

'Nor has it been easy here without you.'

'No, I am sorry,' she offered.

'Please, don't apologise,' he said hastily. 'I am very happy

you are back.' He smiled tentatively. 'I have missed you, Izabela.'

'Thank you, Gustavo. Now, I must get ready for dinner,
and so must you.'

He nodded at her, and made his way towards the bathroom, closing the door behind him.

Bel walked to the window, observing that the qualities of
the light had subtly altered since the seasons had changed. It
was past seven o'clock in the evening, but the sun was only
just starting to descend to the earth. Bel realised it was mid-
October and the height of spring in Rio. Turning back
towards the bed, still dazed by her realisation in the bath, she
saw that Loen had laid out a dress that she rarely wore, due
to its flowing design – Gustavo preferred his wife to wear
clothes which defined her comely figure – and her eyes filled
with tears at her maid's thoughtfulness. Once dressed, she left
Gustavo upstairs and walked down the stairs to the drawing
room, preferring that option to facing her husband alone. As
she reached the bottom, she eyed the front door, wishing with
all her heart that she could open it and run now to Laurent.
For there was no doubt in her mind that the child she carried
inside her was his.

Over dinner that night, Bel realised that little had changed
here since she'd been away. Luiza was still cold and patronising, hardly offering a word of sympathy for her loss. Maurício
was a little more forthcoming, but spent most of the evening
discussing the financial intricacies of Wall Street and some-

thing called the Dow Jones Index with Gustavo, which had apparently seen a mass selling of stocks last Thursday.

'I thank God I decided to sell the stocks I held last month. I hope your father did the same,' said Maurício. 'Luckily, I didn't have many to begin with. Never did trust those Yankees. They're trying to shore up the market at the moment, hoping it will have settled over the weekend, but I doubt we've seen the worst yet. Long term, however, if the market does crash, it will have a devastating effect on our coffee industry. The demand from America, which accounts for most of our produce, is sure to fall like a stone. Especially with the mass overproduction Brazil has seen in the past few years,' he added gloomily.

'It seems a blessing that our family got out of the American markets when we did,' said Luiza pointedly, shooting a glance at Bel. 'I've always believed the avaricious get their just deserts sooner or later.'

Bel chanced a glance at her husband, who returned an unusually sympathetic smile at his mother's inference.

'We may no longer be rich, my dear, but at least we are stable,' said her father-in-law neutrally in response.

On the way up to bed that evening, Bel turned to Gustavo.

'How bad is this situation in America? Do you know? I'm obviously concerned for my father. What with him being out of Rio for the past week, he may not know much of any of this.'

'As I'm sure you realise, I didn't follow the markets previously,' Gustavo admitted as he opened the door to their bedroom. 'But from what my father says, and based on the facts that I'm only just beginning to understand, it's very serious indeed.'

Bel went into the bathroom, her mind whirling with the events of the past few hours. She undressed and once again could not help but stare at the small but visible bump, still hoping she'd somehow been mistaken earlier. As she donned her nightgown, she simply had no idea what she should do. But the one thing she *did* know was that she couldn't bear her husband to touch her tonight. Taking as long as she could with her ablutions, she left the bathroom, hoping and praying Gustavo would have fallen asleep. But he was lying in bed wide awake, watching her.

'I've missed you, Izabela. Come to your husband.'

Climbing tentatively into bed beside him, a million excuses went through her mind. But not one of them was sufficient to give to a husband who'd been without his wife for the past two months.

She realised Gustavo was still staring at her.

'Izabela, you look terrified. Do I frighten you that much?'

'No, no . . . of course not.'

'*Querida*, I understand that you are grieving and perhaps need some time before you are able to fully relax. So let me simply hold you.'

Gustavo's words were a complete surprise to her. And, given the realisation of her current condition earlier, the pain of watching her mother die and the news over dinner of the situation in America, his empathy was enough to bring further tears to her eyes.

'Please, Izabela, don't be frightened of me. I promise I only wish to comfort you tonight,' he reiterated as he reached to turn out the light.

She allowed Gustavo to pull her into his arms, and lay there on his chest, staring wide-eyed into the darkness. She felt his hand stroking her hair, and, as she thought of the tiny heartbeat inside her, her emotions see-sawed towards guilt.

'While you were away, I had plenty of time to think,' Gustavo said softly. 'I remembered how we were when we first met, how we used to talk about art and culture and laugh together. But since we married, I feel we have been drifting apart, and I take a lot of responsibility for that. I understand I've been spending far too long at my club. Partly, if I'm honest, to get me out of this house. We both know the atmosphere is somewhat . . . austere.'

Bel lay in the dark listening to what he was saying, but decided to make no comment until he had finished.

'But that again is my fault. I should have been firmer with my mother when I married you. Told her point-blank that you would now be running the household and that she must retire gracefully into the background to allow you to do so. Forgive me, Izabela, I have been weak and have not stood up for you, or for myself, when it was needed.'

'Gustavo, it's hardly your fault that Luiza dislikes me.'

'I doubt it's *you* she dislikes,' he replied bitterly. 'She wouldn't take to anyone who threatened her position in the household. She even suggested to me that, given the fact that you'd not yet managed to conceive a child since we were married, she could speak to the bishop and have our marriage annulled. On the grounds that we had obviously not shared intimate relations.'

Bel could not help a gasp of horror at Gustavo's words, given what currently lay secretly inside her. Gustavo took her reaction as shock at his mother's dreadful damning of their marriage and pulled her closer to him.

'Of course I was furious with her and told her that if she

ever uttered such blasphemy again, it would be *her* who was out on the street, not my wife. After that,' Gustavo continued, 'I decided I must act. I have asked my father to transfer this house into my name, something I should have insisted on the moment we married, since it is the normal protocol. He has agreed, and will also pass over the running of the family finances to me once I feel equipped and knowledgeable enough to handle them. Therefore, for the next few weeks I will be with my father for much of the time, learning from him rather than wasting my days at the club. Once all that happens, I will be passing responsibility for all domestic matters over to you. And my mother will have no choice but to accept the situation.'

'I see.' Bel noted the new determination in his voice and wished that she could find comfort in it.

'So, later than it should have been, we will finally be in joint control of our own household. As for my drinking, I know it has been excessive recently, Izabela, and I swear to you that for the past few weeks I have only been taking a little wine with dinner and no more. Can you forgive your husband for not acting sooner? I can understand how difficult the past few months must have been for you. But as you have just heard, I am determined to make a fresh start. I hope you can too, because I love you so very much.'

'Of . . . of course I can forgive you,' she stammered, unable to utter any other response to his heartfelt words.

'And from now on, there will be no more forced' – Gustavo searched for an appropriate phrase – 'bedroom activity. If you tell me you do not wish to make love with me, I will accept it. Although I hope that sometimes in the future, once you have seen how I mean to continue, you will wish for it.

There, that is all I have to say. And now, *querida*, after the dreadful few weeks you have had, I hope I can hold you in my arms until you fall asleep.'

A few minutes later, Bel heard Gustavo snoring gently and moved out of his arms to roll onto her side. Her heart pounded and butterflies circled around the pit of her stomach as she contemplated her situation. Was there any chance this baby could be her husband's? She thought back desperately to the last time they had successfully made love, and knew there was not.

As the night hours dragged on and she tossed and turned in misery, Bel knew she must make an immediate decision. After all, Laurent might be horrified if she told him she was pregnant and that the baby was his. This had never been part of the plan for either of them, which was why Laurent had taken all the care he could to protect her from it. Bel's mind went back to Margarida's original words of warning: that men such as Laurent did not want or wish for any ties of a permanent nature.

As the dawn began to glow through the cracks in the shutters, all Bel's old insecurities about Laurent returned with a vengeance. There was only one thing she could do, and that was to see him as soon as possible.

42

'Where are you off to today, *meu amor*?' Gustavo asked, smiling at his wife as he helped himself to more coffee from the silver pot on the breakfast table.

'I'm going for my final fitting at Madame Duchaine's before the new season begins,' Bel smiled brightly. 'I hope the garments will be ready for me to collect at the end of the week.'

'Good, good,' he said.

'And if I may, I would like to miss luncheon to visit my father. I telephoned him earlier and Gabriela told me that he hadn't even dressed and wasn't planning on going into the office today.' Bel's features creased into a frown. 'I'm obviously very concerned about his state of mind.'

'Of course,' agreed Gustavo. 'I am going with my father to the senate building. President Washington Luís has called an emergency meeting of all the coffee barons to discuss the continuing crisis in America.'

'I thought your father no longer had an interest in coffee farming?' queried Bel.

'He has very little, but as a senior member of the community here in Rio, the President has asked for him to be there.'

'Surely my father should also be attending?'

'Yes, he should, of course. The situation is deteriorating by the day. But please tell him that I will be happy to brief him on what is said. I will see you before dinner, *querida*.' Gustavo kissed Bel gently on the cheek and rose from the table.

Once Gustavo had left with his father for the senate and she knew Luiza was sequestered in the kitchen with the cook organising the menus for the next week, Bel hurried upstairs to find her address book. Running back downstairs to the hall, her hands shaking, she picked up the receiver and asked to be put through to the number Laurent had given her.

'Please be at home,' she whispered as she heard the line ring at the other end.

'*Ici* Laurent Brouilly.'

The sound of his voice made her stomach churn with nerves and anticipation. 'It's Izabela Aires Cabral,' she replied, just in case Luiza decided to emerge unexpectedly from the kitchen and into the hall. 'Is it possible for me to book an appointment for this afternoon at two o'clock?'

There was a pause before Laurent answered. 'Madame, I am sure I can accommodate that. Will you be coming here?'

'Yes.'

'Then I will look forward very much to seeing you again.'

She could almost hear the wry smile in his voice as he joined in with the game. 'Goodbye then.'

'*A bientôt, ma chérie*,' he whispered as Bel abruptly replaced the receiver.

Her fingers hovered over it for a few seconds as she thought of calling Madame Duchaine to book an appointment with her as an alibi, but she knew that she could not yet chance Madame's beady eyes falling on her newly rounded stomach and gossiping to others about it. So she called and made an appointment for two days' time instead. Grabbing her hat and informing Luiza she was on her way to see her father and then on to her dressmaker, Bel climbed into the back of the car and asked Jorge to take her to Mansão da Princesa.

Gabriela was at the front door before she had even climbed the steps, her face full of concern.

'How is he?' Bel asked as she walked inside the house.

'Still in bed, saying he hasn't the energy to get up. Shall I tell him you are here, senhora?'

'No, I will go and see him myself.'

Knocking on her father's bedroom door, and receiving no response, she opened it and walked inside. The shutters were tightly closed against the bright midday sun, and she could barely make out the shape huddled under the covers.

'Pai, it is me, Izabela. Are you ill?'

There was a grunt from the bed, but nothing more.

'I'm going to open the shutters so that I can take a look at you,' she said, going over to the windows and throwing them wide. She turned and saw her father was feigning sleep, so she walked over to the bed and sat down on it.

'Pai, please tell me, what is wrong with you?'

'I cannot go on without her,' Antonio moaned. 'What is the point in anything if she is not here?'

'Pai, you promised Mãe on her deathbed that you would carry on. She is probably looking down on you now from the heavens this very moment, shouting at you to get up!'

'I don't believe in the heavens, or God,' he growled morosely. 'What kind of deity would remove from the earth my precious Carla, who had never done a single bad thing in the whole of her life?'

'Well, she *did* believe, and so do I,' Bel replied staunchly.

'We both know there is never a reason behind these things. You had twenty-two wonderful years together. Surely you must be grateful for them? And try to fulfil her wish that you carry on in memory of her?'

Her father did not respond, so Bel tried another tack.

'Pai, you must know what is happening in America at present? Maurício said last night that they think another crash might happen on Wall Street at any moment. The senate is holding an emergency meeting right now to discuss the impact on Brazil. All the major coffee producers are there. Surely you should be there too?'

'No, Bel, it is too late,' sighed Antonio. 'I didn't sell the stocks I had when I should have done, believing others were panicking. Yesterday, after you left, my stockbroker called to tell me that the market had fallen and many of my shares were already worth nothing. He says there is worse to come today. Izabela, most of our cash was invested in Wall Street. I have lost everything.'

'Pai, surely that can't be true? Even if you have lost your stocks, you own many farms that must be worth a lot of money? Even if coffee doesn't sell so well now and in the future, you have the properties themselves?'

'Izabela,' Antonio sighed quietly, 'please do not begin to try and understand business. I borrowed money from the banks to buy those farms. And they were very willing to lend it to me while coffee yields and the sale price of the beans was so high. As those prices have dropped, I've struggled to keep on top of the repayments. The banks wanted more security and so I had to give them this house as collateral against any default. Izabela, do you understand? Now they will take everything I own to pay off my debts. If my stocks in America have gone as well, I have nothing left, not even a roof over my head.'

Bel listened, aghast at what her father was telling her, and berated herself for her shallow fiscal understanding. If she were more adept in these matters, perhaps there would be something she could say to give Antonio the hope he needed.

'But Pai, surely it's all the more reason why you should be at the senate today? You're not the only one in this position and you've told me before that Brazil's economy is based on coffee production. Surely the government will not allow it to simply collapse?'

'*Querida*, there is a very simple equation here: if no one has any money to buy our beans, there is nothing that *any* government can do about it. And I can assure you that those in America will simply be thinking about how they can survive rather than the luxury of enjoying a cup of coffee.' Antonio rubbed his forehead in agitation. 'Of course, the senate are trying to look as if they are doing something about the crisis. But every one of them knows it is already too late. So, thank you for telling me of the meeting, but I will tell you now that it is a fruitless gesture.'

'At the very least I will ask Maurício to tell you what was discussed,' said Bel resolutely. 'Besides, even if you're right and you are left with nothing, remember that it is I who owns the *fazenda*. You will not be homeless, dearest Pai. And I'm sure that given the fact that you made such a generous payment to Gustavo when he married me, he would be prepared to make sure that you don't starve.'

'And what would you have me do all alone at the *fazenda*?' Antonio asked her bitterly. 'With no business to run or the company of my precious wife?'

'Pai, enough! As you said yourself, many will be affected by this situation, made destitute even, so you must count yourself lucky that you won't be. You are only forty-eight years old. Surely there is plenty of time to start again?'

'Izabela, my reputation is ruined. Even if I wanted to start again, no bank in Brazil would lend me the money I would need to do so. It is all over for me.'

Bel watched as her father closed his eyes once more. She thought back to only a few months ago, when Antonio had walked her so proudly down the aisle. Even though she'd always hated the blatant way her father had liked to show off his newly gained wealth, she wished with all her heart that she could retrieve it for him. It was only now that she realised his entire self-esteem had been built on it. Add that to the loss of his beloved wife and she could understand why he felt he had nothing left.

'Pai, you have me,' she said quietly. 'And I need you. Please believe me when I say that I don't care whether you have everything or nothing. I still love you and respect you as my father.'

For the first time, as Antonio's eyes flickered open, Bel saw a hint of a smile in them. 'Yes, you're right, I do,' he agreed. 'And you, *princesa*, are the one thing in my life that I am truly proud of.'

'Then you will hear me when I tell you, just as Mãe would, that you are not yet beaten. Please Pai, rouse yourself, and together we can work out what is to be done. I will help you in any way I can. I have my own jewellery and Mãe's, which you know she left to me. Surely if we sold it, that would raise a considerable amount for you to put into a new business?'

'If there is anyone with the cash left to buy anything at the end of this financial holocaust,' Antonio said brutally. 'Now Izabela, I thank you for coming and I am embarrassed that you have had to see me like this. And I promise you that I will rise from my bed the moment you leave. But right now, I would simply like to be alone to think.'

'You promise, Pai? I warn you, I will call Gabriela later to make sure you have done as you are promising me. And I'll be back tomorrow to see how you are.' Bel bent to kiss him and he smiled at her.

'Thank you, *princesa*. I'll see you tomorrow.'

Bel spoke briefly to Gabriela and said she'd telephone her later, then climbed into the waiting car and directed Jorge to Madame Duchaine's salon in Ipanema. Telling him as usual to return for her at six, Bel went through the rigmarole of waiting until he had pulled away, then turned from the doorstep and walked as fast as she could in the direction of Laurent's apartment building.

'*Chérie!*' Laurent said as he pulled her through the door and into his arms, covering her face and neck with kisses. 'You have no idea how much I have missed you.'

Melting into him with relief, Bel did not protest as he picked her up and carried her into the bedroom. And for a few precious minutes, all the dreadful thoughts whirling around her head disappeared in the ecstasy of being one with him again.

Afterwards, they lay together in the tangle of sheets and Bel answered many of the gentle questions Laurent put to her about the past few weeks.

'And what of you, Laurent?' she asked eventually. 'You have managed to keep yourself busy?'

'Sadly, since Alessandra Silveira, I have been unable to secure a further commission. Everyone is nervous about the situation with the coffee in Brazil and the stock market in New York. They are no longer spending their money on frippery such as sculptures. So for the past month I have done little more than eat, drink and take a swim in the sea. Izabela,' Laurent said, his face becoming serious, 'apart from the fact that the situation in Brazil worsens by the day, I feel that I have stayed here as long as I can. I miss France and it is time that I stopped treading water. *Chérie*, forgive me, but I must return home.' He reached for her hand and kissed it. 'The question is, will you come with me?'

Bel found herself unable to reply. She lay silently in his arms, eyes tightly closed, feeling as though all the elements which made up her life were rising to an unbearable crescendo.

'Senhor da Silva Costa has booked me a cabin on a steamer that leaves on Friday,' he continued, urgency in his voice. 'I must take it, as many of the shipping companies are owned by Americans. If the financial situation worsens further, there may be no boats leaving the port in Rio for many months.'

Bel listened to Laurent, finally realising just how deep this crisis in America went. 'You sail on Friday? In three days' time?' she finally managed to whisper.

'Yes. And I beg you, *mon amour*, to join me. I think it is time for you to follow *me*,' he urged. 'However much I love you, there is nothing for me here: no life, and certainly not one we could share together, given your circumstances. I feel guilty for forcing a decision on you when your precious *maman* is barely cold in her grave. But I hope you can understand why I must go.' His eyes searched her face for an answer.

'Yes, you've waited for me long enough.' Bel sat upright and pulled the sheet across her naked breasts. 'Laurent, there is something I must tell you . . .'

Gustavo emerged from the crowded senate building with relief. Inside, both the temperature and the tension had reached boiling point as desperate coffee producers demanded to know what the government would do to save them. There had even been some brawling – civilised men driven to violence at the thought of their fortunes dwindling to nothing overnight.

He had lasted as long as he could, wanting to at least show his support but feeling he had little to offer in the way of advice. Now more than anything he wanted a drink. Turning in the direction of his club and walking a few paces, he checked himself.

No. He must resist or he would be back to where he started, and he had promised Izabela only last night that he was a reformed character.

Then he remembered her telling him over breakfast that she was going to her dressmaker's in Ipanema for a fitting. The salon was only a ten-minute walk from here and he suddenly thought how nice it would be to surprise her. Perhaps they could take a walk along the promenade, sit in one of the beachside cafés and simply watch the world go by. That was the kind of thing husbands and wives who enjoyed each other's company did, wasn't it?

He turned left and headed in the direction of Ipanema.

Fifteen minutes later, Gustavo emerged from Madame Duchaine's salon confused. He swore Izabela had said earlier that this was where she was headed after visiting her father, but Madame Duchaine had assured him that no appointment had been booked that afternoon by his wife. Shrugging, Gustavo walked along the street and hailed a cab to take him home.

Laurent was staring at her, utter shock on his face.

'And you are sure the baby is mine?'

'I have gone over and over any occasion in my mind which could have made it possible for it to be Gustavo's, but as you have said yourself, unless there is proper . . . *entry*, it is impossible to make a baby.' Bel was blushing with embarrassment at talking so intimately about her relationship with her husband. 'And in the two months before I left for the *fazenda* with my mother, there . . . was none. Not that my husband would have noticed one way or the other,' she added.

'You think you are about three months pregnant?'

'Maybe more, but I cannot be sure. I could hardly go to the family doctor until I'd spoken to you about it.'

'Can I see?' he asked her.

'Yes, although there is little showing.'

Bel watched as Laurent took the sheet from her body and put his hand gently on the tiny bump. His eyes left her belly and travelled upwards to hers. 'And you can swear to me that you are as sure as you can be the child is mine?'

'Laurent' – Bel held his gaze – 'there is no doubt in my mind. If there was, I simply would not be here.'

'No. Well . . .' he sighed. 'Given the circumstances we were discussing before this news, it makes it more imperative that we leave together for Paris as soon as possible.'

'You are saying you want our child?'

'I am saying that I want *you*, my Izabela. And if that,' he said, pointing to the bump, 'is part of you and me – however unexpected – then yes, of course I do.'

Bel's eye's blurred with tears. 'I thought you might not. I was steeling myself for it.'

'Admittedly, if it arrives and resembles a ferret, I may have second thoughts, but of course I believe you, Bel. I can think of no good reason why you would lie to me, given the life I can offer a child compared to your husband.' Laurent dropped his gaze from her and sighed. 'You must realise I have no idea how we will survive. Even I can see that bringing up a baby in my garret in Montparnasse is not suitable for it. Or for you.'

'I have jewellery that I could sell,' Bel offered for the second time that day. 'And a little money to get us started.'

Laurent looked at her in wonder. '*Mon Dieu!* You have already thought about this.'

'Every minute since I knew for certain,' she admitted. 'But . . .'

'There is always a "but".' He rolled his eyes. 'And what is yours?'

'I saw my father before I came here to you. He wouldn't stir from his bed, he is so depressed. He told me that he has lost everything in the American stock market. He is ruined and broken by this and my mother's death.'

'So now you are no longer just feeling guilty about your husband, but about leaving your father?'

'Of course!' Bel said, frustrated that he didn't seem to understand the enormity of her decision. 'If I go with you, Pai really will feel he has lost everything.'

'And if you don't, our baby will have lost its papa. And you and I, each other,' countered Laurent. '*Chérie*, I can't help you make your decision. All I can say is that I travelled half-way across the world to be with you, and have sat here in this apartment for the past nine months living only for the moments we are together. Of course I would understand if you decided to stay, but it seems to me that there is always a reason for you not to consider your own happiness.'

'I loved my mother so very much, and I love my father still. Please remember it was not Gustavo who drew me back to Rio from Paris,' Bel begged him, tears pricking at her eyes. 'I did not wish to break my parents' hearts.'

'I think, Izabela, that you need some more time to think about this.' Laurent tipped her chin towards him and kissed her lightly on her lips. 'Once the decision is made, there is no going back. Either way.'

'At the moment, I confess that I'm not sure which way to turn.'

'Sadly, I doubt that there will ever be a better "moment" in the future to make a choice such as this. There never is. However,' he sighed, 'I suggest we meet again here in two days' time. And then you will tell me of your decision and we will make a plan.'

Bel had climbed off the bed and was already dressing. Pinning on her hat, she nodded.

'Whatever happens, *querida*, I will be here at two o'clock on Thursday.'

When she arrived home at the Casa, Bel telephoned Gabriela to ask after her father. Gabriela said that he had indeed risen from his bed and had left the house, telling her he was going to the office for the afternoon. Relieved, she decided that rather than going upstairs immediately, she'd ask Loen to bring her some mango juice out to the terrace and enjoy the softness of the evening sun.

'Is that all you need, Senhora Bel?' Loen asked her as she placed the glass and jug on the table beside her mistress.

Bel was tempted to confide about the dreadful quandary she was in. But she knew that even though Loen was the closest friend she had, she could not burden her maid with the truth.

'Yes thank you, Loen. Could you draw my bath for me in ten minutes? I'll be up later.'

Bel watched her disappear round the side of the house and into the kitchen. Now her mother was gone, she knew this was a decision she had to take on her own. Bel sipped her mango juice and tried to rationalise the facts. Even though Gustavo's behaviour in the past twenty-four hours had been a marked improvement on the previous few months, from his past history, Bel had to believe it was temporary. Whatever he'd promised, she doubted her husband had the spine to stand up to Luiza.

And more to the point, she felt nothing for him, and not even a trace of guilt any longer. If she *did* leave him, it seemed his mother already had a fail-safe option in place. The marriage could be annulled and Gustavo would be free to find a more suitable wife than herself. And Bel was sure that this time his mother would choose the bride for him.

Her father was a different matter. She agonised that her mother would never forgive her for deserting Antonio in his hour of need. She also remembered her mother's words to her just before she'd died – how following her heart to Laurent could only end in disaster.

And now, of course, there was a new presence in her life that she must consider. She must think what would be better for the little one growing inside her. If she stayed with Gustavo, she could give the baby security and a family name which would carry her child comfortably through its life. And of course, Bel thought, she could imagine the look on Pai's face if she told him he was expecting his first grandchild. That alone would surely give him a reason to live.

But would she want any baby of hers brought up under the emotionless, austere roof of the Aires Cabrals? The child would be saddled with a mother who would spend the rest of her life regretting her decision to stay, secretly dreaming of another world she had rejected. And a father who was only that in name . . .

Bel sighed in desperation. Whichever way she turned, she could not come to a resolution.

'Hello, Izabela.' Gustavo appeared on the terrace from around the corner of the house. 'What are you doing out here?'

'Enjoying the coolness of the evening air,' she said abruptly, unable to stop herself outwardly blushing from the hidden thoughts inside her head.

'Yes,' he said, sitting down. 'It certainly became heated in the senate today. Apparently on Wall Street, they're calling today "Black Tuesday". The Dow Jones has lost an additional thirty points from yesterday and the Rockefeller family has been buying large amounts of stocks to shore up the market. I don't think it's worked, but we won't know until tomorrow exactly how much has been lost. Anyway, at least my father seems to have made some sensible decisions over the past few months, unlike others. How was your father today?' he asked her.

'Dreadful. I think he is one of those you just mentioned who has gambled and lost.'

'Well, he mustn't feel ashamed. There are many of them in the same boat. They weren't to know. None of us were.'

Bel turned to him, appreciating his calm words of wisdom. 'Perhaps you would go and see my father. Tell him what you've just told me.'

'Of course.'

'It is almost seven and my bath will be getting cold,' she said, standing up from the bench. 'Thank you, Gustavo.'

'For what?'

'For understanding.'

Bel made to walk around the corner of the house and back inside.

'By the way, how was your fitting at the dressmaker's?' he asked her, watching as she paused at his words, her back to him.

'It was most successful. Thank you for asking.' She turned and smiled at him before disappearing out of sight.

43

After a further restless night, Bel awoke groggy and exhausted, having finally fallen asleep as dawn broke. She saw the space where Gustavo lay was empty next to her. As she made her way to the bathroom, she thought how this was unusual in itself; Gustavo was never normally up before her. Perhaps he really did mean to turn over a new leaf. When she went downstairs for breakfast, she found only Luiza at the table.

'My husband and yours are together in the study looking at the morning papers. You will have heard from Gustavo yesterday, I'm sure, that Wall Street crashed again. They will both be heading back to the senate soon to discuss what can be done to save the coffee industry in the wake of this disaster. Will you be going to the Igreja da Glória today?' Luiza queried blandly, as if nothing had changed since yesterday and half the world hadn't woken to find themselves bankrupted this morning.

'No. I must go and see my father. As you can imagine, he is currently . . . out of sorts,' Bel replied in a similarly neutral tone.

'Of course. Well, everyone reaps what they sow, as I've said before.' Luiza stood up. 'Then I shall continue in your absence to do our family duty and take your place at the church.'

Bel watched the woman as she swept from the room, and felt breathless with astonishment at Luiza's insensitivity. Made even more unbearable by the fact that her mother-in-law's continuing financial stability – including this recently renovated house – had been aided and paid for by Antonio and his hard work.

Bel took an orange from the bowl and threw it against the wall in frustration, just as Gustavo entered the room.

He raised an eyebrow as the orange rolled back towards her under the table. 'Good morning, Izabela,' he said as he knelt to retrieve the fruit and put it back in the bowl on the table. 'Practising your tennis?'

'Forgive me, Gustavo. I'm afraid your mother made a particularly insensitive comment.'

'Ah yes, well, that will probably be due to the fact that my father informed her before breakfast this morning that you will be taking over the household accounts from now on. As you can imagine, she hasn't taken it well. I'm afraid you will simply have to ignore any tantrums the news has solicited.'

'I'll do my best,' she agreed. 'I hear you're going to the senate again this morning?'

'Yes. News is gradually trickling through from New York. Apparently, yesterday was a bloodbath,' Gustavo sighed. 'There were men throwing themselves out of windows all along Wall Street. Thirty billion dollars has been wiped off the value of stocks. Within a few hours, the price of coffee per pound plummeted.'

'Then my father was right to think it was all over for him?'

'It's certainly a huge disaster for every producer, and, more importantly, for Brazil's economy as a whole,' Gustavo explained. 'Can I suggest that your father joins us for dinner tonight? Perhaps I can find a means of helping him in some way. At the very least, my father and I can tell him what the government is saying, if he can't face appearing at the senate himself.'

'That would be most kind, Gustavo. I'm going to visit him later and I will suggest it,' Bel replied gratefully.

'Good. And may I say how very beautiful you look this morning.' Gustavo kissed her gently on the top of her head. 'I will see you at luncheon.'

Having telephoned Gabriela to be told that Antonio had ventured into the office this morning, she told her to inform him of the dinner invitation for this evening. Climbing back up the stairs to her bedroom, Bel watched from the window as Jorge returned from chauffeuring Maurício and Gustavo to the senate building in Rio. Then, twenty minutes later, the car left again with Luiza inside it.

Bel walked back downstairs and wandered along the hall, glad to have the house to herself. On the silver tray, she saw a letter addressed to her. Picking it up, she opened the front door and walked round to the bench on the back terrace to read.

> *Apartment 4*
> *48, Avenue de Marigny*
> *Paris*
> *France*

> *5th October 1929*

My dearest Bel,

    I can hardly believe it is over a year since I last saw you and you left Paris. I write to tell you that we are on our way back home to Rio, as Pai has finished his computations for the Cristo and wishes to return to oversee the final stages of its construction. By the time you read this, we will be somewhere on the Atlantic Ocean. You'll be pleased to hear that I will be able to converse with you in French, as my lessons and my work at the hospital have made me proficient, if not fluent. I leave Paris with mixed emotions. When I first arrived, you will remember that I was almost afraid of it; but now, I can honestly say I will miss it – in all its complexity – and perhaps find Rio claustrophobic in comparison. However, there is much I am looking forward to, including seeing you, my dearest friend.

How is your mother's health? You wrote of concerns about her in your last letter and I hope she is fully recovered. Speaking of health, I have written to the Santa Casa de Misericórdia Hospital and I am enrolling on their nurses' training programme on my return. This will keep me out of trouble, I'm sure. Sadly, I did not meet my French count while I was here, and no man has shown interest in me, so I have decided that I will be wedded, certainly for the time being, to my career.

How is Gustavo? Will we soon be hearing the patter of tiny feet? You must long to be a mother, and certainly it is the one part of marriage that I long for too.

Our steamer docks in the middle of November. I shall call on you when I'm home and we can catch up properly.

By the way, Margarida sends her best love too.
She is still in Paris pursuing her artistic talents. She
also said that Professor Landowski had asked after
you. I hear Monsieur Brouilly is now in Rio, working
on the Cristo project. Have you seen him?
With best regards,
Your friend, Maria Elisa

Sadness overwhelmed Bel as she remembered how relatively simple life had seemed when she'd left for Paris eighteen months ago. Her parents had been well, alive and contented and her future – albeit one she hadn't relished – had been planned out for her. Now, as she sat here, the wife of one man, the lover of another, with one parent dead, the other bankrupt and broken, and with a child growing in her belly that she must protect at all costs, Bel felt that life was a see-saw of pleasure and pain. From one day to the next it never remained the same, and nothing was ever certain.

She pondered how there were thousands – perhaps millions – of people who had been financially secure and happy a few days ago, and had woken this morning to discover they had lost everything.

And here was she, sitting in this beautiful house, with a husband who might not be the handsome prince she had imagined when she was younger, but who provided her with everything she wanted. How on earth did she have a right to complain? And how could she even *consider* leaving her poor father, when it was he who had worked so hard to put her where she was now?

As for her baby, the idea of running to Paris to an uncertain future that might well subject her child to poverty when it could enjoy security here caused her to realise just how selfish her love for Laurent had made her.

However desolate the thought made her, Bel forced her mind to contemplate staying where she was. Even though she was sure the baby was not Gustavo's, there was enough evidence to have him believe it was. She imagined his face when she told him she was pregnant. His talk of a new start yesterday would only be enhanced by her news, and it would put Luiza in her place once and for all.

Bel stared into the distance. Of course, it would mean giving up the one person in her life who she loved more than any other . . . and any chance of the happiness they'd both dreamt of so often. But was life simply about personal happiness? And how happy would she ever be anyway, knowing she'd deserted her widowed father in his hour of need? Bel knew that she wouldn't be able to forgive herself for that.

'Senhora Bel? Can I get you a drink? The sun is very hot this morning.' Loen appeared on the terrace.

'Thank you, Loen. I'd like some water.'

'Of course. Senhora, are you all right?'

Bel paused before she answered. 'I will be, Loen. I will be.'

That evening, Antonio came round for dinner. Gustavo welcomed him warmly and the three men closeted themselves in Maurício's study for an hour. Antonio emerged looking far calmer, with Gustavo following behind him.

'It seems this kind husband of yours might be able to help me. He has some ideas at least. It is a start, Izabela, and I am grateful to you, senhor,' her father added, bowing to Gustavo.

'Think nothing of it, Antonio. You are family, after all.'

Bel took a deep breath, knowing that she must say the words now or her courage might fail her and she would change her mind.

'Gustavo, may I speak with you for a few minutes alone before dinner?'

'Of course, my dear.'

Maurício and Antonio continued to the dining room as Bel led Gustavo into the drawing room and shut the door.

'What is it?' said Gustavo, his forehead creased into a worried frown.

'Please, it's nothing to be concerned about,' Bel assured him hastily. 'In fact, I hope you will think it is good news. I wanted to tell you now, so that perhaps we could announce the news together over dinner. Gustavo, I am with child.'

Bel watched her husband's reaction swing immediately from concern to joy. 'Izabela, you're telling me you are pregnant?'

'Yes.'

'*Meu Deus!* I can hardly believe it! My clever, clever girl!' he said as he came to embrace her. 'This news will silence my mother forever.'

'And hopefully will please her son,' she replied with a smile.

'Of course, of course, *querida*.' Gustavo was now grinning from ear to ear. 'I doubt I have ever felt so happy. And it is news that could not have come at a better moment for everyone in our family. And for you, Izabela, who has suffered such a recent loss. And of course, for your father, whom my father and I think we may be able to help. I insisted on it,' he added.

'It is only right, given his generosity in the past. Are you absolutely certain you are pregnant, Izabela?'

'Yes. It has been confirmed by the doctor. I went to see him yesterday and he telephoned me earlier today.'

'That explains it!' said Gustavo, relief crossing his face. 'Yesterday afternoon I went to collect you from your dressmaker's after the senate meeting. Madame Duchaine told me that you had no appointment booked and that you hadn't been to her salon. You were seeing the doctor, weren't you?'

'Yes,' Bel lied, fear clutching at her heart.

'For a few minutes, as I stood outside wondering why on earth you had lied to me, I even wondered if you had taken a lover,' Gustavo chuckled as he kissed her on the forehead. 'I couldn't have been more wrong. Do you know when the baby is due?'

'In about six months.'

'Then you are over the danger time, and yes, of course, we must announce it,' he said, almost skipping like an excited child as he led her to the door. 'Oh my beautiful Izabela, you have made me the happiest man in the world. And I swear to you now that I will do everything to be the father that our child deserves. Now, make your way through to the dining room while I go down to the cellar and open a bottle of our finest champagne!'

Gustavo blew her a kiss as he left, and Bel stood for a few seconds, knowing that her path was now set. And whatever it took, she would have to live with the duplicity of her actions until the day she died.

Over dinner that night, celebrations ensued, and the look of joy on her father's face when Gustavo announced their news confirmed to Bel that she had made the right decision. Luiza's wintry expression meanwhile had given her a tiny inner glow of satisfaction. After dinner, Gustavo turned to Bel.

'It is past ten, my dear, and you must be exhausted. Come,' he said as he pulled back her chair and helped her up from it, 'I will accompany you upstairs.'

'Really,' muttered Bel, embarrassed, 'I'm feeling extremely well.'

'No matter. You and the baby have had a difficult few weeks and we must all look after you now,' he added, looking directly at his mother.

Bel said her goodnights, and then walked around the table to hug her father tightly, not caring for protocol. 'Goodnight, Pai.'

'Sleep well, Izabela, and I promise that the little one's grandfather will make him proud,' he whispered, indicating her stomach. 'Come and visit me soon.'

'I will, Pai.'

Upstairs, Gustavo followed his wife into the bedroom and stood there uncertainly. 'Izabela, now that you are . . . in this condition, you must tell me if you'd prefer to sleep alone until the child is born. I believe that is what married couples usually do in these circumstances.'

'If you feel that would be more appropriate, then yes,' she agreed.

'And from now on, you must rest as often as you can. You mustn't tire yourself.'

'Gustavo, I promise you I am not unwell, just pregnant.

And I wish to carry on my life as normally as possible. Tomorrow afternoon, I really must go to see Madame Duchaine and ask her to alter my wardrobe to fit my growing shape.' She smiled shyly at him.

'Yes, of course. Well then.' He walked to her and kissed her on both cheeks. 'I shall say goodnight.'

'Goodnight, Gustavo.'

Bel watched as he smiled at her then left the bedroom. She sank down onto the edge of the bed, her heart a mixture of conflicting emotions. Her thoughts travelled to Laurent and the fact that he was expecting her at his apartment tomorrow afternoon. Rising, Bel walked to the window and looked out at the stars, which reminded her poignantly of the nights they had shone so brightly above Landowski's *atelier* in Boulogne-Billancourt. She remembered in particular the evening she had found the young boy under the bushes in the garden, and how his suffering had provided a catalyst for the start of her love affair with Laurent.

'I will always love you,' she whispered to the stars.

Bel readied herself for bed, then walked over to the writing bureau that sat beneath the window. Given that Gustavo had followed her to Madame Duchaine's yesterday – albeit it purely out of loving motives, not suspicious ones – Bel knew she couldn't risk meeting Laurent at his apartment tomorrow. Instead, she would attend an appointment at the dressmaker's and send Loen as her emissary, carrying with her the letter she would write now . . .

Taking a sheet of notepaper from the drawer and a pen, Bel sat staring out into the starlit night, asking the heavens to help her compose the last words she would ever say to Laurent.

Two hours later, she read the letter through one last time.

Mon *chéri*,
     The very fact that by now you have been handed an envelope by Loen will have told you that I cannot come with you to Paris. Even though my heart breaks as I write this, I know where my duty lies. And I cannot, even for my love of you, shirk it. I only hope and pray that you understand my decision is made purely on this basis, and not out of any lessening of love and desire. I yearn to be with you for all eternity. I sit here looking up at the stars and wish with all my heart we had met at a different moment in time, for I have no doubt that if we had, we would be together now.
     But this was not our fate. And I hope you will, just as I must, accept it. Be assured that every day of my life, I will wake thinking of you, praying for you and loving you with all my heart.
     My deepest fear is that any love for me you have presently may turn to hate for my betrayal of it. I beg you, Laurent, not to hate me, but to carry what we had in your heart and move on to the future, which I can only hope will eventually bring you happiness and contentment.
     Au revoir, mon amour
     Your Bel

Bel folded the letter and sealed it in an envelope, putting no name on the front of it for fear of it being discovered. Opening the drawer, she secreted it at the back under a stack of fresh envelopes.

As she closed it, her eye caught the soapstone triangle, which she'd been using to stand her inkpot on. Taking it in her hands, she touched its softness. Then, on impulse, she turned it over and dipped her pen in the ink once more.

30th October 1929
Izabela Aires Cabral
Laurent Brouilly

Then, painstakingly, she wrote one of her favourite quotations from a parable by Gilbert Parker underneath their names.

Once the ink was dry, she hid the tile with the letter at the bottom of the envelope pile. When Loen came in to dress her in the morning, she would tell her what she must do with them. If the tile could not be placed onto the *Cristo*, then at least it would serve as a perfect memory for Laurent of the moment in time they had once shared together.

Bel stood up slowly from the desk and climbed into bed, curling up like the foetus inside her, as if the arms that crossed her chest could somehow hold together her broken heart.

44

'Is Izabela not joining us for breakfast this morning?' asked Luiza of her son.

'No, I asked Loen to take her a tray upstairs,' replied Gustavo, as he joined his mother at the breakfast table.

'Is she unwell?'

'No, Mãe, but for the past two months she was nursing her poor mother night and day. Which, as you can imagine, has taken its toll on her.'

'I hope that she will not be too precious about her pregnancy,' said Luiza. 'I certainly wasn't during mine.'

'Really? I was talking to Father only last night and he mentioned how you were as sick as a dog for weeks when you were carrying me, and how you rarely rose from your bed,' he countered as he poured himself some coffee. 'Anyway, it is the news you have longed for, isn't it? You must be overjoyed.'

'I am, but . . .'

Gustavo watched as Luiza signalled for the maid to leave.

'Close the door behind you, if you please,' she added.

'What is it now, Mãe?' Gustavo asked her with a weary sigh.

'This morning, I prayed long and hard in the chapel, asking for guidance as to whether I should tell you what I know or not.'

'Well, given you've just requested the maid to leave us alone, I presume you have made your decision. And I assume it will be to do with some kind of misdemeanour you believe my wife has committed. Would I be right?'

Luiza's face displayed an exaggeratedly pained expression. 'Sadly, you would be, yes.'

'Well then, spit it out. I have a busy day ahead of me.'

'I have reason to believe that your wife has not been . . . faithful to you during your marriage.'

'What?' Gustavo exclaimed angrily. 'Mãe, I seriously think you are becoming deluded! What evidence do you have of this?'

'Gustavo, I understand your disbelief and anger, but I can assure you that I am not deluded. And yes, I do have proof.'

'Really? And what is that?'

'Our driver, Jorge, who you are aware has worked for me for many years, has seen Izabela entering the apartment building of a certain young' – Luiza sniffed – 'gentleman.'

'You mean Jorge has driven her somewhere in the city to visit a friend perhaps, and you have twisted this into some kind of ridiculous accusation?' said Gustavo, standing up from the table. 'I wish to hear no more of this bile! What do you hope to achieve?'

'Please, Gustavo, I beg you to sit down and listen,' Luiza entreated him. 'Your wife has never asked Jorge to take her directly to this particular young man's address. In fact, she has had him drop her off in front of Madame Duchaine's salon. Then one afternoon, when he was stuck fast in traffic, he saw Izabela leave the dressmaker's a few minutes after she'd arrived, and hurry off into the streets of Ipanema.'

Gustavo sat down heavily. 'So, Jorge came to you with this information of his own volition, did he?'

'No,' Luiza admitted. 'My own suspicions were raised when I went one afternoon in May to the Igreja da Glória, where your wife had told me she was going when she'd left the house an hour earlier. She wasn't there. I obviously asked Jorge that evening where Izabela had asked him to collect her from. He told me that it was from Madame Duchaine's salon and confessed to me what I have just told you. I instructed him that the next time he drove her there and saw her leave after a few minutes, he was to follow your wife and find out where it was she was going.'

'You mean, you asked Jorge to spy on her?'

'If you wish to put it like that, then yes. However, I was only trying to protect you, my dear son, and you must accept my motives are well intentioned. There was something that had been worrying me since the start of your marriage.'

'And what was that?'

'I . . .' Luiza had the grace to blush. 'Obviously I'm your mother and I wished to make sure your wedding-night coupling had been successful. I asked the chambermaid at the Copacabana Palace to tell me if it had.'

'You did *what*?' Gustavo was on his feet and walking around the table towards his mother, fury in his eyes.

'Please, Gustavo!' Luiza put up her arms to protect herself. 'Your wife had just been away to Paris for many months. I felt it my duty to make sure that she was still . . . pure. The chambermaid informed me that there was no sign of a bloodstain on the sheets or the counterpane.'

'You bribed a maid for information about my wife's purity?' Gustavo shook his head, trying to maintain his anger with his mother, but at the same time knowing she spoke the truth about their wedding night.

'Well,' Luiza eyed him, 'were the sheets stained?'

'How dare you ask me that!' Gustavo rallied. 'It is a private matter between me and my wife!'

'I take it they weren't,' said Luiza, almost contentedly. 'So, Gustavo, do you want me to continue? I can see how agitated you are becoming. We can leave the subject there, if you wish.'

'No, Mãe, you've gone too far for that. And I'm sure you are desperate to tell me who it is Izabela has been meeting in secret.'

'I can assure you that it gives me no pleasure at all to tell you' – the triumphant expression in Luiza's eyes suggested the opposite – 'but the . . . "person" in question is someone we all know.'

Gustavo racked his brains to come up with a name before his mother could produce it, but he failed to do so.

'Who is it?'

'A young gentleman who has enjoyed hospitality here under our own roof. In fact, someone to whom you paid a great deal of money, as you wished to give your wife a special wedding present. The apartment Izabela has been visiting regularly is none other than that of Senhor Laurent Brouilly, the sculptor.'

Gustavo opened his mouth to speak, but no words came out.

'I understand this is the most dreadful shock for you, Gustavo, but given the fact that your wife is with child – after months of being unable to conceive – I felt it was only right to tell you.'

'Enough!' cried Gustavo. 'I agree it is possible that Izabela has visited this man while he has been here in Brazil. They became friends in Paris. And you yourself sent Alessandra Silveira to have Brouilly sculpt her. But even you, Mãe, could not have been in the bedroom with them. And to even insinuate that the child my wife carries is illegitimate is frankly obscene!'

'I can understand your reaction,' said Luiza calmly. 'And if I'm right, it is indeed obscene.'

Gustavo was pacing up and down, trying to calm himself. 'Then tell me *why* you put this man – whom you obviously suspected was my wife's lover – under your patronage? It was *you* who introduced him to society, helped him gain commissions through your recommendations. And, if I remember correctly, even provided him with a soapstone block from our family's mines to enable him to continue his work! *You* prolonged his stay here in Rio. Why on earth would you do that if you were suspicious of his relationship with Izabela?' Gustavo eyed her furiously. 'Because, Mãe, I believe you actually wanted to help discredit my wife. You've disliked her from the start. You've spent every day of her married life here at the Casa patronising her and treating her as if she was simply an irritation to be borne. It wouldn't surprise me if you wanted our marriage to fail before it had even begun!' Gustavo was now shouting across the table at Luiza. 'I will hear no more of this. And I can tell you that I mean to make sure Izabela assumes her rightful position in this house as soon as possible. If you interfere in our marriage any further, I will have you out! Do you understand?'

'I do,' Luiza replied without a flicker of emotion. 'Besides, you need worry no longer about Senhor Brouilly. He is leaving tomorrow for Paris.'

'You are still spying on him?' Gustavo raged.

'Not at all. I halted my patronage as soon as your wife left for the *fazenda* with her mother. Without a commission, and your wife gone from Rio, I knew it would not be long before he decided to return to Paris. He wrote me a letter only two days ago informing me of his departure and thanking me for my assistance. Here,' Luiza said, handing him an envelope, 'you can read it for yourself. You will note the address of his apartment in Ipanema at the top of it.'

Gustavo grabbed the envelope from his mother and stared at her in hatred. His hands were shaking so much that he had difficulty stuffing the envelope into his trouser pocket.

'Although you say you did this out of love for me, there is not one part of your son who believes you did. And I will not hear another word about any of it. Do I make myself clear?'

'Yes.'

With a small smile, Luiza watched her son leave the room.

Somehow, Gustavo managed to maintain an outwardly calm demeanour as Izabela left with her maid to visit Madame Duchaine. As he watched the car snaking down the drive, he thought that one way of discovering immediately whether there was any substance to his mother's story was to ask Jorge, the driver. But given that Jorge had worked for Luiza for over thirty years, Gustavo couldn't trust him to tell the truth. Walking into the drawing room, his first instinct was to grab the whisky bottle, but he refrained, knowing if he took a little, it would not be enough and he needed a clear head to think now.

Pacing back and forth across the drawing room, wondering how the joy he'd woken to this morning could have dissipated into such anger and uncertainty two hours later, he tried to rationalise everything his mother had said. Even if there was a grain of truth in her story, to accuse Izabela of foisting another man's baby upon him was surely the ranting of a lunatic? After all, many married women had admirers and Gustavo was not stupid enough to think that his beautiful wife did not have her fair share too. Perhaps this Brouilly had grown fond of her during their time in Paris – had even asked her to sit for him again here in Rio – but he could not bring himself to believe that she had surrendered physically to him.

However, one thing his mother *had* said to him which had made him uneasy was the lack of bloodstain after they had made love on their wedding night. Gustavo was no biologist and perhaps Izabela had been telling him the truth that night, but . . .

Gustavo slumped into a chair, his head cradled desperately in his hands.

If she had lied, the depth of betrayal was simply too awful to contemplate. He had encouraged Izabela to go to Paris out of purely altruistic reasons, because he truly loved her and trusted her.

Surely, he thought, the best thing to do was to leave the whole sordid matter be? The letter he'd read from Brouilly to his mother indeed confirmed he was travelling back to Paris by steamer tomorrow. Whatever might have passed between the two of them, surely it was over now?

Yes, Gustavo decided, as he stood up and walked determinedly to his father's study to read the newspapers. He would forget all about his mother's nonsense, he told himself sternly. But as he sat trying to concentrate on the financial carnage, both in Brazil and in America, he found he could not. His mother's words had sown unstoppable seeds of doubt in his mind, as she had known they would. And until he knew for certain, Gustavo realised he could not rest. Seeing that Jorge had returned from taking Izabela into the city, he grabbed his hat and climbed into the car to follow her.

Bel stood in front of the mirror as Madame Duchaine showered her with congratulations and assured her it was a simple enough job to alter the clothes she had made to fit her burgeoning body over the coming months.

'I always think the shape of a pregnant woman has a magic all of its own,' Madame Duchaine twittered as Bel caught Loen's eye and gave her a barely perceptible nod.

Loen stood up from her chair and walked towards her mistress. 'Senhora, I should go and collect the tonic your doctor has suggested you should take from the pharmacy. It is only around the corner, and I shall be back as fast as I can.'

Bel suppressed a painful smile as her maid repeated parrot-fashion the sentence she had suggested she say to her. 'I'm sure I will be fine in Madame Duchaine's capable hands,' she replied.

'Of course she will.' Madame Duchaine smiled benignly at Bel.

As Loen nodded and left the salon, Bel could see that her

eyes were large with trepidation. It was a lot to ask of her maid, but what choice did she have? 'God speed,' she whispered inwardly, then took a deep breath and turned back to the mirror.

Gustavo had ordered Jorge to take him to his club, which was only a few minutes' walk from Madame Duchaine's salon, and the address of the apartment where Brouilly apparently resided. He left the club and walked briskly along the street, deciding that as he was twenty minutes behind his wife, he would go directly to Brouilly's apartment block. Finding there was a café on the other side of the road, Gustavo secreted himself in a corner of the pavement terrace and, feeling foolish, used his newspaper to disguise himself. Above the pages, his eyes flicked nervously back and forth along the busy street. The waitress came to take his order, and without diverting his gaze, he asked for a coffee.

Twenty minutes later, there was still no sign of his wife scurrying along the road to attend a rendezvous with her supposed lover. Every instinct in him wanted to leave, forget the whole thing. But, he rationalised, perhaps Bel would have a fitting first, giving her an alibi. So he gritted his teeth and forced himself to stay where he was.

And not long afterwards, Gustavo spied a familiar face walking fast along the street. It was not that of his wife, but her maid, Loen. Standing upright and knocking over his still full cup of coffee with a clatter, he threw some coins onto the table and darted through the traffic to the other side of the road. Walking past the apartment block and away from Loen, who was approaching tentatively, stopping occasionally as if she was unsure of her destination, Gustavo secreted himself inside the doorway next to the entrance of Brouilly's apartment.

Let this be a coincidence, he prayed, but a few seconds later, as Loen halted outside the next-door entrance just a few feet away from him, he knew it was not. Just as she made to enter the building, Gustavo stepped out in front of her.

'Hello, Loen,' he said as pleasantly as he could. 'And where are you headed?'

If Gustavo wanted proof of his wife's guilt, it was there in the terror that showed on her maid's face as she stared at him.

'I . . .'

'Yes?' Gustavo crossed his arms and waited for her reply.

'I . . .'

Then he noticed that one of her hands was held protectively over the pocket of her apron. From the shape of it, it looked like it contained an envelope.

'Perhaps you are delivering something for your mistress?'

'Senhor, I thought this was the entrance to the pharmacy. I . . . have got the wrong address. Forgive me . . .'

'Really? You have a prescription to collect for my wife?'

'Yes.' There was a sudden look of relief in her eyes that he'd managed to find an explanation for her. 'It must be further along the street.'

'As a matter of fact, I know exactly where it is. So, why don't you hand it over to me and I will deliver it to the pharmacist myself?'

'Senhor, Senhora Bel made me swear I would deliver this . . . prescription to the pharmacy with my own hands.'

'And as I'm her husband, I'm sure she would feel it was safe in *mine*, don't you?'

'Yes.' The maid lowered her eyes in resignation. 'Of course.'

Gustavo put out his palm and Loen pulled the envelope out of her pocket, her eyes agonised and pleading as he took it from her.

'Thank you,' he said, tucking it into the top pocket of his jacket. 'I promise you I will deliver it safely to the correct recipient. Now, run along back to your mistress, who is surely wondering where you have got to.'

'Senhor, please . . .'

Gustavo's palm halted any further remonstrations. 'Senhorita, unless you want to be thrown out onto the street without a reference the moment I arrive home, I suggest you do not discuss this meeting with my wife. No matter how loyal you are to her, it is I who decides who we employ to serve our household. Do you understand me?'

'Yes, senhor, I do,' the maid answered, her voice quavering and her eyes full of tears.

'Now, I suggest you run along back to Madame Duchaine's and collect the necessary medicine from the pharmacy, which I believe is only a few doors down from the salon, to sustain your alibi.'

'Yes, senhor.'

Loen dropped a shaky curtsey, and turned away from him to walk back the way she had come.

Immediately, Gustavo hailed a passing cab. Knowing that whatever this envelope contained he would need a strong whisky to enable him to open it, he directed the driver towards his club.

Loen had hidden herself round the corner, due to the fact her legs would carry her no further as they were shaking like saplings in a hurricane. She was slumped in a doorway when she saw Gustavo pass right by her in the back of a cab.

Burying her head between her legs and taking some deep breaths, Loen tried to clear her mind of the shock at what had just taken place. Even though she couldn't know for sure what the envelope contained, she could imagine only too well. She had no idea what she should do and only wished Bruno was with her to advise her now.

She too had her own problems presently – which she'd felt unable to speak of to her mistress, who had been so grief-stricken by her mother's death, and then the realisation that she was with child.

The truth was that Senhora Bel was not the only female living at the Casa in a similar predicament. She herself had known that she was carrying a child for the past three weeks. She'd told Bruno just before she'd left the *fazenda* and he had made her promise that she would speak to Bel. She'd been intending to beg her mistress to let her work permanently at the farm so the two of them could marry and raise their child there.

Loen had no idea who owned the *fazenda*, but she had an inkling that normally a man inherited his wife's assets on marriage. If this was the case, Gustavo had it in his power to ensure that neither she nor Bruno ever worked for the family again. Which meant any plans they had for the future would be turned to dust. They would be just another impoverished black couple, turned out on the streets, with her pregnant and penniless, headed for the *favelas* that were expanding daily with their starving inmates.

All this would happen . . . *if* she told her mistress what had just taken place.

As her breathing began to slow and Loen began to think more clearly, her fingers touched the unfamiliar outline of the life that was growing inside her. Just like Bel, she too had a decision to make. And quickly. The master had asked her to stay silent – in essence, to betray the trust her mistress had always placed in her. In any other circumstances, she would not have adhered to his wishes, whatever the cost. She would have run straight back to Madame Duchaine's, then asked Senhora Bel to take a short walk as she informed her of what had happened so that her mistress could prepare for what she might face when she returned home.

After all, she had been with Senhora Bel since she was a child. And owed everything she had – as did her mother – to the Bonifacio family.

But now Loen knew she must think of herself. Her fingers moved from her belly and into the other pocket of her apron. They touched the smoothness of the tile that lay within it. Perhaps it would be easier for her to lie if she had at least completed half of her mission.

Making her decision and knowing that Senhor Gustavo would not be back from wherever he had gone in the cab for the next few minutes, Loen stood up and ran blindly in the direction of Laurent Brouilly's apartment.

A few minutes later, she arrived breathless outside his front door and knocked loudly.

The door opened immediately and a pair of arms reached out to her.

'*Chérie*, I was beginning to worry, but—'

As Laurent Brouilly realised that it was not his love, Loen saw his joyful expression contract into a mask of immediate and horrified understanding.

'She has sent you? On her behalf?' he said, staggering a little and holding on to the door for support.

'Yes.'

'Then she is not coming?'

'No, senhor, I am sorry. She asked that I bring something to you.'

Loen held out the soapstone tile to him and watched as he took it from her. 'I believe there is a message on the back,' she whispered.

Laurent turned it over slowly in his hands and read the inscription. He looked up at her and she saw the tears appearing in his eyes.

'*Merci* . . . I mean, *obrigado.*'

And then the door was slammed in her face.

Gustavo sat down in a quiet part of the library, thankful that the room was virtually empty, as it had been since the Wall Street crisis had struck. He ordered himself the whisky he so badly needed as he studied the envelope that sat on the table next to him. He downed the drink in one gulp and immediately asked for a replacement. Once that was by his side, he took a deep breath and opened the letter.

A few minutes later, he asked the waiter for a third whisky and sat, catatonic, staring into space.

Whatever the letter did or didn't prove with regard to

what his mother had insinuated, it did tell him without a doubt that his wife had been passionately in love with another man. So passionately in love that she had even been contemplating running away to Paris with him.

This in itself was damning enough, but reading between the lines, it also told Gustavo something more: if Izabela had been serious in her intentions of leaving with Brouilly, surely it meant that her lover must have known of her current physical state? Which in turn meant that the child his wife carried was almost certainly her lover's . . .

Gustavo reread the letter, grasping at the thought that it could perhaps also be interpreted as a means to get rid of Brouilly once and for all, without the need for public revelation on his part. Faced with the knowledge that Izabela would love him forever, but that their situation was impossible, an ardent and desperate suitor might be pacified enough to leave quietly of his own accord, realising it simply couldn't be.

Gustavo sighed and realised he was clutching at straws. He pictured Brouilly in his mind's eye and saw his fine physique and handsome Gallic features. He was without doubt a man whom any woman could easily find attractive, and to many his talent would be a further aphrodisiac. Bel had sat for hours in his studio in Paris . . . God only knew what had passed between them while she'd been there.

And he had let her go, like a lamb to the slaughter, just as his mother had always suspected would be the case.

During the following half hour, as he downed one whisky after the other, Gustavo ran through a gamut of emotions: from sorrow and despair to dreadful anger at the thought of how his wife had made a cuckold of him. He knew he was absolutely within his rights to go home, show Izabela the letter and throw her out on the streets then and there. He had even offered her father a decent sum of money to put him back on his feet and clear some of his debts, so that Antonio could at least have a fighting chance of a future. With the letter as his evidence, he could destroy his wife's and his father-in-law's reputation for good and divorce her on the grounds of adultery.

Yes, yes, he could do all these things, Gustavo thought, rallying. He wasn't the meek, frightened little boy his mother made him out to be.

But then the smug look of satisfaction on Luiza's face if he told her that she'd been right about Izabela all along was simply too much to bear . . .

He could also go and confront Brouilly – after all, he now knew exactly where he lived. Few would blame him if he shot the man where he stood. At the very least, he could ask for the truth. And he knew he'd get it, since Brouilly had nothing more to lose by confessing. Because Izabela was staying with her husband.

She is staying with me . . .

This thought calmed Gustavo. Despite professing her enormous love for Brouilly, his wife had not surrendered to it and was not leaving him to run off to Paris. Perhaps Brouilly did *not* know that Izabela was pregnant. After all, if she truly believed that Brouilly was the father of her child, surely she *would* have gone with him, whatever the ramifications.

By the time Gustavo left the club an hour later, he had managed to convince himself that whatever had occurred between his wife and the sculptor, it was *he*, her husband, she had chosen out of the two of them. Brouilly was on his way back to Paris tomorrow and was disappearing from both of their lives for good.

As he staggered down the steps of the club and walked through the streets towards the beach to try and sober up, Gustavo knew he had come to a decision.

Whatever his wife might or might not have done, there was no apparent benefit to himself if he declared that he knew and threw her out. She would obviously run to Brouilly in Paris and that would be the end of their marriage.

Other women in society had affairs, he rationalised. *And other men*, he thought, as he recalled a particular peccadillo of his father's, whom he'd once met at a charity dance. The woman had made it obvious there was more between the two of them than simply friendship.

Ultimately, it would give him more satisfaction to return home and tell his mother he had investigated the situation and found not a shred of substance than it would to confront Izabela with the letter.

Gustavo looked at the waves pounding relentlessly against the fragile softness of the sand and sighed in resignation.

Whatever she had done, he loved her still.

Taking the letter from his pocket, he walked nearer to the shore, tore the page into pieces and threw them into the air, watching them flutter like miniature kites before they fell towards earth and disappeared into the sea.

45

'So, Brouilly, you're back in one piece.' Landowski eyed him as Laurent walked into his *atelier*. 'I had written you off for good, thinking you'd joined some Amazonian tribe and married the chief's daughter.'

'Yes, I'm back,' Laurent agreed. 'Is there still a place for me here?'

Landowski turned his attention from the enormous stone head of Sun Yat-sen and studied his erstwhile assistant. 'Perhaps,' he said, turning to the young boy, who had grown and filled out since Laurent had last set eyes on him. 'What do you think? Have we work for him here?'

Laurent felt the boy's eyes on him. Then he turned to Landowski, and with a smile, he nodded.

'So, the boy says yes. And from what I can see, it seems there's not much left of you and that it is your turn to require feeding up. Was it dysentery or love?' Landowski asked him.

Laurent could only shrug miserably.

'I believe your smock is still on the hook where you left it.

524

Go and put it on and come and help me with that eyeball you worked so hard on before you left us for the jungle.'

'Yes, professor.' Laurent made to move towards the hooks by the door.

'And Brouilly?'

'Yes, professor?'

'I am sure that you will be able to pour all your recent experiences – good and bad – into your sculpture. You were technically competent before you left. Now, you have the ability to be a master. One must always suffer to achieve greatness. Do you understand me?' Landowski asked him gently.

'Yes, professor,' Laurent replied with a catch in his voice. 'I do.'

Later that evening, Laurent sighed and wiped his hands on his smock. Landowski had left the *atelier* to return next door to his wife and children hours ago. As he made his way by candle-light towards the kitchen to wash the clay from his hands, he stopped suddenly in his tracks. From somewhere close by, he could hear the faint but exquisite sound of a violin. The violinist was playing the mournful first few bars of *The Dying Swan*.

His hands paralysed under the tap, Laurent felt tears he still had not shed prick his eyes. And there, in the tiny kitchen, which was the place he'd watched Izabela care so tenderly for a suffering child and known then that he loved her, Laurent wept. For him, for her, for all that could have been, but never would be now.

As the music drew to its poignant finale, he dried his eyes roughly on a cloth, and walked out of the kitchen in search of the musician who had allowed him to break the dam that had sat inside him ever since Loen had delivered the soapstone tile from Izabela in Rio.

The tune on the violin had changed and he could now hear the haunting melody of Grieg's *Morning Mood*, evoking – as it always had for him – a sense of a new day and new beginnings. Comforted somewhat, he followed his ears and took his candle, making his way outside into the garden, then held it up to illuminate the player.

The young boy was sitting on the bench outside the *atelier*. In his hands was a battered fiddle. But the sound coming from the instrument belied its shabby appearance. It was pure, sweet and extraordinary.

'Where did you learn to play like that?' he asked the boy in astonishment when the piece had ended.

As usual, he received only a piercing gaze in return.

'Who gave you the fiddle? Landowski?'

His question elicited a nod.

Recalling Landowski's words, Laurent surveyed the boy carefully. 'I see,' he said quietly, 'that like any artist, you speak through your craft. Truly, you have a gift. Treasure it, won't you?'

The boy nodded, and gave him a sudden smile of gratitude. Laurent placed a hand on his shoulder, and, with a small wave of goodbye, he wandered off to further contemplate his own misery in the bars of Montparnasse.

Maia

July 2007

Last Quarter

16; 54; 44

46

I stared at Yara as she finally lapsed into silence, then looked up at the portrait of Izabela that hung on the wall above the fireplace, thinking of the dreadful decision my great-grandmother had been forced to make. I simply had no idea what I would have done in the circumstances. Even though we'd lived at different times, in different cultures, the underlying dilemmas had not changed at all, especially for women . . .

'So did Gustavo ever mention what he had discovered to Bel?' I asked Yara.

'No, never. But even though he may not have outwardly spoken the words, my mother always said she could see the pain in his eyes. Especially when he looked at his daughter.'

'Senhora Carvalho? Her first name is Beatriz, isn't it?'

'Yes. I myself remember Senhor Gustavo once entering the drawing room when the two of us were ten or eleven. He stared at his daughter for a long time, almost as though she was a stranger. I didn't think much of it at the time, but I think now that perhaps he was trying to decide whether she could possibly be his blood. Senhora Beatriz was born with green eyes, you see, which my mother once said were reminiscent of Senhor Laurent's.'

'So your mother suspected that he was Beatriz's natural father?'

'When she told me the story before she died, she said she had never been in any doubt,' Yara explained. 'According to her, Senhora Beatriz was the image of Senhor Brouilly and she also had artistic talents. She was only just in her teens when she painted that portrait of Izabela.' Yara pointed to the painting. 'I remember her saying that she wanted to do it in memory of her poor dead mother.'

'Izabela died while Beatriz was still a child?'

'Yes,' Yara nodded. 'We were both eighteen months old and it was just when the *Cristo* was being blessed and inaugurated on Corcovado Mountain in 1931. There was an outbreak of yellow fever in Rio and Senhora Beatriz and I were confined to the house. But of course, Senhora Izabela insisted on going to watch the *Cristo* ceremony. Given her history, it obviously meant a lot to her. Three days later, she went down with the fever and never recovered. She was only twenty-one.'

My heart contracted at the thought of it. Even though Floriano had shown me the birth and death dates from the register, I hadn't taken them in at the time. 'After all that turmoil and tragedy, to die so young,' I said, a catch in my voice.

'Yes. But . . . forgive me, Lord, for saying so' – Yara crossed herself – 'the only blessing was that the fever also took Senhora Luiza a few days later. They were interred together in the family mausoleum at a joint funeral.'

'My God, poor Bel, destined to lie next to that woman for all eternity,' I murmured.

'And it left her little girl without a mother, living in a household of men,' Yara continued. 'From what I have said, you can understand how distraught her father was after the death of his wife. He still loved her, you see, despite everything. And as you might imagine from what I've told you, Senhor Gustavo took comfort in the bottle and sank deeper and deeper into himself. Senhor Maurício did his best with his granddaughter – he was always a kind man, especially after his own wife died – and at least he organised a tutor to come in to give Senhora Beatriz lessons, which was more than her father could manage.'

'Were you living here in the Casa at the time?' I asked.

'Yes. When my mother told Senhora Izabela that she too was pregnant and requested a transfer to the *fazenda* to be with my father, Izabela could not bear to let her go. So instead she arranged for Bruno, my father, to come here and work as a handyman and driver for the family, as Jorge was close to retirement. This was my childhood home too,' Yara mused. 'And I think that it holds much happier memories for me than it does for my mistress.'

'I'm surprised that Gustavo agreed to Izabela's request that Loen stay here. After all, she was the only other person who knew the truth,' I queried.

'Perhaps he felt he *had* to agree.' Yara's eyes were knowing. 'With the secret they shared, each held power over the other, whether or not they were master and servant.'

'So you grew up with Beatriz?'

'Yes, or perhaps it would be more accurate to say that she grew up with us. She spent more time in our little house – which Senhora Izabela insisted be built for my parents and me at the bottom of the garden here – than she did in the Casa. And my family became the closest thing she had to one of her own. She was such a sweet little girl, affectionate and loving. But so lonely,' Yara added sadly. 'Her father was too drunk to know whether she was there at all. Or maybe he ignored her because she was a constant reminder of the doubts he always harboured in his mind about his dead wife. It was something of a blessing that he died when Senhora Beatriz was seventeen. She inherited the house and the family stocks and shares. Up until then, Senhor Gustavo had refused to let her pursue her passion for art, but when he passed on, there was nothing to stop her,' Yara explained.

'I can understand why Gustavo wasn't supportive of his daughter's creative ability. It must have rubbed salt into an already open wound. Actually, Yara, I can't help but feel sympathy for him,' I admitted.

'He wasn't a bad man, Senhorita Maia, just weak,' Yara agreed. 'So when Beatriz turned eighteen, she told her grandfather she was going to Paris to enrol at the École Nationale Supérieure des Beaux-Arts, just as she knew her mother had done before her. She stayed in Paris for over five years, only returning to Rio when she heard that Maurício, her grandfather, had died. I think she had many adventures,' smiled Yara wistfully. 'And I was happy for her.'

The picture Yara was painting of the woman I had met five days ago here in the garden was so different from the one I had conjured up in my mind. I realised I had imagined her to be far more like Luiza. But perhaps that was simply because she was old and had been so determined not to acknowledge me.

'And what happened to Antonio?' I asked.

'Oh, he recovered, as my mother always thought he would,' Yara said with a smile. 'He went to live at the Fazenda Santa Tereza, and with the small amount of money he'd been handed by Gustavo to start again, he bought a tomato farm. You might remember I told you before that they are the financial mainstay of Paty do Alferes. With his head for business, by the time Antonio died, he had what you might call a tomato empire, owning most of the local farms surrounding the *fazenda*. I remember that like Senhora Izabela before her, Senhora Beatriz used to love it there when she visited. Her grandfather adored her and taught her to ride and swim. He left the farms to her, and it is those that have provided the source of her income since her husband passed on. It's not much, but it has paid the bills here.'

'Who was Beatriz's husband, my grandfather?' I asked her.

'Evandro Carvalho, and he was a very talented pianist. He was a good man, Senhorita Maia, and it was a true love match. After Senhora Beatriz's difficult childhood, our family were so pleased to see her happy. And the Casa finally came back to life. Beatriz and Evandro held soirées for the creative community here in Rio. They also set up a charity to raise money for the city's *favelas*. I can assure you, Senhorita Maia, that while age and pain have affected her as she nears the end, she really was very beautiful when she was younger. Everyone who knew her respected and loved her.'

'Then it's such a pity that I will never see that side of her,' I mused.

'No . . .' Yara sighed heavily. 'But death comes to us all.'

'And . . .' I steeled myself to ask the question that had been burning through my brain for the past ten minutes. 'Beatriz and Evandro had a child, didn't they?'

I saw Yara's eyes dart uncertainly around the room. 'Yes.'

'Just one?'

'There was another, a boy, but he died in infancy. So yes,' she agreed, 'one.'

'A girl?'

'Yes.'

'And her name was Cristina?'

'Yes, Senhorita Maia. It was I who helped bring her up.'

I paused, uncertain of what to say next. The words that had poured out of Yara like a babbling brook for the past hour had suddenly dried up too. I looked up at her expectantly, willing her to continue.

'Senhorita, I don't believe I have done damage by telling you the past, but . . .' she sighed, 'I do not think it is my place to say any more. The rest is not my story to tell.'

'Then whose is it?' I begged her.

'It is Senhora Beatriz's.'

Desperate as I was to press her further, I could see that Yara had begun to look anxiously at the clock ticking on the wall.

'I have something for you,' she said, putting a hand into one of her voluminous pockets and handing four envelopes to me. Almost, I felt, as a peace offering for being unable to tell me more. 'Those are the letters sent via my mother by Laurent Brouilly to Senhora Izabela, when they stayed at the *fazenda* in Senhora Carla's last days. They will show better than I ever could the feeling that existed between the two of them.'

'Thank you,' I said as I watched her stand. I suppressed an urge to hug her, so grateful was I to finally hear of my ancestry and the tragic story that lay behind it.

'I must return to Senhora Beatriz,' she said.

'Of course,' I said, rising too, stiff after sitting so tensely while trying to catch every word Yara had spoken.

'I will show you out, senhorita,' she said.

'It would be easy for us to drive you up to the convent,' I suggested to her as we walked along the corridor, across the entrance hall and Yara opened the front door. 'I have a car waiting for me outside.'

'Thank you, but I still have things to do here.' She looked at me expectantly, as I hesitated beside her.

'Thank you for all you've told me. Is it possible that I might just ask you one last question?'

'It depends what it is,' she said, as I felt her eyes willing me to cross the threshold and leave.

'Is my mother still alive?'

'I do not know, Senhorita Maia,' Yara sighed. 'And that is the truth.'

I knew that the meeting was at an end and she would say no more.

'Goodbye, Yara,' I said as I reluctantly made my way down the steps. 'Please send my best wishes to Senhora Beatriz.'

She did not reply as I began to walk away, and it was only as I was passing by the crumbling stone fountain that she spoke again.

'I will speak to her, senhorita. Goodbye.'

I heard the front door being shut and rebolted as I continued down the drive. My hands touched the hot iron of the rusting metal gate and as I opened then closed it behind me and crossed the road, I looked up at the heavy sky and saw there was a storm brewing.

'How was it?' Floriano had resorted to sitting on a grass verge in the shade. I could see a pile of cigarette butts next to him.

'I learnt a lot,' I said, as he stood up and unlocked the car.

'Good,' he said as we both climbed inside and he started the engine. He didn't question me further as we drove back towards Ipanema, perhaps sensing that I needed some time to come back into the present from the past. I was silent for the rest of the journey, mulling over the story I'd been told. When we arrived on the forecourt of my hotel, Floriano turned to me. 'I'm sure you feel exhausted and need some time alone. You know where I'll be if you want some food and company later. And I promise it'll be me, not my daughter, who's the chef tonight,' he assured me with a wink.

'Thank you,' I said, climbing out of the car. 'For everything,' I added as he nodded at me and reversed out onto the street. As I walked into the hotel, I didn't understand why my legs felt as though they were two deeply rooted tree trunks that I had to drag out of the earth every time I asked them to take a step forward. I crossed the lobby slowly, took the lift upstairs and walked almost drunkenly to my suite. Expending my last burst of energy on unlocking my door, I entered the room, staggered to the bed and slept where I lay.

I awoke two hours later, feeling as though I was experiencing a giant hangover, and took an ibuprofen and a large slug of water for my aching head. Lying on my bed, I could hear the approaching storm rumbling ominously overhead in the grey-blue sky, and watched the clouds gathering in preparation. Too exhausted to move, I slept again and awoke an hour later to see it beginning in earnest. Jagged bolts of lightning split the dusky sky above the now frantic waves, and claps of thunder – the likes of which I'd never heard – boomed in my ears.

As the first pattering of raindrops began to land on the narrow windowsill outside, I looked at my watch and saw it was almost seven in the evening. I pulled up a chair right in front of the window and sat down in wonder to watch the storm take hold. The slanting rain was so heavy it bounced off every solid surface at right angles, the roads and pavements becoming streams of boiling, bubbling water below me. Sliding the window open, I stuck my head out and felt the cool, clear drops pelting on to my hair and drenching my shoulders.

I laughed out loud suddenly, almost euphoric at the magnificence of the sheer force of nature on display. In that moment, I felt as if I too were part of the maelstrom, intrinsically attached to both the heavens and the earth, unable to comprehend the miracle that created it, just exhilarated knowing I belonged to it.

Realising I was about to be drowned if I didn't close the window and pull my upper half back inside, I ran to the bathroom, scattering drops across the carpet, and took a shower. I emerged, headache gone and feeling as refreshed as the storm-cleansed air around me. Lying on the bed, I looked at the letters that Yara had given me and tried to make sense of all she had told me earlier. But my thoughts kept spinning back to Floriano, to the patient way he had waited for me all afternoon and the sensitivity he'd shown afterwards. And I realised that whatever these envelopes contained, I wanted – *really* wanted – to share the contents with him. I picked up my mobile and scrolled down to find his number.

'*Olá*, Floriano, it's Maia here,' I said when he answered.

'Maia, how are you?'

'Watching the storm. I've never seen anything quite like it before.'

'It's certainly one of the things that we *cariocas* can say we do spectacularly well,' he agreed. 'Do you want to come round and have some supper? It's pretty basic, I'm afraid, but you're very welcome.'

'If the rain stops, then yes, I'd like to.'

'I'd give it another nine minutes or so, looking at the sky. So I'll see you in twenty, okay?'

'Yes, thank you, Floriano.'

'Enjoy the puddles.' I heard the smile in his voice. '*Tchau*.'

Exactly nine minutes later, I ventured downstairs and outside, my Havaianas and ankles submerged in the deluge of water that was still flowing off the pavements and down into the inadequate drains. There was a wonderful freshness to the air and as I walked, I saw more and more locals emerging back onto the streets.

'Come up,' Floriano said when I rang his intercom.

Arriving at the top of the stairs, he met me with his finger to his lips. 'I've just got Valentina to bed. She'll be up immediately if she thinks you're here,' he whispered.

Nodding silently, I followed him upstairs to the roof terrace, which was miraculously snug and dry beneath the sloped roof.

'Help yourself to some wine and I'll go downstairs and organise supper.'

I poured myself a small glass of red, feeling guilty I had come without an offering and promising myself I'd take Floriano out for dinner the next time we met to repay him for his hospitality. He'd already lit candles on the table, for darkness had fallen in earnest now, and there was the sound of soft jazz music playing from hidden speakers in the eaves above me. The atmosphere was tranquil, which was surprising, placed as it was in the centre of such a throbbing city.

'Enchiladas with all the trimmings,' he said as he appeared with a tray. 'I went to Mexico a few years ago and fell in love with their cuisine.'

I stood up and helped him unload the steaming dish of enchiladas and bowls of guacamole, sour cream and salsa, wondering if he ate like this every night.

'Please, help yourself,' he encouraged as he sat down.

I ate hungrily, impressed by his culinary prowess. I doubted if I could serve even a simple meal such as this with the same ease. In fact, I thought miserably, I hadn't held a dinner party since I moved into the Pavilion in Geneva thirteen years ago.

'So,' said Floriano, when we'd finished eating and he had lit a cigarette, 'did you discover all you needed to today?'

'I discovered many things, but sadly, not the one thing I came to Brazil to find out.'

'You're referring to your mother, I presume?'

'Yes. Yara said that wasn't her story to tell.'

'No. Especially if your mother is still alive,' agreed Floriano.

'Yara said when I asked her that she didn't know. And I think I believe her.'

'So . . .' Floriano studied me with interest. 'Where will you go from here?'

'I'm not sure. I remember you saying that you could find no record of Cristina's death on the register.'

'No, I couldn't, but for all we know she left Brazil and

went abroad. Maia, would it be a trial for you to tell me the story that Yara told you today?' he asked me. 'I confess, having come this far, I'm eager to know.'

'As long as you don't do what you threatened and put it into one of your novels,' I said, only half in jest.

'I write fiction, Maia. This is reality, and you have my word.'

For the next half an hour, I briefed Floriano on as much as I could remember of what Yara had told me. Then I reached into my handbag and drew out the four envelopes she had given me when I was about to leave.

'I haven't opened these yet. Perhaps I'm nervous, like Gustavo was when he opened the letter he took from Loen,' I conceded as I handed them to him. 'Yara said they're written from Laurent to Izabela during the time she was away nursing her mother at the *fazenda*. I want you to read one first.'

'I'd be delighted,' he said, his eyes lighting up as I'd known they would at discovering solid evidence of a piece of the historical puzzle.

I watched as he pulled the yellowing sheet of paper out of the first envelope and began to read. Eventually, he looked up at me, obviously moved by what he'd read. 'Well, Monsieur Laurent Brouilly may have been a great sculptor, but judging from this, he had a way with words too.' Floriano cocked his head to one side. 'Why does anything written in French seem more poetic? Here,' he said, handing it to me. 'You read this, while I struggle on through the next one with the aid of my schoolboy language skills.'

'*Meu Deus*, these letters almost bring tears to an old cynic's eyes,' he said a few minutes later, echoing my thoughts exactly.

'I know. Even though I heard from Yara of the love Bel and Laurent shared, somehow reading the actual words brings it to life,' I whispered. 'In some ways, even though her story ended in such tragedy, I envy Bel,' I admitted, pouring myself another glass of wine.

'Have you ever been in love?' Floriano asked me in his usual blunt fashion.

'Yes, once. I think I mentioned it to you,' I said hurriedly. 'And told you it didn't work out.'

'Ah, yes, and that one experience has apparently scarred you for life.'

'It was a little more complicated than that,' I countered defensively.

'These situations always are. Look at Bel and Laurent. If you read these, you might presume they were simply a young man and woman in love.'

'Well, that's how my first love affair began, but not how it ended.' I shrugged as I watched him reach for another cigarette. 'Do you mind if I have one too?'

'Not at all. Please, go ahead,' he said as he proffered the pack.

I lit the cigarette, inhaled and smiled at him. 'I haven't had one of these since university.'

'Well, I wish I could say the same. Valentina is forever trying to persuade me to give them up. And maybe one day I will,' he said taking a deep drag. 'So, this love of yours who broke your heart . . . do you want to tell me what happened?'

After fourteen years of remaining completely silent on the subject, and, in fact, doing anything and everything to avoid talking about it, I wondered what on earth I was doing on a roof terrace in Rio with a man I hardly knew feeling almost ready to tell him.

'Really, Maia, you don't have to,' Floriano said, seeing the fear in my eyes.

But instinctively, I knew that this was the reason why I'd come to him tonight. The story I'd been hearing over the past few days – coupled with Pa Salt's death – had unleashed the pain and guilt of what I had once done. Then there was Floriano, of course, whose life circumstances had held up an unflattering mirror to my own sad, solitary life.

'I will say it,' I blurted out before I lost my nerve. 'When I was at university, I met someone. He was a couple of years older than me and I met him in the last semester of my second year. He was in his final year and about to leave. I fell in love with him and was very careless and stupid. When I went home for the summer, I realised I was pregnant. But it was too late to do anything about it. So,' I sighed, knowing I must tell the story quickly and get to the end before I broke down, 'Marina, the woman I've mentioned to you, who brought all us six girls up, helped me arrange to go away and have the baby. Then' – I paused, garnering every ounce of courage I had to speak the words – 'when he was born, I gave him up immediately for adoption.'

Taking a large gulp of wine, I screwed my fists into my eyes to dam the torrent that was in danger of flooding out of them.

'Maia, it's okay, cry if you want. I understand,' he said softly.

'It's just that . . . I haven't ever told anyone this,' I admitted, feeling my heart palpitating in my chest. 'And I'm so ashamed . . . so ashamed . . .'

The tears began to fall, even though I'd done my best to stop them. Floriano came to sit next to me on the sofa and took me into his arms. He stroked my hair as I babbled incoherently about how I should have been stronger and kept the child, whatever it took. And how not a single day had gone by since they took my baby away from me a few minutes after I'd given birth to him that I hadn't relived that terrible moment.

'They never even let me see his face . . .' I moaned. 'They said it was for the best.'

Floriano offered no sympathy or platitudes, until the last shred of despair left me like the final whistle of air from a popped balloon and my entire body sagged in exhaustion. I lay there silently against his chest, wondering what on earth had possessed me to tell him my terrible secret.

Floriano remained silent. Eventually, I asked in desperation, 'Are you shocked?'

'No, of course not. Why would I be?'

'Why *wouldn't* you be?'

'Because,' he sighed sadly, 'you did what you thought was right at the time, under the circumstances you faced. And there's no crime in that.'

'Perhaps murderers also think what they did was right,' I countered morosely.

'Maia, you were very young and very frightened, and I presume the father was not around to make an honest woman of you? Or to even support you?'

'God no,' I said with a shudder as I remembered my last conversation with Zed at the end of that summer term. 'To him, we were no more than a fling. He was leaving university and about to begin his future. He told me he felt long-distance relationships rarely worked and that it had been fun, but it was best if it ended there. While we were still friends,' I added with a grim chuckle.

'And you never told him you were pregnant?'

'I didn't realise I was for sure until I arrived home and Marina took one look at me and carted me off to the doctor's. By that time, I was too far gone to do anything but have it. I was so naive, so stupid,' I berated myself. 'And so in love that I was prepared to do anything he wanted me to.'

'Which I presume meant not spoiling his enjoyment of you with contraception?'

'Yes.' I hid my blushes in his shirt. 'But I should have – *could* have – protected myself more carefully. I wasn't a child, after all, but I suppose I just didn't believe it would happen to me.'

'Many inexperienced young women don't, Maia. Especially in the first flush of love. Did you speak to your father about it?' he asked. 'It sounds as though the two of you were very close.'

'We were, but not in *that* way. It's impossible to explain, but I was his little girl, his first child. And he had such high hopes for me. I was flying at the Sorbonne and was expected to gain a first-class degree. To be honest, I would have died rather than ever tell him how stupid I'd been.'

'What about Marina? Did she not try to persuade you to tell your father?'

'Yes, she did, but I was adamant that I couldn't. I know it would have broken his heart.'

'So instead, you broke your own,' Floriano countered.

'It was the best option at the time.'

'I understand.'

We sat there on the sofa in silence for a while, and I stared at the candle flickering in the darkness, reliving the pain of the decision I'd made.

'It must have occurred to you at some point that your father had adopted six girls of his own,' Floriano ventured suddenly. 'And that perhaps he, of all people, would understand the predicament you were in?'

'It didn't at the time.' My shoulders slumped in renewed despair. 'But of course, since he died, I've thought about it constantly. Even so, I can't explain who he was to me. I idolised him and wanted his approval.'

'More than his help,' Floriano clarified.

'It wasn't *his* fault, it was mine,' I said, brutal with the truth. 'I didn't trust him, didn't trust in his love for me. And I'm sure now that if I *had* told him, he would have been there for me, he would have . . .' My voice trailed off to a whisper as fresh tears sprang to my eyes. 'And I look at you and Valentina, in similar circumstances, and see how my life might have been now if I'd had the guts to be stronger, and think what a mess I've made of things so far.'

'We all do things we regret, Maia,' Floriano said sadly. 'I wish every day that I'd been firmer with the doctors who told me to take my wife home from the hospital, when I knew instinctively that she was desperately ill. Perhaps if I had, my daughter would still have a mother, and I'd have a wife. But where does self-recrimination get us?' he sighed. 'Nowhere.'

'But to give up my child, especially when the reasons were purely selfish and not motivated by poverty or war, has to be the worst crime of all,' I stated.

'Each of us thinks that our own mistake is the worst, because *we* have made it. We all live with guilt for our actions, Maia. Especially if we have chosen to keep them inside us for as long as you have. I'm sitting here feeling only sadness for you, not disapproval. And I really think that anyone else who heard your story would feel the same. It's only you who blames yourself. Can't you see that?'

'I suppose so, but what can I do about it?'

'Forgive yourself. It's really as simple as that. Until you do, you won't be able to move on. I know. I've been there.'

'Every day I think about where my son might be, whether he's happy and if the parents he went to are loving him. I sometimes hear him crying for me in my dreams, but I can never find him . . .'

'I understand, but remember that you too are adopted, *querida*. Do you think you have suffered because of it?' Floriano asked me.

'No, because I haven't known any other life.'

'Exactly,' he said. 'You've just answered your own question. You've told me once before that you didn't think it mattered who brought up a child, as long as it was loved. It will be the same for your son, wherever he is. I'd wager that the only person truly suffering because of all this is you. Now, I think I could do with a brandy.' He released himself from around me and went to a narrow shelf to retrieve a bottle. 'Want some?' he asked me as he poured a small amount into a glass.

'No thanks.' I watched him as he wandered across the terrace to light a cigarette and stood there looking out into the darkness. Eventually, feeling vulnerable and insecure, I went to join him.

'You do realise,' he said eventually, 'that all this revelation about your own heritage has made you think even more about your son?'

'Yes,' I acknowledged. 'After all, Pa Salt has allowed all of his adopted girls to discover their origins if they wish. Surely my child has a right to discover his too?'

'Or at least a right to *choose* if he wishes to,' Floriano corrected me. 'You said yourself you were reticent about digging into your background. And besides, you were told from the start that you were all adopted. Perhaps your son hasn't been given that information. It's entirely possible that he is unaware.'

'I just wish I could see him once, to know that he is safe . . . happy.'

'Of course you do. But perhaps you should put him first and realise that it may not be the best thing for him,' he said gently. 'Now, it's past one in the morning and I have to be up bright and early for the little senhorita downstairs.'

'Of course,' I said, turning round immediately, crossing the terrace and retrieving my bag from under the table. 'I'll go.'

'Actually, Maia, I was going to suggest you stay here. I don't think you should be alone tonight.'

'I'll be fine,' I said, panicked by his suggestion and heading for the door.

'Wait.' Floriano chuckled as he caught up with me. 'I didn't mean you should stay with *me*. I meant that you could sleep in Petra's room. She's gone home to Salvador to see her family for a week. Really, please stay here. I'll worry about you if you don't.'

'Okay,' I agreed, feeling too exhausted to argue. 'Thank you.'

Floriano blew out the candles and switched off his computer, then we both walked downstairs and he pointed me in the direction of Petra's room.

'You'll be glad to know I changed the sheets and vacuumed after she left, so it's quite presentable for a change. The bathroom is just along there on the right. Ladies first. Goodnight, Maia,' he said, coming towards me and dropping a gentle kiss on my forehead. 'Sleep well.'

With a wave he disappeared back upstairs and I went to use the bathroom. Entering Petra's room a few minutes later, I looked at the biology text books stacked on rough shelves above a desk, saw the jumble of cosmetics strewn over the dressing table and a pair of jeans tossed haphazardly onto a chair. As I stripped down to my T-shirt and climbed into the narrow bed, I remembered that I too had once been a carefree student with my whole life ahead of me – a pristine canvas waiting for me, the artist, to paint upon it – until I'd found out I was pregnant.

And with that thought, I fell asleep.

47

I was woken by the sound of a door opening and the feeling that I was not alone in the room. I opened my eyes and saw Valentina standing at the end of the bed, staring at me.

'It's already ten o'clock. Papai and I just made pound cake for breakfast. Will you get up now and help us eat it?'

'Yes,' I agreed, still coming to, having obviously slept deeply. Valentina nodded in satisfaction then left the room and I rolled out of bed and dressed quickly. As I walked along the narrow corridor, a delicious smell of baking filled my nostrils, reminding me of Claudia's kitchen at Atlantis. Following the sound of Valentina's chatter, I climbed the stairs to the roof terrace and found father and daughter already seated and tucking in with relish to the circular ring of cake that sat in the centre of the table.

'Good morning, Maia. How did you sleep?' asked Floriano, wiping crumbs from his mouth as he pulled out the rickety wooden chair for me to sit down on.

'Very well indeed.' I smiled at him as he cut me a slice of cake and smeared butter all over it.

'Coffee?' he asked.

'Yes please,' I said, biting into the still warm cake. 'Is this what you get for breakfast every morning, Valentina? It beats the boring cereal and toast I eat at home every day.'

'No,' she sighed. 'Only today. I think Papai is showing off for you.' She shrugged nonchalantly.

Floriano raised his eyebrows helplessly at his daughter's words, although I did notice a faint tinge of colour come to his cheeks. 'So, Valentina and I were just discussing how we thought you needed some fun.'

'Yes, Maia,' Valentina interrupted. 'If my papai had gone to heaven, I would be very sad and need cheering up.'

'So, between us we've come up with a schedule,' Floriano said.

'No, Papai, *you* have.' Valentina frowned at me. 'I suggested you go to the fun fair and then to see a Disney film, but Papai said no, so you're doing boring things instead.' She lifted her small palms upwards and sighed again. 'Don't blame me.'

'Well, maybe we can do some of both,' I conciliated. 'I happen to love Disney films too.'

'Well, I'm not even coming with you, because Papai is going to Paris tomorrow for his book and has some work he needs to do before he leaves. So I'm going to stay with avô and vovó.'

'You're going to Paris?' I asked Floriano in surprise, experiencing a sudden, irrational stab of fear at the news.

'Yes. Remember the email I sent you a few weeks ago? You're invited too, don't forget,' he said, smiling at me.

'Oh yes, of course,' I said, recalling his message.

'I'm not,' Valentina said, pouting. 'Papai thinks I'll get in the way.'

'No, *querida*, I think you'll get very bored. Remember

how you haté it when you come to my readings and book signings here? The minute we arrive, you're tugging on my arm asking when we can go home.'

'But they're *here*, not in Paris. I'd love to go to Paris,' Valentina said wistfully.

'And one day,' replied Floriano, leaning towards her and kissing her on top of her dark, shiny hair, 'I promise I'll take you. Right,' he said, 'your grandparents will be here any minute. Have you packed your case?'

'Yes, Papai,' she said obediently.

'Maia, while I clear up breakfast, would you mind going with Valentina and checking that she has enough clothes and a toothbrush for the next two weeks?' Floriano asked me. 'She can be a little . . . haphazard with her packing.'

'Of course,' I agreed, and followed Valentina down the stairs and into her tiny bedroom. Everything in it was pink – walls, duvet cover, and even some of the teddy bears that sat in a row at the bottom of the bed. As Valentina gestured at me to sit down and hauled the case onto the bed for me to inspect its contents, I smiled at the cliché, finding it comforting at the same time. Pink seemed to simply be part of a little girl's genetic make-up. It had been my colour of choice too.

'Everything I need is in there, I promise,' said Valentina, folding her little arms defensively as I opened the lid. Barbie dolls, DVDs, colouring books and loose felt-tip pens had been stuffed inside. As had one T-shirt, a pair of jeans and some trainers.

'Do you think you might need some underwear?' I ventured.

'Oh yes,' Valentina said, going to a drawer. 'I forgot about that.'

'And maybe these pyjamas?' I suggested, reaching for the ones Valentina had obviously thrown on the floor when she'd dressed this morning. 'And perhaps some more clothes?'

Ten minutes later, I heard the intercom buzz and Floriano's footsteps coming down the stairs.

'They're here. I hope you're ready, Valentina,' he called from the corridor.

'I don't want to go,' she said, looking up from the pictures she'd been showing me that she'd coloured in.

Instinctively, I put an arm round her small shoulders. 'I'm sure it'll be great fun. I bet your grandparents spoil you rotten.'

'They do, but I will miss Papai.'

'Of course you will. I used to hate it when my father went away. And he did, a lot.'

'But you had lots of sisters to keep you company. I don't have anyone.' With a sigh of resignation, Valentina stood up and I closed her suitcase and zipped it up.

She watched me as I pulled the suitcase from the bed, tugged out the handle and wheeled it towards the door. 'There, I think you're all ready to go.'

'Will I see you when I get back home, Maia?' she asked me plaintively. 'You're much nicer than Petra; she just spends all her time on the phone talking to her boyfriend.'

'I hope so, *querida*, I really do. Now,' I said as I kissed her, 'you go off and have a wonderful time.'

'I will try.' Valentina took hold of the handle of the case and moved to open the door. 'Papai really likes you, you know.'

'Does he?' I smiled at her.

'Yes, he told me so himself. Bye bye, Maia.'

I watched her leave the bedroom, and thought how her demeanour resembled that of a modern-day refugee. Not wanting to intrude on the goodbye between father and daughter, or embarrass Floriano in front of his dead wife's parents, I sat on the bed with my hands in my lap. I thought yet again how difficult it was for the two of them and how much I admired Floriano for juggling his life between his daughter and his work. I also experienced more than a tinge of pleasure at the fact that Valentina had told me her father liked me. And I admitted to myself how much I liked him too.

A few minutes later, Floriano knocked on the door and poked his head around it.

'It's okay, you can come out now. I thought you'd accompany Valentina and meet Giovane and Lívia, but you didn't appear. Anyway,' he continued, taking my hand and pulling me from the bed, 'as I said to you over breakfast, I think it's time you had some fun. Can you remember what that is?'

'Of course I can!' I said defensively.

'Good. Then on the way to where I'm taking you, you can tell me the last fun thing you did.'

'Floriano, please don't patronise me!' I said crossly as I followed him out of the bedroom. He stopped abruptly in the corridor and turned so I almost bumped into him.

'Maia, please, lighten up, I'm teasing you. Even I, with a propensity for navel-gazing, know that I mustn't take myself too seriously. You've been alone too long, it's as simple as that. At least I have my daughter to constantly pull me up and out of myself,' he explained. 'And just for today, I want you to cast off your woes and *live*. Okay?'

I hung my head, feeling awkward and uncomfortable. I

realised it was a very long time since I'd last let another human being in close enough to lecture me on my failings.

'I just want to show you *my* Rio. I can assure you, I need time out as much as you,' Floriano added as he opened the front door and ushered me through it.

'Okay,' I agreed.

'Good,' he said as he marched down the stairs and we arrived at the front door. He offered me the crook of his arm. 'Shall we?'

'Yes.'

Floriano led me out of the building and along the streets of Ipanema to a café already buzzing with locals drinking beer.

Floriano said hello to the bartender, who obviously knew him, then ordered us both a *caipirinha* as I looked on in shock.

'It's only half past eleven in the morning!' I said as he handed me mine.

'I know. We are being reckless and debauched beyond belief.' He nodded sagely. 'Now,' he said, clinking his glass against mine, 'down it in one.'

When we had, and the acidic yet sickly-sweet alcohol had slid down my throat and into my stomach, and I'd thanked God the cake was already in there to soak it up, he paid and pulled me up from my bar stool. 'Right, we go.' He hailed a cab and we climbed inside.

'Where are we going?'

'I'm taking you to meet a friend of mine,' he said mysteriously. 'There's something you should see before you leave Rio.'

The cab drove us out of the city, and twenty minutes later

we alighted at what I realised was the entrance to a *favela*. 'Don't worry,' he said as he paid the driver, 'you won't get shot or offered a gram of cocaine by one of the local drug barons.' He put an arm around my shoulder and we began the long climb up the steps and into the village. 'I promise that Ramon, my friend, is as civilised as we are.'

I could already hear the faint throbbing of the surdo drums as we reached the top and entered the *favela*. The alleyways were so narrow that I could put my arms out and touch the brick shacks built on either side of them. Down here on the ground it was dark, and I glanced up to see a strange mixture of buildings built on top of the street-level homes.

Floriano followed my eyeline and nodded. 'The residents on the ground floor sell the space in the air to other families, and they build their homes above,' he explained as we walked up and up the winding streets.

Even I, who prided myself on the ability to take the heat, found myself sweating profusely and feeling light-headed in the claustrophobic, airless atmosphere. Floriano noticed immediately and at the top of one of the alleyways, stopped and plunged into a dark doorway. Which I realised as I followed him inside was a shop of sorts, albeit just a concrete space with a few shelves holding canned goods and a fridge in the corner. Having paid for a bottle of water, which I drank thirstily, we continued upwards, finally arriving at a brightly painted blue door. Floriano knocked, and immediately a dark-skinned man opened it. I watched as the two men embraced with much playful back-slapping and arm-punching, and we entered the house. I was surprised to see a computer blinking in one corner of the narrow room, and also a big television screen. The room was sparsely furnished but spotlessly clean.

'Maia, this is Ramon. He's been a resident of the *favela* since the day he was born, but now he works for the government as a' – Floriano stared at his friend for inspiration – 'a peacemaker.'

The man's white teeth flashed as his lips parted and he threw his head back with laughter. 'My friend,' he said in a deep, rich voice, 'you are definitely a novelist. Senhorita,' he continued, extending his hand to me, 'it is a pleasure to meet you.'

During the following two hours, as we walked around the *favela*, stopping to eat and drink beer at a ramshackle café that some entrepreneurial resident had set up in the tiny space they owned, I learnt a lot about *favela* life.

'Of course, there is still crime and poverty in the streets of every *favela* in Rio,' Ramon explained to me. 'And there are some places even I would not dare to venture near, especially at night. But I have to believe that things are improving, admittedly far more slowly than they should. And as everyone now has the opportunity to gain an education, and with it a sense of self-worth, I hope my grandchildren will experience a better childhood than I had.'

'How did you two meet?' I asked as I baked in the stifling heat.

'Ramon won a scholarship to my university,' Floriano explained. 'He was majoring in social science, but he nodded his head in the direction of history too. He's far cleverer than I am. I keep telling him he should write a book about his life.'

'You know as well as I do that no one would publish it here in Brazil,' said Ramon, suddenly serious. 'But perhaps one day, when I'm old and the political situation is different, I will. Now, I'm taking you to see my favourite project.'

As we followed Ramon along the maze of alleyways, Floriano explained quietly that Ramon's mother had been forced into prostitution by his father, who'd been a known drug baron and was now serving a life sentence for a double murder.

'Ramon had six little brothers and sisters to bring up alone when his mother died of a heroin overdose. He's an amazing man. The kind who makes you feel hopeful about human nature,' he mused. 'He works ceaselessly to lobby on behalf of the residents for some form of basic healthcare and better facilities for the children here. He's dedicated his life to the *favelas*,' Floriano added as he took my arm to guide me down the uneven stone steps.

From far below I could hear the sound of the drums getting louder, pulsating through my body as we continued to descend the steps. I watched the way Ramon was greeted with respect and affection from every narrow doorway by the residents, and by the time we reached the bottom and he led us through a wooden door surrounded by high walls, my own respect for him had multiplied. I thought how he'd turned round his own life using his own dreadful circumstances to improve those of others, and felt humbled by his dedication and strength of character.

Inside the courtyard we'd entered, I saw twenty or so children – several even younger than Valentina – all dancing to the strong rhythm of the drums. Ramon led us discreetly around the wall and into the shade that the building above us provided. He indicated the children.

'They are preparing for Carnival. You know the *favelas*

are where it all began?' he whispered, offering me a warped plastic chair so that I could sit down and watch.

The tiny bodies of the children seemed to throb instinctively to the beat of the drums. I watched their rapt faces, many of them with their eyes closed, as they simply moved to the music.

'They are learning something we call *samba no pé*. It was what saved me when I was a child,' Ramon said quietly into my ear from behind me. 'They are dancing for their lives.'

I wished later that I had taken some form of photographic record of the event, but maybe it could never have captured the ecstasy that I saw on the children's faces. I knew what I was witnessing would be burned into my memory forever.

Eventually, Ramon indicated it was time to leave, and I stood up reluctantly. We waved goodbye to the children and walked away from them through the wooden door.

'Are you okay?' asked Floriano, again placing a protective arm around my shoulder.

'Yes,' I managed, my voice breaking with emotion. 'It's the most beautiful thing I've ever seen.'

We left the *favela* and hailed a cab back into the city, my heart and senses still full of the sheer, joyous abandon of the children's dancing.

'Are you sure everything's all right, Maia?' Floriano asked as he reached over and took my hand solicitously.

'Yes,' I said. 'Honestly, I'm fine.'

'You liked watching the samba?'

'I loved it.'

'Good, because that's exactly what *we're* going to do later on tonight.'

I looked at him in horror. 'Floriano, I can't dance!'

'Of course you can, Maia. Everybody can, especially *cariocas*. It's in your blood. Now,' he said, halting the cab at the square in Ipanema that was filled with market stalls, 'we need to find you something suitable to wear. Oh, and a pair of samba shoes.'

I followed him like a lamb through the market as he went through racks of dresses and picked out the ones he deemed suitable for me to choose from.

'I think the peach would suit your skin colour best,' he said, proffering a figure-hugging wrap dress made of silky-soft material.

I frowned. It was exactly the kind of thing I would never pick out for myself, considering such styles far too revealing.

'Come on, Maia, you promised me that you'd live a little today! You dress like my mother at the moment!' he teased me.

'Thanks,' I said flatly, as he insisted on paying the few reais for the dress to the vendor.

'Right, now for the shoes,' he said as he took my hand once more and we weaved through the streets of Ipanema, alighting in front of a tiny shop that looked similar to a cobbler's.

Ten minutes later, I emerged with a pair of Cuban-heeled leather shoes that were held in place with a button securing the strap over the arch of my foot.

'Now these really *are* something that Marina would wear,' I said, as I pressed him to take some money from me for the shoes, which I knew had been expensive. He refused and instead stopped in front of an ice-cream kiosk, its display offering endless different flavours.

'What do you want?' he asked me. 'I promise you this place sells the best in Rio.'

'Whatever you're having,' I answered. Once the cones were handed over, we wandered across the main road and sat on a bench looking down on the beach, licking the delicious ice cream with relish before it melted.

'Right,' he said as we wiped our sticky mouths, 'it's past six o'clock, so why don't you wander up to your hotel and get ready for your dancing debut tonight? I must go home to write some emails and pack for Paris tomorrow. I'll pick you up in the hotel lobby at eight thirty.'

'Okay, and thank you for a lovely day,' I called as he walked away from me and I crossed the street to return to my hotel.

'It's not over yet, Maia,' he shouted back at me with a smile.

As I asked for my room key from the reception desk, I was greeted by a concerned face.

'Senhorita D'Aplièse, we were worried about you. You didn't return home last night.'

'No, I stayed the night with a friend.'

'I see. Well, there was a phone call for you earlier. The operator couldn't get hold of you, so the caller dictated a message. She said it was urgent.' The receptionist handed an envelope over to me.

'Thank you,' I said as I took it from her.

'And if possible, next time you decide to stay out overnight, perhaps you can let us know? Rio can be a dangerous city for foreigners, you see. Any longer and we would have had to call the *polícia*.'

'Of course,' I said, faintly embarrassed as I walked to the lift, musing on the fact that Rio might well be a dangerous city for foreigners. But for a native like me, it felt completely safe.

Up in my room, I tore open the envelope, wondering who could have left me a message of urgency, and read the typed words.

> *Dear Senhorita Maia,*
> *Senhora Beatriz says she would like to see you.*
> *She is growing weaker every day and it is imperative*
> *that you come as soon as you can. Tomorrow*
> *morning at ten o'clock would be the best time.*
> *Yara Canterino*

Having taken a whole day out and forgotten completely for a few precious hours about my unknown past *and* uncertain future, it took a while for my brain to compute what this letter meant. As I ran the shower and stepped into the warm water, letting it cascade over my body, I decided that whatever tomorrow would bring, I would think about it then, not tonight.

I put on the dress Floriano had bought me, sure that it would look dreadful, but as I donned the shoes and stepped before the mirror to take a look, I was surprised by the result. The crossover bodice accentuated my full breasts and my slim waist, and the wrap skirt that fell away in soft folds from my lower thighs gave a glimpse of my legs, their length accentuated by the dainty Cuban heels.

The time in Rio had given my skin some colour, and as I

blow-dried my hair and piled it on top of my head, then added some eyeliner, mascara and a deep red lipstick I'd once bought on a whim and had never used, I chuckled at how my sisters would hardly recognise me. Floriano's teasing comment on my style of dress had stung me, but was not, I realised, far off the mark. Everything I wore was sober, designed to help me melt into a crowd. Here in Rio I knew women celebrated the sensuousness of their bodies and their sexuality, whereas I had spent years hiding mine.

In the half hour I had before I was due to meet Floriano I wrote a burst of emails to my sisters, telling them what a wonderful time I was having and how much better I was feeling. Sipping a glass of wine from the bottle I'd taken from the mini bar, I was amazed at how I meant every word I'd written. It was as if a huge boulder-sized weight had been lifted from my shoulders, and tonight I felt as light as air. Perhaps it had been as simple as my confession to Floriano, but an inner voice told me it was more than that.

It was him too.

His energy, positivity and down-to-earth common sense, not to mention the way he handled his daughter and their domestic arrangements with such dexterity, was a life lesson I'd needed to learn. If nothing else, he had provided me with a role model, one that I realised I desperately wanted to aspire to. Next to him, my own life seemed like a dull grey facsimile and I was aware that Floriano – even if sometimes his comments had been painful – had made me realise I was simply *surviving*, not living.

And somehow the combination of this city and this man had cracked the invisible protective shell that I'd been hiding in. I chuckled at the analogy, thinking that I did indeed feel like a newly hatched chick.

And yes, I admitted that I probably *was* a little in love with him. As I looked at my watch and realised it was time to go downstairs, I decided that even if I never saw Floriano again, he'd given me my life back. And tonight I would celebrate my rebirth without fearing for tomorrow.

'Wow!' Floriano stared at me in blatant admiration as I appeared in the lobby. 'Talk about a phoenix emerging from the ashes.'

Instead of blushing and trying to bat away his compliment, I smiled warmly at him.

'Thank you for the dress. You were right, it does suit me.'

'Maia, you look absolutely stunning, and believe me,' he said as he took my arm and we walked outside, 'all I've done is enhance what you seem to have been so determined to hide.' Standing at the top of the steps, he glanced at me. 'Shall we go?'

'Yes.'

We hailed a cab and Floriano directed it to a district called Lapa, which he said was one of the old parts of the city where the Bohemian set used to hang out.

'Not safe alone, mind you,' he warned me as we emerged into a cobbled street, lined with old brick buildings. 'But tonight you have me to protect you,' he said, as I held on to him in my unfamiliar heels, stepping carefully over the uneven surface. Pavement cafés were packed with drinkers and diners, but we turned off from the main street and eventually he led me down a staircase and into a basement.

'This is the oldest samba club in Rio. No tourists here; it's for the real *cariocas* who just want to dance to the best samba music in town.'

A waitress smiled at him, kissed him on both cheeks, then led us to a battered leather booth in a corner. He ordered two beers, announcing that the wine was undrinkable as the waitress proffered us menus.

'Please, Floriano, tonight is on me,' I said, glancing at the dance floor, where the musicians were already gathered, setting up their instruments.

'Thank you.' He nodded graciously in acceptance. 'And by the way, anything you want to say, Maia, say it in the next hour. After that, neither of us will be able to hear a word.'

Once we had ordered the house speciality, which Floriano had recommended, our beers arrived and he toasted his bottle to mine.

'Maia, it's been a pleasure to spend time with you. And I'm only sorry that it has to be cut short by me flying to Paris tomorrow.'

'And I want to say thank you to you too. You've been wonderful to me, Floriano, really.'

'So, you'll agree to do my next translation?' he joked.

'I'd be insulted if you didn't ask me. By the way,' I said as some kind of bean stew arrived in front of both of us, 'Yara had left a message for me when I arrived back at the hotel this evening. Apparently, Senhora Beatriz wishes to see me tomorrow morning,' I announced as casually as I could.

'Really?' said Floriano between mouthfuls. 'And how do you feel about that?'

'You told me today was for fun,' I reminded him playfully. 'So I haven't thought about how I feel.'

'Good. But I can't help wishing I could be there with you. Or at least to act as your chauffeur. It's quite a journey we've been on in the last few days. And I've enjoyed being your passenger. Do you promise to tell me what she says?'

'I'll send you an email, of course.'

There was a sudden tense atmosphere between us, which we both filled with finishing the delicious stew in front of us. Floriano ordered another beer from the attentive waitress, but I refrained, settling for a glass of 'undrinkable' wine instead. In the background, the band began to play the sensuous music of the hills, and two couples took to the floor. I focused on them as they began to dance, their careful movements mirroring the exquisite tension that hung between Floriano and me.

'So,' I said, as more couples began to take to the floor, 'will you teach me how to dance the samba?' I offered my hand across the table to him, and he nodded. Without speaking, we rose and joined the crowd.

Putting one arm around my waist and using his other hand to encircle my fingers with his own, he whispered in my ear. 'Just feel the rhythm running through you, Maia, that is all you need to do.'

I did as he suggested, and the pulse began to move through my body. My hips started to sway in time with his and our feet began to move, mine clumsily at first as I studied his and the other dancers' around me. But soon, something instinctive took over and I relaxed and let my body move with his to the rhythm.

I'm not sure how long we danced together that night. As

the floor became more crowded, I felt that we had all become a single homogenous mass; moving as one, a group of human beings simply celebrating the joy of being alive. I'm sure that to any professional outsider, my samba was amateurish and imperfect, but for the first time in my life, I didn't care what anyone thought. Floriano steered and twirled me and held me close until I was laughing out loud with the sheer exhilaration of the moment.

Eventually, with both of us sweating profusely, he led me from the dance floor, grabbed the water from our table and drew me up the steps into the street for some fresh air, immediately polluting it by lighting a cigarette.

'*Meu Deus*, Maia! For a beginner, that was incredible! You are a true *carioca*.'

'Tonight I feel it, thanks to you.' I moved my fingers towards him to take the cigarette and a puff of it. I felt him watch me as I did so.

'Do you know how beautiful you look at this moment?' he murmured. 'Far more beautiful than your great-grandmother. Tonight, you have a light burning inside you.'

'Yes,' I said, 'and it's thanks to you, Floriano.'

'Maia, I've done nothing. It's you who has decided to live again.'

Suddenly, he pulled me into his arms, and before I knew it, he was kissing me. And I was responding with equal fervour.

'Please,' he whispered as we pulled away to take a breath, 'come home with me tonight.'

We left the club and barely made it up the stairs to his apartment before he pulled my dress from my shoulders and took me then and there in the narrow hall, with the music of the hills still ringing in my ears. Eventually we climbed into his bed, and made love again, this time more slowly, but with equal passion.

Afterwards, he propped himself up on his elbow and stared down at me with his familiar, intense gaze. 'How you have changed,' he said. 'When I first met you, I acknowledged your beauty, as any man would, but you were so closed, so tense. And look at you now,' he said as he kissed the hollow at the base of my neck and moved to caress my breasts. 'You are . . . delicious. And after months of wishing that tomorrow was the day I was flying to Paris, tonight, with only hours to go, all I want to do is to stay right here with you. Maia, I adore you.' He moved on top of me suddenly, pushing his nakedness against mine and gazing down at me. 'Come to Paris with me,' he urged.

'Floriano, tonight is our night,' I whispered. 'You are the one who has taught me to take each moment as it arrives. Besides, you know I can't.'

'No, not tomorrow, but please, once you have spoken to the old lady, get on a plane and join me there. We could have a few wonderful days together. A moment in time,' he encouraged me.

I didn't answer him, not even wanting to contemplate tomorrow just now. Eventually, he fell asleep next to me, and I watched him, bathed in the moonlight that was shining through the window. I reached out to touch his cheek gently with my fingers.

'Thank you,' I whispered. 'Thank you.'

48

Surprisingly, given that I hadn't slept in the same bed as anyone else for over fourteen years, I didn't stir until I felt a gentle nudge on my shoulder and opened my eyes to see Floriano looking down at me, already dressed.

'I brought you some coffee,' he said, indicating the mug perched on the bedside table beside me.

'Thank you,' I replied sleepily. 'What time is it?'

'Eight thirty. Maia, I have to leave for the airport now. My flight departs for Paris in three hours' time.'

'And I have to run back to my hotel and change,' I said, making to climb out of the bed immediately. 'I have to be up at the convent at ten.'

Floriano put a hand on my arm to stop me. 'Listen, I don't know what your plans are once you've seen Beatriz, but I wanted to reiterate what I said last night. Come to Paris, *querida*. I'd love you to be with me. Promise me you'll think about it?'

'Yes,' I agreed. 'I promise I will.'

'Good.' Floriano scratched his nose as a wry smile spread across his lips. 'I hate to say it, but I can't help feeling there are shades of Bel and Laurent in this conversation. I'd like to think that we could pursue a happier ending than they had.' He reached out a hand and smoothed some stray hair from my forehead, then bent and kissed me gently upon it. '*A bientôt*, and good luck this morning. Now, I really must go.'

'Have a safe journey,' I said as I watched him walk to the door.

'Thank you. Just pull the door closed behind you when you leave. Petra will be back in the next couple of days. Goodbye, *querida*.'

I heard the front door click a few seconds later and I jumped out of bed to dress. I left the apartment and walked fast through the streets of Ipanema to my hotel. I strode through the lobby with my head held high and asked for my key at the desk, ignoring the sweep of the receptionist's eyes as she took in my dishevelled appearance, and asked her if Pietro was available in twenty minutes to drive me up to the convent.

Upstairs in my suite, I took a hasty shower, part of me not wishing to remove the scent of Floriano from my body, dressed quickly in something more appropriate and was back down in the lobby fifteen minutes later. I could see Pietro waiting for me outside and he smiled at me as I climbed into the car.

'Senhorita D'Aplièse, how are you? I haven't seen you for a few days. We're going up to the convent hospital, yes?' he confirmed.

'Yes,' I said as we drove off, before turning my attention to clearing my jumbled brain for the meeting ahead.

When we arrived, Yara was already waiting for me nervously outside.

'Hello, Senhorita Maia. Thank you for coming.'

'Thank you for arranging it.'

'As a matter of fact, it had nothing to do with me. It was Senhora Beatriz who asked without prompting if I could contact you. She knows she only has a short time left. Are you ready?' I read sympathy in Yara's eyes.

I said I was and she led me along wide, dark corridors towards the hospital wing. As she pushed open the double doors and we walked through, I smelt disinfectant mixed with another, indefinable aroma that seemed to pervade all the hospitals I'd ever visited. The last time I'd been in one was when I'd given birth to my baby boy.

'Senhora Beatriz is in here.' Yara indicated a door at the end of the corridor. 'I will just go and see if she is prepared.'

I sat on the bench outside, thinking that no matter what Beatriz told me today, it would not bring me down. The past was the past, and yesterday I'd finally begun to have a future.

The door to Beatriz's room opened and Yara beckoned me in. 'She's very alert this morning. She told the nurse she didn't want any drugs until she'd spoken with you so that her mind would be clear. You'll have about an hour until the pain will be too much for her.' She ushered me into the room, which was bright and airy with a beautiful view of the mountains and the sea below. Even though Beatriz's bed was of hospital design, everything else resembled an ordinary bedroom.

'Good morning, Maia.'

Beatriz, who was sitting in a chair by the window, greeted me with surprising warmth. 'Thank you for coming to see me. Please, sit down.' She indicated a wooden chair opposite her. 'Yara, you can leave us now.'

'Yes, senhora. Press the bell if you need anything,' Yara said as she left the room.

While mistress and maid had been conversing, I'd taken the opportunity to study Beatriz. And after what Yara had said about her, I attempted to see her in a new light. Certainly physically, she didn't resemble Izabela, her mother, without doubt leaning more towards the paler, European features of her father. I also noticed for the first time the still vivid green of her eyes, huge in her emaciated face.

'Firstly, Maia, I want to apologise to you. Seeing you walk into my garden, looking as you do – the living image of my mother – was a shock. And of course, the necklace you wear . . . I, like Yara, recognised it immediately. It was left to me by my mother, Izabela, and is the same one I gave to my own daughter on her eighteenth birthday.' Beatriz's eyes clouded suddenly with pain or emotion – I wasn't sure which. 'Forgive me, Maia, but I had to take some time to decide what was best to do about your sudden arrival, so close to my own . . . departure.'

'Senhora Beatriz, as I said to you before, I'm not here for money or an inheritance or—'

Beatriz held up a shaking hand to silence me. 'Firstly, please call me Beatriz. I think, sadly, that it's a little late for "grandmother", don't you? And secondly, although I was aware that the timing of your visit seemed rather too convenient to be a coincidence, that did not worry me unduly. If necessary, it is possible these days to take tests to prove a genetic link. Besides, your heritage shines out of every feature. No,' she sighed, 'it was something else that made me hesitate.'

'And what was that?'

'Maia, every child who is either adopted or loses a parent

young is able to place their biological creator on a pedestal. I know I did with my own mother. In my imagination, Izabela became a madonna, a perfect woman. Although I'm sure that in reality, she had many faults, as we all do,' Beatriz admitted.

'Yes, I suppose you're right,' I agreed.

She paused for a moment, studying my face thoughtfully. 'So, when I saw your understandable desperation to know of your *own* mother and the reasons why she had put you up for adoption, I knew that I wouldn't be able to lie to you if I agreed to answer your questions. And that if I told you the truth, then I would sadly destroy any image you had naturally built up about her in your mind.'

'I'm beginning to see what a dilemma it must have been for you,' I said, trying to reassure her. 'But perhaps I should tell you that up until my adoptive father died, I'd rarely thought about who my real mother was. Or my father, for that matter. I had a very happy upbringing. I adored my father, and Marina, the woman who brought me and my sisters up, could not have been more caring. And still is,' I added.

'Well, I suppose that helps somewhat,' Beatriz agreed. 'Because I'm afraid to say that the story leading up to your adoption is not a pretty one. It's a dreadful thing for a mother to admit that she struggled to like her own child, but I'm sad to tell you that is how I came to feel about Cristina, your mother. Forgive me, Maia, the last thing I want to do is to cause you further grief. But you are obviously an intelligent woman and it would be wrong for me to throw you platitudes and lies. You would see through them, I'm sure. But you must remember that, just as parents can't choose their children, neither can children choose their parents.'

Understanding what Beatriz was trying to tell me, I wavered for a few moments, wondering if it was best, after all, if I didn't know. But I'd come this far, and perhaps, for Beatriz's *own* sake, she should be allowed to explain. I took a deep breath. 'Why don't you tell me about Cristina?' I said quietly.

Beatriz saw I'd made my decision. 'Very well. Yara says she's told you already about my life, so you will have heard that my husband – your grandfather – and I were very happily married. And the icing on our cake was when we discovered I was pregnant. Our first son died a few weeks after he was born, so when I finally gave birth to Cristina a few years later, she was even more precious to us.'

I took a deep breath, my thoughts flying momentarily to my own lost son.

'And after the experiences of my own childhood,' Beatriz continued, 'I was determined to make sure that my baby would be brought up with as much love as I and her father could give her. But to be blunt, Maia, Cristina was difficult from the day she was born. She rarely slept through the night, and by the time she was a toddler she had become prone to huge tantrums which would sometimes last for hours without abating. When she went to school, she was constantly in trouble, her teachers sending letters home saying she had bullied this girl or that and reduced them to tears. It's a terrible thing to admit' – Beatriz's voice was quavering now at obviously painful memories – 'but Cristina seemed to have no compunction about hurting people, no remorse at all after the act.' She looked up at me, her eyes full of agony. 'Maia, my dear, please tell me if you wish me to stop.'

'No, keep going,' I encouraged numbly.

'And of course, her teenage years were the worst. Her father and I despaired of her total lack of respect for authority, whether it was us or anyone else who had dealings with her. The tragedy of it all was that she was extremely bright, as her teachers never stopped reminding us. Her IQ had been tested when she was younger and it was far above average. In the past few years, as mental health issues have been investigated more thoroughly, I've read articles about a syndrome called Asperger's. Have you heard of it?' she asked me.

'Yes, I have.'

'Well, apparently the sufferer almost always has a high level of intelligence, and they also seem to show little sensitivity or empathy towards others. And that is the best way I can think of to describe your mother. Although Loen, Yara's mother, always told me that Cristina reminded her of my grandmother, Luiza, whom I barely remember. She died when I was two, you see, at the same time as my mother.'

'Yes, Yara told me.'

'So, whether it was genetic, or would these days be termed a syndrome – or perhaps a mixture of both – Cristina's personality made her almost impossible to deal with. And none of the many experts we consulted could offer any solutions.' Beatriz shook her head sadly. 'When she was sixteen, she began to stay out, frequenting some of the seedier bars in the city and falling into the wrong company. Which, as you can imagine in Rio – especially thirty-five years ago – could be extremely dangerous. On more than one occasion, she was brought home by the *polícia*, drunk and dishevelled. They threatened her with prosecution for underage drinking and that calmed her down for a while. But then we discovered that she was not attending school, and instead meeting her friends – many of whom lived up in the *favelas* – and spending her time there with them.'

Beatriz paused and stared out of the window at the distant mountains before turning her gaze back to me. 'Eventually, the school had little choice but to expel her. She'd been caught with a bottle of rum in her school bag and had plied the other girls with it. Subsequently, they'd all arrived for afternoon lessons drunk. Her father and I employed a private tutor so that she could at least finish her examinations and we could keep a closer eye on her activities too. Sometimes, we even resorted to locking her in her room when she insisted she wanted to go out for the night, but the rages that ensued would be cataclysmic. And besides, she would always find a way to escape. She was completely out of control. My dear, could you possibly pass me the water from my bedside table? All this talking is making my mouth quite dry.'

'Of course,' I said, going to fetch the beaker and straw from the table and handing it to her. As she attempted to hold it, I saw her hands were shaking too much to do so, so I put the straw to her lips and held it there while she sucked.

'Thank you,' she said, as her green eyes looked up at me in distress. 'Are you sure you can cope with hearing more, Maia?'

'Yes,' I said, putting the cup down and returning to my chair.

'Well, one day I discovered that my mother's emeralds – the necklace and earrings she had been given by her parents on her eighteenth birthday and which were worth a fortune – had disappeared from my jewellery box. Nothing else had been taken, so it was unlikely there'd been a burglary at the Casa. By now, Cristina was spending almost all her time at the *favela* – her father and I deduced that there was some man involved – and I began to notice how her eyes seemed permanently glazed and the pupils enlarged. I consulted a doctor friend of mine, and he told me it was likely that Cristina was taking some form of drugs.' Beatriz shivered at the thought. 'And of course, when he told me how much such substances cost, it explained the missing emeralds. We believed she'd stolen them, then sold them on to pay for her habit. By this time, her father and I were on the brink of divorce. Evandro had had enough and something had to give. Cristina had turned eighteen a couple of months before – I remember so vividly giving her my mother's moonstone for her birthday and her face falling because she knew it was not of any great value. That,' Beatriz said, as tears came to her eyes for the first time, 'was perhaps the most upsetting of all the terrible things she had done. It was my most precious possession, because I knew my father had once given it to my mother, and I discovered later that he had passed it on to me after she died. I gave it to my daughter, who could only wonder how many reais it would raise at a second-hand jewellery shop to fund her habit. Excuse me, Maia dear,' she said as she fumbled for a handkerchief in the pocket of her robe.

'Please, Beatriz, don't apologise. I understand how upsetting it must be to tell me this. But try and remember that you're describing a stranger to me, whether good or bad. I can't feel love for her, because I never knew her,' I comforted her softly.

'Well, I will now tell you that my husband and I decided we had to confront Cristina and warn her that unless she stopped taking drugs and stealing from us, we would have no choice but to ask her to leave the Casa. At the same time, we offered as much help and support as she needed, if only she would try to help herself. But by then she was addicted, and besides, her life was elsewhere, up in the hills with her *favela* friends. So eventually, we packed her suitcase and asked Cristina to leave our house.'

'Beatriz, I'm so sorry. That must have been unimaginably hard for you,' I said, reaching towards her and squeezing her hand gently in sympathy.

'It was,' she agreed with a deep sigh. 'We impressed upon her that if she ever wished to return to us and try to stop her habit, we would welcome her back with open arms. I remember her coming down the stairs with her suitcase as I stood by the front door. She walked straight past me, then turned back, just for a second. The hatred in her eyes for me at that moment has haunted me to this day. And' – Beatriz was weeping openly now – 'I'm afraid to say, that is the last time I ever set eyes on my daughter.'

We both sat in silence for a while, lost in our own thoughts. Despite my protestations that whatever Beatriz told me would not upset me, given the story she'd just related, it was an impossible task. Because somewhere in my veins ran Cristina's blood. Was I too as flawed as she was?

'Maia, I know what you are thinking,' Beatriz said suddenly as she dried her eyes and surveyed me. 'And let me assure you that from what I have seen of you and from what Yara has told me, there is not one iota of your character that reminds me of your mother. They say that genes skip generations and you truly are the living image of my mother, Izabela. And from what everyone told me of her, very like her in personality.'

I knew Beatriz was trying to be kind. And yes, right from

the start, from when I'd first heard about my great-grand-mother and seen how physically alike we were, I *had* felt a natural empathy towards her. But it still didn't change the fact that my birth mother had been as she was.

'So, if you never saw Cristina again, how do you know she had me?' I asked, wildly grasping at straws in the hope that there was some mistake. And that I wasn't after all related to this family. Or my mother.

'I wouldn't have known, my dear, had it not been for a friend of mine who worked as a volunteer at one of the many orphanages in Rio around that time. Most of the babies came from the *favelas* and my friend happened to be there when Cristina brought you in. She didn't give her name, just left the baby and ran, as many of the mothers did. It took my friend a few days to realise where she recognised Cristina from – apparently she was painfully thin and had lost some of her teeth.' Beatriz's voice cracked with emotion. 'But eventually, she remembered. She came to see me to tell me you'd been left with a moonstone necklace which, when she described it, I realised was the one I'd given my daughter. Immediately, I went up to the orphanage with Evandro to claim you and to bring you home, so that I and your grandfather could take care of you as our own. But even though it had been less than a week since you'd been brought in, you'd already gone. My friend was very surprised because, as she said, there were a large number of newborn infants in the orphanage at the time. It often took many weeks for a baby to be adopted – if they ever were. Perhaps it was because you were a very pretty baby, my dear,' Beatriz smiled.

'So,' I said shakily, knowing I had to ask the question that was hanging on my lips, 'does that mean your friend saw my adoptive father?'

'Yes,' Beatriz confirmed, 'and also the woman who came with him to collect you. My friend assured me that they both seemed very kind. Inevitably, Evandro and I pleaded with her to tell us where you'd been taken, but she was only a volunteer and wasn't able to provide such information.'

'I see.'

'However, there was one thing that she *was* able to provide, Maia. In that drawer' – Beatriz pointed to it – 'you'll find an envelope. The orphanage took a photograph of each baby that arrived in it for their records. As you'd gone and the file was closed, my friend asked the director of the orphanage if she could bring it to me as a keepsake. There, take a look for yourself.'

I went to the drawer and pulled out the envelope that sat inside it. Drawing out the photograph, I saw a blurred black-and-white image of a baby with a shock of dark hair and huge, startled eyes. I'd seen a number of photographs of myself lying contentedly in Marina's arms or being cradled by Pa Salt when I was tiny. And I knew without a doubt that this photograph was of me.

'So you never discovered who it was that adopted me?' I asked Beatriz.

'No. Although I hope you can imagine how hard we tried to. We explained to the director that we were your grandparents and had been intending to adopt you and bring you up as our own child. She asked what proof we had that you were even our grandchild. Sadly there was none,' Beatriz said, sighing deeply, 'because the birth mother was unnamed on your file. And even when I showed her a photograph of myself wearing the moonstone necklace, she said it didn't count as proof in the eyes of the law. I asked her – no, *begged* her – to let me at least make contact through her with the family who had taken you. She refused, saying that it had been proven disruptive in the past to put relatives of the old family in touch with the new. And their policy was firm and unbreakable. My dear,' she sighed, 'despite all our efforts, we came to a dead end.'

'Thank you for trying,' I whispered.

'Maia, you must believe me when I say that if your adoptive father had not arrived as promptly as he did, both of our lives would have been very different.'

I tucked the photograph back into the envelope for want of something to concentrate on. Standing up, I moved to put it back into the drawer.

'No, my dear, you keep it. I've no need of it now. I have my real, living, breathing granddaughter standing in front of me.'

I saw Beatriz wince in pain and knew that my time was running out.

'So, you never discovered who my real father was?' I asked her.

'No.'

'And Cristina? Do you know what became of her?'

'Sadly, as I said, I never heard a word from her again. So I'm afraid I can't even tell you whether she's dead or alive. After she took you to the orphanage, she simply disappeared into thin air. As many did in Rio in those days,' Beatriz sighed. 'Perhaps, if you wanted to pursue it further, you might have more luck. These days, I know the authorities are more open to helping those in search of a long-lost parent. My instinct, if a mother really does have such a thing, is that Cristina is dead. Those on a mission to destroy themselves usually succeed. Yet it still breaks my heart to think about her.'

'Of course it must,' I replied softly, knowing only too well what that felt like. 'But please, Beatriz, you should at least take some comfort from the fact that she took the moonstone necklace with her when she left the Casa. And then passed it on to me. The connection it held to you must have been important to her, despite everything that happened before and since. Maybe more than anything, it shows that underneath, she did love you.'

'Perhaps.' Beatriz nodded slowly, the ghost of a smile touching her dry lips. 'And now, my dear, may I ask you to ring the bell for the nurse? I'm afraid I must surrender and take one of those ghastly pills which knock me out, but at least allow me to tolerate the pain.'

'Of course.' I pressed the bell and watched as Beatriz held out a hand weakly to me.

'Maia, please tell me that you won't let the story I've told you interfere with your future. Your mother and father may have let you down, but you must know that myself and your grandfather never stopped thinking of you and loving you. And your reappearance means I can be finally at peace.'

I moved towards her and put my arms around her, for the first time embracing the physical presence of a blood relative. And only wishing that we had more time left together.

'Thank you for seeing me. And although I didn't find my mother, I found you. And that's enough,' I said gently.

The nurse arrived in the room. 'Maia, are you here in Rio tomorrow?' Beatriz asked me suddenly.

'I can be, yes.'

'Then come back and visit me again. I have told you about the bad things, but if you can spare the time, let's use what we have left to get to know each other better. You can't imagine how much I've longed to discover who you are.'

I watched as Beatriz opened her mouth obediently to take the pills the nurse was proffering. 'See you at the same time tomorrow,' I said.

Her hand fluttered a weak goodbye, and I left the room.

49

Back at the hotel, I lay down on my bed, curled up into a ball and fell fast asleep. When I woke, I lay thinking about Beatriz and what she had told me, probing my newly opened consciousness for an emotional reaction. Surprisingly, I found little pain, even though the story my grandmother had related was dreadful by anyone's standards.

I began to think about the profound reaction I'd had to the children I'd seen only yesterday at the *favela*, dancing for their lives, and realised that it had perhaps been the result of a connection I had with them that I hadn't understood at the time; I was now almost certain that I too had been born in a *favela*. My mother's actions – whatever her motivation at the time – had undoubtedly saved me from a desperately uncertain future. And besides, whoever my mother had been, or my father, I had found a blood grandmother who genuinely seemed to care for me.

I pondered whether I would try to search my mother out. And decided that I wouldn't. It was obvious from what Beatriz had described that I had only been a biological by-product of her life and was, as such, unwanted. Yet, this train of thought inevitably led me to the fact that *I* had ostensibly done the same as far as my *own* child was concerned. So how could I judge my mother harshly or believe she never loved me, not knowing the full circumstances of her decision?

However, if nothing else, the events of today had made me realise that the one thing I did want to do was to leave my son something that explained why I had made my decision. There was no moonstone necklace or grandparent desperate to adopt him. No clues as to where he'd originally come from. As Floriano had pointed out, there was every chance that the adoptive parents he'd gone to would not have told him his true birth story. But just in case they had, or would in the future and one day he went searching, I wanted to make sure there was a trail for him to follow.

Just like the one Pa Salt had left his six daughters.

I understood now why Pa Salt's coordinates had led me back to A Casa das Orquídeas rather than an orphanage. Even though I hadn't been born there, perhaps he'd known I would find and meet Beatriz, the only relative from my past who'd cared enough to search for me.

I also pondered again why Pa Salt had been in Rio at the time I was born and *why*, out of all the babies available to adopt, it had been me that he'd chosen. Beatriz had mentioned nothing about a soapstone tile being left with me when my mother had deposited me at the orphanage. So just how had Pa Salt got hold of that?

It was another conundrum I knew I would never find the answer to. And I decided that I must stop asking 'why', and simply accept that I'd been blessed to have had him as a wonderful mentor and loving father, who had always been there for me whenever I'd needed him. And that I must learn the lesson of trust in another human being's goodness.

Which, naturally, brought me back to the subject of Floriano.

Instinctively, I looked out of the window and moved my eyeline up to the skies. By now, he was somewhere over the Atlantic Ocean. It was odd, I thought, after spending fourteen years existing in a void, having absolutely nothing to ponder, or if I did, not wishing to, that I found myself with so many emotions to deal with now. The feelings I had for Floriano had emerged suddenly – like the tight bud of a rose that blossoms magically overnight into glorious colour – and felt overwhelming, but also completely natural.

I missed him, I admitted, not because of some transient passion, but with a quiet recognition that he was now part of me. And somehow, I knew that I was part of him too. Instead of a mad desperation, I felt a calm acceptance of something that had begun between us, which needed nurturing if it wasn't to wither and die.

Grabbing my laptop, I opened it, and as I'd promised him I would, I wrote Floriano an email. I explained to him as succinctly as possible what Beatriz had told me this morning. And that I was going back to the convent to see her again tomorrow.

Rather than hesitating as I would normally over my closing statement, I followed my instincts. And pressed 'send' without editing it. Then I left the hotel and crossed the road to have a swim in the bracing waves that flung themselves onto Ipanema Beach.

The following morning, Yara was waiting for me in the entrance hall of the convent, as she had been the day before.

Today, however, she greeted me with a bright smile and reached shyly to clasp my hand.

'Thank you, senhorita.'

'What for?' I asked her.

'For bringing the light back to Senhora Beatriz's eyes. Even if only for a short time. And you are feeling all right after what she had to tell you?'

'To be honest, Yara, it wasn't what I was expecting, but I'm coping.'

'She did not deserve that child as a daughter, nor did you deserve her as a mother,' Yara muttered tensely.

'I think we often don't deserve what we get. But then, maybe in the future we get what we deserve,' I said, almost to myself as I began to follow her along the corridor.

'Senhora Beatriz is lying down, but she still insisted that she wanted to see you. Shall we go in?' she asked me.

'Yes.'

And today, for the first time, we walked into the room together, without any need for Yara to check first that her mistress was prepared for me. Beatriz was in bed looking dreadfully frail, but her features broke into a smile when she saw me.

'Maia.' She indicated for Yara to pull up a chair by her bed. 'Come and sit down. How are you today, my dear? I was concerned for you overnight. What I told you must have been such a shock.'

'I'm fine, Beatriz, really,' I said as I sat down by her and patted her hand tentatively.

'Then I am glad. I think you are a strong person and I admire you for it. Now,' Beatriz said, 'enough of the past. I wish to hear about your life. Tell me, Maia, where do you live? Are you married? Do you have children yet? An occupation?'

For the next half an hour, I told my grandmother everything I could think of about myself. About Pa Salt, and my sisters and our beautiful home on the shores of Lake Geneva. I told her about my translating career, and was half tempted to tell her about Zed and confide in her about my subsequent pregnancy and the adoption of my baby. But I realised instinctively that all she wanted to hear was that I'd been happy, so I didn't elaborate.

'And what about the future? Tell me about that very attractive man who accompanied you to see me at the Casa. He's quite famous here in Rio. Is he just a friend?' She eyed me slyly. 'Something told me he was more than that.'

'Yes, I like him,' I confessed.

'So, what will you do from here, Maia? Will you return to Geneva, or stay in Rio with your young man?'

'As a matter of fact, he flew to Paris yesterday morning,' I explained.

'Ah, Paris!' Beatriz clasped her hands together. 'One of the happiest times of my life. And, as you already know, your great-grandmother visited when she was younger. I believe you've seen the sculpture of her in the garden that my father had shipped over from Paris as her wedding gift?'

'Yes, I did notice it,' I confirmed lightly, wondering where this conversation would lead.

'When I was in Paris and studying at the Beaux-Arts school, the sculptor responsible for it was one of my professors. So I introduced myself to him one day after class and told him I was Izabela's daughter. To my surprise, Professor Brouilly said he recalled her most clearly. And when I told him of her death, he seemed genuinely grief-stricken. After that, he seemed to take me under his wing, or at least developed a special interest in me, inviting me to his beautiful house in Montparnasse and taking me for lunch at La Closerie des Lilas. He said it was where he'd once spent a splendid lunch with my mother. He even took me to the *atelier* of Professor Paul Landowski and introduced me to the great man himself. By then, of course, Landowski was old and rarely sculpting, but he showed me photographs of the time when the moulds for the *Cristo* were prepared in his *atelier*. Apparently, my mother was there too while Landowski and Professor Brouilly were working on it. He also found a mould from his store cupboard that he said he'd taken of my mother's hands as a possible prototype for the *Cristo*'s.' Beatriz smiled in fond remembrance. 'Professor Brouilly was so generous to me with both his time and affection. And for years afterwards, we corresponded, right up until his death in 1965. The kindness of strangers,' Beatriz mused. 'So, Maia, my dear, are you to follow in your great-grandmother's and grandmother's footsteps and make the journey from Rio to Paris? It is certainly easier to get there than it used to be. It took me and my mother almost six weeks to get there. By this time tomorrow you could be sitting in La Closerie des Lilas sipping absinthe! Maia, dear? Did you hear me?'

After what Beatriz had just related to me, I was too choked to speak. No wonder Yara had been so wary of telling me the story of my past. It was clear that this woman knew nothing of the father who had originally given her life.

'Yes. Perhaps I will go to Paris,' I agreed, trying to recover my equilibrium.

'Good.' Beatriz seemed satisfied with my answer. 'And

now, Maia, I'm afraid we must move to more serious matters. This afternoon, I have a *notário* coming to see me. I am intending to rewrite my will and leave most of what I have to you, my granddaughter. It isn't a lot, sadly, just a house that is falling down and needs many hundreds of thousands of reais to renovate it. Money which you don't have, I'm sure. So perhaps you may want to sell it and I wish you to know that I don't mind in the least if you do. But I do have one condition, and that is that you allow Yara to live in it until her death. I know how frightened she is about the future, and I want to reassure her that she will be taken care of. And the Casa is as much her home as it has been mine. She will be left a bequest, a sum of money that should see her through the rest of her life. But if it does not, and she lives longer, I trust that you will take care of her. She is my closest friend, you see. We grew up as sisters.'

'Of course I will,' I said, trying to hold back my tears.

'I do have some jewellery too that belonged to me and to your great-grandmother. And the Fazenda Santa Tereza, my mother's childhood home. I run a small charity which helps women from the *favelas*. The charity uses the farm as a place of refuge for them. If you were able to keep that going, I would be very happy.'

'Of course I will, Beatriz,' I whispered, my throat constricting at her words. 'Beatriz, I really feel I don't deserve this. Surely you have friends, family—'

'Maia! How can you say that you don't deserve it!' There was real passion in Beatriz's voice now. 'Your mother gave you away at birth, denied you your heritage, which, might I add, once upon a time meant something here in Rio. You are a continuation of the Aires Cabral line, and although money can never make up for the loss you have suffered, it is the least I can do. And should do,' she underlined.

'Thank you, Beatriz.' I could see that she was becoming agitated and I didn't want to upset her further.

'I trust that you will use the legacy wisely,' she said, as I saw the now familiar wince of pain.

'Shall I call for the nurse?'

'In a few moments, yes. But first, Maia, before you're tempted to say that you will stay with me until the end, I will tell you equally firmly that after today, I do not want you to come and visit me again. I know where I'm headed and I don't wish for you to witness my final demise, especially as you are still grieving for your adoptive father. Yara will be with me and she is all I need.'

'But Beatriz—'

'No buts, Maia. The pain is so dreadful now that even though I have resisted so far, this afternoon I will ask the nurse for some morphine. And then the end will come quickly. So . . .' Beatriz forced a smile. 'I am only happy that I have been lucky enough to share my last lucid moments with my beautiful granddaughter. And you *are* beautiful, my dear Maia. I wish so many things for your future. But most of all, I wish that you will find love. It is the only thing in life that makes the pain of being alive bearable. Please remember that. Now, you may call for that nurse.'

A few moments later, I hugged Beatriz to me and we said our final goodbyes. As I left the room, I could see that her eyelids were already drooping and she managed a fragile wave as I closed the door behind me. Sinking onto the bench, I put my head in my hands and sobbed quietly. I felt an arm wrap around my shoulder and looked up to see that Yara had sat down beside me.

'She never knew that Laurent Brouilly was her father, did she?'

'No, Senhorita Maia, she didn't.'

Yara took my hand and we sat together, both of us mourning the tragedy of the situation.

After I wrote down my address, telephone number and email on a piece of paper that Yara had handed to me, she walked me outside to the waiting car.

'Goodbye, senhorita. I'm glad that all was resolved between you and Senhora Beatriz before it was too late.'

'It's all down to you, Yara. Beatriz is very lucky to have had you as a companion.'

'And I her,' Yara countered as I climbed into the car.

'Please promise to let me know when . . .' I couldn't bring myself to say the words.

'Of course. Now, you go off and live your life, senhorita. As perhaps you have learnt from your own family's story, every moment of it is precious.'

Taking Yara at her word, back at the hotel I checked my emails with far more anticipation than usual. And managed a smile when I saw that Floriano had replied. Paris was wonderful, he said, but he needed an interpreter to help him with his bad French.

I have also discovered something you should see, Maia. Please let me know when you will be arriving.

I laughed to myself as I read this, for he wasn't asking me whether I *would* arrive, but when. I called down to the concierge and asked them to check whether there was availability on a flight from Rio to Paris, and they called up ten minutes later to tell me there was only room in the first-class cabin. I gulped as I heard the cost, but then agreed and asked them to book the seat. And felt Pa Salt, Beatriz and Bel cheering me on.

I then left the hotel and went deep into Ipanema, back to the market, and bought a number of 'unsuitable' dresses that the former Maia would have been horrified at. But this was the new Maia, who thought that, just maybe, she was loved by a man, and she wanted to please him and look her best.

No more hiding, I told myself firmly as I also purchased two pairs of shoes with a heel to them and walked along the road to a pharmacy to test out some scent, something I hadn't worn for years. I then bought a new red lipstick.

That night, I went upstairs to the hotel roof terrace to catch a last glimpse of the *Cristo* as the sun began to set. Sipping a glass of chilled white wine, I thanked Him and the heavens for bringing me back to myself.

And as I left Rio early the next morning with Pietro, I looked back at Him, high above me on Corcovado Mountain, feeling with a strange certainty that I'd be back in His embrace very soon.

50

'Hello?' said a familiar voice at the other end of the phone line.

'Ma, it's me, Maia.'

'Maia! How are you, *chérie*? It seems an age since I heard from you last,' Marina added with a hint of reproach in her voice.

'Yes, I'm sorry I've been bad at keeping in touch, Ma. I was . . . busy,' I said, trying not to giggle as a hand snaked up my naked stomach. 'I just wanted to let you know that I'll be home tomorrow around teatime. And that' – I swallowed hard before I announced it – 'I'll be bringing a guest with me.'

'Shall I make a room up in the house, or will she stay with you in the Pavilion?'

'My guest will be staying with me at the Pavilion.' I turned to Floriano and smiled.

'Lovely,' her bright voice answered. 'Shall I have supper ready for you?'

'No, please don't worry. I'll call you tomorrow and let you know exactly what time we'll need Christian to meet us.'

'I'll wait to hear from you. Goodbye, *chérie*.'

'Goodbye.' I replaced the receiver in its cradle on the

bedside table and fell back into Floriano's arms, wondering what on earth he would make of my childhood home.

'You mustn't be shocked, or think I'm grand or anything. It's just the way my life has been,' I explained.

'*Querida*,' he said as he pulled me into his arms, 'I am fascinated to see how you live now. But always remember I know where you come from. Now, on our last day here in Paris, I'm taking you to see something very special.'

'Do we have to go?' I asked him, stretching my body languidly into his.

'I think we should,' said Floriano, 'eventually . . .'

Two hours later we dressed, left the hotel and Floriano hailed a cab. He even managed to give the driver a coherent address in French.

'We're going to somewhere off the Champs-Élysées?' I confirmed, as much for the driver's sake as my own.

'Yes. Do you doubt me and my prowess at my favourite new language?' He smiled.

'No, of course not,' I said. 'But are you sure you meant a park?'

'Hush, Maia,' he said, putting a finger to my lips, 'and trust me.'

Sure enough, we alighted next to the iron railings of a small, square expanse of green just off the Avenue de Marigny. Floriano paid the driver, then took my hand and led me through the gate and along the path that took us to the centre of the gardens. A pretty fountain played there, and Floriano pointed up to a bronze statue of a reclining, nude woman which sat atop it. Accustomed to seeing many erotic images all over Paris, I turned to Floriano askance.

'Look at her, Maia, and tell me who she is.'

I did as he bid, and suddenly I saw her. Izabela, my great-grandmother, naked and sensuous, her head thrown back in pleasure, her hands thrown out, her palms facing upwards to the heavens.

'Do you see now?'

'Yes, I do,' I whispered.

'Then it will be no surprise to you that I discovered this sculpture is by none other than Professor Laurent Brouilly, your great-grandfather. I can only believe it is his silent tribute to his love for your great-grandmother. And now, Maia, look at her hands.'

I looked, and saw the palms and the delicate fingertips. And yes, I did see.

'They are much smaller, of course, to fit the size of this sculpture, but I have compared them to the *Cristo*'s hands, and I am convinced they are identical. I will show you the photographic evidence later, but for me, there is no doubt. Especially as it is the very gardens where Izabela told Loen she met Laurent for the last time here in Paris.'

I looked up at Izabela and wondered how she would feel if she could see how she'd been once again immortalised; no longer the innocent virgin as in the first sculpture, but subtly, sensuously, by a man who had truly loved her. And a father who, through the hands of fate, had also been able to know and love the daughter they had conceived together.

Floriano placed an arm around my shoulder as we eventually walked away. 'Maia, we are not saying goodbye here like

Bel and Laurent once had to. And you must never believe we will. Do you understand?'

'Yes.'

'Good, then we can leave Paris. And one day,' he whispered into my ear, 'I will write a beautiful book as my tribute to *you*.'

I watched Floriano's face as we sped across Lake Geneva towards my home. Even though it felt to me as though I had been away for many months, in reality, it was only three weeks. The lake was busy with tiny craft, their sails fluttering in the breeze like angels' wings. The day was still very warm, even though it was past six in the evening, and the sun hung clear and golden above us in a cloudless blue sky. As I saw the familiar wall of trees in the distance, I felt as though I had lived another lifetime since I'd left Atlantis.

Christian steered the boat in to the pier, secured it and then helped us both out. I saw Floriano reach for our luggage, and Christian stop him. 'No, monsieur. I'll bring those up to the house for you later.'

'*Meu Deus!*' he commented as we walked across the lawns. 'You truly are a princess returning to your castle,' he teased me.

Up at the main house I introduced Floriano to Marina, who did her best to hide her surprise at the fact my guest was a 'he' not a 'she'. Then I took him on a tour of the house and gardens, and through his eyes I saw the beauty of my home anew.

As the sun began to dip below the mountains on the other

side of the lake, we took a glass of white wine for me and a beer for Floriano and I led him down to Pa Salt's secret garden by the water's edge. It was a riot of July colour, each plant and flower at the peak of its beauty. It reminded me today of a famous garden I'd seen once somewhere in the south of England when I had visited it with Jenny and her parents: everything laid out so perfectly, its intricate parterres lined by immaculately clipped box hedges.

We sat together on the bench under the gorgeous, fragrant rose arbour overlooking the water – the spot where so many times in the past I'd found my father deep in contemplation – and toasted each other.

'Here's to your last night in Europe,' I said, with a slight catch in my voice. 'And to the success of your book. As it's already number six on the bestseller list in its first week in France, it might go to number one.'

'You never know.' Floriano shrugged casually, although I knew he'd been overwhelmed by the positive reaction from the French media and the bookshops. 'And of course, it's all due to the wonderful translation. What is that?' he asked me, pointing to the centre of the terrace.

'It's called an armillary sphere. I think I told you that it appeared in the garden soon after Pa Salt died. It has all of our names engraved on a band and a set of coordinates for each sister. And an inscription written in Greek,' I explained.

Floriano stood up and wandered over to inspect it. 'Here you are.' He indicated one of the bands. 'And what does your inscription read?'

'*Never let fear decide your destiny.*' I gave him an ironic smile.

'I think your father knew you well,' he said, turning his

attention back to the armillary sphere. 'And what about this band? There's nothing on it.'

'No. Pa named us all after The Seven Sisters stars, but even though we all expected one more to arrive, she didn't. So there have only ever been six of us. And now,' I mused sadly, 'there'll never be a seventh.'

'It's a beautiful parting gift to give his daughters. Your father sounds as if he was an interesting man,' Floriano said, sitting down again next to me.

'He was, even though since his death I've realised we girls knew so little about him. He was an enigma,' I shrugged. 'And admittedly, I keep asking myself what he was doing in Brazil when I was born. And why it was *me* he chose.'

'That's a little like asking why a soul chooses its parents, or why it was you who was chosen to translate my book, which is where it all began for us. Life is random, Maia, a lottery.'

'Maybe it is, but do you believe in fate?' I asked him.

'A month ago, I'd almost certainly have said no. But I'll let you into a little secret,' he said, taking my hand. 'Just before I met you, it was the anniversary of my wife's death and I was feeling very low. Remember, like you, I'd been alone for a long time. I remember standing on the edge of my roof terrace, and gazing up at the *Cristo* and the stars above it. I called out to Andrea and asked her to send someone to me who would give me a reason to go on. A day later, my publisher passed on your email, asking me to take care of you while you were in Rio. So yes, Maia, I believe you *were* sent to me. And I to you.' He squeezed my hand, then in the way he always did when a moment had become too serious, lightened the mood by saying, 'Although having seen the way you live, I'm not expecting you back at my tiny apartment any time soon.'

Eventually, we walked back and Marina, even though I'd told her not to bother with supper, intercepted us on the way up to the Pavilion.

'Claudia has made a bouillabaisse which is on the warmer in the kitchen if either of you are hungry.'

'I am,' Floriano said eagerly. 'Thank you, Marina. Will you join us?' he asked her in stilted French.

'No thank you, Floriano, I've already eaten.'

We sat in the kitchen eating the delicious bouillabaisse, both suddenly aware that this would be our last supper together. As he had already extended his time in Europe, with Valentina's grandparents kindly agreeing to have her a little longer, I knew he must return home to his daughter. And I . . . well, I didn't know.

After supper, I took him into Pa's study to show him what I'd always thought was the best photograph of him and us six girls. And I named all my sisters for him.

'You're all so very different,' he commented. 'And your father was an attractive man too, wasn't he?' Floriano added as he replaced the photograph on the shelf. As he did so, something caught his attention. He stood for a few seconds staring at it intently. 'Maia, have you seen this?' He beckoned me over and pointed to the statuette sitting on the shelf amongst Pa Salt's collected personal treasures. I stared at it, realising why he had asked me.

'Yes, many times, but it's just a copy of the *Cristo*.'

'I'm not so sure . . . May I take it down?'

'Of course,' I said, wondering why he seemed so interested

in a statuette that was sold by the thousand for a few reais in any tourist shop in Rio.

'Look how finely this is sculpted,' he said, his fingers brushing the grooves of the *Cristo*'s robe. 'And look here.' He pointed to the base, which I could see had an inscription on it.

Landowski

'Maia,' he said, his eyes full of genuine wonder. 'This isn't any old mass-produced copy. It's signed by the sculptor himself! Don't you remember in Bel's letters to Loen that she talked of the miniature versions Heitor da Silva Costa had Landowski make before they settled on the final design? Here,' he said as he passed it to me and I took it into my hands carefully, surprised at its heaviness. My own fingers traced the delicately sculpted features of the *Cristo*'s face and hands. And I knew Floriano was right, that this was the work of a master craftsman.

'But how on earth would Pa have got hold of it? Maybe he bought it at auction? Or maybe it was a gift from a friend? Or . . . I really don't know,' I said as I lapsed into a frustrated silence.

'Those might be possibilities. But apart from those owned by the Landowski family, the only other two known surviving statuettes are owned by Heitor da Silva Costa's relatives. It would have to be authenticated, of course, but what a find!'

I saw the excitement brimming in Floriano's eyes. I understood he was seeing this through an historian's eyes, whereas I was merely trying to work out how my father had come across it in the first place. 'I'm sorry, Maia, I'm getting carried away,' Floriano apologised, 'and I'm sure you'll want to keep it anyway. Would anyone mind if we took it with us into your Pavilion just for tonight? I'd like the privilege of staring at it for at least a while longer.'

'Of course we can. Everything in this house belongs to us sisters now, and I doubt the others would mind.'

'Then let's go to bed,' he whispered, reaching out to stroke one of my cheeks gently with his fingers.

I slept badly that night, a pall falling over me at the thought of Floriano leaving tomorrow. Even though I'd told myself firmly to take our relationship one moment at a time, as the hours ticked past towards morning, I found I could not. I turned over and watched Floriano sleeping peacefully next to me. And then thought of how, when he left Atlantis, my life here would revert to exactly how it had been before I left for Rio.

Floriano and I had barely talked of the future, and certainly not in terms of concrete plans. Even though I knew he *did* feel something for me, as he'd told me so many times when he'd made love to me, it was very early days in our relationship. And given we lived on opposite sides of the world, I had to accept that the chances were that it would simply peter out and become no more than a fond memory.

I thanked God when the alarm went off and the long night was finally over. I jumped out of bed immediately and went to shower as Floriano dozed on, frightened of any post-mortem or meaningless conciliatory words he might speak to me on the imminent parting of our ways. Dressing quickly, I announced to him that I was off to the kitchen to make breakfast, as Christian would be waiting at the launch in twenty minutes. Then, as he appeared in the kitchen a few minutes later, I left the room hurriedly, telling him I had to go up to the main house and that I'd see him down by the pier in ten minutes.

'Maia, please . . .' I heard him call, but I was already out of the front door and walking fast along the path towards the house. When I got there, unable to face Marina or Claudia, I locked myself in the downstairs cloakroom, willing the minutes on my watch to pass so that the moment he left would be over soon. With only a few seconds to spare until the launch left, I emerged, opened the front door and walked down across the lawns, seeing Floriano was already there talking to Marina.

'Where have you been, *chérie*? Your friend has to board the launch immediately or he will miss his flight.' Marina gave me a quizzical stare before turning her attention to Floriano. 'It's been a pleasure to meet you and I hope we'll be seeing you back at Atlantis soon. Now, I'll leave you two to say goodbye.'

'Maia,' Floriano said as Marina left us. 'What is it? What's wrong?'

'Nothing, nothing . . . Look, Christian is waiting for you. You'd better go.'

He opened his mouth to say something, but I abruptly left his side and walked in front of him along the pier towards the launch, giving Floriano no choice but to follow me. Christian handed him into the boat and started the motor.

'*Adeus*, Maia,' Floriano said, his eyes full of sadness. The launch began to move away from the pier, and the engines churned noisily.

'I'll write to you!' he shouted to me above the roar. Then he said something else which I didn't catch as the launch sped away from Atlantis. And from me.

I walked miserably back towards the house, berating myself for my childish behaviour. I was a grown woman, for God's sake, and should be able to cope with what I had known from the start was this inevitable parting. Rationally, I knew it was a knee-jerk reaction to my past, the pain of the parting with Zed still – after all these years – burning laser-like into my psyche.

Marina was waiting for me in front of the Pavilion, arms crossed and a frown on her face.

'What was all that about, Maia? Had you two had an argument? Floriano seemed like such a nice young man. You hardly said goodbye. Neither of us knew where you were.'

'I had . . . something to do. Sorry.' I shrugged, feeling like a petulant teenager being told off for bad manners. 'By the way, I'm going into Geneva to see Georg Hoffman. Is there anything you need?' I asked her pointedly, changing the subject.

Marina looked at me, and I saw something that resembled despair in her eyes. 'No thank you, dear. Nothing.'

She walked away from me, and I felt as ridiculous as I knew my behaviour had been.

Georg Hoffman's offices were situated in the business district of Geneva, just off the Rue Jean-Petitot. Georg's office was sleek and modern, with huge floor-length windows giving an aerial view of the harbour in the distance.

'Maia,' he said as he stood up from his desk to greet me. 'This is an unexpected pleasure.' He smiled as he ushered me to a black leather sofa and we both sat down. 'I hear you've been away.'

'Yes. Who told you?'

'Marina, of course. Now, what can I do for you?' he asked.

'Well . . .' I cleared my throat. 'I suppose it's two things really.'

'Right.' Georg steepled his fingers. 'Fire away then.'

'Do you have any idea how Pa Salt came to choose me as his first adopted girl?'

'Goodness, Maia.' I saw his face register surprise. 'I'm afraid I was your father's lawyer, not his emotional confidant.'

'But I thought the two of you were friends?'

'Yes, we were, I suppose, from my point of view at least. But as you know, your father was a very private individual. And even though I'd like to think he regarded me as trustworthy, at the end of the day, I was an employee first and foremost and it was never my place to question him. The first I knew about you was when he contacted me to register your adoption with the Swiss authorities, and fill in the necessary forms for your first passport.'

'So you have no idea what his connection with Brazil might have been?' I persisted.

'On a personal level, none at all. Although he did have a number of business interests there, of course. But then he had similar interests in many places across the world,' Georg clarified. 'So I'm afraid I really am unable to help you on that matter.'

Disappointed, but not entirely surprised by his response, I pressed on with my line of enquiry.

'When I was in Brazil, thanks to the clues Pa left me, I met my grandmother, who sadly passed away only a few days ago. She told me that when my father arrived to adopt me, he was accompanied by a woman. The orphanage assumed the woman was his wife. Was he married?'

'Never, as far as I know.'

'Then could this woman have been a girlfriend of his at the time?'

'Maia, forgive me, but I really have no idea about your father's private life. I'm sorry not to be able to help you further, but there we are. Now, what was the other matter you mentioned that you wanted to discuss with me?'

As it was obvious I wasn't going to get any further, I surrendered to the inevitable realisation that I would never know the full circumstances of my adoption. Then I took a deep breath to say what else I needed to. 'I told you a few moments ago that my maternal grandmother died recently. She left me two properties in Brazil and a small amount of income in her will.'

'I see. And you'd like me to act on your behalf during probate?'

'Yes, but in fact, more importantly, I want to make a will too. And leave the properties to a . . . relative.'

'I see. Well, that's not a problem. And in fact, it's one thing that I would recommend to all my clients, whatever their age. If you write a list of who exactly you'd like to leave anything you own to, and include small bequests to friends, et cetera, I can turn it into the necessary legalese.'

'Thank you.' I hesitated for a moment, trying to decide

how best I could phrase what I wanted to say next. 'I also wanted to ask you how difficult it is for parents who have given up their babies for adoption to trace their children.'

Georg studied me thoughtfully, but didn't seem remotely surprised by the question. 'Extremely difficult, for the parent that is,' he clarified. 'As you can imagine, a child who is adopted, especially at a very young age, needs to feel settled and secure. Adoption authorities won't take the risk of natural parents regretting their decision after the fact and introducing themselves to the child. You can imagine how disruptive it would be. And, of course, for the adoptive parents themselves, who have loved the child as their own, the reappearance of the natural mother or father would be very distressing, unless they agreed to it beforehand. However, if, like yourself, the adopted child wishes to seek out their natural parents once they are legally able to do so, then that's a different story.'

I listened intently to what Georg was telling me. 'So, if an adopted child *did* want to seek out their natural mother or father, where would they go?'

'To the adoption authorities. These days, here in Switzerland at least, they keep a very careful record of these things. He would go there. I mean' – Georg corrected himself immediately – 'that is where any adopted child would need to begin.'

I watched a faint blush of colour tinge his pale cheeks. And in that moment, I realised he knew.

'So, if a natural parent was – just for example – going to make a will and leave the child they'd given up for adoption a bequest, what would happen then?'

I watched Georg pause as he thought about his words

carefully. 'A lawyer would use the same route as any adopted child. He'd go to the adoption authorities and explain the situation. They would then – if the child was over sixteen years of age – contact the child, or, I should say, young adult concerned.'

'And if the child wasn't over sixteen?'

'Then the authorities would contact the adoptive parents, who have the right to decide whether it would be beneficial for their child to know of the bequest at the time.'

'I see.' I nodded, now feeling oddly in control. 'And if the adoption authorities were unable to trace the child concerned, and a lawyer had to use less . . . *conventional* means to find them, how easy would that be?'

Georg stared at me. And in that moment, his eyes told me everything his words couldn't say. 'For a competent lawyer, Maia, it would be easy, very easy indeed.'

I told Georg that I would do as we had discussed and construct a will. I also told him I would be sending him a letter, to be held by him and passed over in the event that any adoption agency, or male with the birth date I would give him, ever made contact. Then I left his office.

Outside, unwilling to go home before I'd had a chance to digest what I had just learnt, I parked myself at a table of a café that overlooked the lake and ordered a beer. I normally hated beer, but somehow as I put the bottle to my mouth, refusing the glass the waitress brought with it, the taste was reminiscent of Rio and it comforted me.

If Georg knew about my son, then so did Pa Salt. I

remembered the words that had upset and destabilised me so much in his parting letter to me.

Please believe me when I say that family is everything. And that the love of a parent for a child is the most powerful force on earth.

As I sipped my beer in the sunshine, I was convinced I could now walk back to Georg's office and confront him. Ask him to tell me exactly who it was that had adopted my son and where in the world he was. But I also knew that what Floriano had said to me made sense. However much I longed to tell my beloved son why I had given him up, and to achieve some form of redemption for myself, currently it was a purely selfish need.

A sudden burst of anger filled me as I thought of the unseen and all-powerful hand of Pa Salt, who still seemed to control my life from beyond the grave. And maybe, I realised, that of my son too.

What right did he have to know things about myself that even *I* didn't?

And yet, just like those who went to pray at the altar of an invisible power that they trusted implicitly – purely on human instinct and little factual evidence – I too felt comforted by Pa Salt's omnipotence. If my father had known – and the guilt in Georg's eyes after he'd made his very human error had confirmed he did – then I knew for certain that my boy was somewhere on the planet being cared for.

It had not been my father who had lacked trust in our relationship. It had been me. I could see clearly now that he'd also understood the reasoning behind my decision not to confide in him and accepted it. He'd allowed me to make my own choice which – I admitted brutally – had not just been about fear of his parental reaction. It had been about me too. Nineteen years old, experiencing freedom for the first time, with what I'd been sure was a brilliant future in front of me, the last thing I'd wanted was the responsibility of bringing up a child alone. And perhaps, I mused, if I *had* gone to Pa then, confessed and talked over the options with him, I might well have come to the same conclusion anyway.

I thought about my own mother. A similar age, in a similar dilemma, albeit at a different moment in time.

'I forgive you,' I said suddenly. 'Thank you,' I added, knowing that whatever her motivation, her decision had been right for *me*, her daughter.

My thoughts flashed back once again to Pa Salt. I gave a small chuckle as I thought that I wouldn't have put it past him to have interviewed the prospective adoptive parents himself.

Maybe he had, maybe he hadn't, but in that moment, as I sat draining my beer, I felt at peace for the first time since my baby had been born thirteen years ago.

And now . . . I realised that in giving me my past, Pa Salt had probably offered me my future too. I quailed as I recalled my behaviour towards Floriano this morning.

Maia, what have you done?

Calling Christian on my mobile, I asked him to meet me at the pontoon in fifteen minutes. As I walked through the hectic streets of Geneva, I longed for the relaxed atmosphere of Rio. The people worked and they played and they also respected what they could not change or understand. And if I had messed up my future by letting old fears get the better of me, I accepted responsibility for it.

For as I stepped onto the pontoon and boarded the launch, I knew that although my life had been shaped by events out of my control, it was *I* who had made the decision to react to them in the way I had.

A very familiar but equally unexpected figure greeted me on the pier as Christian pulled the launch into Atlantis.

'Surprise!' she said, throwing her arms open to embrace me as I climbed out of the boat.

'Ally! What are you doing here?'

'Strangely enough, this is my home too,' she said with a grin as we walked up to the house together arm in arm.

'I know, but I wasn't expecting you.'

'I had a few days off, so I thought I'd come and check on how Ma was while you were away. I imagine it's been hard on her too since Pa died.'

Instantly, I felt guilty at my own selfishness. I hadn't spoken to Ma once during my time in Rio. Or even given her much more than a casual 'hello' since I'd arrived yesterday.

'You look wonderful, Maia! I hear you've been busy.' Ally nudged me affectionately. 'Ma tells me you had a guest here last night. Who is he?'

'Just someone I met in Rio.'

'Well, let's get ourselves a cool drink and you can tell me all about it.'

We sat at the table on the terrace, enjoying the sunshine. And as my usual initial ambivalence towards my 'perfect' sister abated after a few minutes in her easy company, I began to relax and tell her what had happened in Brazil.

'Wow,' she said as I paused for breath and took a sip of the home-made lemonade Claudia knew we both loved. 'What an adventure you've been on. And it's so brave of you to have gone there and discovered your past. I'm not confident that I'd be able to cope with finding out the reasons why I was put up for adoption in the first place, even though I did get lucky with Pa Salt and all my sisters afterwards. Didn't it hurt when your grandmother told you about your mother?' she asked me.

'Yes, of course it did, but I understand. And Ally, there's something else I want to tell you. That perhaps I should have told you a long time ago . . .'

I told her about my son then, and how I'd made the terrible decision to give him up. Ally looked genuinely shocked and I saw tears appear in her eyes.

'Maia, how dreadful that you had to go through that all alone. Why on earth didn't you tell me? I was your sister! I always thought we were close. I would have been there for you, I really would.'

'I know, Ally, but you were only just sixteen at the time. And besides, I was ashamed.'

'What a burden you've had to carry,' she breathed. 'By the way, if you don't mind me asking, who was the father?'

'Oh, no one you'd know. He was someone I met at university called Zed.'

'Zed Eszu?'

'Yes. You may have heard his name on the news. His father was the tycoon who committed suicide.'

'And whose boat I saw close to Pa's that terrible day when I heard he'd died, if you remember.' Ally shuddered.

'Of course,' I acknowledged, having completely forgotten that detail in the maelstrom of the past three weeks. 'Ironically, it was Zed who inadvertently forced me onto the plane to Rio when I was originally deciding whether to go or not. After fourteen years of silence, he left me a voicemail message out of the blue, saying he had to come to Switzerland and asking if we could meet up.'

Ally looked at me oddly. 'He wanted to meet *you*?'

'Yes. He said he'd heard about Pa's death and suggested that perhaps we could cry on each other's shoulders. If anything was going to send me scurrying away from Switzerland, that was it.'

'Does Zed know that he was the father of your child?'

'No. And if he did, I doubt he'd care.'

'I think you are definitely best rid of him,' Ally said darkly.

'You know him then?'

'Not personally, no. But I have a . . . friend who does. Anyway,' she said, recovering somewhat, 'it sounds as though getting on that plane was the best thing you've ever done. Now, you still haven't told me about this gorgeous Brazilian you had in tow. I think Ma rather fell for him. When I arrived earlier, she could talk of nothing else. He's a writer apparently?'

'Yes. I translated his first novel for him. It was published in Paris last week to rave reviews.'

'You were with him there?'

'Yes.'

'And?'

'I . . . like him a lot.'

'Marina says he liked you too. A lot,' Ally emphasised. 'So, where do the two of you go from here?'

'I don't know. We didn't really make any future plans. He has a six-year-old daughter, you see, and he lives in Rio, and I'm here . . . Anyway, how about you, Ally?' I said, not wishing to discuss Floriano any further.

'The sailing's going well, and I've been asked to join the crew of the Fastnet Race next month. Also, the coach of the Swiss national sailing team wants to put me through my final paces. If I'm in, it would mean training from autumn with the rest of the squad for next year's Olympics in Beijing.'

'Ally! That's fantastic! Do let me know, won't you?'

'Of course I will.'

I was just about to question her further when Marina came out onto the terrace. 'Maia, *chérie*, I didn't know you were home until I saw Claudia just now. Christian gave me this, I'm afraid I forgot to give it to you.' Marina handed me an envelope. I looked down at the writing and recognised it instantly as Floriano's.

'Thank you, Ma.'

'Will you two girls be wanting supper?' she asked us.

'If there's any going, absolutely. Maia?' Ally looked at me. 'Will you join me? It's not often we get the chance for a catch-up these days.'

'Yes, of course,' I said, standing up. 'But if you don't mind, I'm going back to the Pavilion for a while.'

The two women looked at me and the letter knowingly.

'See you later, *chérie*,' said Marina.

Back at the Pavilion, my fingers trembling, I opened the envelope.

I drew out a piece of tatty paper that looked as if it had been hastily torn from a notepad.

On the boat
Lake Geneva

Mon amour Maia,

I write to you in what you know is my bad French, and although I cannot be poetic in the language the way that Laurent Brouilly was to Izabela, the feeling behind the words is just the same. (And forgive the bad writing, the launch is a little bumpy across the water.) Chérie, I understood your distress this morning and wished to comfort you, but perhaps you still struggle to trust me. So I will tell you in writing that I love you. And even though we have spent such a short time together so far, I believe our story has only just begun. If you'd stayed with me long enough this morning before I left, I would have told you that I wish more than anything for you to come to be with me in Rio. So we can eat burnt bean stew, sip undrinkable wine and dance the samba together every night of our lives. It is a lot to ask of you, I know, for you to give up your life in Geneva and come to me here. But, just as Izabela had a child to think of, so do I. And Valentina needs her family close. Certainly for now, at least.

I will leave you to think about it, for it is a big decision. But please, I'd be grateful if you could put me out of my misery sooner rather than later. Tonight

*is too long to wait, but, under the circumstances, will
be acceptable.*

*Also, I enclose the soapstone tile. My friend at the
museum finally managed to decipher the quotation
that Izabela wrote for Laurent.*

Love knows not distance;
It hath no continent;
Its eyes are for the stars.

*Goodbye for now. I'll wait to hear.
Floriano X*

Ally

July 2007

New Moon

12; 04; 53

51

Marina and I waved and blew kisses as we watched Maia leave Atlantis. Her two suitcases were filled to the brim with her most treasured possessions. *And* three hundred Twinings English Breakfast teabags, which she said were impossible to find in Rio. Even though she'd assured us she'd be back very soon, somehow we knew she wouldn't be. And so we both felt emotional as we watched my big sister disappear from view to begin her new life.

'I'm so happy for her,' said Marina, surreptitiously wiping her eyes as we turned and walked back to the house. 'Floriano is such a lovely man, and Maia tells me his young daughter is beautiful too.'

'It seems as if she's found herself a ready-made family,' I commented. 'Maybe it will make up for what she lost.'

Marina shot me a glance as we entered the house. 'Maia told you?'

'Yes, yesterday. And I admit I was shocked. Not so much by what had happened, but by the fact she'd kept it to herself for all these years. As a matter of fact,' I said, 'selfishly, I felt very hurt that she'd been unable to trust me with her secret.

Presumably you knew?' I asked Ma as I followed her into the kitchen.

'Yes, *chérie*, I was the one who helped her. Anyway, what's done is done. And Maia, finally, has found herself a life. To be honest,' Marina admitted as she switched the kettle on to boil, 'sometimes I despaired she ever would.'

'I think we all did. I remember her being so happy and positive when she was younger, but then she seemed to change overnight. I went to visit her once when she'd returned to continue her third year of university at the Sorbonne. She was so quiet . . . closed,' I sighed. 'It was a very boring week-end because Maia didn't want to go anywhere, whereas I was sixteen and in Paris for the first time. Now I understand why. You know how I idolised her when I was younger. It really upset me as I knew she had shut me out.'

'I think she shut us all out,' Marina comforted me. 'But if anyone can bring her back and teach her to trust, it's that young man she's found herself. Tea? Or something cooler?'

'Water will be fine, thanks. Honestly, Ma, I think you have a serious crush on Floriano!' I teased her, as she passed me a glass of water.

'Well, he's certainly very attractive,' Marina agreed with-out guile.

'I can't wait to meet him. But now Maia's gone, what will you do here?'

'Oh, don't you worry, I have lots of things to keep me busy. It's amazing how often you girls fly back to the nest. Usually at short notice.' She smiled at me. 'I had Star here last week, as a matter of fact.'

'Did you? Without CeCe?'

'Yes.' Marina tactfully refrained from commenting further.

'But you know it's a pleasure to have any of you at home with me.'

'It does feel so different here without Pa,' I said suddenly.

'Yes, of course it does. But can you imagine how proud he would be if he could see what you are doing tomorrow? You know how much he loved his sailing.'

'Yes,' I said, smiling sadly. 'Changing the subject, you obviously know that the father of Maia's son was Kreeg Eszu's boy, Zed?'

'I do, yes. Anyway' – Marina abruptly changed the subject – 'I'll ask Claudia to make sure supper's ready by seven tonight. I know you have an early start in the morning.'

'Yes, and I must go and check my emails. Is it okay if I use Pa's study?'

'Of course it is. Remember, this is yours and your sisters' house now,' Marina said patiently.

Taking my laptop from my bedroom, I went downstairs, opened the door to my father's study, and for the first time in my life, sat down tentatively in Pa Salt's chair. I stared into space as my laptop went through the process of opening, and gazed blankly at the cornucopia of objects Pa had kept on his shelves.

The laptop then decided to tell me it wanted to shut down, having just opened up, so while I waited for it to reboot, I stood up and went over to Pa's CD player. All of us had tried to move him on to an iPod, and even though he had a raft of sophisticated computers and electronic communication equipment in his study, he'd said he was too old to change, and preferred to physically 'see' the music he wanted to play. As I switched the CD player on, fascinated to discover what Pa Salt had been listening to last, the room was suddenly filled with the beautiful opening bars of Grieg's *Morning Mood* from the Peer Gynt Suite.

I stood, rooted to the spot, as a wave of memories assailed me. It had been Pa's favourite orchestral piece, and he'd often asked me to play the opening bars for him on my flute. It had become the theme tune of my childhood and it reminded me of all the glorious sunrises we'd shared when he'd taken me out on the lake and patiently taught me to sail.

I missed him so very much.

And I also missed someone else.

As the music swelled from the hidden speakers, filling the room with glorious sound, on instinct, I picked up the receiver of the phone on Pa's desk to make a call.

Holding it to my ear as I made to dial the number, I realised someone else in the house was already on the line. The shock of hearing the familiar, resonant tones of the voice that had comforted me from childhood forced me to interrupt the conversation.

'Hello?' I said, hurriedly reaching over and turning the CD player down to make absolutely sure it was him.

But the voice at the other end had become a monotonous bleeping, and I knew he had gone.

Author's Note

The 'Seven Sisters' series is loosely based on the mythology of The Seven Sisters of The Pleiades, the well-known star constellation next to the famous belt of Orion. From the Mayans to the Greeks to the Aborigines, The Seven Sisters stars are noted in inscriptions and in verse. Sailors have used them as guiding lights for thousands of years and even a Japanese brand of car, 'Subaru', is named after the *six* sisters . . .

Many of the names in the series are anagrams for the characters that populate the legends, with relevant allegorical phrases used throughout, but it is not important to know anything about these to enjoy the books. However, if you are interested in reading more about 'Pa Salt', Maia and her sisters, then please visit my website, www.lucindariley.com, where the many legends and stories are revealed.

Acknowledgements

Firstly, I would like to thank Milla and Fernando Baracchini and their son Gui, as it was at their dining-room table in Ribeirão Preto that I first came up with the idea of writing a story set in Brazil. And the wonderful Maria Izabel Seabra de Noronha, the great-granddaughter of Heitor da Silva Costa, the architect and engineer of *Christ the Redeemer*, for so generously sharing her time and knowledge as well as her documentary *De Braços Abertos* (*Arms Wide Open*). And then sparing the time to read through the manuscript to check all the details were correct. However, this is a work of fiction, wrapped around real historical figures. And my portrayal of both Paul Landowski and the da Silva Costa family and his staff is down to my imagination, rather than fact. Valeria and Luiz Augusto Ribeiro for offering me their *fazenda* up in the mountains above Rio to write in – I never wanted to leave – and especially to Vania and Ivonne Silva for the pound cake and so much more. Suzanna Perl, my very patient guide to Rio and its history, Pietro and Eduardo, our lovely drivers, Carla Ortelli for her magnificent organisation – nothing was ever too much trouble – and Andrea Ferreira for being at the other end of the phone whenever I needed her to translate for me.

I would also like to thank all my publishers around the world for their support and encouragement when I announced to them that I would be writing a series of seven books based on The Seven Sisters of the Pleiades. Particularly Jez Trevathan and Catherine Richards, Georg Reuchlein and Claudia Negele, Peter Borland and Judith Curr, Knut Gørvell, Jorid Mathiassen and Pip Hallén.

Valérie Brochand, my neighbour in the South of France, who so kindly went to the Landowski museum for me in Boulogne-Billancourt and took hundreds of photos, and Adriana Hunter, who translated Landowski's enormous biography and collated the important facts. David Harber and his staff, who helped me understand the workings of the armillary sphere.

My ever-supportive mother, Janet, my sister, Georgia, and her son Rafe, who, at the age of nine, made *The Midnight Rose* his school reading book! Rita Kalagate, for telling me I *would* go to Brazil the night before I received an offer from my publishing house, and Izabel Latter for keeping me going in Norfolk and listening to me chunter on as she gently manipulates an aching body that has flown thousands of miles across the world or been hunched over a manuscript 24/7.

Susan Moss, my best friend forever and now partner in crime on the detail of the manuscript, Jacquelyn Heslop, my 'sis' in another life, and my PA, Olivia Riley, who miraculously manages to decipher my scribble and introduced me to the concept of an armillary sphere.

It was a starlit night in early January 2013 when I first

came up with the idea of writing allegorically about my seven mythical sisters. I called the family together and sat by the fire, bubbling over with excitement and trying to explain what I wanted to do. To give them credit, not a single one of them said I was mad – though I must have sounded so at the time as the ideas began to grow. So it is to them I owe the biggest thank you for what has happened since. My darling husband and agent, Stephen – we have been on an exhilarating journey together in the past year and both learned a lot. And my fantastic children: Harry, who makes all my wonderful films; Leonora, who came up with the very first anagram – 'Pa Salt'; Kit, my youngest who can always make me laugh; and of course Isabella Rose, my amazing 'high-voltage baby' of eighteen, to whom this book is aptly dedicated.

Bibliography

The Seven Sisters is a work of fiction set against a historical and mythological background. The sources I've used to research the time period and detail on my characters' lives are listed below:

Munya Andrews, *The Seven Sisters of the Pleiades* (Spinifex Press, 2004)

Dan Franck, *Bohemian Paris* (Grove Press, 2001)

Robert Graves, *The Greek Myths* (Penguin, 2011)

Robert Graves, *The White Goddess, a Historical Grammar of Poetic Myth* (Faber and Faber, 1975)

Michèle Lefrançois, *Paul Landowski: L'oeuvre sculpté* (Crèaphis editions, 2009)

Jeffrey D. Needell, *A Tropical Belle Époque* (Cambridge, 2009)

Maria Izabel Noronha, *De Braços Abertos* (documentary) (2008)

Maria Izabel Noronha, *Redentor: De Braços Abertos* (Reptil Editora, 2011)

Peter Robb, *A Death in Brazil* (Bloomsbury, 2005)

Nigel Spivey, *Songs of Bronze* (Faber and Faber, 2005)

Read on for an extract of

The Storm Sister,

the second book in the spellbinding
Seven Sisters series

1

The Aegean Sea

I will always remember exactly where I was and what I was doing when I heard that my father had died.

I was lying naked in the sun on the deck of the *Neptune*, with Theo's hand resting protectively on my stomach. The deserted curve of golden beach on the island in front of us glimmered in the sun as it sat nestled in its rocky cove. The crystal-clear turquoise water was making a lazy attempt at forming waves as it hit the sands, foaming elegantly like the froth on a cappuccino.

Becalmed, I'd thought, *like me.*

We'd dropped anchor in the small bay off the tiny Greek island of Macheres at sunset the night before, then waded ashore to the cove carrying two cool boxes. One was filled with fresh red mullet and sardines that Theo had caught earlier that day, the other with wine and water. I'd set down my load on the sand, panting with effort, and Theo had kissed my nose tenderly.

'We are castaways on our very own desert island,' he'd announced, spreading his arms wide to gesture at the idyllic setting. 'Now, I'm off in search of firewood so we can cook our fish.'

I'd watched him as he turned from me and walked towards the rocks forming a crescent around the cove, heading for the tinder-dry sparse bushes that grew in the crevices. Given he was a world-class sailor, his slight frame belied his strength. Compared to the other men I crewed with in sailing competitions who seemed to be all rippling muscles and Tarzan-like chests, Theo was positively diminutive. One of the first things I'd noticed about him was his rather lopsided gait. He'd since told me how he'd broken his ankle falling out of a tree as a child and how it had never mended properly.

'I suppose it's another reason why I was always destined for a life on the water. When I'm sailing, no one can tell how ridiculous I look walking on land,' he'd chuckled.

We'd cooked our fish and later made love under the stars. The following morning was our last aboard together. And just before I'd decided I absolutely had to resume contact with the outside world by switching on my mobile, and then subsequently discovered my life had shattered into a million tiny pieces, I'd lain there next to him perfectly at peace. And, like a surreal dream, my mind had replayed the miracle of Theo and me, and how we'd come to be here in this beautiful place . . .

I'd first set eyes on him a year or so ago at the Heineken Regatta in St Maarten in the Caribbean. The winning crew was celebrating at the victory dinner and I was intrigued to discover that their skipper was Theo Falys-Kings. He was a celebrity in the sailing world, having steered more crews to victory in offshore races during the past five years than any other captain.

'He isn't what I imagined at all,' I commented under my breath to Rob Bellamy, an old crewmate with whom I'd sailed for the Swiss national team. 'He looks like a geek with those horn-rimmed glasses,' I added as I watched him stand up to move across to another table, 'and he has a very odd walk.'

'He's certainly not your average brawny sailor, admittedly,' agreed Rob. 'But Al, the guy is a total genius. He has a sixth sense when it comes to the water and there's no one I'd trust more as my skipper on stormy seas.'

I was introduced to Theo briefly by Rob later that evening and I noticed his hazel-flecked green eyes were thoughtful as he shook my hand.

'So, you're the famous Al D'Aplièse.'

Behind his British accent, his voice was warm and steady. 'Yes, to the latter part of that statement,' I said, embarrassed at the compliment, 'but I think it's *you* who's famous.' Doing my best not to let my gaze waver under his continued scrutiny, I saw his features soften as he let out a chuckle.

'What's so funny?' I demanded.

'To be frank, I wasn't expecting *you*.'

'What do you mean "*me*"?'

Theo's attention was diverted by a photographer wanting a team photo, so I never did get to hear what it was he meant.

After that, I began to notice him across the room at various social events for the regattas we took part in. He had an indefinable vibrancy about him and a soft, easy laugh that, despite his outwardly reserved demeanour, seemed to draw people to his side. If the event was formal, he was usually dressed in chinos and a crumpled linen jacket as a nod to protocol and the race sponsors, but his ancient deck shoes and unruly brown hair always made him look as if he'd just stepped off a boat.

On those first few occasions, it seemed as if we were dancing around each other. Our eyes met often, but Theo never attempted to continue our first conversation. It was only six weeks ago, when my crew had claimed victory in Antigua and we were celebrating at the Lord Nelson's Ball that marked the end of race week, when he tapped me on the shoulder.

'Well done, Al,' he said.

'Thanks,' I replied, feeling gratified that our crew had beaten his for a change.

'I'm hearing many good things about you this season, Al. Do you fancy coming to crew for me in the Cyclades Regatta in June?'

I'd already been offered a place on another crew, but had yet to accept. Theo saw my hesitation.

'You're already taken?'

'Provisionally, yes.'

'Well, here's my card. Have a think about it and let me know by the end of the week. I could really do with someone like you aboard.'

'Thanks.' I mentally pushed aside my hesitation. Who on earth turned down the chance to crew for the man currently known as 'The King of the Seas'? 'By the way,' I called out as he began to walk away from me, 'last time we talked, why did you say you weren't expecting "me"?'

He paused, his eyes sweeping briefly over me. 'I'd never met you in person; I'd just heard titbits of conversation about your sailing skills, that's all. And as I said, you aren't what I was expecting. Goodnight, Al.'

I mulled over our conversation as I walked back to my room in a little inn by St John's harbour, letting the night air wash over me and wondering why it was that Theo fascinated me so much. Street lights bathed the cheerful multi-coloured house fronts in a warm nocturnal glow, and from a distance, the lazy hum of people in the bars and cafés drifted towards me. I was oblivious to it all, exhilarated as I was by the race win – and by Theo Falys-King's offer.

As soon as I entered my room, I made a beeline for my laptop and wrote him an email to accept his offer. Before I sent it, I took a shower, then stopped to read it through again, blushing at how eager I sounded. Deciding to save it in my drafts folder and send it in a couple of days, I stretched out on my bed, flexing my arms to relieve the tension and soreness from the race that day.

'Well, Al,' I muttered to myself with a smile, '*that* will be an interesting regatta.'

I sent the email as planned and Theo contacted me immediately, saying how pleased he was I could join his crew. Then just two weeks ago, I found myself inexplicably nervous as I stepped aboard the race-rigged Hanse 540 yacht in Naxos harbour to begin training for the Cyclades Regatta.

The race was not overly demanding as competitive racing went, the entrants comprising a mix of serious sailors and weekend enthusiasts, all buoyed up by the prospect of eight days' fabulous sailing between some of the most beautiful islands in the world. And as one of the more experienced crews involved, I knew we were strongly fancied to win.

Theo's crews were always notoriously young. My friend

Rob Bellamy and me, both thirty, were the 'senior' members of the team in terms of age and experience. I'd heard that Theo preferred to recruit talent in the early stages of a sailor's career to prevent bad habits. The rest of the crew of six were in their early twenties: Guy, a burly Englishman; Tim, a laid-back Aussie; and Mick, a half-German, half-Greek sailor who knew the waters of the Aegean like the back of his hand.

Although I was eager to work with Theo, I hadn't stepped into it blindly; I'd done my best beforehand to gather information on the enigma that was 'The King of the Seas', by looking on the internet and talking to those who had crewed with him previously.

I'd heard that he was British and had studied at Oxford, which would account for his clipped accent, but on the internet, his profile said that he was an American citizen who had captained the Yale varsity sailing team to victory many times. One friend of mine had heard he came from a wealthy family, another that he lived on a boat.

'Perfectionist', 'Control freak', 'Hard to please', 'Workaholic', 'Misogynist' . . . These were other comments I had gathered, the latter coming from a fellow female sailor who claimed she'd been sidelined and mistreated on his crew, which did give me pause for thought. But the overwhelming sentiment was simple:

'Absolutely the best bloody skipper I have ever worked for.'

That first day aboard, I began to understand why Theo was afforded so much respect from his peers. I was used to shouty skippers, who screamed instructions and abuse at one and all, like bad-tempered chefs in a kitchen. Theo's understated approach was a revelation. He said very little as he put us through our paces, just surveyed us all from a distance. When the day was over, he gathered us together and pin-pointed our strengths and weaknesses in his calm, steady voice. I realised he'd missed nothing and his natural air of authority meant we hung on every word he said.

'And by the way, Guy, no more sneaking a cigarette during a practice under race conditions,' he added with a half-smile as he dismissed us all.

Guy blushed to the roots of his blond hair. 'That guy must have eyes in the back of his head,' he mumbled to me as we trooped off the boat to shower and change for dinner.

That first evening, I headed out from our pension with the rest of the crew, feeling happy I'd made the decision to join them in the race. We walked along Naxos harbour, the ancient stone castle lit up above the village and a jumble of twisting alleys winding down between the white-washed houses. The restaurants along the harbour front were teeming with sailors and tourists enjoying the fresh seafood and raising endless glasses of ouzo. We found a small family-run establishment in the back streets, with rickety wooden chairs and mismatching plates. The home-cooked food was just what we needed after a long day on the boat, the sea air giving us all a ravenous appetite.

My obvious hunger elicited stares from the men as I tucked into the moussaka and generous helpings of rice. 'What's the problem? Have you never seen a woman eat before?' I com-mented sarcastically, as I leant forward to grab another flatbread.

Theo contributed to the banter with the occasional dry observation, but left immediately after dinner, choosing not to participate in the post-supper bar crawl. I followed him shortly afterwards. Over my years as a professional sailor, I'd learnt that the boys' antics after dark were not something I wished to witness.

In the next couple of days, under Theo's thoughtful green gaze, we began to pull together and quickly became a smoothly efficient team, and my admiration for his methods grew apace. On our third evening on Naxos, feeling particularly tired from a gruelling day under the searing Aegean sun, I was the first to stand up from the dinner table.

'Right lads, I'm off.'

'Me too. Night boys. No hangovers aboard tomorrow, please,' Theo said, following me out of the restaurant. 'Can I join you?' he asked as he caught up with me in the street outside.

'Yes, of course you can,' I agreed, feeling suddenly tense that we were alone together for the first time.

We walked back to our pension along the narrow cobbled streets, the moonlight illuminating the little white houses with their blue-painted doors and shutters on either side. I did my best to make conversation, but Theo only contributed the odd 'yes' or 'no', and his taciturn responses began to irritate me.

As we reached the lobby of the pension, he suddenly turned to me. 'You really are an instinctive seaman, Al. You beat most of your crewmates into a cocked hat. Who taught you?'

'My father,' I said, surprised by the compliment. 'He took me out sailing on Lake Geneva from when I was very small.'

'Ah, Geneva. That explains the French accent.'

I readied myself for the typical 'say something sexy in French' type of comment that I usually got from men at this point, but it didn't come.

'Well, your father must be one hell of a sailor – he's done an excellent job on you.'

'Thanks,' I said, disarmed.

'How do you find being the only woman aboard? Although I'm sure it's not a one-off occurrence for you,' he added hastily.

'I don't think about it, to be honest.'

He looked at me perceptively through his horn-rimmed glasses. 'Really? Well, forgive me for saying so, but I think you do. I feel you sometimes try to overcompensate for it and that's when you make errors. I'd suggest you relax more and just be yourself. Anyway, goodnight.' He gave me a brief smile then mounted the white-tiled stairs to his room.

That night, as I lay in the narrow bed, the starched white sheets itched against my skin and my cheeks burnt at his criticism. Was it *my* fault that women were still a relative rarity – or, as some of my male crewmates would undoubtedly say, a novelty – aboard professional racing boats? And who did Theo Falys-Kings think he was?! Some kind of pop psychologist, going around analysing people who didn't need to be analysed?

I'd always thought I handled the woman-in-a-male-dominated-world thing well, and had been able to take friendly jibes and asides about my female status on the chin. I'd built myself a wall of inviolability in my career, and two different personas: 'Ally' at home, 'Al' at work. Yes, it was often hard and I'd learnt to hold my tongue, especially when the comments were of a pointedly sexist nature and alluded to my supposed 'blonde' behaviour. I'd always made a point of warding off such remarks by keeping my red-gold curls scraped back from my face and tied firmly in a ponytail, and by not wearing even a smidgen of make-up to accentuate my eyes or cover up my freckles. And I worked just as hard as any of the men on the boat – perhaps, I fumed inwardly, harder.

Then, still sleepless with indignation, I remembered my father telling me that much of the irritation people feel at personal observations was usually because there was a grain of truth in them. And as the night hours drew on, I had to concede that Theo was probably right. I wasn't being 'myself'.

The following evening, Theo joined me again as I walked back to the pension. For all his lack of physical stature, I found him hugely intimidating and I heard myself stumble over my words. As I struggled to explain my dual personas, he listened quietly before responding.

'Well, my father – whose opinion I don't normally rate to be fair,' he said, 'once stated that women would run the world if they only played to their strengths and stopped trying to be men. Maybe that's what you should try to do.'

'That's easy for a man to say, but has your father ever worked in a completely female-dominated environment? And would he "be himself" if he did?' I countered, irritated at being patronised.

'Good point,' Theo agreed. 'Well, at least it might help a little if I called you "Ally". It suits you far better than "Al". Would you mind?'

Before I had a chance to answer, he halted abruptly on the picturesque harbour front, where small fishing boats rocked gently between the larger yachts and motor cruisers as the soothing sounds of a calm sea lapped against their hulls. I watched him look up to the skies, his nostrils flaring visibly as he sniffed the air, checking to see what the dawn would bring weather-wise. It was something I had only ever seen old sailors do, and I chuckled suddenly at the projected image of Theo as an ancient, grizzled sea dog.

He turned to me with a puzzled smile. 'What's so funny?'

'Nothing. And if it makes you feel better, you're welcome to call me "Ally".'

'Thanks. Now, let's get back and grab some sleep. I have a hard day planned for us all tomorrow.'

Again that night, I was restless as I replayed our conversation in my mind. *Me*, who usually slept like a log, especially when I was training or competing.

And rather than Theo's advice helping me, over the next couple of days I made numerous silly mistakes, making me feel more like a rookie than the professional I was. I castigated myself harshly; but ironically, even though my crewmates teased me good-naturedly, never once was there a word of criticism from Theo.

On our fifth night, feeling horribly embarrassed and confused by my uncharacteristically sloppy performance level, I didn't even join the rest of the crew for dinner. Instead, I sat on the small terrace of the pension eating bread, feta cheese and olives provided by the kind owner. I drowned my sorrows in the rough red wine she poured me, and after a number of glasses, began to feel decidedly queasy and sorry for myself. I was just lurching unsteadily from the table, headed for bed, when Theo arrived on the terrace.

'Are you all right?' he asked, sliding his glasses up his nose to see me properly. I squinted back at him, but his outline had become inexplicably blurry.

'Yes,' I replied thickly, sitting back down hurriedly as everything I tried to focus on started to sway.

'Everyone was worried about you when you didn't turn up tonight. You're not sick, are you?'

'No.' I felt the burning sensation of bile rising in my throat. 'I'm fine.'

'You know, you can tell me if you are sick and I swear I won't count it against you. Can I sit down?'

I didn't answer. In fact, I found I couldn't as I struggled to control my nausea. He sat down in the plastic chair across the table from me anyway.

'So what's the problem?'

'Nothing,' I managed.

'Ally, you're an awful colour. Are you sure you're not ill?'

'I . . . Excuse me.'

With that, I staggered up and just made it to the edge of the terrace before I vomited over it onto the pavement below.

'Poor you.' I felt a pair of hands clasp me firmly around my waist. 'You're obviously not well at all. I'm going to help you to your room. What number is it?'

'I am . . . perfectly well,' I muttered stupidly, horrified beyond measure at what had just happened. And all in front of Theo Falys-Kings, who, for some reason, I was desperate to impress. All things considered, it could not have been worse.

'Come on.' He hoisted my limp arm over his shoulder and half-carried me past the disgusted gaze of the other guests.

Once in my room, I was sick a few more times, but at least it was into the toilet. Each time I emerged, Theo was waiting for me, ready to help me back to the bed.

'Really,' I groaned, 'I'll be fine in the morning, I promise.'

'You've been saying that in between rounds of vomit for the past two hours,' he said pragmatically, wiping the sticky sweat from my forehead with a cool, damp towel.

'Go to bed, Theo,' I murmured groggily. 'Really, I'm fine now. Just need to sleep.'

'In a while, I will.'

'Thanks for looking after me,' I whispered as my eyes began to shut.

'That's okay, Ally.'

And then, as I drifted in the half here, half there world of the few seconds before sleep, I smiled. 'I think I love you,' I heard myself say before I descended into oblivion.

I woke the next morning feeling shaky but better. As I climbed out of bed, I tripped over Theo, who had used a spare pillow and was curled up on the floor fast asleep. Shutting the bathroom door, I sank onto the edge of the bath and remembered the words I'd thought – or Christ, had I actually *spoken* them? – last night.

I think I love you.

Where on earth had that come from? Or had I dreamt I'd said it? After all, I'd been very unwell and might have been hallucinating. *God, I hope so*, I groaned to myself, my head in my hands. But ... if I hadn't actually said it, why could I remember those words so vividly? They were ridiculously inaccurate, of course, but now Theo might think that I actually meant them. Which of course I didn't, surely?

Eventually, I emerged sheepishly from the bathroom and saw that Theo was about to leave. I couldn't meet his eye as he told me he was going to his own room to take a shower, and would come back to collect me in ten minutes to take me down for breakfast.

'Really, you go on your own, Theo. I don't want to risk it.'

'Ally, you have to eat something. If you can't keep food

down for an hour afterwards, I'm afraid you're banned from the boat until you can. You know the rules.'

'Okay,' I agreed miserably. As he left, I wished with all my heart that I could simply become invisible. Never in my life had I wanted to be somewhere else as much as I did at that moment.

Fifteen minutes later, we walked onto the terrace together. The other crew members looked up at us from the table with knowing smirks on their faces. I wanted to punch each and every one of them.

'Ally has a stomach bug,' Theo announced as we sat down. 'But by the looks of it, Rob, you missed out on some beauty sleep too.' The assembled crew members chuckled at Rob, who shrugged in embarrassment as Theo proceeded to talk calmly about the practice session he had planned.

I sat silently, appreciating that he'd moved the conversation on, but I knew what the others were all thinking. And the irony was, they were so, so wrong. I'd made a vow never to sleep with a crewmate, knowing how quickly women could get a reputation in the close-knit world of sailing. And now, it seemed I'd acquired one by default.

At least I was able to keep my breakfast down and was allowed aboard. From that moment on, I went out of my way to make it clear to everyone – especially to him – that I was not the slightest bit interested in Theo Falys-Kings. During the practices, I kept as far away from him as was possible on a small craft, and answered him in monosyllables. And in the evenings, after we finished dinner, I gritted my teeth and stayed on with the crew as he rose to leave and return to the pension.

Because, I told myself, I did not love him. And I did not

wish for anyone else to think I did either. However, as I set about convincing everyone around me, I realised there was no real conviction in my own mind. I found myself staring at him when I didn't think he was looking. I admired the calm, measured way he dealt with the crew and the perceptive comments he made that pulled us together and made us work better as a team. And how, despite his comparatively small stature, his body was firm and muscled beneath his clothes. I watched him as he proved himself time and again to be the fittest and strongest of all of us.

Every time my treacherous mind wandered in *that* direction, I did my best to reel it firmly back in. But I'd suddenly started noticing just how often Theo walked around without a shirt on. Granted, it was extremely hot during the day, but did he really have to be topless to look at the race maps . . . ?

'Do you need anything, Ally?' he asked me once, as he turned around to find me staring at him.

I don't even remember what I mumbled as I turned away, my face bright red with shame.

I was only relieved that he never mentioned what I may have said to him on the night I was so ill, and began to convince myself that I really must have dreamt it. But still, I knew something irrevocable had happened to me. Something that, for the first time in my life, I seemed to have no control over. As well as my usual clockwork sleeping pattern deserting me, my healthy appetite had disappeared too. When I did manage to doze off, I had vivid dreams about him, the kind that made me blush when I awoke and made my behaviour towards him even more awkward. As a teenager, I'd read love stories and dismissed them, preferring meaty thrillers. Yet, as I mentally listed my current symptoms, sadly, they all seemed to fit the same bill: I'd somehow managed to develop a massive crush on Theo Falys-Kings.

On the last night of training, Theo rose from the table after supper and told us we'd all done a spectacular job and that he had high hopes for winning the forthcoming regatta. After the toast, I was just about to depart for the pension when Theo's gaze fell on me.

'Ally, there's something I wanted to discuss with you. The regulations say we have to have a member of the crew who's in charge of first aid. It means nothing, just red tape and a case of signing a few forms. Would you mind?' He indicated a plastic file, then nodded to an empty table.

'I know absolutely nothing about first aid. And just because I'm a woman,' I added defiantly as we sat down at the table away from the others, 'doesn't mean I can nurse anyone better than the men. Why not ask Tim or one of the others to do it?'

'Ally, please shut up. It was just an excuse. Look.' Theo showed me the two sheets of blank paper he'd just taken out of his file. 'Right,' he said, handing me a pen, 'for the sake of form, particularly yours, we will now conduct a discussion about your responsibilities as the appointed crew member in charge of first aid. And at the same time, we will discuss the fact that on the night you were so ill, you told me that you thought you loved me. And the fact is, Ally, I think I might feel the same about you too.'

He paused and I looked at him in total disbelief to see if he was teasing me, but he was busy pretending to check the pages.

'What I'd like to suggest is that we find out what this means for both of us,' he continued. 'As from tomorrow, I'm taking my boat and disappearing for a long weekend. I'd like you to come with me.' Finally, he looked up at me. 'Will you?'

My mouth was opening and closing, probably in a very good impression of a goldfish, but I simply didn't know how to answer him.

'For goodness' sake, Ally, just say yes. Forgive the feeble analogy, but we're both in the same boat. We both know that there's something between us and has been ever since we first met a year ago. To be frank, from what I'd heard about you, I'd been expecting some muscly "he-she". And then you turned up, all blue eyes and gorgeous Titian hair, and completely disarmed me.'

'Oh,' I said, totally lost for words.

'So.' Theo cleared his throat and I realised that he was equally nervous. 'Let's go and do what we both love best: spend some time mucking about on the water and give whatever this "thing" is a chance to develop. If nothing else, you'll like the boat. It's very comfortable. And fast.'

'Will there . . . be anyone else on-board?' I asked him, eventually finding my voice.

'No.'

'So, you'll be skipper and I'll be your only crew?'

'Yes, but I promise I won't make you climb the rigging and sit in the crow's nest all night.' He smiled at me then, and his green eyes were full of warmth. 'Ally, just say you'll come.'

'Okay,' I agreed.

'Good. Now, perhaps you can sign on the dotted line to . . . er, seal the deal.' His finger indicated a spot on the blank sheet of paper.

I glanced at him and saw that he was still smiling at me. And finally, I offered him a smile back. I signed my name and passed the sheet of paper over to him. He studied it in a show of seriousness, then returned it to the plastic file. 'So, that's all sorted,' he said, raising his voice for the benefit of our fellow crew members, whose ears were no doubt on elastic. 'And I'll see you down at the harbour at noon to brief you on your duties.'

He gave me a wink and we walked sedately back to join the others, my measured pace belying the wonderful bubble of excitement I felt inside me.